THE
BROWNSON READER

This is a volume in the
Arno Press collection

THE AMERICAN CATHOLIC TRADITION

Advisory Editor
Jay P. Dolan

Editorial Board
Paul Messbarger
Michael Novak

See last pages of this volume
for a complete list of titles.

The

BROWNSON READER

Orestes Augustus Brownson

Edited by

ALVAN S. RYAN

ARNO PRESS
A New York Times Company
New York • 1978

Editorial Supervision: JOSEPH CELLINI

———◆———

Reprint Edition 1978 by Arno Press Inc.

Copyright © 1955 by P.J. Kenedy & Sons

Reprinted by permission of the
    Macmillan Publishing Co., Inc. and
    Alvan S. Ryan

THE AMERICAN CATHOLIC TRADITION
ISBN for complete set: 0-405-10810-9
See last pages of this volume for titles.

Manufactured in the United States of America

———◆———

The Brownson Reader

The

BROWNSON READER

Edited, with an Introduction, by

ALVAN S. RYAN

Associate Professor of English
The University of Notre Dame

New York

P. J. KENEDY & SONS

ACKNOWLEDGMENTS

I wish to thank the following authors and publishing houses for the use of quotations: the Columbia University Press for passages from *The Letters of Ralph Waldo Emerson,* edited by Ralph L. Rusk; the Duke University Press for quotations from C. L. F. Gohdes' *The Periodicals of American Transcendentalism;* Harcourt, Brace and Company for a quotation from T. S. Eliot's *Essays Ancient and Modern;* the Harvard University Press for a passage from Perry Miller's *The Transcendentalists;* Longmans, Green and Company for quotations from Denis Gwynn's *A Hundred Years of Catholic Emancipation,* Newman's *Apologia Pro Vita Sua,* edited by C. F. Harrold, and Wilfrid Ward's *Life of John Henry Cardinal Newman;* The Macmillan Company for quotations from Theodore Maynard's *Orestes Brownson: Yankee, Radical, Catholic;* Arthur Schlesinger, Jr., for passages from his *Orestes A. Brownson: A Pilgrim's Progress;* Sheed and Ward for quotations from Christopher Dawson's *Progress and Religion* and Daniel Sargent's *Four Independents;* and Odell Shepard for a passage from his *Pedlar's Progress: The Life of Bronson Alcott.*

I am also indebted to the Reverend Thomas T. McAvoy, C.S.C., and to Miss Elizabeth Brownson for their many courtesies.

Finally, I wish to express my gratitude to my wife, Pauline Hillberg Ryan, for her typing and proofreading of the entire manuscript, and to Professor M. A. Fitzsimons of the Notre Dame history department for his reading of a substantial part of the material.

CONTENTS

The Brownson Reader

INTRODUCTION

I

O RESTES AUGUSTUS BROWNSON was a seeker, with all the enthusiasm and the passionate intensity of men of that stamp. He was, as Arthur Schlesinger, Jr. saw so clearly, a Pilgrim in search of the Celestial City.[1] The urbanities and the graces were not for one born at the outset of the nineteenth century in an isolated farming community in northern Vermont, and virtually orphaned at the age of four. No Lord Chesterfield ever wrote him letters saying, "Sacrifice to the graces, my son, sacrifice to the graces." What Brownson missed in his early life can be suggested by Matthew Arnold's distinction between the provincial spirit and the urbane spirit, the tone of the city, of the center, the tone of the writer—Arnold singles out John Henry Newman as an example—who has shared the advantages of a cultivated community, London or Paris, or a university like Oxford. Such a writer is continually checked and corrected in a hundred ways by the intelligence, the taste, the critical pressure around him.

Brownson in his formative years enjoyed no such advantage. His early experience was provincial and sectarian. The cost to Brownson was immense. Largely self-taught, and self-supporting from an early age, first a schoolmaster then later a minister in frontier or rural communities, he was deprived of the assurances enjoyed by an Emerson in Cambridge and Concord, an Arnold at Oxford. His search for truth was an independent

---

[1] Arthur M. Schlesinger, Jr., *Orestes A. Brownson, A Pilgrim's Progress* (Boston, 1939).

search and a lonely one. To say that he often showed the head-
long impetuosity of an Oedipus in his desire to know would go
far to explain his tortured career. So urgent was Brownson for
answers, and so intense was his passion to formulate at each step
of the way what partial truth he had apprehended, that he could
be said to have embraced at one time or another most of the
intellectual errors possible for a nineteenth-century man. But he
also embraced profound truths—truths hidden from more
cautious men who for fear of speaking falsely speak not at all.
And in his best work he expressed these truths with rare force
and clarity. He committed himself as few men do; he was, in
the existentialist phrase, thoroughly engaged in his time and
place, yet always seeking absolutes. Controversy was meat and
drink to him; logic, not sweet reasonableness, was his weapon.

Provincial as were his beginnings, Brownson eventually
moved into the larger intellectual world around Boston (and
later in New York), and through his voracious reading of contemporary European religious, philosophical, political, and social
thinkers, not only overcame many of his initial handicaps, but
became, as editor of the *Boston Quarterly Review*, a leading
spokesman of the Transcendentalist movement. After his conversion, Brownson's awareness of European intellectual currents
acquired a new immediacy. Sharing with Europeans and with
Catholics throughout the world membership in the universal
Church, he came to know intimately the divergent understand-
ings of the relation of the Church to society, to civilization, to
contingent and constantly shifting political problems. He entered the turbulent disputes that marked the pontificate of
Pius IX. But always Brownson was most concerned with American society in all its dimensions, and he strove especially to see in
its true perspective the relation of the Catholic Church to
America.

His important work is that of the general critic and journalist.

Nearly all of his writing, except for a few separately published volumes, appeared in periodical reviews, chiefly in two which he himself edited, the *Boston Quarterly Review* (1838–1842) and *Brownson's Quarterly Review* (1844–1864; 1873–1875). His work covers a span of more than forty years, and because he wrote on subjects of perennial interest, and tried to bring philosophical principles to bear on the questions of the day, much of his work transcends the limitations of journalism.

I have called him a general critic. By general criticism I mean criticism of the type practiced by Matthew Arnold, as in *Culture and Anarchy*, which proliferates in many directions, into philosophy, theology, education, political and social questions; by Irving Babbitt in *Rousseau and Romanticism*, and *Democracy and Leadership;* or by Christopher Dawson in nearly all of his work. However diverse the conclusions of these writers, they ask similar questions. Concerned with the inner life of society, they continually bring religious, philosophical, and ethical standards to bear upon social and political problems. Brownson was constantly occupied with these very problems, and if we take into account the particular conditions under which he worked, if we think of him as a journalist for whom religion and civilization were abiding concerns, the comparison with these critics can aid in the measuring of his achievement.

Brownson was a journalist in a double sense. He was often the sole author of an entire issue of his *Review*, and a single number would usually include lengthy essays on political, social, literary, and theological questions. Compelled, like any journalist, to meet a deadline, he rarely had an opportunity to write at a leisurely pace. He often found it necessary to present his first thoughts and impressions, and it is no wonder that as his thought developed and as events and history unfolded, he seemed continually to change. "To live is to change," said Newman, "and to be perfect is to have changed often." Change is, at least, the mark of our imperfection. Brownson justified the bold and forth-right method which characterizes nearly all of his work by say-ing that his purpose was to stimulate thought, to get great issues before a serious reading public. In the dialectic of debate, so he hoped, truth would be arrived at and error exposed.

When, holding such a conception of journalism, an editor fills issue after issue of his review with his own work, it becomes a journal in another sense. He keeps his private journal in public, and forfeits the chance to change a line. He records the very process of his thinking. His thoughts cannot be recalled, and at his own risk he writes for all to see the record of his own in-tellectual and spiritual odyssey. By contrast, an Emerson or a Thoreau keeps a private journal as a storehouse of ideas and im-pressions which only after long reflection find their way into es-says and books. To follow Brownson's essays on a given subject over a period of years is often to experience an inner dialectic, lacking, to be sure, the form, the drama, and the excitement of a Platonic dialogue, yet yielding an excitement of its own and a grasp at the end of complex truths seen in dialectical harmony.

What is the central concern of his life? It is, as I have sug-gested, twofold. There is Brownson's quest for religious cer-tainty, for the truth of his personal relation to God and to the Church. And there is Brownson's concern about temporal and contingent realities: justice between man and man, political liberty and order, the good of the earthly city. For him the two could not be separated, and the double quest led him into the Catholic Church at the age of forty-one. After his conversion he was no less concerned to understand the doctrine and the life of the Church, and the light they throw on every area of human ex-perience. To do justice to both spiritual and temporal realities was the whole purpose of all his work.

Had Brownson lacked the passion for social reform he might have come to a position akin to that of Thoreau, or as a Catholic he might have accepted with relative equanimity a dualism which left the great social and political questions of the day unanswered, or answered with little reference to religion. On the other hand, the Utopian socialism of his early years, had it been divorced from Christian inspiration, might eventually have led him in the direction of dialectical materialism.

Brownson could not accept such a dualism. He was involved in the great struggle of his age between Liberalism and Christianity, the struggle which, through the Oxford Movement, brought Newman into the Catholic Church. His most Utopian schemes in his early life were inspired, however confusedly, by religious motives. He was always trying to see authority and freedom, the spiritual and the temporal, Church and state, in their mutual relations. And when he became a Catholic he knew himself to be a member of a Church *semper eadem,* clothed with authority to teach an unchanging truth through all the centuries, conservative and traditional in the root meanings of these two terms. But he knew also that this same Church had the mission of regenerating mankind, bringing justice and charity into the dealings of man with man. It was tied to no social or political forms merely because they were old. It was as creative as it was conservative. How to bring the tradition and the life of the Church into creative relation with the manifold problems of the age was his predominant concern.

II

BROWNSON was born in Stockbridge, Vermont, September 16, 1803. He and his twin sister, Daphne, were the youngest among six children of Sylvester and Relief Metcalf Brownson. His father had come to Stockbridge from Hartford County, Connecticut, where the Brownsons were among the earliest settlers, his mother from Keene, New Hampshire. Stockbridge was then a frontier town, having been first settled only twenty years before Orestes' birth, and had less than one hundred inhabitants. Orestes' father died when the boy was very young, and poverty forced his mother to send Orestes to live with foster parents in nearby Royalton, Vermont. Religious sects flourished here in this period of evangelical fervor—there were Congregationalists, Methodists, Baptists, Universalists, and a sect founded in 1800 which called themselves "Christ-yans." The stern Congregational morality of his foster parents made an indelible impression on the boy, though he was left to understand that conversion must come as a personal rebirth. His early schooling was acquired at home through his own reading of the Bible and the few English classics he found there or could borrow. The dominant impressions of his childhood were religious, and when very young he was imbued with the ambition to become a minister.

Moving at the age of fourteen to Ballston Spa in northern New York with his mother, he attended the local academy, and worked in a printing office as apprentice and then journeyman. At the age of nineteen he joined the Presbyterian Church, and for a time taught school in Stillwater, near Ballston Spa. Unable to reconcile himself to the doctrine of unconditional election, and convinced that to accept the Calvinistic teaching was to do violence to his reason, he rejected Presbyterianism and in 1824 became a Universalist. The next two years find him teaching school for a time near Detroit, Michigan, then in Elbridge, New York, where he fell in love with Sally Healy, one of his pupils in the country school. In the summer of 1826, in Jaffrey, New Hampshire, he was ordained a Universalist preacher. His marriage to Sally Healy occurred in June, 1827.

Brownson preached for short periods in New Hampshire and Vermont, then for longer periods in Ithaca and Auburn, New York. He first contributed to, and later edited, *The Gospel Advocate*, the chief publication of the Universalist society. It was soon apparent, however, that Brownson's Universalist career would not be long. The sensitivity to social injustice that makes his youthful diaries read so much like early Carlyle was quickened by his reading of William Godwin's *Political Justice*. Then, quite by chance, he heard Fanny Wright lecture in Utica, New York, in the fall of 1829. He was captivated by her eloquence and her Utopian schemes. She, in turn, saw in him a valuable ally. He became for a short time a contributing editor to the *Free Inquirer*, published in New York by Fanny Wright and Robert Dale Owen. For a brief period he was also a member of the Workingmen's party in New York, dedicated to social democracy. Brownson's socialistic enthusiasms did not please the Universalists. He was, in fact, preaching socialism rather than Christianity the last two years of his ministry, and later spoke of the years 1829–1831 as the most anti-Christian period of his life. His association with Fanny Wright had precipitated a crisis in his religious beliefs. Realizing that he no longer believed what he was expected to preach, he left the Universalists and in February, 1831, began preaching as an independent minister in Ithaca, New York. In his first sermon he declared: "I do not wish to be called a Universalist. Should I assume the name of any party, it should be Unitarian. . . . Unitarian discourses are mostly practical; their lessons inculcate charity, a refined moral feeling, and universal benevolence." [2]

Late in 1831, upon hearing a friend read to him a sermon by William Ellery Channing, the noted Boston Unitarian, Brownson's hitherto vague acceptance of Unitarianism was suddenly kindled to enthusiasm. In 1832 he applied for the Unitarian pulpit in Walpole, New Hampshire, and was accepted. The two years in Walpole were years of intensive study. He learned French, read the five octavo volumes of Benjamin Constant's *Religion Considered in Its Origin, Its Forms, Its Developments*, and found here confirmation of his own confi-

[2] Henry F. Brownson, *Orestes A. Brownson's Early Life* (Detroit, 1898), pp. 51–2.

dence in intuition. Thenceforth for many years French philosophy and social theory—Saint-Simon, Victor Cousin, Jouffroy—became one of his chief enthusiasms. Brownson's sermons and his intellectual vigor began to be recognized more widely. From Walpole he frequently traveled the ninety miles to Boston for Lyceum lectures, met Channing and George Ripley, with both of whom he exchanged pulpits, and so began to be known among the leading Unitarians around Boston. Ripley became his closest friend, and at Ripley's suggestion he moved to Canton, Massachusetts, in 1834 as Unitarian minister.

Brownson plunged into his work in Canton with prodigious energy. He often preached three or four sermons a week; he gave Lyceum lectures, and devoted especial attention to the situation of the workingmen around Boston. In fact, it was Brownson's earlier connection with the Workingmen's party that led Channing to believe him particularly fitted to win to Christianity the industrial workers of the city. In 1834, in *The Christian Examiner*, Brownson outlined his plan for his "Church of the Future," in which Christianity became essentially a doctrine of social reform. He was, as he said later in *The Convert*, working for "the progress of man and society, and the realization of a heaven on earth." [3]

In 1836 he moved to Chelsea, across the Mystic River from Boston, where he would be even closer to the laboring men to whom he felt he had a special mission, and began to preach in the Lyceum Hall and the Masonic Temple. He also edited the *Boston Reformer*. "Even in Boston," wrote Harriet Martineau, "as far behind the country as that city is, a notable change has taken place. A strong man, full of enlarged sympathies, has not only discerned the wants of the time, but set himself to do

[3] *The Works of Orestes A. Brownson* (Detroit, 1882–1887), V, 74. Henceforth these twenty volumes collected and arranged by Henry F. Brownson will be referred to as *Works*.

what one man may to supply them." [4] The reference is to Brownson's discourse on "The Wants of the Times," delivered in May, 1836, in which he declared the old churches to be failures. "All over the Christian world," Brownson declared, "a contest is going on . . . between the people and their masters, between the many and the few, the privileged and the underprivileged." In this contest, religion must ally itself with the cause of the people. Jesus is "the prophet of the workingmen." [5] This was the doctrine of Brownson's "Church of the Future," and in July he established his Society for Christian Union and Progress as a beginning. In his first book, *New Views of Christianity, Society, and the Church* (1836), drawing heavily from Saint-Simon and Cousin, he attempted to show how the "Church of the Future" would combine the spirituality of Catholicism with the humanitarianism of Protestantism in a new synthesis. He was already, like so many of his associates, looking beyond Unitarianism.

This same year, 1836, saw the publication of Emerson's first notable work, the slim volume called *Nature*, and the appearance of Bronson Alcott's *Conversations*. In the fall at Ripley's home occurred the first meeting of the so-called Transcendental Club, or as Emerson always called it, for one of its members, F. H. Hedge, the "Hedge Club." Brownson attended several of the meetings, and some of them were held at his home in Chelsea. He was already recognized as one of the leaders of the new school, and his influence continued to increase in the next few years.

The establishment of the Club by no means signalized that the Transcendentalist group was thoroughly homogeneous. The movement assimilated myriad influences from Europe, while retaining its American flavor. Emerson, Alcott, Ripley, Brown-

[4] Schlesinger, *Orestes A. Brownson*, p. 45.
[5] *Ibid.*, p. 53.

son, F. H. Hedge, Convers Francis—each brought through personality, temperament, or background—a different emphasis to the movement. Dissatisfaction with the orthodoxy of Harvard Unitarianism was for many, at least, their point of departure. Emerson had left the ministry to become a lay prophet. Thoreau, who, after living with Brownson and tutoring his children for several weeks in 1836, had called these weeks "an era in my life—the morning of a new *Lebenstag*" [6]—would go his way, and so of the others. They were more united in what they opposed than in what they professed. Philosophically, the enemy was eighteenth-century rationalism and the school of Locke, as it was with Coleridge and Wordsworth and many others of the English Romantic movement. Spiritual reality was deeper and richer than anything imagined by Unitarianism or by the rationalists.

Brownson's chief contribution to the movement was as the expositor of European philosophy and social thought, and as a leader in bringing religion to bear upon social problems. Whereas Emerson addressed the individual, and was suspicious of social reformers, Brownson became convinced that social institutions must be altered. In 1838 he founded the *Boston Quarterly Review* and for five years filled most of its pages with his own writing. Through these years Brownson's attempts to further his social ideals occupied nearly all of his energies. Religion was primarily a social evangel to be spread by independent Christians like himself who were dissatisfied with all existing churches. He became, much like Thomas Carlyle, whose influence on him during this period was pronounced, something of a lay prophet.

His essay on "The Laboring Classes" in the July, 1840, issue of his *Review* brought this phase of his thought to its climax. Carlyle's *French Revolution* had appeared in 1837. In it Carlyle had tried to show England an image of its own social conditions

[6] *Brownson's Early Life*, p. 204.

as in a glass, and to warn England of the imminent danger of revolution. Brownson had reviewed it enthusiastically. And when Carlyle's *Chartism* came out in Boston in 1840, Brownson made it the occasion of stating in the boldest terms his radical social doctrines. In England laboring men and factory workers were rioting; Chartism as a socialistic movement was short-lived but for a time threatened revolution. Carlyle in his pamphlet attacked *laissez-faire* economic theory vigorously, but saw no real solution in Chartism. Brownson, however, went far beyond Carlyle. He saw in the depression and panic of 1837 in America a parallel with what Carlyle called The-Condition-of-England-Question. The class war was entering an acute phase. Industrialism had brought on evils worse than those of slavery. "Wages," Brownson declared, "is a cunning device of the devil, for the benefit of tender consciences, who would retain all the advantages of the slave system, without the expense, trouble, and odium of being slave-holders." [7] He ridiculed theories about freedom of opportunity in the factories and on the frontier. There was not even true *laissez faire;* the power had already passed to corporations. "The proletaries" must be emancipated, monopoly and privilege must go, the inheritance of property be abolished. On the positive side, what Brownson asked for was the restoration to the workingman of his dignity as a person, a return to genuine free competition, and the opportunity for every man to own his own shop or his own farm.

The essay created a sensation, coming as it did from an editor who had declared himself in this election year for the Democratic candidate, Van Buren. The Whig politicians used it skillfully as evidence of the socialistic leanings of the Democratic party, giving it wide distribution during the campaign.

Aside from the inadequacies of some of Brownson's positive suggestions, like Carlyle and Ruskin in England he saw early

[7] *Boston Quarterly Review*, III, 370.

the gross injustices of the industrial system. Schlesinger calls the
Brownson of this period "the nearest forerunner"[8] of Marx
in America. In the light of Brownson's conversion four years
later, however, his indignation, if not his entire social theory,
seems prophetic, for it should be remembered that neither in
England nor in New England, where the factory system was developing most rapidly, had the Catholic Church yet developed
any specific social program. The Catholic hierarchy was not even
restored to England until 1850, and in New England Catholicism was still engaged in the vital mission of preserving the faith
of immigrants who were beginning to come here in vast numbers
to escape oppressive conditions in the Old World. But by 1874
Cardinal Manning was delivering such addresses as his "Rights
and Dignity of Labor," claiming for labor "not only the rights
of property but the right of unionization, the right to strike, and
the right to have recourse to the civil authorities."[9] Not until
1891, however, with Leo XIII's *Rerum Novarum* do we have
a positive and explicit Catholic social doctrine.

With the outcry against his essay on "The Laboring Classes,"
Brownson began to re-examine his religious position. Both his
Unitarian and Transcendental assumptions gradually gave way.
His study of Leroux, he tells us, gave him the sense of hierarchy, which disposed him to look more favorably on the Catholic Church, and gave him also the doctrine of communion—that
man lives by communion with realities outside himself, with
nature, his fellow man, and God. For Brownson this meant a
significant step beyond the subjectivism of his earlier religious
views. It suggested to him, he says in *The Convert*, the Catholic
doctrine of grace. Moreover, Leroux's treatment of the function
of providential men led him to a different view of the historical
church. "The Mediatorial Life of Jesus" (1842) is further testimony to Brownson's rejection of Unitarian doctrine. He now

[8] *Orestes A. Brownson*, p. 100.
[9] J. J. O'Connor, *The Catholic Revival in England* (New York, 1942), p. 92.

saw that his efforts to establish a new church as the foundation for a renewal of society were presumptuous. He was trying to lift himself by his own bootstraps. Man was no church builder. By April, 1844, he had concluded that "either there is already existing the divine institution, the church of God, or there are no means of reform." [10] Nothing is more characteristic of Brownson than this indication that his "passion for reforming the world," to use Shelley's phrase, should lead him to examine the credentials of the Catholic Church.

Brownson tells the story of his conversion in *The Convert* and elsewhere, but even his own account is not entirely satisfying. To reconstruct the complex processes by which he was led to the Church is extremely difficult. As Maynard says, "it was an ecumenical council composed of such queerly assorted figures as William Godwin, and Robert Owen, and Benjamin Constant, and Saint-Simon, and Cousin, and Leroux—all presided over by Dr. Channing—that gave Brownson his faith, in so far as this came from natural sources." [11]

During these years prior to Brownson's conversion he was by no means concerned solely with his personal religious situation. His friend George Ripley inaugurated the Brook Farm venture, and while Brownson was not an ardent supporter of the project, he showed a wary interest in it, and visited the Farm often. But Brownson's true feeling may have been expressed in a letter he wrote in 1843 to Isaac Hecker, later the founder of the Paulist Congregation in America. Commenting on Hecker's stay at the Farm, he remarked, "after all, these communities are humbugs." [12] Yet he sent his son Orestes there, and Hecker himself had gone there at Brownson's suggestion.

This period was also one of stormy political debates for

---

[10] *Works*, IV, 511.

[11] Theodore Maynard, *Orestes Brownson: Yankee, Radical, Catholic* (New York, 1943), p. 123.

[12] Orestes A. Brownson to Isaac T. Hecker, September 2, 1843, University of Notre Dame Archives.

Brownson. The year 1842 saw the end of the *Boston Quarterly* and the start of Brownson's connection with J. L. O'Sullivan's *Democratic Review*, for which he wrote until he revived his own review, as *Brownson's Quarterly*, in 1844. His selection of metaphysical subjects for articles and his increasingly severe criticism of what he held to be myths as to the nature of democracy were no more pleasing to O'Sullivan, the editor, than was O'Sullivan's practice of appending objections to the essays to Brownson. And Brownson's admiration for John C. Calhoun and his states' rights doctrine was such that he was already working to insure the nomination of Calhoun as Democratic candidate for the presidency in 1844. In severing connections with the *Democratic Review* and establishing *Brownson's Quarterly*, he was able to put his own review behind Calhoun's candidacy.

Brownson saw Bishop Fenwick of Boston in the spring of 1844 and began taking instructions in the Catholic faith some time in May. The rapport between Brownson and the Bishop's coadjutor, Bishop Fitzpatrick, who gave him his instructions, was at first minimal. The steps by which Brownson had come to the door of the Church seemed of no interest to Fitzpatrick, who insisted that Brownson simply follow the traditional course of instruction. Difficulties were at length overcome, and Brownson was received into the Church October 20, 1844. Like Newman, whose conversion came a year later almost to the day, Brownson carried others with him, humanly speaking, into the Church. Isaac Hecker entered before Brownson, but largely because of his influence. Sophia Ripley, wife of George Ripley, the founder of Brook Farm, was another; and some others of the Brook Farm group owed their conversion to Brownson.

Though Brownson thought seriously of abandoning his review, now *Brownson's Quarterly Review*, and studying law, Bishop Fitzpatrick urged him to continue his work and as a Catholic journalist to bring Catholic principles to bear on the questions of the day. Brownson, a neophyte in the Church, without formal education in theology or philosophy, faced the prospect with misgivings. He was not prepared for such a task. Yet he became "a defender of the Catholic Faith, its champion in the printed word, two months after his conversion, without even a spiritual retreat in which to collect his thoughts." [13]

Under Bishop Fitzpatrick's guidance, Brownson began an intensive study of St. Thomas, St. Augustine, and manuals of scholasticism. He virtually repudiated most of what he had written prior to his conversion, so intent was he to demonstrate his obedience. It is clear, however, that Brownson even then wished it might have been otherwise, and in retrospect he speaks of his attitude as mistaken. It was the Bishop who insisted that Brownson put aside all the thinking by which he had been led into the Church, and employ in his writing only the traditional arguments for belief. Thus Brownson tried, with the Bishop as censor of his theological articles, to make a new beginning. His old friends and readers saw no connection between his former and present opinions. In his *Fable for Critics* (1848) James Russell Lowell describes Brownson after Emerson and Alcott:

> He shifts quite about, then proceeds to expound
> That 'tis merely the earth, not himself, that turns round,
> And wishes it clearly impressed on your mind
> That the weathercock rules and not follows the wind;
> Proving first, then as deftly confuting each side,
> With no doctrine pleased that's not somewhere denied,
> He lays the denier away on the shelf
> And then—down beside him lies gravely himself.

Brownson had been, up to his conversion, in the main stream of American Protestantism, and a leading figure in the movement party of New England. He knew the Protestant mind as

[13] Daniel Sargent, *Four Independents* (New York, 1935), p. 237.

only one can who has himself passed through a series of religious crises on the road to Rome. It is not surprising, then, that immediately after his conversion he addressed himself to those outside the Church, and entertained great hope of leading them along the way he had traveled. What is surprising is the tone and the strategy of his appeal to Protestants. His tone was militant, his strategy was, in Schlesinger's words, to destroy "all the strongholds between atheism and Catholicity where Protestants might seek shelter." [14] His method was chiefly logical, and his language was frequently the newly acquired terminology of scholastic philosophy, with which his readers were as unfamiliar as he had been a year earlier. He analyzed and refuted errors, often with devastating logic, when he might better have pointed out what Protestants held that was true. Years later, in 1856, he concluded in a letter to Father Hewit that his approach was mistaken. "My own conviction," he wrote, "is that our true policy in dealing with the American mind is to study first to ascertain, not its errors, but the truth it still maintains, and to show it that that truth can find its unity and its integrity only in the Catholic Church. . . . My own method, I believe, is the worst of all, that of logic." [15]

His articles on Transcendentalism, brilliant and searching in many ways, failed to recognize that in many of those who still remained Transcendentalists there might be the same mental disposition of openness to the claims of the Catholic Church which was his own a few years earlier. In his criticism of Newman's *Development of Christian Doctrine* he charged Newman's theory with being "essentially anticatholic," insisting that Newman repudiate it now that he had embraced the Catholic Faith. Again, Brownson's interpretation of the doctrine "no salvation

---

[14] *Orestes A. Brownson*, p. 196.
[15] H. F. Brownson, *Orestes A. Brownson's Latter Life* (Detroit, 1900), p. 60.

outside the Church" was frequently expressed in language that left little room for the necessary theological distinctions.

In all of this there was no effort on Brownson's part to say only what would please Catholics. On the contrary, his articles on Native Americanism and on the Know-Nothing party, while they opposed the injustice and bigotry of these movements in courageous fashion, succeeded in stirring up against him the wrath of many Irish Catholics. Henry F. Brownson suggests his father's situation under a crossfire of criticism during this period, when he says that Brownson defended against Americans his right to be a Catholic, and against Catholics, his right to be an American.[16]

How much of Brownson's manner and method is to be attributed to his own judgment, and how much to Bishop Fitzpatrick's direction as censor of the *Review* is difficult to decide. Isaac Hecker in his articles after Brownson's death, and Brownson's son, Henry, in the biography, place much of the responsibility on the Bishop. Whatever the truth may be, Brownson had been requested to fulfill a most delicate function, and one for which he was not, nor could be expected to be, adequately prepared. He believed that on many issues it was his duty to present not his own ideas but rather the position of his Bishop, and as a recent convert he was not sufficiently aware that full acceptance of the teaching authority of the Church still left ample room for differences of opinion in the domain of prudential judgments. As he put it himself in 1862: "Having experienced the need of authority, having suffered more than we care to repeat for the lack of some infallible teacher, we thought, and could think, only of asserting authority in season and out of season." [17] He had been for many years a liberal Christian in theology, and had virtually

---

[16] *Orestes A. Brownson's Middle Life* (Detroit, 1899), p. 528.
[17] *Works*, XX, 251.

substituted a secular vision of the kingdom of God on earth for the supernatural life; his present harshness toward all merely secular reform programs was a repudiation of his own earlier social philosophy.

More important, Brownson saw, after becoming a Catholic, that while his own earlier social theories were neither inspired by nor tried to foment a hatred of the Catholic Church, these same theories on the continent of Europe were often so motivated. In his zeal to attack anti-Christian socialism, he seemed to lose sight also of what had once been his greatest hope: to bring Christian principles into a creative relation with the social problems of the time.

In the next ten years after his conversion, Brownson gradually regained for his *Review* a new reading public. A letter of general approbation from the American bishops for his work was signed in 1849, and appeared on the inside cover of the *Review* until 1855. Partly as a result of this recognition, and in spite of vigorous criticism of much that Brownson wrote, by 1853 his *Review* had a larger circulation than in 1845. In 1855, however, Bishop Kenrick of Baltimore, wishing to dissociate himself from some of Brownson's recent pronouncements, especially on the temporal power of the Church, suggested to Brownson that the Bishop's endorsement of 1849 be dropped, and later the Bishop of Pittsburgh asked that his name be omitted. Brownson complied, offended though he was by their attitude, and omitted the letter from subsequent volumes of the *Review*. As Maynard points out, the letter cut both ways in terms of Brownson's position. It set his *Review* apart from other Catholic publications, and probably aroused the jealousy of editors who were not so favored.

Favorable recognition came to Brownson from abroad. Late in 1853 Newman invited him to join the faculty of his new university in Ireland, though in the heat of the controversy in

1854 over Brownson's attitude on the issue of Native American-ism, Newman deemed it best to withdraw the invitation. An English edition of the *Review* began to be published in 1853, and in 1854 Pope Pius IX sent him his apostolic blessing for his work.

While Bishop Fitzpatrick was in Europe in 1854, Brownson's articles were censored by a substitute, but upon the Bishop's return, Brownson did not resume the practice of submitting his articles. The tension between them soon led him to reconsider Hecker's earlier suggestion that he move with his *Review* to New York, and in October, 1855, he did so. But soon he was having difficulties with his new Bishop, Archbishop Hughes. Brownson's articles of 1854 on the spiritual and temporal power of the Pope had not pleased Hughes, and he had written to Brownson on the subject. In 1856 Brownson published his essay on "The Mission of America," developing the thesis, later pre-sented at the close of *The American Republic* (1866), that America has a providential destiny "far higher, nobler, and more spiritual" than the "Manifest Destiny" usually spoken of—"the realization . . . of the Christian ideal of society for both the Old World and the New." [18] Brownson's implication, in May-nard's words, "that a new sort of leadership was necessary for the Church in the United States" [19] irked the Bishop, who sug-gested to Brownson that he stop agitating the question of Ameri-canizing the Church.

While a change in emphasis and direction is apparent in Brownson's whole attitude during the 1850's, it is difficult to ascertain the specific causes for the change. His son calls it a gradual change, while Maynard says it began "the moment that Bishop Fitzpatrick sailed for Europe in 1854." [20] Brownson him-self said in retrospect that at about this time he began to reassert

[18] *Works*, XI, 567.
[19] *Orestes Brownson*, p. 251.
[20] *Ibid.*, p. 256.

his own identity. Actually the causes are complex and to be looked for both in the movement of events and in the progress of Brownson's own thought. He began to feel that, his apprenticeship now being over, he could reassess his earlier attitudes. By 1857, when he wrote *The Convert*, he had come to believe that he had been wrong to repudiate so completely in 1844 the philosophical, religious, and social thought which had led him to the Church. Indeed, Maynard makes very convincing his thesis that Brownson wrote *The Convert* largely to assert the validity of his personal approach to the Church. Maynard's interpretation is borne out by much that Brownson wrote in the 1850's and early 60's. In essay after essay he insisted on the distinction between Catholic tradition and the traditions of Catholics, and on the danger of confusing "what is of religion and what pertains only to the social life, nationality, or secular habits, customs, and usages of Catholics." [21] He finds many Catholics "not up to the level of the church," but "merely men of routine, creatures of the traditions and associations inherited from their ancestors, and which they seldom ever dream of distinguishing from their religion itself." [22]

Brownson's sympathies during this period were increasingly with those European Catholic thinkers whose political views were liberal. Add to this the fact that he had begun to criticize scholastic philosophy as not being adapted to meet the real philosophical problems of the age, and had begun to speculate in a way that brought upon him the charge of ontologism, and it can be understood why he was under suspicion in certain quarters for his theological, political, and social thought. Finally, when in 1860 Brownson wrote on the "Rights of the Temporal" in a way that seemed to some of his critics as minimizing the temporal power of the Church, his writings on the subject were re-

[21] *Works*, XII, 140.
[22] *Ibid.*, 142.

ferred to the Congregation *de Propaganda Fide*. Cardinal Barnabo, the Prefect of Propaganda, gave Brownson an opportunity to explain his position more clearly. No grounds for condemnation were found, and the matter was dropped.

In these years up to 1864, Brownson ventured into very troubled waters. This was just the time when in England, in Ireland, and on the Continent, Catholic reviews were involved in the great struggle between the liberal and conservative forces within the Church that took place during the papacy of Pius IX (1846–1878). Brownson's position is best understood when seen in this larger context. To state in simple terms relationships that were often complex, the *Dublin Review*, the French publication *Univers*, and in Rome the journal *Civiltà Cattolica* represented the extreme conservative position, while Montalembert's *Le Correspondant* and the reviews with which Newman was associated in an advisory capacity and briefly as editor—*The Rambler*, and *The Home and Foreign Review*—were liberal. A single statement by the editors of *The Rambler* will indicate the direction of their thought: "Modern society has developed no security for freedom, no instrument of progress, no means of arriving at truth, which we look upon with indifference or suspicion." [23] Newman, for example, like Brownson during this period, saw the need of a review in which Catholic writers could address themselves freely to the philosophical, social, and political problems which critical minds were bound to consider, and he strenuously opposed the attitude of publicists like W. G. Ward who wanted every question settled authoritatively from Rome. But at the same time Newman was aware of the recklessness of the extreme liberals. He, like Montalembert, Lacordaire, and Bishop Dupanloup favored the liberal reviews, but he tried without success to moderate their tone. Papal censure would have

[23] Wilfrid Ward, *William George Ward and the Catholic Revival* (London, 1893), p. 139.

terminated *The Rambler* had its editors not discontinued it, and did terminate *The Home and Foreign Review*. It is one of the great tragedies of this period that men who tried to make Catholicism a creative and revivifying force in every field of activity were too often silenced because of their errors, instead of being given the positive guidance that they looked for. Even in 1882 Newman writes in a letter of "what may be called Nihilism in the Catholic Body and in its rulers. They forbid, but they do not direct or create." [24]

Brownson was by 1855 well aware of this struggle in Europe. He was with those Catholics who, like Newman, might be called the moderate liberals, but he certainly never for a moment defended religious liberalism. In his essay on "Lacordaire and Catholic Progress" (1862) he declared himself an ally of Lacordaire and Montalembert. He wrote eloquently of their work and of that of Ozanam. "How often," he says of Lacordaire, "have we heard him traduced, denounced as a radical, a Jacobin, a socialist, concealing the *bonnet rouge* under the friar's hood. Yet he persevered, held fast to his integrity, held fast to his convictions, and continued on in the line of duty marked out for him, unshaken and unruffled, calm and serene. . . ." [25] And referring to what Montalembert called the Catholic renaissance in France, Brownson says: "Our own country presents a fair and open field for this *renaissance*, for the union of religion with civilization, and that new Catholic development which will restore to the church the nations she has lost, give her back the leadership of human intelligence, and secure her the willing obedience and love of mankind." [26]

I have tried to illustrate by these quotations the direction of Brownson's thought during these years; I could quote from a dozen articles: "Separation of Church and State," "The Rights

[24] Wilfrid Ward, *Life of Cardinal Newman* (London, 1912), II, p. 486.
[25] *Works*, XX, 272.
[26] *Works*, XX, 278.

of the Temporal," "Christian Politics," "Civil and Religious Freedom," and many others to indicate Brownson's position on the issues that were then so sorely dividing Catholic opinion. But Brownson's views were by now the object of widespread attack from ultra-conservatives. The time was not right for such ideas, and there is no denying that Brownson was at times far too blunt in his manner. Yet it is well to remember that even Newman, a far more moderate and restrained controversialist than Brownson, was about this time "denounced in Rome, and even delated to the Holy See, as the most formidable agent of Catholic Liberalism in England." [27]

Even though Brownson's essays on European politics and on the relation of Church and state were the chief targets of criticism from Catholic quarters, he did not confine himself to such subjects during this period. On the contrary, the domestic issues raised by the Civil War occupied much of his attention, and he called the 1864 volume of the *Review* the "National Series" to emphasize its concern with domestic problems. Though he had little respect for Lincoln's statesmanship, Brownson's allegiance to the Union had led him to support Lincoln and the Republican party in 1860, and he continued throughout the war to defend the Union cause and to attack those sections of the Catholic press which he believed were lukewarm in the struggle. Finally, in 1864, after at first deciding to support Lincoln for re-election, he switched to General John C. Fremont, whose withdrawal from the campaign left Brownson stranded. Later Brownson said in a letter, "My Review died of Fremont. . . . I stopped it because I had sacrificed my position, and had no party to fall back upon." [28] The Fremont fiasco certainly influenced, if it did not determine, Brownson's decision to suspend the *Review*. Under the pressure of criticism, Brownson, now sick and weary, his

[27] Denis Gwynn, *A Hundred Years of Catholic Emancipation* (London, 1929), pp. 169–70.
[28] *Latter Life*, p. 450.

eyesight failing, his two sons recently killed in the war, ended his *Review* with the October, 1864, issue.

A few weeks later, December, 1864, Pope Pius IX handed down the encyclical *Quanta Cura* and had the *Syllabus of Errors* published at the same time. In such condemned theses as No. 80 of the *Syllabus:* "The Roman Pontiff can and ought to reconcile himself to, and agree with, progress, liberalism, and civilization as lately introduced," Brownson's critics thought they read a condemnation of his work of the past several years. The conclusion was undoubtedly false, but Brownson saw that his influence was at least temporarily destroyed. Moreover, he himself seemed to interpret the *Syllabus* as a condemnation of his most recent thought. Instead of examining it with his usual capacity for making distinctions, instead of recognizing it for what it was, an index of references to the various encyclicals and allocutions of recent decades—as did Bishop Dupanloup and Newman —Brownson capitulated to the critics who had opposed him for years, and from 1864 to the end of his life continued to do penance for his "liberal period." Nothing, in fact, more clearly reveals Brownson's loss of confidence after 1864 than to compare his understanding of the *Syllabus* with Newman's, as expressed in personal letters in 1864 and later in his *Letter to the Duke of Norfolk* (1875). Newman, for example, saw immediately the harm that would be done by extremists, both within and outside the Church, through misinterpretation of the *Syllabus*, and refused to be stampeded. Brownson, on the other hand, in taking the *Syllabus* as a condemnation of his writings of recent years, was really accepting the interpretation of it sanctioned by his opponents.

In the period immediately after the suspension of his *Review*, Brownson planned a whole series of volumes in which he hoped to give systematic expression to his thought. Of these, only one, *The American Republic* (1866), was brought to completion.

Work on the others was deferred in favor of numerous essays he contributed to *The Catholic World*, the newly established *Ave Maria* at Notre Dame, and the New York *Tablet*, to the latter of which he was a regular contributor. Brownson was, to the end, a journalist, and he was unable in advanced years to change the writing habits of a lifetime. Nor was he, now that he was no longer in the editor's chair, happy about the revisions to which some of his essays were subjected. He wanted one more opportunity to speak out in his own review. His wife's request, just before her death in 1872, that he revive *Brownson's Quarterly Review*, was all that he needed, and in 1873 he began the "Last Series."

In the first issue of the revived *Review* Brownson wrote:

I willingly admit that I made many mistakes; but I regard as the greatest of all the mistakes into which I fell during the last three or four years that I published my *Review*, that of holding back the stronger points of the Catholic faith, on which I had previously insisted. . . . I have no ambition to be regarded as a *liberal* Catholic. A *liberal* Catholic I am not, never was, save in appearance for a brief moment, and never can be. . . . What is most needed in these times . . . is the truth that condemns, point-blank, the spirit of the age, and gives no quarter to its dominant errors. . . .[29]

With this tone he carried on the *Review* for three years, until the autumn of 1875. As an affirmation of his orthodoxy and of his submission of all he had written to the judgment of the Church these last essays have some interest. But his best work had been done.

In the autumn of 1875, after the final number of his *Review* was finished, Brownson left Elizabeth, New Jersey, and went to live with his son Henry in Detroit, Michigan. He had been in poor health for more than fifteen years. Even as early as 1857

[29] *Works*, XX, 382.

he had begun to suffer from gout of the eyes, and later his joints had been affected. Reading became difficult, and at times his hand was too crippled to hold a pen. He often had to dictate his articles, and in his last years even fell back on the re-publication of earlier essays to fill the pages of his revived *Review*. After moving to Detroit, Brownson was able to complete only one article, "The Philosophy of the Supernatural." From Christmas on into the spring the physical and intellectual energy that had sustained him through years of writing and lecturing waned rapidly. On Easter Sunday he received the Sacraments of Holy Communion and Extreme Unction. He died early the next morning, April 17, 1876, and was buried in Detroit.

Brownson had for many years known Father Edward Sorin, the first president of the University of Notre Dame. In 1862 Brownson had been invited to join the Notre Dame faculty, and though he declined at the time for reasons of health, his writings for the *Ave Maria* from 1865 to 1872 were the occasion of frequent correspondence with Father Sorin. In 1872, after the death of Brownson's wife, Father Sorin invited him to come to live at the University, but he had already decided to revive his *Review*, and felt it would be difficult to conduct it from there. Ten years after his death, Brownson's remains were removed from Detroit to Notre Dame, where they now repose in a crypt in the center aisle of the Brownson Memorial Chapel in Sacred Heart Church.

III

Brownson has been denounced by liberals for his conservatism; by conservatives for his liberalism. Liberals who acclaim his keenness of mind and courage in his early liberal period often look sadly upon his conversion as a retreat, and lament that one who was a "forerunner of Marx" in the 1830's should end as a reactionary Catholic. Conservatives who approve not only his

American Republic (1866) but even his abandonment in old age of any interest in political and social reform seem too ready to place him among the ultra-conservatives within the Church whose influence he continued to oppose for nearly ten years prior to the publication of the *Syllabus*.

These, I believe, are gross oversimplifications. They ignore the whole context of Brownson's work: the hammering out of his thought in journalistic essays, the hazards and risks he took, perhaps too hastily at times, in laying before the public the very process of his own self-education, his development in the milieu of New England Protestantism, and then his entering the lists, so suddenly and so unprepared in many ways, as a champion of Catholic orthodoxy. More important, the isolation of what may loosely be called the two conservative or the two liberal phases of his thought from contemporary American and European movements makes his vacillations, as they are often called, far less understandable than they really are. The dialectic of Brownson's thought mirrors in many ways the intellectual dialectic of the middle half of the nineteenth century. And finally, to ignore the relation of Church history to these movements, and especially during the papacy of Pius IX, which, except for two years, covers Brownson's entire Catholic life, is at least to miss the drama of his intellectual changes.

Society and Politics

SOCIETY AND POLITICS

EDITOR'S PREFACE

BROWNSON began as radical social reformer, in whom a vague religious impulse and a passion for reforming the world now conflicted and now were merged into a temporary harmony. Around the year 1828 the Utopian experiments and the writings of Robert Owen first attracted Brownson's attention, as he says in *The Convert,* "to the question of reorganizing society and creating a paradise on earth." (*Works,* V, 43.) He reread Godwin's *Enquiry Concerning Political Justice* and was profoundly influenced by it. Thenceforth for some ten years he allied himself with the cause of the workingman. His brief association with Fanny Wright and Robert Dale Owen, and with the Workingmen's party, represented his furthest movement toward a purely secular approach to social reform. Yet as an independent and then a Unitarian minister, Brownson's chief interest continued through the thirties to be in the condition of the laboring classes. His religion was humanitarianism, the God he worshiped was the God in man.

His political thinking up to 1838 was unsystematic and inchoate. "Democracy" was a rallying cry, carrying emotional overtones that remained unanalyzed. He made none of his later distinctions between the conditions that led to the French Revolution and the American Revolution nor between the European and American conceptions of democracy. Instead, he interpreted the impulse toward freedom, equality, and "progress" according to his own personal understanding of Christianity, and such continental thinkers as Lamennais and Saint-Simon molded much of his thought. His political writings proper began with "Democracy" (1838). Here he repudiated egalitarian theories of democracy, affirming that true democracy makes justice and law, not the general will, sovereign. Yet in 1839 he hailed Andrew Jackson as the champion of the masses, and wrote of the Democratic party: "Through it now speaks the voice of eternal principle, which is the voice of the people; and the voice of the people is the voice of God; and when God speaks, who dare deny that he will be heard and obeyed?" (*Works*, XV, 44.)

Brownson's decision to support the Democratic party in the election campaign of 1840, and the violent attacks upon his essay, "The Laboring Classes," led him to his first serious confrontation of the problems of political philosophy. "I read for the first time Aristotle on Politics; I read the best treatises, ancient and modern, on government within my reach; I studied the constitutions of Greece and Rome . . . and came to the conclusion that the condition of liberty is order, and that in this world we must seek, not equality, but justice. . . . Liberty is not in the absence of authority, but in being held to obey only just and legitimate authority. Evidently, I had changed systems, and had entered another order of ideas. . . . I became henceforth a conservative in politics, instead of an impracticable radical, and through political conversation I advanced rapidly towards religious conservatism." (*The Convert*, *Works*, V, 120–1.)

The essays Brownson wrote from 1841 to his conversion in 1844 developed the distinction between radical democracy and constitutional republicanism. He now became a constitutionalist for whom the American Constitution represented one of the great achievements in the history of government. He analyzed the contract theories of Locke and Rousseau, and repudiated them as inadequate to establish legitimate authority in government. Even in the common interpretation of the natural-rights doctrine of the Declaration of Independence he saw a doctrinaire element close to the French conception of democracy but alien to the American. While Brownson was soon accused of adopting a reactionary political philosophy, he insisted that he was still of the movement party, that he would never be a Whig, and that the conservative view he developed in these essays was the only safeguard of genuine liberty. His political sympathies remained Democratic, even while he was increasingly critical of the Jacksonian type of democracy. His opposition both to industrialism and to excessive centralization of power led him to embrace Calhoun's states' rights doctrine and to support Calhoun as Democratic candidate for the presidency in 1844. If he now seemed less concerned with social justice, it was partly because in his approach toward the Catholic Church during these years he was attempting, as he affirmed in the essay, "No Church, No Reform" (1844), to find a true basis for reform.

As a Catholic, Brownson developed his theory of the providential constitution, and continued to deny all undelegated authority whether of king, nobility, or the people. All authority was ultimately from God, and politics was subject to the moral order. Up to 1851 he saw the chief danger in European politics in the false theories of liberty of the revolutionary parties, which would replace one form of despotism with another. Yet while many American Catholics applauded as favorable to the French Church the *coup d'état* of 1851 by which Louis Napoleon became Emperor of France, Brownson immediately warned of the new trend in Europe toward absolutism. He became a friend and champion of Count Montalembert, who opposed the monarchists rallying around Louis Veuillot, the editor of the *Univers*. From 1855 to 1864 he showed increasing sympathy with the Catholic liberals of Europe, as some of the essays included in this volume under "Christianity and Civilization" make clear, and in doing so came into continual conflict with many American Catholics. During this period he moderated his criticism of liberalism and socialism, attempting to distinguish the excesses of these movements from the truths they embraced. After 1864, Brownson's political and social thought became much more conservative, though it should be emphasized that the fullest exposition of his political theory during this later period, *The American Republic* (1866), is in part a development and revision of his essays on the "Origin and Ground of Government" published in 1843.

As Russell Kirk has recognized in his valuable recent study, *The Conservative Mind* (Chicago, 1953), much of Brownson's later political thought is in the tradition of Burke's conservatism. Even more striking are the similarities between Brownson's analysis of the types of political thinking and that developed by Irving Babbitt in *Democracy and Leadership* (Boston, 1924), though the differences are not to be minimized. Brownson's constitutional theory and his organismic idea of the community are in the conservative tradition, as is his whole later critique of the doctrinaire approach to reform which he had once adopted. In a sense, he traversed the whole distance between Thomas Paine and Edmund Burke. Since he looked to conservative principles as the true foundation of improvement and progress, it is unfortunate that Brownson lost interest in the situation of the workingman, and turned his attention so exclusively to religious, philosophical, and political issues. Though it is true that from 1855 to 1864 he devoted much of his effort to bringing the vital conservatism of the Catholic tradition to bear on contemporary problems, he failed to recognize that his own earlier social thought, freed of its errors, might have been developed into such a Catholic social philosophy as was finally enunciated in Pope Leo XIII's encyclical on the Condition of Labor, *Rerum Novarum* (1891).

Among recent studies of Brownson's social and political

thought, the following are especially useful: M. A. Fitzsimons, "Brownson's Search for the Kingdom of God: The Social Thought of an American Radical," *Review of Politics,* XVI (1954), pp. 22–36; Stanley J. Parry, C.S.C., "The Premises of Brownson's Political Theory," *Review of Politics,* XVI (1954), pp. 194–211. Lawrence Roemer's recent volume, *Brownson on Democracy and the Trend Toward Socialism* (New York, 1953), brings Brownson's *American Republic* into relation with some of his earlier essays. For an adverse evaluation of Brownson's later political and religious thought, see Carl F. Krummel, "Catholicism, Americanism, Democracy, and Orestes Brownson," *American Quarterly,* VI (1954), pp. 19–31.

DEMOCRACY
[1838]

[*This essay appeared in the first number of Brownson's* Boston Quarterly Review, *January, 1838.* (Works, *XV, 1–34*) *It shows that even in his early period he held that in democracy there must be a source of authority above the mere will of the majority. In the words of Schlesinger:* "*It soon became evident that Brownson looked to the state-rights doctrine as the guardian of liberty. The people could not control the government, he thought, unless the states retained their integrity; for centralization would open the way to control by a small group. The American democracy had started from the distribution of powers. The assurance of liberty must lie in keeping local authorities independent.*" (Orestes A. Brownson, *pp. 76–77.*) *Brownson's argument in the following essay suggests comparison with that of de Tocqueville, whose* Democracy in America *was published in two parts in 1835 and 1840.*]

DEMOCRACY, in the sense we are now considering it, is sometimes asserted to be the sovereignty of the people. If this be a true account of it, it is indefensible. The sovereignty of the people is not a truth. Sovereignty is that which is highest, ultimate; which has not only the physical force to make itself obeyed, but the moral right to command whatever it pleases. The right to command involves the corresponding duty of obedience. What the sovereign may command, it is the duty of the subject to do.

Are the people the highest? Are they ultimate? And are we bound in conscience to obey whatever it may be their good pleasure to ordain? If so, where is individual liberty? If so, the people, taken collectively, are the absolute master of every man taken individually. Every man, as a man, then, is an absolute slave. Whatever the people, in their collective capacity, may demand of him, he must feel himself bound in conscience to give. No matter how intolerable the burdens imposed, painful and needless the sacrifices required, he cannot refuse obedience without incurring the guilt of disloyalty; and he must submit in quiet, in silence, without even the moral right to feel that he is wronged. . . .

The majority will always have the physical power to coerce the minority into submission; but this is a matter of no moment in comparison with the doctrine which gives them the right to do it. We have very little fear of the physical force of numbers, when we can oppose to it the moral force of right. The doctrine in question deprives us of this moral force. By giving absolute sovereignty to the majority, it declares whatever the majority does is right, that the majority can do no wrong. It legitimates every possible act, for which the sanction of a majority of voices can be obtained. Whatever the majority may exact, it is just to give. Truth, justice, wisdom, virtue can erect no barriers to stay its progress; for these are the creations of its will, and may be made or unmade by its breath. Justice is obedience to its decrees, and injustice is resistance to its commands. Resistance is not crime before the civil tribunal only, but also *in foro conscientiae.* Now this is what we protest against. It is not the physical force of the majority that we dread, but the doctrine that legitimates each and every act the majority may choose to perform; and therefore teaches them to look for no standard of right and wrong beyond their own will.

We do not believe majorities are exceedingly prone to encroach on the rights of minorities; but we would always erect a bulwark of justice around those rights, and always have a moral power which we may oppose to every possible encroachment. The majority, we believe, always leaves the minority in possession of the greater part of their rights, not, however, as rights, but as favors. It is to this we object. We cannot, and will not, consent to receive as a boon what we may demand as a right. Our liberties belong to us as men; and we would always feel that we hold them as our personal property, of which he who despoils us is a thief and a robber. . . .

There is within every man, who can lay any claim to correct moral feeling, that which looks with contempt on the puny creature who makes the opinions of the majority his rule of action. He who wants the moral courage to stand up "in solitary grandeur," like Socrates in face of the Thirty Tyrants, and demand that right be respected, that justice be done, is unfit to be called a statesman, or even a man. A man has no business with what the majority think, will, say, do, or will approve; if he will be a man, and maintain the rights and dignity of manhood, his sole business is to inquire what truth and justice, wisdom and virtue demand at his hands, and to do it, whether . . . he stand alone "in solitary grandeur," or be huzzaed by the crowd, loaded with honors, held up as one whom the young must aspire to imitate, or be sneered at as singular, branded as a "seditious fellow," or crucified between two thieves. Away then with your demoralizing and debasing notion of appealing to a majority of voices! Dare be a man, dare be yourself, to speak and act according to your own solemn convictions, and in obedience to the voice of God calling out to you from the depths of your own being. Professions of freedom, of love of liberty, of devotion to her cause, are mere wind when there wants the power to live, and to die, in defense of what one's own heart tells him is just and true. A free government is a mockery, a solemn farce, where every man feels himself bound to consult and to conform to the opinions and will of an irresponsible majority. Free minds, free hearts, free souls are the materials, and the only materials, out of which free governments are constructed. And is he free in mind, heart, soul, body, or limb, he who feels himself bound to the triumphal car of the majority, to be dragged whither its drivers please? Is he the man to speak out the lessons of truth and wisdom when most they are needed, to stand by the right when all are gone out of the way, to plead for the wronged and downtrodden when all are dumb, he who owns the absolute right of the majority to govern? . . .

Democracy, as we understand it, we have said, is, on the one hand, the denial of absolute sovereignty to the state, whatever the form of government adopted, and, on the other hand, the assertion of the absolute sovereignty of justice. It therefore commands both the people and the individual to be just. It subjects both to one and the same law; and, while it commands the citizen to obey and serve the state with all fidelity, so long as it keeps within its legitimate province, it takes care not to forget to remind the state that it must leave the citizen, as a man, free to do or to enjoy whatever justice permits, commands, or does not forbid. . . .

Democracy is the doctrine of true liberty. The highest conception of liberty is that which leaves every man free to do whatever it is just to do, and not free to do only what it is unjust to do. Freedom to do that which is unjust according to the laws of God or,—which is the same thing,—the law of nature, is license, not liberty, and is as much opposed to liberty as lust is to love. "A free government," say the old English lawyers, "is a government of laws," and they say right, if law is taken absolutely, and not merely as the enactment of the human legislature. Where there is an arbitrary will above the law, be it the will of the one, the few, or the many, there is, in theory at least, absolutism, and the room for pure despotism. A free government must be a government, not of the will of one man, nor of the will of any body of men, but a government of law; not of a law which a human authority may make or unmake, but of that which is law in the very nature, constitution, and being of this system of things to which we belong. Under a government of law in this sense, where authority may never do, command, or permit, except what the immutable law of justice ordains, men are free; they live under the "perfect law of liberty," and may attain to the full and harmonious development of all their faculties. . . .

Democracy takes care not to lose the man in the citizen. In the free states, or rather free cities, of antiquity there were rights of the citizen, but no rights of man. As a citizen, the individual might use his personal influence and exertions in making up the decision of the city; but when the decision was once made up, he was bound in conscience, as well as compelled by physical force, to yield it, whatever it might be, the most unqualified submission. He had no rights sacred and inviolable, beyond the legitimate authority of the city. In a question between the city and himself, he could demand nothing as his right. The city was in no way responsible to him; but he owed it everything he had, even to his life. Athens condemns Socrates to death, and sends him to prison to await his execution. His friends provide the means, and urge him to escape. No; Socrates is a conscientious man. He knows his duty. Athens has condemned him to die, and he is bound, as a good citizen, to submit to her sentence. He drinks, therefore, the hemlock at the appointed time, of his own accord, and dies in discharge of his duty to the laws of the city of which he acknowledged himself a citizen. As a citizen of Athens, Socrates knew he could not save his life, without incurring the guilt of disloyalty. He had no rights as a man, that he might plead. He felt himself as much the slave of Athens, as the Persian was of the "Great King." His rights as a man were sunk in those of the citizen, and those of the citizen were sunk in those of the city.

Here was the great defect of ancient democracy. In Athens, in any of the ancient republics, there was no personal liberty. One individual might indeed call in the city to maintain his rights, in a dispute with another individual; but beyond this, he had no rights. There was municipal liberty, but no individual liberty. The city could bind or loose the individual at its will, declare him a citizen, or degrade him to a slave, just as she deemed it most expedient. The city differed in no respect from an absolute monarchy, save in the fact, that the absolute sovereignty, in the case of the city, was supposed to be vested in the majority of the citizens, instead of being vested in one man, as in the monarchy. But she was as absolute, and in case she could get a majority of voices, she might go as far, and play the tyrant to as great an extent, as the king of Persia himself. Her democracy was then by no means liberty. It was liberty, if you will, for the city, but none for the individual man. The individual man was not recognized as an integer; he was, at best, only a fraction of the body politic. He was, in truth, merely a cypher; without inherent value, augmenting the value of the city, indeed, if placed at her right hand, but counting for nothing if placed at her left hand. But, thanks to the feudal system, and still more to Christianity, an element is introduced into the modern city, which was unknown in the ancient, the element of Individuality, by virtue of which the individual man possesses an intrinsic value which he retains in all positions, and instead of a fraction, becomes a whole.

Modern democracy, therefore, goes beyond the ancient. Ancient democracy merely declared the people the state; the modern declares, in addition, that every man, by virtue of the fact that he is a man, is an equal member of the state,—universal suffrage, and eligibility, two things the ancients never dreamed of,—and that the state is limited by justice, or, what is the same thing, the inalienable Rights of Man. These inalienable rights of

man are something more than the rights of citizenship, or certain
private rights, the rights of one man in relation to another,
which the state is bound to protect; they stretch over nearly the
whole domain of human activity, and are, in the strictest sense of
the word, rights of the individual in relation to the state, rights
of which the state may not, under any pretense whatever, deprive him, and to whose free exercise it may, in no case whatever, interpose any obstruction. In the ancient democracies the
individual, if a member of the ruling race, was a citizen with
duties; in the modern, he adds, in theory, to the citizen with
duties, the man with rights. Democracy, as we understand it,
does not give all the rights to the state and impose all the duties
on the individual. It places the state under obligation to the
citizen, in the same manner, and to the same extent, that it
places the individual under obligation to the state. . . .

The great error of government, in all ages of the world, has
been, that of counting itself the real owner and sovereign dis-
poser of the individual,—that of disfranchising all individuals,
and then pretending to redistribute individual rights, according
to its own caprice, interests, or necessities. To put an end to this
system of privilege is now the great aim of democracy. Its object
is to restrict governments, whether royal, aristocratical, or popular, to their legitimate province, and individuals to their natural
rights, and to teach both to perform those duties, and those
duties only, which everlasting and immutable justice imposes.
To this it steadily makes its way; for this it struggles; and this it
will ultimately achieve.

The reduction to practice of the theory we have now imperfectly, but we hope distinctly, set forth, will demand great
changes, and more changes, perhaps, than anyone can foresee;
and changes, too, which can be introduced at once, in no country,
without violence, and probably not without bloodshed and great
suffering. He who pleads for justice will not be anxious to pro-

mote violence, bloodshed, or suffering. There may be times when the kingdom of heaven must be taken by violence, and when a people should rise up and demand its rights, at whatever sacrifice it may be. But there is and there can be, in this country, no occasion for any but orderly and peaceful measures, for the acquisition of all we have supposed. We must not dream of introducing it all at once. We must proceed leisurely. Let the men of thought speculate freely, and speak boldly what comes to them as truth; but let the men of action, men who have more enthusiasm than reflection, greater hearts than minds, and stronger hands than heads, guard against impatience. Practical men, men of action, are, after all, the men who play the most mischief with improvements. Our principle is, no revolution, no destruction, but progress. Progress is always slow, and slow let it be; the slower it is the more speed it makes. So long as we find the thinkers busy canvassing all great matters, discussing all topics of reform, and publishing freely to the world the result of their investigations, we have no fears for the individual, none for society. Truth is omnipotent. Let it be uttered; let it spread from mind to mind, from heart to heart, and in due season be assured that it will make to itself hands, erect itself a temple, and institute its worship. Set just ideas afloat in the community, and feel no uneasiness about institutions. Bad institutions, before you are aware of it, will crumble away, and new ones and good ones supply their places.

We hold ourselves among the foremost of those who demand reform, and who would live and die for progress; but we wish no haste, no violence in pulling down old institutions or in building up new ones. We would innovate boldly in our speculations; but in action we would cling to old usages and keep by old lines of policy, till we were fairly forced by the onward pressure of opinion to abandon them. We would think with the radical, but often act with the conservative. When the time comes to abandon an old practice, when new circumstances have arisen to demand a new line of policy, then, we say, let no attachments to the past make us blind to our duty or impotent to perform it. All we say is, let nothing be done in a hurry, and let no rage for experiments be encouraged.

THE LABORING CLASSES
[1840]

["*The Laboring Classes,*" *which began as a review of Carlyle's* "*Chartism*" (*1839*), *appeared in the July, 1840, number of the* Boston Quarterly (*III, 358–95*). *Replying to the storm of criticism his essay aroused, Brownson elaborated on his thought in a second essay in the October number* (*III, 420–510*). *Unfortunately, neither of the two essays, totaling over one hundred pages, is included in the collected* Works. *I have reduced the first essay to one fourth its original length, but have included nothing from the second.*

The country was still suffering from the results of the financial panic of 1837. Moreover, 1840 was an election year, and Brownson's review was supporting the Democratic candidate Van Buren for re-election against the Whig candidate Harrison. The Whigs reprinted Brownson's essay and gave it wide distribution to show what it was the President and his party really held. While Brownson said Van Buren attributed his defeat to the essay, historians do not accord "The Laboring Classes" that much importance. Emerson's comment in a letter to Margaret Fuller was surprisingly favorable: "The hero wields a sturdy pen which I am very glad to see. I had judged him from some old things & did not know he was such a Cobbett of a scribe. Let him wash himself and he shall write for the immortal Dial." (*Quoted from Emerson's* Letters, *II, p. 273, by Maynard,* Orestes Brownson, *p. 96.*)

Later Brownson came to refer to the articles as his "Horrible Doctrines" and dated his "convalescence" from their publication. (The Convert, Works, *V, 99–121.*) *Schlesinger's illuminating discussion of this phase of Brownson's thought* (Orestes A. Brownson, *pp. 88–111*) *should be consulted.*]

THOMAS CARLYLE unquestionably ranks among the ablest writers of the day. His acquaintance with literature seems to be almost universal, and there is apparently no art or science with which he is not familiar. He possesses an unrivaled mastery over the resources of the English tongue, a remarkably keen insight into the mysteries of human nature, and a large share of genuine poetic feeling. His works are characterized by freshness and power, as well as by strangeness and singularity, and must be read with interest, even when they cannot be with approbation. . . .

He is good as a demolisher, but pitiable enough as a builder. No man sees more clearly that the present is defective and unworthy to be retained; he is a brave and successful warrior against it, whether reference be had to its literature, its politics, its philosophy, or its religion; but when the question comes up concerning what ought to be, what should take the place of what is, we regret to say, he affords us no essential aid, scarcely a useful hint. He has fine spiritual instincts, has outgrown materialism, loathes skepticism, sees clearly the absolute necessity of faith in both God and man, and insists upon it with due sincerity and earnestness; but with feelings very nearly akin to despair. . . .

He disheartens and enfeebles us; and while he emancipates us from the errors of tradition, he leaves us without strength or courage to engage in the inquiry after truth. We rise from his writings with the weariness and exhaustion one does from the embraces of the Witch Mara. It is but slowly that our blood begins to circulate again, and it is long before we recover the use of our powers. Whether his writings produce this effect on others or not, we are unable to say; but this effect they do produce on us. We almost dread to encounter them. . . .

The object of the little work before us, is one of the weightiest which can engage the attention of the statesman or the philanthropist. It is indeed, here, discussed only in relation to the working classes of England, but it in reality involves the condition of the working classes throughout the world,—a great subject, and one never yet worthily treated. Chartism, properly speaking, is no local or temporary phenomenon. Its germ may be found in every nation in Christendom; indeed wherever man has approximated a state of civilization, wherever there is inequality in social condition, and in the distribution of the products of industry. And where does not this inequality obtain? Where is the spot on earth, in which the actual producer of wealth is not one of the lower class, shut out from what are looked upon as the main advantages of the social state? . . .

There is no country in Europe, in which the condition of the laboring classes seems to us so hopeless as in that of England. This is not owing to the fact, that the aristocracy is less enlightened, more powerful, or more oppressive in England than elsewhere. The English laborer does not find his worst enemy in the nobility, but in the middling class. . . . The middle class is always a firm champion of equality, when it concerns humbling a class above it; but it is its inveterate foe, when it concerns elevating a class below it. Manfully have the British Commoners struggled against the old feudal aristocracy, and so successfully that they now constitute the dominant power in the state. . . .

But this class has done nothing for the laboring population, the real *proletarii*. It has humbled the aristocracy; it has raised itself to dominion, and it is now conservative,—conservative in fact, whether it call itself Whig or Radical. From its near relation to the workingmen, its kindred pursuits with them, it is altogether more hostile to them than the nobility ever were or ever can be. This was seen in the conduct of England toward the French Revolution. . . . England fought in the ranks, nay, at the head of the allies, not for monarchy, not for nobility, nor yet for religion; but for trade and manufactures, for her middle class, against the rights and well-being of the workingman; and her strength and efficiency consisted in the strength and efficiency of this class.

Now this middle class, which was strong enough to defeat nearly all the practical benefit of the French Revolution, is the natural enemy of the Chartists. . . . No one can observe the signs of the times with much care, without perceiving that a crisis as to the relation of wealth and labor is approaching. It is useless to shut our eyes to the fact, and like the ostrich fancy ourselves secure because we have so concealed our heads that we see not the danger. We or our children will have to meet this crisis. The old war between the King and the Barons is well nigh ended, and so is that between the Barons and the Merchants and Manufacturers,—landed capital and commercial capital. The businessman has become the peer of my Lord. And now commences the new struggle between the operative and his employer, between wealth and labor. Every day does this struggle extend further and wax stronger and fiercer; what or when the end will be God only knows. . . .

What we would ask is, throughout the Christian world, the actual condition of the laboring classes, viewed simply and exclusively in their capacity of Laborers? They constitute at least a moiety of the human race. We exclude the nobility, we exclude also the middle class, and include only actual laborers, who are laborers and not proprietors, owners of none of the funds of production, neither houses, shops, nor lands, nor implements of labor, being therefore solely dependent on their hands. We have no means of ascertaining their precise proportion to the whole number of the race; but we think we may estimate them at one half. In any contest they will be as two to one, because the large class of proprietors who are not employers, but laborers on their own lands or in their own shops, will make common cause with them.

Now we will not so belie our acquaintance with political economy, as to allege that these alone perform all that is necessary to the production of wealth. We are not ignorant of the fact, that the merchant, who is literally the common carrier and exchange dealer, performs a useful service, and is therefore entitled to a portion of the proceeds of labor. But make all necessary deductions on his account, and then ask what portion of the remainder is retained, either in kind or in its equivalent, in the hands of the original producer, the workingman? All over the world this fact stares us in the face, the workingman is poor and depressed, while a large portion of the non-workingmen, in the sense we now use the term, are wealthy. It may be laid down as a general rule, with but few exceptions, that men are rewarded in an inverse ratio to the amount of actual service they perform. Under every government on earth the largest salaries are annexed to those offices, which demand of their incumbents the least amount of actual labor either mental or manual. And this is in perfect harmony with the whole system of repartition of the fruits of industry, which obtains in every department of society. Now here is the system which prevails, and here is its result. The whole class of simple laborers are poor, and in general unable to procure anything beyond the bare necessaries of life. . . .

Now, what is the prospect of those who fall under the operation of this system? We ask, is there a reasonable chance that any considerable portion of the present generation of laborers, shall ever become owners of a sufficient portion of the funds of production, to be able to sustain themselves by laboring on their own capital, that is, as independent laborers? We need not ask this question, for everybody knows there is not. Well, is the condition of a laborer at wages the best that the great mass of the working people ought to be able to aspire to? Is it a condition,—nay can it be made a condition,—with which a man should be satisfied; in which he should be contented to live and die?

In our own country this condition has existed under its most favorable aspects, and has been made as good as it can be. It has reached all the excellence of which it is susceptible. It is now not improving but growing worse. The actual condition of the workingman today, viewed in all its bearings, is not so good as it was fifty years ago. If we have not been altogether misinformed, fifty years ago, health and industrious habits, constituted no mean stock in trade, and with them almost any man might aspire to competence and independence. But it is so no longer. The wilderness has receded, and already the new lands are beyond the reach of the mere laborer, and the employer has him at his mercy. If the present relations subsist, we see nothing better for him in reserve than what he now possesses, but something altogether worse. . . .

Now the great work for this age and the coming is to raise up the laborer, and to realize in our own social arrangements, and in the actual condition of all men, that equality between man and man, which God has established between the rights of one and those of another. In other words, our business is to emancipate the proletaries, as the past has emancipated the slaves. This is our work. There must be no class of our fellow men doomed to toil through life as mere workmen at wages. If wages are tolerated it must be, in the case of the individual operative, only under such conditions that by the time he is of a proper age to settle in life, he shall have accumulated enough to be an independent laborer on his own capital,—on his own farm or in his own shop. Here is our work. How is it to be done?

Reformers in general answer this question, or what they deem its equivalent, in a manner which we cannot but regard as very unsatisfactory. They would have all men wise, good, and happy; but in order to make them so, they tell us that we want not external changes, but internal; and therefore instead of declaiming against society and seeking to disturb existing social arrangements, we should confine ourselves to the individual reason and conscience; seek merely to lead the individual to repentance, and to reformation of life; make the individual a practical, a truly religious man, and all evils will either disappear, or be sanctified to the spiritual growth of the soul. . . .

For our part, we yield to none in our reverence for science and religion; but we confess that we look not for the regeneration of the race from priests and pedagogues. They have had a fair trial. They cannot construct the temple of God. They cannot conceive its plan, and they know not how to build. They daub with untempered mortar, and the walls they erect tumble down if so much as a fox attempt to go up thereon. In a word, they always league with the people's masters, and seek to reform without disturbing the social arrangements which render reform necessary. They would change the consequents without changing the antecedents, secure to men the rewards of holiness, while they continue their allegiance to the devil. We have no faith in priests and pedagogues. They merely cry peace, peace, and that too when there is no peace, and can be none. . . .

The truth is, the evil we have pointed out is not merely individual in its character. It is not, in the case of any single individual, of any one man's procuring, nor can the efforts of any one man, directed solely to his own moral and religious perfection, do aught to remove it. What is purely individual in its nature, efforts of individuals to perfect themselves, may remove. But the evil we speak of is inherent in all our social arrangements, and cannot be cured without a radical change of those arrangements. . . . The only way to get rid of its evils is to change the system, not its managers. The evils of slavery do not result from the personal characters of slave masters. They are inseparable from the system, let who will be masters. Make all your rich men good Christians, and you have lessened not the evils of existing inequality in wealth. The mischievous effects of this inequality do not result from the personal characters of either rich or poor, but from itself, and they will continue, just so long as there are rich men and poor men in the same community. You must abolish the system or accept its consequences. No man can serve both God and Mammon. If you will serve the devil, you must look to the devil for your wages; we know no other way.

Let us not be misinterpreted. We deny not the power of Christianity. Should all men become good Christians, we deny not that all social evils would be cured. But we deny in the outset that a man, who seeks merely to save his own soul, merely to perfect his own individual nature, can be a good Christian. The Christian forgets himself, buckles on his armor, and goes forth to war against principalities and powers, and against spiritual wickedness in high places. No man can be a Christian who does not begin his career by making war on the mischievous social arrangements from which his brethren suffer. He who thinks he can be a Christian and save his soul, without seeking their radical change, has no reason to applaud himself for his proficiency in Christian science, nor for his progress toward the kingdom of God. Understand Christianity, and we will admit, that should all men become good Christians, there would be nothing to complain of. But one might as well undertake to dip the ocean dry with a clam shell as to undertake to cure the evils of the social state by converting men to the Christianity of the Church. . . .

For our part we are disposed to seek the cause of the inequality of conditions of which we speak, in religion, and to charge it to the priesthood. . . . We object not to religious instruction; we object not to the gathering together of the people on one day in seven, to sing and pray, and listen to a discourse from a religious teacher; but we object to everything like an outward, visible church; to everything that in the remotest degree partakes of the priest. A priest is one who stands as a sort of mediator between God and man; but we have one mediator, Jesus Christ, who gave himself a ransom for all, and that is enough. It may be supposed that we, protestants, have no

priests; but for ourselves we know no fundamental difference between a catholic priest and a protestant clergyman, as we know
no difference of any magnitude, in relation to the principles on
which they are based, between a protestant church and the
catholic church. Both are based on the principle of authority;
both deny in fact, however it may be in manner, the authority of
reason, and war against freedom of mind; both substitute dead
works for true righteousness, a vain show for the reality of piety,
and are sustained as the means of reconciling us to God without
requiring us to become godlike. Both therefore ought to go by
the board. . . .

In every age the priests, the authorized teachers of religion,
are the first to oppose the true prophet of God, and to condemn
his prophecies as blasphemies. They are always a let and a
hindrance to the spread of truth. Why then retain them? Why
not abolish the priestly office? Why continue to sustain what the
whole history of man condemns as the greatest of all obstacles to
intellectual and social progress? . . .

The next step in this work of elevating the working classes
will be to resuscitate the Christianity of Christ. . . . According
to the Christianity of Christ no man can enter the kingdom of
God, who does not labor with all zeal and diligence to establish
the kingdom of God on the earth; who does not labor to bring
down the high, and bring up the low; to break the fetters of the
bound and set the captive free; to destroy all oppression,
establish the reign of justice, which is the reign of equality, between man and man; to introduce new heavens and a new earth,
wherein dwelleth righteousness, wherein all shall be as brothers,
loving one another, and no one possessing what another lacketh.
No man can be a Christian who does not labor to reform society,
to mould it according to the will of God and the nature of man;
so that free scope shall be given to every man to unfold himself
in all beauty and power, and to grow up into the stature of a

perfect man in Christ Jesus. No man can be a Christian who does not refrain from all practices by which the rich grow richer and the poor poorer, and who does not do all in his power to elevate the laboring classes, so that one man shall not be doomed to toil while another enjoys the fruits; so that each man shall be free and independent, sitting under "his own vine and figtree with none to molest or to make afraid." We grant the power of Christianity in working out the reform we demand; we agree that one of the most efficient means of elevating the workingmen is to christianize the community. But you must christianize it. It is the Gospel of Jesus you must preach, and not the gospel of the priests. . . . We must preach no gospel that permits men to feel that they are honorable men and good Christians, although rich and with eyes standing out with fatness, while the great mass of their brethren are suffering from iniquitous laws, from mischievous social arrangements, and pining away for the want of the refinements and even the necessaries of life. . . .

Having, by breaking down the power of the priesthood and the Christianity of the priests, obtained an open field and freedom for our operations, and by preaching the true Gospel of Jesus, directed all minds to the great social reform needed, and quickened in all souls the moral power to live for it or to die for it; our next resort must be to government, to legislative enactments. Government is instituted to be the agent of society, or more properly the organ through which society may perform its legitimate functions. It is not the master of society; its business is not to control society, but to be the organ through which society effects its will. Society has never to petition government; government is its servant, and subject to its commands. . . .

But what shall government do? Its first doing must be an *un*doing. There has been thus far quite too much government, as well as government of the wrong kind. The first act of government we want is a still further limitation of itself. It must begin by circumscribing within narrower limits its powers. And then it must proceed to repeal all laws which bear against the laboring classes, and then to enact such laws as are necessary to enable them to maintain their equality. We have no faith in those systems of elevating the working classes, which propose to elevate them without calling in the aid of the government. We must have government, and legislation expressly directed to this end.

But again what legislation do we want so far as this country is concerned? We want first the legislation which shall free the government, whether State or Federal, from the control of the Banks. The Banks represent the interest of the employer, and therefore of necessity interests adverse to those of the employed; that is, they represent the interests of the business community in opposition to the laboring community. So long as the government remains under the control of the Banks, so long it must be in the hands of the natural enemies of the laboring classes, and may be made, nay, will be made, an instrument of depressing them yet lower. . . . The present character, standing, and resources of the Bank party, prove to a demonstration that the Banks must be destroyed, or the laborer not elevated. Uncompromising hostility to the whole banking system should therefore be the motto of every workingman, and of every friend of Humanity. The system must be destroyed. On this point there must be no misgiving, no subterfuge, no palliation. The system is at war with the rights and interest of labor, and it must go. Every friend of the system must be marked as an enemy to his race, to his country, and especially to the laborer. No matter who he is, in what party he is found, or what name he bears, he is, in our judgment, no true democrat, as he can be no true Christian.

Following the destruction of the Banks, must come that of all monopolies, of all PRIVILEGE. There are many of these. We cannot specify them all; we therefore select only one, the greatest of them all, the privilege which some have of being born rich while others are born poor. It will be seen at once that we allude to the hereditary descent of property, an anomaly in our American system, which must be removed or the system itself will be destroyed. . . . A man shall have all he honestly acquires, so long as he himself belongs to the world in which he acquires it. But his power over his property must cease with his life, and his property must then become the property of the state, to be disposed of by some equitable law for the use of the generation which takes his place. Here is the principle without any of its details, and this is the grand legislative measure to which we look forward. We see no means of elevating the laboring classes which can be effectual without this. And is this a measure to be easily carried? Not at all. It will cost infinitely more than it cost to abolish either hereditary monarchy or hereditary nobility. It is a great measure, and a startling. The rich, the business community, will never voluntarily consent to it, and we think we know too much of human nature to believe that it will ever be effected peaceably. It will be effected only by the strong arm of physical force. It will come, if it ever come at all, only at the conclusion of war, the like of which the world as yet has never witnessed, and from which, however inevitable it may seem to the eye of philosophy, the heart of Humanity recoils with horror.

We are not ready for this measure yet. There is much previous work to be done, and we should be the last to bring it before the legislature. The time, however, has come for its free and full discussion. It must be canvassed in the public mind, and society prepared for acting on it. No doubt they who broach it, and especially they who support it, will experience a due share of contumely and abuse. They will be regarded by the part of the community they oppose, or may be thought to oppose, as "graceless varlets," against whom every man of substance should set his face. But this is not, after all, a thing to disturb a wise man, nor to deter a true man from telling his whole thought. He who is worthy of the name of man, speaks what he honestly believes the interests of his race demand, and seldom disquiets himself about what may be the consequences to himself. Men have, for what they believe the cause of God or man, endured the dungeon, the scaffold, the stake, the cross, and they can do it again, if need be. This subject must be freely, boldly, and fully discussed, whatever may be the fate of those who discuss it.

DEMOCRACY AND LIBERTY
[1843]

[*Brownson gave up the* Boston Quarterly *in 1842, combining it with J. L. O'Sullivan's* Democratic Review, *for which he became a contributing editor. His strictures against democracy pleased neither O'Sullivan nor the readers, and when the following essay appeared in the* Democratic Review *for April, 1843, O'Sullivan appended to it a dissenting "Note" which Brownson promptly answered in the May issue by developing with more precision the argument of his first essay. (See* Works, *XV, 281–96.) When O'Sullivan's notes continued to appear throughout the year, Brownson decided to revive his own review. Since O'Sullivan's publishers would not release the original name, Brownson called it* Brownson's Quarterly Review, *and brought out the first number in January, 1844.*

In The Convert, *and in many other passages, Brownson repeats what he says here about the effect of the campaign of 1840 upon his political thought.*]

OUR DEMOCRATIC BRETHREN are upon the whole a fine set of fellows, and rarely fail to take whatever turns up with great good humor; otherwise we should expect to lose our ears, if not our head, for the many severe things we intend in the course of our essay to say to them and about them. We shall try them severely; for we intend to run athwart many of their fondly cherished prejudices, and to controvert not a few of their favorite axioms; but we trust they will be able to survive the trial, and to come forth as pure and as bright as they have from that which the Whigs gave them in 1840.

Mentioning this 1840, we must say that it marks an epoch in *our* political and social doctrines. The famous election of that year wrought a much greater revolution in us than in the government; and we confess, here on the threshold, that since then we have pretty much ceased to speak of, or to confide in, the "intelligence of the people." The people, the sovereign people, the *sovereigns*, as our friend Governor Hubbard calls them, during that campaign presented but a sorry sight. Truth had no beauty, sound argument no weight, patriotism no influence. They who had devoted their lives to the cause of their country, of truth, justice, liberty, humanity, were looked upon as enemies of the people, and were unable to make themselves heard amid the maddened and maddening hurrahs of the drunken mob that went for "Tippecanoe, and Tyler too." It was a sorry sight, to see the poor fellows rolling huge balls, and dragging log cabins at the bidding of the demagogues, who were surprised to find how easily the enthusiasm of the people could be excited by hard cider and doggerel rhymes. And we confess that we could hardly forbear exclaiming, in vexation and contempt, "Well, after all, nature will out; the poor devils, if we but let them alone, will make cattle of themselves, and why should we waste our time and substance in trying to hinder them from making themselves cattle?"

An instructive year, that 1840, to all who have sense enough to read it aright. What happened then may happen again, if not in the same form, in some other form equally foolish, and equally pernicious; and, therefore, if we wish to secure to ourselves and our posterity the blessings of freedom and good government, we must secure stronger guaranties than popular suffrage and popular virtue and intelligence. We for one frankly confess,—and we care not who knows it,—that what we saw during the presidential election of 1840, shook, nay, gave to the winds, all our remaining confidence in the popular democratic doctrines—not *measures*—of the day; and we confess, further-more, that we have seen nothing in the conduct of either party since that has tended to restore it. During the extra session of congress in the summer of 1841, the Democratic delegations in both houses behaved nobly, and acquitted themselves like men; they won the victory for their country, as well as lasting honor and gratitude for themselves from the wise and good every-where; but our friends seem to have been more successful in gaining the victory than in securing its fruits. The rapid and overwhelming successes which have followed in the state elec-tions seem to have intoxicated the whole Democratic party, and unless God sends us some sudden and severe rebuke, there is great danger that we shall go into power again in 1845, without having been in the least instructed by defeat, or purified by ad-versity. Adversity is easy to bear; it is prosperity that tries the man. But enough of this. . . .

We assure our democratic brethren, then, in the Old World as well as in the New, that if we have words of rebuke for them, we have no words of consolation or of hope for their enemies. Thank God, we are neither traitors nor deserters; we stand by our colors, and will live or die, fighting for the good old cause, the CAUSE OF THE PEOPLE. But if our general made an un-successful attack yesterday, and was repulsed with heavy loss, and all in consequence of not choosing the best position, or of not taking the necessary precautions for covering his troops from the enemy's batteries, we hope we may in the council held today, without any dereliction from duty, advise that the attack be re-newed under an officer better skilled to conduct it, or at least that it be renewed from a more advantageous position. We see in the fact that democracy has hitherto failed, no reason for deserting its standard, but of seeking to recruit its forces; or, without a figure, we see in our ill success hitherto, simply the necessity of obtaining new and stronger guaranties than popular suffrage can offer, even though coupled with popular intelligence. We would not, we cannot dispense with popular suffrage and intelligence, and we pray our readers to remember this; but they are not alone sufficient, and we must have something else in *addition* to them, or we shall fail to secure those results from the practical working of the government, which every true-hearted democrat is laboring with all his might to secure.

We have not erred in laboring to extend popular suffrage,— though thus far its extension has operated almost exclusively in favor of the business classes, or rather of the money power,—but in relying on it as alone sufficient. There is not a tithe of that virtue in the ballot box which we, in our Fourth-of-July orations and caucus speeches, are in the habit of ascribing to it. The virtue we have been accustomed to ascribe to it, we have claimed for it on the ground that the people always know what is right, and will always act up to their knowledge. That is to say, suffrage rests for its basis, as a guaranty of freedom and good government, on the assumed intelligence and virtue of the people. Its grand maxim is, "The people can do no wrong." Now, this may be very beautiful in theory, but when we come to practice, this virtue and intelligence of the people is all a humbug. We beg pardon of the sovereign people for the treasonable speech; but it is true, true as Holy Writ, and there is neither wisdom nor virtue in pretending to the contrary. Perhaps, however, our remark is not quite true, *in the sense in which it will be taken*, without a word or two by way of explanation.

To the explanation, then. We are in this country, we democrats and all, most incorrigible aristocrats. We are always using the word *people* in its European sense, as designating the unprivileged many, in distinction from the privileged few. But this sense of the word is with us really inadmissible. We, *we* the literary, the refined, the wealthy, the fashionable, we are people as well as our poorer and more coarsely mannered and clad neighbors. We are all *people* in this country, the merchant, the banker, the broker, the manufacturer, the lawyer, the doctor, the officeholder, the office seeker, the scholar, and the gentleman, no less than the farmer, the mechanic, and the factory operative. We do well not to forget this. For ourselves, we always remember it, and therefore when we speak slightingly of the intelligence and virtue of the people, it is of the whole people, not of any particular class; in a sense which includes necessarily us who speak as well as those to whom we speak. When, then, we call what is usually said about the virtue and intelligence of the people all a humbug, we do not use the word in its European sense, and mean to speak disparagingly of the intelligence of plebeians as distinguished from patricians, of the "base-born" as distinguished from the "well-born"; for the distinctions here implied do not exist in this country, and should not be recognized even in our speech. When it comes to classes, we confess that we rely as much on the virtue and intelligence of proletaries as on the virtue and intelligence of capitalists, and would trust our mechanics as quick and as far as we would our merchants and manufacturers. . . .

But once more. What is the ground of this confidence in the virtue, intelligence, and capacity of the people? Do we really mean to say that the people acting individually or collectively never do, and never can do, any wrong? Whence, then, comes all this wrong of which everybody is complaining? The people are virtuous,—whence, then, the vice, the crime, the immorality, the irreligion which threaten to deluge the land? What need of swords, pistols, bowie knives, jails, penitentiaries, pains, penalties, laws, judges, and executioners? What need of schools, churches, teachers, preachers, prophets, and rulers? Nobody is so mad as really to pretend that nothing among us is wrong. Let alone private life, go merely into public life, enter the halls of justice and legislation—is all right here? No; everybody complains, everybody finds somewhat to condemn; some one thing, some another. And yet who has done this of which everybody is complaining? The people. What hear we from every quarter, but denunciations of this or that measure of public policy; of the profligacy of the government, or of its administration? And after all who is in fault? Whose is the government? The people's. The people are sovereign, and of course the government and its administration, the laws and their execution, are just what the people will they should be. Is it not strange, if the people always perceive the right, and perceiving, always do it, that nevertheless where they are supreme, and whatever is done, is done by them, there yet should be so much wrong done? . . .

The great end with all men in their religious, their political, and their individual actions, is FREEDOM. The perfection of our nature is in being able "to look into the perfect law of liberty," for liberty is only another name for power. The measure of my ability is always the exact measure of my freedom. The glory of humanity is in proportion to its freedom. Hence, humanity always applauds him who labors in right-down earnest to advance the cause of freedom. There is something intoxicating to every young and enthusiastic heart in this applause—always something intoxicating, too, in standing up for freedom, in opposing authority, in warring against fixed order, in throwing off the restraints of old and rigid customs, and enabling the soul and the body to develop themselves freely and in the natural proportions. Liberty is a soul-stirring word. It kindles all that is noble, generous, and heroic within us. Whoso speaks out for it can always be eloquent, and always sure of his audience. One loves so to speak if he be of a warm and generous temper, and we all love him who dares so to speak.

In consequence of this, we find our young men—brave spirits they are too—full of a deep, ardent love of liberty, and ready to do battle for her at all times, and against any odds. They, in this, address themselves to what is strongest in our nature, and to what is noblest; and so doing become our masters, and carry us away with them. Here is the danger we apprehend. We fear no attacks on liberty but those made in the name of liberty; we fear no measures but such as shall be put forth and supported by those whose love of freedom, and whose impatience of restraint, are altogether superior to their practical wisdom. These substitute passion for judgment, enthusiasm for wisdom, and carry us away in a sort of divine madness whither we know not, and whither, in our cooler moments, we would not. It is in the name of liberty that Satan wars successfully against liberty. . . .

We solemnly protest against construing one word we have said into hostility to the largest freedom for all men; but we put it to our young friends, in sober earnest, too, whether with them freedom is something positive; or whether they are in the habit of regarding it as merely negative? Do they not look upon liberty merely as freedom from certain restraints or obstacles, rather than as positive ability possessed by those who are free? They assume that we have the ability, the power, both individually and collectively,—when once the external restraints are taken off,—to be and to do all that is requisite for our highest individual and social weal. Is this assumption warrantable? Is man individually or socially sufficient for himself? Should not our politics, as well as our religion, teach us that it is not in man that walketh to direct his steps, and that he can work out his own salvation, only as a higher power, through grace, works in him to will and to do. . . .

Democracy is construed with us to mean the sovereignty of the people as the body politic; and the sovereignty of the people again is so construed that it becomes almost impossible to draw any line of distinction between the action of the people legally organized as the state, and the action of the people as a mob. The *people* in a legal or political sense, properly speaking, have no existence, no entity, therefore no rights, no sovereignty, save when organized into the body politic; and then their action is legitimate only when done through the forms which the body itself has prescribed. Yet we have seen it contended, and to an alarming extent, that the people, even outside and independent of the organism, exist as much as in it, and are as sovereign; and that a majority—aye, a bare majority counted by themselves— of the inhabitants of any given territory have the right, if dissatisfied with the existing organism, to come together, informally, without any reference to existing authorities, and institute a new form of government, which shall *legitimately* supersede the old, and to which all the inhabitants of the territory shall owe allegiance! Admit this doctrine, and we ask our friends who have, we must believe, hastily and without reflection adopted it, what distinction they would make between the people and the mob? . . .

Democracy, in our judgment, has been wrongly defined to be a *form* of government; it should be understood of the *end*, rather than of the *means*, and be regarded as a principle rather than a form. The end we are to aim at, is the freedom and progress of all men, especially of the poorest and most numerous class. He is a democrat who goes for the highest moral, intellectual, and physical elevation of the great mass of the people, especially of the laboring population, in distinction from a special devotion to the interests and pleasures of the wealthier, more refined, or more distinguished few. But the means by which this elevation is to be obtained, are not necessarily the institution of the purely democratic form of government. Here has been our mistake. We have been quite too ready to conclude that if we only once succeed in establishing democracy,—universal suffrage and eligibility, without constitutional restraints on the

power of the people,—as a form of government, the end will
follow as a matter of course. The considerations we have ad-
duced, we think prove to the contrary.

In coming to this conclusion, it will be seen that we differ from
our friends not in regard to the end, but in regard to the means.
We believe, and this is the point on which we insist, that the end,
freedom and progress, will not be secured by this loose radical-
ism with regard to popular sovereignty, and these demagogical
boasts of the virtue and intelligence of the people, which have
begun to be so fashionable. They who are seeking to advance the
cause of humanity by warring against all existing institutions,
religious, civil, or political, do seem to us to be warring against
the very end they wish to gain.

It has been said that mankind are always divided into two parties, one of which may be called the stationary party, the other the
movement party, or party of progress. Perhaps it is so; if so, all
of us who have any just conceptions of our manhood, and of our
duty to our fellow men, must arrange ourselves on the side of
movement. But the movement itself is divided into two sections,
—one the radical section, seeking progress by destruction; the
other the conservative section, seeking progress through and in
obedience to existing institutions. Without asking whether the
rule applies beyond our own country, we contend that the
conservative section is the only one that a wise man can call his
own. In youth we feel differently. We find evil around us; we
are in a dungeon; loaded all over with chains; we cannot make a
single free movement; and we utter one long, loud, indignant
protest against whatever is. We feel then that we can advance religion only by destroying the church; learning only by breaking
down the universities; and freedom only by abolishing the state.
Well, this is one method of progress; but, we ask, has it ever
been known to be successful? Suppose that we succeed in de-
molishing the old edifice, in sweeping away all that the human

race has been accumulating for the last six thousand years, what have we gained? Why, we are back where we were six thousand years ago; and without any assurance that the human race will not reassume its old course and rebuild what we have destroyed.

As we grow older, sadder, and wiser, and pass from idealists to realists, we change all this, and learn that the only true way of carrying the race forward is through its existing institutions. We plant ourselves, if on the sad, still on the firm reality of things, and content ourselves with gaining what can be gained with the means existing institutions furnish. We seek to advance religion through and in obedience to the church; law and social well-being through and in obedience to the state. Let it not be said that in adopting this last course, we change sides, leave the movement, and go over to the stationary party. No such thing. We do not thus in age forget the dreams of our youth. It is because we remember those dreams, because young enthusiasm has become firm and settled principle, and youthful hopes positive convictions, and because we would realize what we dared dream, when we first looked forth on the face of humanity, that we cease to exclaim "Liberty *against* Order," and substitute the practical formula, "LIBERTY ONLY IN AND THROUGH ORDER." The love of liberty loses none of its intensity. In the true manly heart it burns deeper and clearer with age, but it burns to enlighten and to warm, not to consume.

Here is the practical lesson we have sought to unfold. While we accept the end our democratic friends seek, while we feel our lot is bound up with theirs, we have wished to impress upon their minds, that we are to gain that end only through fixed and established order; not against authority, but by and in obedience to authority, and an authority competent to ordain and to guaranty it. Liberty without the guaranties of authority would be the worst of tyrannies.

THE AMERICAN REPUBLIC
[1866]

[*The complete text of* The American Republic *runs to over two hundred pages in Vol. XVIII of Brownson's* Works. *I have tried in the following selection to represent the gist of the argument of the second half of the book, with the hope that the interested reader may be led back to the full text. The first part contains Brownson's most penetrating criticisms of the theories of Locke, Hobbes, and Rousseau on the origin and constitution of government. Though he recognized that some of the Founding Fathers accepted the contract theory of government, he was less interested in their theory than in their actual achievement, which he held to be not theirs alone, but also the work of Providence. Anterior to the written constitution, so he maintained, was the providential constitution.*

Brownson's reiteration of the distinction between a constitutional republic and a radical democracy may at times seem to be a mere quibble over terminology. Yet he was astute in analyzing the ambiguities in the term democracy. His attempt to discriminate between the Rousseauistic theory of the general will and American constitutional government, with its roots in classical and Christian thought, has profound meaning today. Rousseau's democracy, as he saw clearly, bore within it the seeds of totalitarianism.

In his preface, Brownson calls The American Republic *"the authentic, and the only authentic statement of my political views and convictions." That it represents an important departure from his earlier thought is seen in his repudiation of the states' rights doctrine he had held up to the Civil War. In the outcome of the war he saw a triumph neither for the northern abolitionists, who would have imposed, so he held, a humanitarian democracy on the South, nor for the personal democracy of the South, but for what he defined as the territorial democracy.*

The best recent analysis of The American Republic *is that by Thomas I. Cooke and Arnaud B. Leavelle in* The Review of Politics, *IV (1942), pp. 77–90 and pp. 173–93.*]

CHAPTER I · INTRODUCTION

THE ANCIENTS summed up the whole of human wisdom in the maxim, Know Thyself, and certainly there is for an individual no more important as there is no more difficult knowledge than knowledge of himself, whence he comes, whither he goes, what he is, what he is for, what he can do, what he ought to do, and what are his means of doing it.

Nations are only individuals on a larger scale. They have a life, an individuality, a reason, a conscience, and instincts of their own, and have the same general laws of development and growth, and, perhaps, of decay, as the individual man. Equally important, and no less difficult than for the individual, is it for a nation to know itself, understand its own existence, its own powers and faculties, rights and duties, constitution, instincts, tendencies, and destiny. A nation has a spiritual as well as a material, a moral as well as a physical existence, and is subjected to internal as well as external conditions of health and virtue, greatness and grandeur, which it must in some measure understand and observe, or become weak and infirm, stunted in its growth, and end in premature decay and death.

Among nations, no one has more need of full knowledge of itself than the United States, and no one has hitherto had less. It has hardly had a distinct consciousness of its own national existence, and has lived the irreflective life of the child, with no severe trial, till the recent rebellion, to throw it back on itself and compel it to reflect on its own constitution, its own separate existence, individuality, tendencies, and end. The defection of

the slaveholding states, and the fearful struggle that has followed for national unity and integrity, have brought it at once to
a distinct recognition of itself, and forced it to pass from thought-
less, careless, heedless, reckless adolescence to grave and reflect-
ing manhood. . . . The change which four years of civil war
have wrought in the nation is great, and is sure to give it the
seriousness, the gravity, and dignity, the manliness it has heretofore lacked.

Though the nation has been brought to a consciousness of its
own existence, it has not, even yet, attained to a full and clear
understanding of its own national constitution. Its vision is still
obscured by the floating mists of its earlier morning, and its
judgment rendered indistinct and indecisive by the wild theories
and fancies of its childhood. The national mind has been quickened, the national heart has been opened, the national disposition
prepared, but there remains the important work of dissipating
the mists that still linger, of brushing away these wild theories
and fancies, and of enabling it to form a clear and intelligent
judgment of itself, and a true and just appreciation of its own
constitution, tendencies, and destiny; or, in other words, of
enabling the nation to understand its own idea, and the means of
its actualization in space and time.

Every living nation has an idea given it by Providence to
realize, and whose realization is its special work, mission, or
destiny. . . .

The United States, or the American republic, has a mission
and is chosen of God for the realization of a great idea. It has
been chosen not only to continue the work assigned to Greece
and Rome, but to accomplish a greater work than was assigned
to either. In art, it will prove false to its mission if it do not rival
Greece; and in science and philosophy, if it do not surpass it. In
the state, in law, in jurisprudence, it must continue and surpass
Rome. Its idea is liberty, indeed, but liberty with law, and law

with liberty. Yet its mission is not so much the realization of liberty as the realization of the true idea of the state, which secures at once the authority of the public and the freedom of the individual—the sovereignty of the people without social despotism, and individual freedom without anarchy. In other words, its mission is to bring out in its life the dialectic union of authority and liberty, of the natural rights of man and those of society. The Greek and Roman republics asserted the state to the detriment of individual freedom; modern republics either do the same, or assert individual freedom to the detriment of the state. The American republic has been instituted by Providence to realize the freedom of each with advantage to the other.

The real mission of the United States is to introduce and establish a political constitution, which, while it retains all the advantages of the constitutions of states thus far known, is unlike any of them, and secures advantages which none of them did or could possess. The American constitution has no prototype in any prior constitution. The American form of government can be classed throughout with none of the forms of government described by Aristotle, or even by later authorities. Aristotle knew only four forms of government: monarchy, aristocracy, democracy, and mixed governments. The American form is none of these, nor any combination of them. It is original, a new contribution to political science, and seeks to attain the end of all wise and just government by means unknown or forbidden to the ancients, and which have been but imperfectly comprehended even by American political writers themselves. The originality of the American constitution has been overlooked by the great majority even of our own statesmen, who seek to explain it by analogies borrowed from the constitutions of other states rather than by a profound study of its own principles. They have taken too low a view of it, and have rarely, if ever, appreciated its distinctive and peculiar merits. . . .

The failure of secession and the triumph of the national cause, in spite of the shortsightedness and blundering of the administration, have proved the vitality and strength of the national constitution, and the greatness of the American people. They say nothing for or against the democratic theory of our demagogues, but everything in favor of the American system or constitution of government, which has found a firmer support in American instincts than in American statesmanship. In spite of all that had been done by theorists, radicals, and revolutionists, no-government men, non-resistants, humanitarians, and sickly sentimentalists to corrupt the American people in mind, heart, and body, the native vigor of their national constitution has enabled them to come forth triumphant from the trial. Every American patriot has reason to be proud of his countrymen, and every American lover of freedom to be satisfied with the institutions of his country. But there is danger that the politicians and demagogues will ascribe the merit, not to the real and living national constitution, but to their miserable theories of that constitution, and labor to aggravate the several evils and corrupt tendencies which caused the rebellion it has cost so much to suppress. What is now wanted is, that the people, whose instincts are right, should understand the American constitution as it is, and so understand it as to render it impossible for political theorists, no matter of what school or party, to deceive them again as to its real import, or induce them to depart from it in their political action.

A work written with temper, without passion or sectional prejudice, in a philosophical spirit, explaining to the American people their own national constitution, and the mutual relations of the general government and the state governments, cannot, at this important crisis in our affairs, be inopportune, and, if properly executed, can hardly fail to be of real service. Such a work is now attempted—would it were by another and abler hand—which, imperfect as it is, may at least offer some useful suggestions, give a right direction to political thought, although it should fail to satisfy the mind of the reader. . . .

CHAPTER IX · THE UNITED STATES

Sovereignty, under God, inheres in the organic people, or the people as the republic; and every organic people fixed to the soil, and politically independent of every other people, is a sovereign people, and, in the modern sense, an independent sovereign nation. . . .

If the Anglo-American colonies, when their independence of Great Britain was achieved and acknowledged, were severally sovereign states, it has never since been in their power to unite and form a single sovereign state, or to form themselves into one indivisible sovereign nation. They could unite only by mutual agreement, which gives only a confederation, in which each retains its own sovereignty, as two individuals, however closely united, retain each his own individuality. No sovereignty is of conventional origin, and none can emerge from the convention that did not enter it. Either the states are one sovereign people or they are not. If they are not, it is undoubtedly a great disadvantage; but a disadvantage that must be accepted, and submitted to without a murmur.

Whether the United States are one sovereign people or only a confederation is a question of very grave importance. If they are only a confederation of states—and if they ever were severally sovereign states, only a confederation they certainly are—state secession is an inalienable right, and the government has had no right to make war on the secessionists as rebels, or to treat them, when their military power is broken, as traitors, or disloyal persons. The honor of the government, and of the people who have sustained it, is then deeply compromised.

What then is the fact? Are the United States politically one people, nation, state, or republic, or are they simply independent

sovereign states united in close and intimate alliance, league, or
federation, by a mutual pact or agreement? Were the people of
the United States who ordained and established the written
constitution one people, or were they not? If they were not before ordaining and establishing the government, they are not
now; for the adoption of the constitution did not and could not
make them one. Whether they are one or many is then simply a
question of fact, to be decided by the facts in the case, not by the
theories of American statesmen, the opinion of jurists, or even by
constitutional law itself. The old articles of confederation and
the later constitution can serve here only as historical documents.
Constitutions and laws presuppose the existence of a national
sovereign from which they emanate, and that ordains them, for
they are the formal expression of a sovereign will. The nation
must exist as an historical fact, prior to the possession or exercise
of sovereign power, prior to the existence of written constitutions
and laws of any kind, and its existence must be established before
they can be recognized as having any legal force or vitality. . . .

In the case of the United States there is only the question of
fact. If they are in fact one people they are so in right, whatever
the opinions and theories of statesmen, or even the decisions of
courts; for the courts hold from the national authority, and the
theories and opinions of statesmen may be erroneous. Certain it
is that the states in the American Union have never existed and
acted as severally sovereign states. Prior to independence, they
were colonies under the sovereignty of Great Britain, and since
independence they have existed and acted only as states
united. . . .

In the declaration of independence they declared themselves
independent states indeed, but not severally independent. The
declaration was not made by the states severally, but by the
states jointly, as the United States. They unitedly declared their
independence; they carried on the war for independence, won it,

and were acknowledged by foreign powers and by the mother country as the *United* States, not as severally independent sovereign states. Severally they have never exercised the full powers of sovereign states; they have had no flag—symbol of sovereignty—recognized by foreign powers, have made no foreign treaties, held no foreign relations, had no commerce foreign or interstate, coined no money, entered into no alliances or confederacies with foreign states or with one another, and in several respects have been more restricted in their powers in the Union than they were as British colonies. . . .

CHAPTER X · CONSTITUTION OF THE UNITED STATES

The constitution of the United States is twofold, written and unwritten, the constitution of the people and the constitution of the government.

The written constitution is simply a law ordained by the nation or people instituting and organizing the government; the unwritten constitution is the real or actual constitution of the people as a state or sovereign community, and constituting them such or such a state. It is providential, not made by the nation, but born with it. The written constitution is made and ordained by the sovereign power, and presupposes that power as already existing and constituted.

The unwritten or providential constitution of the United States is peculiar, and difficult to understand, because incapable of being fully explained by analogies borrowed from any other state historically known, or described by political philosophers. It belongs to the Graeco-Roman family, and is republican as distinguished from despotic constitutions, but it comes under the head of neither monarchical nor aristocratic, neither democratic nor mixed constitutions, and creates a state which is neither a centralized state nor a confederacy. The difficulty of understanding it is augmented by the peculiar use under it of the word *state*, which does not in the American system mean a sovereign community or political society complete in itself, like France, Spain, or Prussia, nor yet a political subordinate to another political society and dependent on it. The American states are all sovereign states united, but, disunited, are no states at all. The rights and powers of the states are not derived from the United States, nor the rights and powers of the United States derived from the states.

The simple fact is, that the political or sovereign people of the United States exists as united states, and only as united states. The Union and the states are coeval, born together, and can exist only together. Separation is dissolution—the death of both. The United States are a state, a single sovereign state; but this single sovereign state consists in the union and solidarity of states instead of individuals. The Union is in each of the states, and each of the states is in the Union.

It is necessary to distinguish in the outset between the United States and the government of the United States, or the so-called federal government, which the convention refused, contrary to its first intention, to call the *national* government. That government is not a supreme national government, representing all the powers of the United States, but a limited government, restricted by its constitution to certain specific relations and interests. The United States are anterior to that government, and the first question to be settled relates to their internal and inherent providential constitution as one political people or sovereign state. The written constitution, in its preamble, professes to be ordained by "the people of the United States." Who are this people? How are they constituted, or what the mode and condition of their political existence? Are they the people of the states severally? No; for they call themselves the people of the *United* States. Are they a national people, really existing outside and independently of their organization into distinct and mutually independent states? No; for they define themselves to be the people of the United *States*. If they had considered themselves existing as states only, they would have said "We, the states," and if independently of state organization, they would have said, "We, the people, do ordain," &c.

The key to the mystery is precisely in this appellation *United States*, which is not the name of the country, for its distinctive name is America, but a name expressive of its political organization. In it there are no sovereign people without states, and no states without union, or that are not *united* states. The term *united* is not part of a proper name, but is simply an adjective qualifying *states*, and has its full and proper sense. Hence while the sovereignty is and must be in the states, it is in the states united, not in the states severally, precisely as we have found the sovereignty of the people is in the people collectively or as society, not in the people individually. . . .

This is not a theory of the constitution, but the constitutional fact itself. It is the simple historical fact that precedes the law and constitutes the lawmaking power. The people of the United States are one people, as has already been proved: they were one people, as far as a people at all, prior to independence, because under the same common law and subject to the same sovereign, and have been so since, for as *united* states they gained their independence and took their place among sovereign nations, and as united states they have possessed and still possess the government. As their existence before independence in distinct colonies did not prevent their unity, so their existence since in distinct states does not hinder them from being one people. The states severally simply continue the colonial organizations, and united they hold the sovereignty that was originally in the mother country. But if one people, they are one people existing in distinct state organizations, as before independence they were one people existing in distinct colonial organizations. This is the original, the unwritten, and providential constitution of the people of the United States.

This constitution is not conventional, for it existed before the people met or could meet in convention. They have not, as an independent sovereign people, either established their union, or distributed themselves into distinct and mutually independent states. . . . The union and the states were born together, are inseparable in their constitution, have lived and grown up together; no serious attempt till the late secession movement has been made to separate them; and the secession movement, to all persons who knew not the real constitution of the United States, appeared sure to succeed, and in fact would have succeeded if, as the secessionists pretended, the union had been only a confederacy, and the states had been held together only by a conventional compact, and not by a real and living bond of unity. The popular instinct of national unity, which seemed so weak, proved to be strong enough to defeat the secession forces, to trample out the confederacy, and maintain the unity of the nation and the integrity of its domain.

The people can act only as they exist, as they are, not as they are not. Existing originally only as distributed in distinct and mutually independent colonies, they could at first act only through their colonial organizations, and afterward only through their state organizations. The colonial people met in convention, in the person of representatives chosen by colonies, and after independence in the person of representatives chosen by states. Not existing outside of the colonial or state organizations, they could not act outside or independently of them. They chose their representatives or delegates by colonies or states, and called at first their convention a congress; but by an instinct surer than their deliberate wisdom, they called it not the congress of the *confederate*, but of the *united* states, asserting constitutional unity as well as constitutional multiplicity. It is true, in their first attempt to organize a general government, they called the constitution they devised articles of confederation, but only because they had not attained to full consciousness of themselves; and that they really meant union, not confederation, is evident from their adopting, as the official style of the nation or new power, *united*, not *confederate* states.

That the sovereignty vested in the states united, and was represented in some sort by the congress, is evident from the fact that the several states, when they wished to adopt state constitutions in place of colonial charters, felt not at liberty to do so without asking and obtaining the permission of congress, as the elder Adams informs us in his *Diary*, kept at the time; that is, they asked and obtained the equivalent of what has since, in the case of organizing new states, been called an "enabling act." This proves that the states did not regard themselves as sovereign states out of the Union, but as completely sovereign only in it. And this again proves that the articles of confederation did not correspond to the real, living constitution of the people. Even then it was felt that the organization and constitution of a state in the Union could be regularly effected only by the permission of congress; and no territory can, it is well known, regularly organize itself as a state, and adopt a state constitution, without an enabling act by congress, or its equivalent. . . .

The formidable rebellion which is now happily suppressed, and which attempted to justify itself by the doctrine of state sovereignty, has thrown, in many minds, new light on the subject, and led them to re-examine the historical facts in the case from a different point of view, to see if Mr. Calhoun's theory is not as unfounded as he had proved Mr. Webster's theory to be. The facts in the case really sustain neither, and both failed to see it: Mr. Calhoun because he had purposes to accomplish which demanded state sovereignty, and Mr. Webster because he examined them in the distorting medium of the theory or understanding of the statesmen of the eighteenth century. The civil war has vindicated the Union, and defeated the armed forces of the state sovereignty men; but it has not refuted their doctrine, and as far as it has had an effect, it has strengthened the tendency to consolidation or centralism.

But the philosophy, the theory of government, the understanding of the framers of the constitution, must be considered, if the expression will be allowed, as *obiter dicta*, and be judged on their merits. What binds is the thing done, not the theory on which it was done, or on which the actors explained their work either to themselves or to others. Their political philosophy, or their political theory, may sometimes affect the phraseology they adopt, but forms no rule for interpreting their work. Their work was inspired by and accords with the historical facts in the case, and is authorized and explained by them. The American people were not made one people by the written constitution, as Mr. Jefferson, Mr. Madison, Mr. Webster, and so many others supposed, but were made so by the unwritten constitution, born with and inherent in them.

CHAPTER XI · CONSTITUTION OF THE UNITED STATES, CONCLUDED.

Providence, or God operating through historical facts, constituted the American people one political or sovereign people, existing and acting in particular communities, organizations, called states. This one people organized as states, meet in convention, frame and ordain the constitution of government, or institute a general government in place of the continental congress; and the same people, in their respective state organizations, meet in convention in each state, and frame and ordain a particular government for the state individually, which in union

with the general government, constitutes the complete and supreme government within the states, as the general government,
in union with all the particular governments, constitutes the
complete and supreme government of the nation or whole country. This is clearly the view taken by Mr. Madison in his letter
to Mr. Everett, when freed from his theory of the origin of
government in compact.

The constitution of the people as one people, and the distinction at the same time of this one people into particular states,
precedes the convention, and is the unwritten constitution, the
providential constitution, of the American people or civil society,
as distinguished from the constitution of the government, which,
whether general or particular, is the ordination of civil society
itself. The unwritten constitution is the creation or constitution
of the sovereign, and the sovereign providentially constituted
constitutes in turn the government, which is not sovereign, but is
clothed with just as much and just so little authority as the sovereign wills or ordains.

The sovereign in the republican order is the organic people, or
state, and is with us the United States, for with us the organic
people exist only as organized into states united, which in their
union form one compact and indissoluble whole. That is to say,
the organic American people do not exist as a consolidated people
or state; they exist only as organized into distinct but inseparable
states. Each state is a living member of the one body, and derives
its life from its union with the body, so that the American state
is one body with many members; and the members, instead of
being simply individuals, are states, or individuals organized
into states. . . .

Such is the sovereign people, and so far the original unwritten
constitution. The sovereign, in order to live and act, must have
an organ through which he expresses his will. This organ, under
the American system, is primarily the convention. The conven-

tion is the supreme political body, the concrete sovereign authority, and exercises practically the whole sovereign power of the
people. The convention persists always, although not in permanent session. It can at any time be convened by the ordinary
authority of the government, or, in its failure, by a plebiscitum.

Next follows the government created and constituted by the
convention. The government is constituted in such manner, and
has such and only such powers, as the convention ordains. The
government has, in the strict sense, no political authority under
the American system, which separates the government from the
convention. All political questions proper, such as the elective
franchise, eligibility, the constitution of the several departments
of government, as the legislative, the judicial, and the executive,
changing, altering, or amending the constitution of government,
enlarging or contracting its powers, in a word, all those questions
that arise on which it is necessary to take the immediate orders
of the sovereign, belong not to the government, but to the convention; and where the will of the sovereign is not sufficiently
expressed in the constitution, a new appeal to the convention is
necessary, and may always be had. . . .

The American system, sometimes called the federal system, is
not founded on antagonism of classes, estates, or interests, and is
in no sense a system of checks and balances. It needs and toler-
ates no obstructive forces. It does not pit section against section,
the states severally against the general government, nor the
general government against the state governments, and nothing
is more hurtful than the attempt to explain it and work it on
the principles of British constitutionalism. The convention created no antagonistic powers; it simply divided the powers of
government, and gave neither to the general government nor to
the state governments all the powers of government, nor in any
instance did it give to the two governments jurisdiction in the
same matters. Hence each has its own sphere, in which it can

move on without colliding with that of the other. Each is independent and complete in relation to its own work, incomplete and dependent on the other for the complete work of government.

The division of power is not between a NATIONAL government and state governments, but between a GENERAL government and particular governments. The general government, inasmuch as it extends to matters common to all the states, is usually called the government of the United States, and sometimes the federal government, to distinguish it from the particular or state governments, but without strict propriety; for the government of the United States, or the federal government, means, in strictness, both the general government and the particular governments, since neither is in itself the complete government of the country. The general government has authority within each of the states, and each of the state governments has authority in the Union. The line between the Union and the states severally, is not precisely the line between the general government and the particular governments. As, for instance, the general government lays direct taxes on the people of the states, and collects internal revenue within them; and the citizens of a particular state, and none others, are electors of president and vice-president of the United States, and representatives in the lower house of congress, while senators in congress are elected by the state legislature themselves. . . .

The division of the powers of government between a general government and particular governments, rendered possible and practicable by the original constitution of the people themselves, as one people existing and acting through state organizations, is the American method of guarding against the undue centralism of which Roman imperialism inevitably tends; and it is far simpler and more effective than any of the European systems of mixed governments, which seek their end by organizing an antagonism of interests or classes. The American method demands no such antagonism, no neutralizing of one social force by another, but avails itself of all the forces of society, organizes them dialectically, not antagonistically, and thus protects with equal efficiency both public authority and private rights. The general government can never oppress the people as individuals, or abridge their private rights or personal freedom and independence, because these are not within its jurisdiction, but are placed in charge, within each state, of the state government, which, within its sphere, governs as supremely as the general government: the state governments cannot weaken the public authority of the nation or oppress the people in their general rights and interests, for these are withdrawn from state jurisdiction and placed under charge of a general government, which, in its sphere, governs as supremely as the state government. . . . The system is no invention of man, is no creation of the convention, but is given us by Providence in the living constitution of the American people. The merit of the statesmen of 1787 is that they did not destroy or deface the work of Providence, but accepted it, and organized the government in harmony with the real order, the real elements given them. They suffered themselves in all their positive substantial work to be governed by reality, not by theories and speculations. In this they proved themselves statesmen, and their work survives; and the republic, laugh as sciolists may, is, for the present and future, the model republic—as much so as was Rome in her day; and it is not simply national pride nor American self-conceit that pronounces its establishment the beginning of a new and more advanced order of civilization; such is really the fact. . . .

No government, whose workings are intrusted to men, ever is or can be practically perfect—secure all good, and guard against all evil. In all human governments there will be defects and abuses, and he is no wise man who expects perfection from imperfection. But the American constitution, taken as a whole, and in all its parts, is the least imperfect that has ever existed, and under it individual rights, personal freedom and independence, as well as public authority or society, are better protected than under any other; and as the few barbaric elements retained from the feudal ages are eliminated, the standard of education elevated, and the whole population americanized, moulded by and to the American system, it will be found to effect all the good, with as little of the evil, as can be reasonably expected from any possible civil government or political constitution of society.

CHAPTER XII · SECESSION

The American system is republican, and, contrary to what some democratic politicians assert, the American democracy is territorial, not personal; not territorial because the majority of the people are agriculturists or landholders, but because all political rights, powers, or franchises are territorial. The sovereign people of the United States are sovereign only within the territory of the United States. The great body of the freemen have the elective franchise, but no one has it save in his state, his county, his town, his ward, his precinct. Out of the election district in which he is domiciled, a citizen of the United States has no more right to vote than has the citizen or subject of a foreign state. This explains what is meant by the attachment of power to the territory, and the dependence of the state on the domain. The state, in republican states, exists only as inseparably united with the public domain; under feudalism, power was joined to territory or domain, but the domain was held as a private, not as a public domain. All sovereignty rests on domain or proprietorship, and is dominion. The proprietor is the dominus or lord, and in republican states the lord is society, or the public, and the domain is held for the common or public good of all. All politi-

cal rights are held from society, or the dominus, and therefore it
is the elective franchise is held from society, and is a civil right,
as distinguished from a natural, or even a purely personal
right. . . .

CHAPTER XIV · POLITICAL TENDENCIES

The most marked political tendency of the American people has
been, since 1825, to interpret their government as a pure and
simple democracy, and to shift it from a territorial to a purely
popular basis, or from the people as the state, inseparably united
to the national territory or domain, to the people as simply population, either as individuals or as the race. Their tendency has
unconsciously, therefore, been to change their constitution from
a republican to a despotic, or from a civilized to a barbaric constitution.

The American constitution is democratic, in the sense that the
people are sovereign; that all laws and public acts run in their
name; that the rulers are elected by them, and are responsible
to them; but they are the people territorially constituted and
fixed to the soil, constituting what Mr. Disraeli, with more propriety perhaps than he thinks, calls a "territorial democracy." To
this territoral democracy, the real American democracy, stand
opposed two other democracies—the one personal and the other
humanitarian—each alike hostile to civilization, and tending to
destroy the state, and capable of sustaining government only on
principles common to all despotisms.

In every man there is a natural craving for personal freedom
and unrestrained action—a strong desire to be himself, not another—to be his own master, to go when and where he pleases,
to do what he chooses, to take what he wants, wherever he can
find it, and to keep what he takes. . . . Restricted in its enjoyment to one man, it makes him chief, chief of the family, the
tribe, or the nation; extended in its enjoyment to the few, it

founds an aristocracy, creates a nobility . . . ; extended to the many, it founds personal democracy, a simple association of individuals, in which all are equally free and independent, and no restraint is imposed on anyone's action, will, or inclination, without his own consent, express or constructive. This is the so-called Jeffersonian democracy, in which government has no powers but such as it derives from the consent of the governed, and is personal democracy or pure individualism—philosophically considered, pure egoism, which says, "I am God.". . . State sovereignty and secession are based on the same democratic principle applied to the several states of the Union instead of individuals.

The tendency of this sort of democracy has been strong in large sections of the American people from the first, and has been greatly strengthened by the general acceptance of the theory that government originates in compact. The full realization of this tendency, which, happily, is impracticable save in theory, would be to render every man independent alike of every other man and of society, with full right and power to make his own will prevail. This tendency was strongest in the slaveholding states, and especially, in those states, in the slaveholding class, which were the American imitation of the feudal nobility of medieval Europe; and on this side the war just ended was, in its most general expression, a war in defense of personal democracy, or the sovereignty of the people individually, against the humanitarian democracy, represented by the abolitionists, and the territorial democracy, represented by the government. This personal democracy has been signally defeated in the defeat of the late confederacy, and can hardly again become strong enough to be dangerous.

But the humanitarian democracy, which scorns all geographical lines, effaces all individualities, and professes to plant itself on humanity alone, has acquired by the war new strength, and is not without menace to our future. The solidarity of the race, which is the condition of all human life, founds, as we have seen, society, and creates what are called social rights, the rights alike of society in regard to individuals, and of individuals in regard to society. Territorial divisions or circumscriptions found particular societies, states, or nations; yet as the race is one, and all its members live by communion with God through it and by communion one with another, these particular states or nations are never absolutely independent of each other, but bound together by the solidarity of the race, so that there is a real solidarity of nations as well as of individuals—the truth underlying Kossuth's famous declaration of "the solidarity of peoples."

The solidarity of nations is the basis of international law, binding on every particular nation, and which every civilized nation recognizes, and enforces on its own subjects or citizens, through its own courts, as an integral part of its own municipal or national law. The personal or individual right is therefore restricted by the rights of society, and the rights of the particular society or nation are limited by international law, or the rights of universal society—the truth the ex-governor of Hungary overlooked. The grand error of gentilism was in denying the unity and therefore the solidarity of the race, involved in its denial or misconception of the unity of God. It therefore was never able to assign any solid basis to international law, and gave it only a conventional or customary authority, thus leaving the *jus gentium*, which it recognized indeed, without any real foundation in the constitution of things, or authority in the real world. . . .

There were greater issues in the late war than negro slavery or negro freedom. That was only an incidental issue, as the really great men of the confederacy felt, who to save their cause were willing themselves at last to free and arm their own negroes, and perhaps were willing to do it even at first. This fact alone proves that they had, or believed they had, a far more important cause than the preservation of negro slavery. They fought for personal democracy, under the form of state sovereignty, against social democracy; for personal freedom and independence against social or humanitarian despotism; and so far their cause was as good as that against which they took up arms; and if they had or could have fought against that, without fighting at the same time against the territorial, the real American, the only civilized democracy, they would have succeeded. It is not socialism nor abolitionism that has won; nor is it the North that has conquered. The Union itself has won no victories over the South, and it is both historically and legally false to say that the South has been subjugated. The Union has preserved itself and American civilization, alike for North and South, East and West. The armies that so often met in the shock of battle were not drawn up respectively by the North and South, but by two rival democracies, to decide which of the two should rule the future. They were the armies of two mutually antagonistic systems, and neither army was clearly and distinctly conscious of the cause for which it was shedding its blood; each obeyed instinctively a power stronger than itself, and which at best it but dimly discerned. On both sides the cause was broader and deeper than negro slavery, and neither the pro-slavery men nor the abolitionists have won. The territorial democracy alone has won, and won what will prove to be a final victory over the purely personal democracy, which had its chief seat in the southern states, though by no means confined to them. The danger to American democracy from that quarter is forever removed, and democracy *à la* Rousseau has received a terrible defeat throughout the world, though as yet it is far from being aware of it.

But in this world victories are never complete. The socialistic democracy claims the victory which has been really won by the territorial democracy, as if it had been socialism, not patriotism, that fired the hearts and nerved the arms of the brave men led by McClellan, Grant, and Sherman. The humanitarians are more dangerous in principle than the egoists, for they have the appearance of building on a broader and deeper foundation, of being more Christian, more philosophic, more generous and philanthropic; but Satan is never more successful than under the guise of an angel of light. . . .

The humanitarian is carried away by a vague generality, and loses men in humanity, sacrifices the rights of men in a vain endeavor to secure the rights of man, as your Calvinist or his brother Jansenist sacrifices the rights of nature in order to secure the freedom of grace. Yesterday he agitated for the abolition of slavery, today he agitates for negro suffrage, negro equality, and announces that when he has secured that he will agitate for female suffrage and the equality of the sexes, forgetting or ignorant that the relation of the equality subsists only between individuals of the same sex; that God made the man the head of the woman, and the woman for the man, not the man for the woman. Having obliterated all distinction of sex in politics, in social, industrial, and domestic arrangements, he must go further, and agitate for equality of property. But since property, if recognized at all, will be unequally acquired and distributed, he must go further still, and agitate for the total abolition of property, as an injustice, a grievous wrong, a theft, with M. Proudhon, or the Englishman Godwin. . . . He can find no limit to his agitation this side of vague generality, which is no reality, but a pure nullity, for he respects no territorial or individual circumscriptions, and must regard creation itself as a blunder. This is not fancy, for he has gone very nearly as far as it is here shown, if logical, he must go.

The danger now is that the Union victory will, at home and abroad, be interpreted as a victory won in the interest of social or humanitarian democracy. It was because they regarded the war waged on the side of the Union as waged in the interest of this terrible democracy, that our bishops and clergy sympathized so little with the government in prosecuting it; not, as some imagined, because they were disloyal, hostile to American or territorial democracy, or not heartily in favor of freedom for all men, whatever their race or complexion. They had no wish to see slavery prolonged, the evils of which they, better than any other class of men, knew, and more deeply deplored; none would have regretted more than they to have seen the Union broken up; but they held the socialistic or humanitarian democracy represented by northern abolitionists as hostile alike to the church and to civilization. For the same reason that they were backward or reserved in their sympathy, all the humanitarian sects at home and abroad were forward and even ostentatious in theirs. The Catholics feared the war might result in encouraging *la république démocratique et sociale;* the humanitarian sects trusted that it would. If the victory of the Union should turn out to be a victory for the humanitarian democracy, the civilized world will have no reason to applaud it.

That there is some danger that for a time the victory will be taken as a victory for humanitarianism or socialism, it would be idle to deny. It is so taken now, and the humanitarian party throughout the world are in ecstasies over it. The party claim it. The European socialists and red republicans applaud it, and the Mazzinis and the Garibaldis inflict on us the deep humiliation of their congratulations. A cause that can be approved by the revolutionary leaders of European liberals must be strangely misunderstood, or have in it some infamous element. It is no compliment to a nation to receive the congratulations of men who assert not only people-king, but people-god; and those Americans who are delighted with them are worse enemies to the American democracy than ever were Jefferson Davis and his fellow conspirators, and more contemptible, as the swindler is more contemptible than the highwayman.

But it is probable the humanitarians have reckoned without their host. Not they are the real victors. When the smoke of battle has cleared away, the victory, it will be seen, has been won by the republic, and that that alone has triumphed. The abolitionists, in so far as they asserted the unity of the race and opposed slavery as a denial of that unity, have also won; but in so far as they denied the reality or authority of territorial and individual circumscriptions, followed a purely socialistic tendency, and sought to dissolve patriotism into a watery sentimentality called philanthropy, have in reality been crushingly defeated, as they will find when the late insurrectionary states are fully reconstructed. The southern or egoistical democrats, so far as they denied the unity and solidarity of the race, the rights of society over individuals, and the equal rights of each and every individual in face of the state, or the obligations of society to protect the weak and help the helpless, have been also defeated; but so far as they asserted personal or individual rights which society neither gives nor can take away, and so far as they asserted, not state sovereignty, but state rights, held independently of the general government, and which limit its authority and sphere of action, they share in the victory, as the future will prove. . . .

The American people will always be progressive as well as conservative; but they have learned a lesson, which they much needed, against false democracy: civil war has taught them that "the sacred right of insurrection" is as much out of place in a democratic state as in an aristocratic or a monarchical state; and that the government should always be clothed with ample authority to arrest and punish whoever plots its destruction. They must never be delighted again to have their government send a national ship to bring hither a noted traitor to his own sovereign as the nation's guest. The people of the northern states are hardly less responsible for the late rebellion than the people of the southern states. Their press had taught them to call every government a tyranny that refused to remain quiet while the traitor was cutting its throat or assassinating the nation, and they had nothing but mad denunciations of the papal, the Austrian, and the Neapolitan governments for their severity against con-spirators and traitors. But their own government has found it necessary for the public safety to be equally arbitrary, prompt, and severe, and they will most likely require it hereafter to co-operate with the governments of the Old World in advancing civilization, instead of lending all its moral support, as hereto-fore, to the Jacobins, revolutionists, socialists, and humanitarians, to bring back the reign of barbarism. . . .

CHAPTER XV · DESTINY—POLITICAL AND RELIGIOUS

It has been said in the Introduction to this essay that every living nation receives from Providence a special work or mission in the progress of society, to accomplish which is its destiny, or the end for which it exists; and that the special mission of the United States is to continue and complete in the political order the Graeco-Roman civilization. . . .

In the Graeco-Roman civilization is found the state proper and the great principle of the territorial constitution of power, instead of the personal or the genealogical, the patriarchal or the monarchical; and yet with true civil or political principles it mixed up nearly all the elements of the barbaric constitution. The gentile system of Rome recalls the patriarchal, and the re-lation that subsisted between the patron and his clients has a striking resemblance to that which subsists between the feudal lord and his retainers, and may have had the same origin. . . . After all, practically the Roman senate was hardly less an estate than the English house of lords, for no one could sit in it unless a landed proprietor and of noble blood. The plebs, though out-

side of the political people proper, as not being included in the
three tribes, when they came to be a power in the republic under
the emperors, and the old distinction of plebs and patricians was
forgotten, were an estate, and not a local or territorial people.

The republican element was in the fact that the land, which
gave the right to participate in political power, was the domain
of the state, and the tenant held it from the state. The domain
was vested in the state, not in the senator nor the prince, and was
therefore *respublica*, not private property—the first grand leap
of the human race from barbarism. In all other respects the Roman constitution was no more republican than the feudal. Athens
went further than Rome, and introduced the principle of territorial democracy. The division into demes or wards, whence
comes the word *democracy*, was a real territorial division, not
personal nor genealogical. And if the equality of all men was
not recognized, all who were included in the political class stood
on the same footing. . . .

The grand error, as has already been said, of the Graeco-
Roman or gentile civilization, was in its denial or ignorance of
the unity of the human race, as well as the unity of God, and
in its including in the state only a particular class of the territorial people, while it held all the rest as slaves, though in different degrees of servitude. It recognized and sustained a privileged class, a ruling order; and if, as subsequently did the Vene-
tian aristocracy, it recognized democratic equality within that
order, it held all outside of it to be less than men and without
political rights. Practically, power was an attribute of birth and
of private wealth. Suffrage was almost universal among freemen,
but down almost to the empire, the people voted by orders, and
were counted, not numerically, but by the rank of the order, and
the *comitia curiata* could always carry the election over the
comitia centuriata and thus power remained always in the hands
of the rich and noble few. . . .

Now, the political destiny or mission of the United States is, in common with the European nations, to eliminate the barbaric elements retained by the Roman constitution, and specially to realize that philosophical division of the powers of government which distinguishes it from both imperial and democratic centralism on the one hand, and, on the other, from the checks and balances or organized antagonisms which seek to preserve liberty by obstructing the exercise of power. No greater problem in statesmanship remains to be solved, and no greater contribution to civilization to be made. Nowhere else than in this New World, and in this New World only in the United States, can this problem be solved, or this contribution be made, and what the Graeco-Roman republic began be completed.   -

But the United States have a religious as well as a political destiny, for religion and politics go together. Church and state, as governments, are separate indeed, but the principles on which the state is founded have their origin and ground in the spiritual order—in the principles revealed or affirmed by religion—and are inseparable from them. . . .

Man, as we have seen, lives by communion with God through the divine creative act, and is perfected or completed only through the incarnation, in Christ, the Word made flesh. True, he communes with God through his kind, and through external nature, society in which he is born and reared, and property through which he derives sustenance for his body; but these are only media of his communion with God, the source of life—not either the beginning or the end of his communion. They have no life in themselves, since their being is in God, and, of themselves can impart none. They are in the order of second causes, and second causes, without the first cause, are naught. . . . As religion includes all that relates to communion with God, it must in some form be inseparable from every living act of man, both individually and socially; and, in the long run, men must conform either their politics to their religion or their religion to their politics. Christianity is constantly at work, moulding political society in its own image and likeness, and every political system struggles to harmonize Christianity with itself. If, then, the United States have a political destiny, they have a religious destiny inseparable from it.

The political destiny of the United States is to conform the state to the order of reality, or, so to speak, to the divine idea in creation. Their religious destiny is to render practicable and to realize the normal relations between church and state, religion and politics, as concreted in the life of the nation.

In politics, the United States are not realizing a political theory of any sort whatever. They, on the contrary, are successfully refuting all political theories, making away with them, and establishing the state—not on a theory, not on an artificial basis or a foundation laid by human reason or will, but on reality, the eternal and immutable principles in relation to which man is created. They are doing the same in regard to religious theories. Religion is not a theory, a subjective view, an opinion, but is, objectively, at once a principle, a law, and a fact, and, subjectively, it is, by the aid of God's grace, practical conformity to what is universally true and real. . . .

The religious destiny of the United States is not to create a new religion nor to found a new church. . . . God has himself founded the church on catholic principles, or principles always and everywhere real principles. . . . Founded on universal and immutable principles, the church can never grow old or obsolete, but is the church for all times and places, for all ranks and conditions of men. Man cannot change either the church or the dogmas of faith, for they are founded in the highest reality, which is above him, over him, and independent of him. Religion is above and independent of the state, and the state has nothing to do with the church or her dogmas, but to accept and conform to them as it does to any of the facts or principles of science, to a mathematical truth, or to a physical law.

But while the church, with her essential constitution, and her dogmas are founded in the divine order, and are catholic and unalterable, the relations between the civil and ecclesiastical authorities may be changed or modified by the changes of time and place. These relations have not been always the same, but have differed in different ages and countries. . . .

It is impossible, even if it were desirable, to restore the mixture of civil and ecclesiastical governments which obtained in the middle ages; and a total separation of church and state, even as corporations, would, in the present state of men's minds in Europe, be construed, if approved by the church, into a sanction by her of political atheism, or the right of civil power to govern according to its own will and pleasure in utter disregard of the law of God, the moral order, or the immutable distinction between right and wrong. It could only favor the absolutism of the state, and put the temporal in the place of the spiritual. Hence, the Holy Father includes the proposition of the entire separation of church and state in the syllabus of errors condemned in the encyclical, dated at Rome, December 8, 1864. Neither the state nor the people, elsewhere than in the United States, can understand practically such separation in any other sense than the complete emancipation of our entire secular life from the law of God, or the divine order, which is the real order. It is not the union of church and state—that is, the union, or identity rather, of religious and political principles—that it is desirable to get rid of, but the disunion or antagonism of church and state. But this is nowhere possible out of the United States; for nowhere else is the state organized on catholic principles, or capable of acting, when acting from its own constitution, in harmony with a really catholic church, or the religious order really existing, in relation to which all things are created and governed. Nowhere else is it practicable, at present, to maintain between the two powers their normal relations.

But what is not practicable in the Old World is perfectly practicable in the New. The state here being organized in accordance with catholic principles, there can be no antagonism between it and the church. Though operating in different spheres, both are, in their respective spheres, developing and applying to practical life one and the same divine idea. The church can trust the state, and the state can trust the church. Both act from the same principle to one and the same end. Each by its own constitution cooperates with, aids, and completes the other. It is true the church is not formally established as the civil law of the land, nor is it necessary that she should be; because there is nothing in the state that conflicts with her freedom and independence, with her dogmas or her irreformable canons. The need of establishing the church by law, and protecting her by legal pains and penalties, as is still done in most countries, can exist only in a barbarous or semi-barbarous state of society, where the state is not organized on catholic principles, or the civilization is based on false principles, and in its development tends not to the real or divine order of things. When the state is constituted in harmony with that order, it is carried onward by the force of its own internal constitution in a catholic direction, and a church establishment, or what is called a state religion, would be an anomaly, or a superfluity. The true religion is in the heart of the state, as its informing principle and real interior life. The external establishment, by legal enactment of the church, would afford her no additional protection, add nothing to her power and efficacy, and effect nothing for faith or piety—neither of which can be forced, because both must, from their nature, be free-will offerings to God. . . .

The religious mission of the United States is not then to establish the church by external law, or to protect her by legal disabilities, pains, and penalties against the sects, however uncatholic they may be; but to maintain catholic freedom, neither absorbing the state in the church nor the church in the state, but leaving each to move freely, according to its own nature, in the sphere assigned it in the eternal order of things. Their mission separates church and state as external governing bodies, but unites them in the interior principles from which each derives its vitality and force. Their union is in the intrinsic unity of principle, and in the fact that, though moving in different spheres, each obeys one and the same divine law. With this the Catholic who knows what Catholicity means, is of course satisfied, for it gives the church all the advantage over the sects of the real over the un-real; and with this the sects have no right to be dissatisfied, for it subjects them to no disadvantage not inherent in sectarianism itself in presence of Catholicity, and without any support from the civil authority.

The effect of this mission of our country fully realized would be to harmonize church and state, religion and politics, not by absorbing either in the other, or by obliterating the natural distinction between them, but by conforming both to the real or divine order, which is supreme and immutable. It places the two powers in their normal relation, which has hitherto never been done, because hitherto there never has been a state normally constituted. . . .

Education

EDUCATION

EDITOR'S PREFACE

THE FOLLOWING ESSAYS, selected from some seventy-five Brownson wrote on education, can only suggest the direction of his thought. His career spanned the period of the development of free public education and the beginnings of Catholic parochial schools and Catholic colleges. His essays were his contribution to the debate on these two developments.

His early writings on education have little consistency. Certain emphases do emerge, however. He insists that education should be an intellectual discipline and an awakening, and opposes narrowly utilitarian and vocational aims. He asks searching questions as to the education best suited to a free society, warning that education can be used to consolidate despotism as well as to develop free citizens. At times he vacillates between emphasis on the intellectual and the moral aim in education. He is convinced that the exclusion of all religious instruction from the public schools leaves the moral and spiritual formation of the pupils incomplete, yet, given the religious division of American society, he can offer no viable solution to the problem. He looks with suspicion on centralized control by the state, and, opposing suggestions for a national system of education, recommends aid by the state, with responsibility shared by local government, parents, and the ministry. There is an unmistakably Emersonian note in his early comments on the proper mode of education. This note is clearly evident in the first essay that follows, with its interweaving of quotations from Emerson's "American

Scholar." The proletarian emphasis found in his early social writings is singularly absent from his early essays on education, and the emphasis on the dangers of the leveling tendency in radical democracy is insistent in "The Scholar's Mission."

Brownson's Catholic career coincided with the expansion of Catholic parochial schools and the establishment of a large number of Catholic colleges and universities. For example, though Georgetown University was founded in 1789, Fordham, Notre Dame, Villanova, and Holy Cross were not established until 1841–1843, while the Catholic University of America was not established until 1887. While Brownson as a Catholic publicist recognized the importance of Catholic education, and wrote many articles to show that its development was imperative if Catholics were really to make their fullest contribution to American society, much of his effort went to pointing out the shortcomings of Catholic schools and colleges as they then existed. As in his political writings, during the fifties and early sixties, he charged that there was too frequently a tendency on the part of Catholics to confuse Catholicism with European social and cultural patterns, and to erect a wall of separation between themselves and non-Catholic Americans. He protested against what he considered extravagant and unwarranted condemnation of the public-school system. His own tone frequently lacked moderation, and thus he was charged with favoring public schools at the expense of the parochial schools. Actually, he was fearful that the founding of large numbers of parochial schools before adequate funds were available would result in an inferior quality of education. The simple establishment of a school under Catholic auspices was to him no guarantee that *ipso facto* it would have more to offer the student, intellectually, than other schools. In his best passages, however, he urged that the Catholic schools and colleges could not rest with the aim of preserving the Faith of the Catholic laity, but must aim at imparting a real intellectual and philosophical formation and an understanding of the role of the Catholic citizen in American society. He lamented the absence of a single Catholic university, and for a time looked to Newman's newly established Dublin University to meet the needs of American Catholics. If much of his criticism was negative, there was also implicit in it a conception of the potentialities of Catholic schools that still has its relevance.

Also relevant to the present is Brownson's discussion of the "separation of Church and state" doctrine as it touched on education. He saw how onerous it was not only for Catholics but for Protestant citizens who wished their children to have religious education to support both the public and the church-affiliated schools. He interpreted "separation" to mean non-establishment, and suggested various ways by which public funds could be apportioned to aid church-affiliated schools of different denominations without doing violence to the conscience of any citizens.

OBSERVATIONS AND HINTS
ON EDUCATION
[1840]

[*The full text of the following essay may be found in the*
Boston Quarterly Review *for April, 1840 (III, 137–166). It
is not included in the standard edition of Brownson's* Works. *He
wrote numerous essays on education prior to 1840, and as early
as 1831 had declared: "Education must wake up a day in the
soul, and give life, activity and energy to the whole intellectual
man, or moral excellence is but a dream." Here he enunciates a
strongly Emersonian theory of education. The emphasis on induction and on the proper use of books recalls Emerson's "Nature" and "The American Scholar," and readers familiar with
"The American Scholar" will recognize nearly all of Brownson's
quotations as coming from that essay. Nature for Emerson is
the primary influence on the scholar, books but secondary. But
Brownson tends here not only to echo Emerson, but to distort
his thought by making specific what Emerson leaves poetic and
suggestive. Brownson himself was largely self-taught, and the
passage, "Great is the theory of self-taught men," can be read
as a comment on his own experience. One wonders whether
Brownson had the passage in mind when in 1847, calling for
more disciplined scholars, he said: "Let the senseless babble, of
which we hear so much, about self-education and self-educated
men, cease. . . ."* (Works, *XIX, 219.) The present essay shows
how pervasive was the emphasis during the period on nature as
the true school of man. For this is also the time when Bronson
Alcott was writing in his* Journal: *"The country is much to every
young soul. . . . It was discipline and culture to me. . . . God
spoke to me while I walked the fields; I read not the gospel of*

wisdom from books written by man, but the page inscribed by the finger of God." (Odell Shepard, Pedlar's Progress, *Boston, 1937, p. 215.)*]

EDUCATION is the great problem of the age. The education of the people is held to be the first condition of the stability of free social institutions; the only efficient means of social progress. Especially is the necessity of popular education in democratic communities insisted on. So imperative is this necessity considered, that the want of education is even sometimes held as a sufficient cause of social, political, and personal disfranchisement. . . .

None but an educated can be a permanently free people. The question is not of the importance of education; but what is education? that which is the support and safeguard of personal and political freedom? . . .

Induction is the foundation of all practical knowledge, and the habit of observation, which it requires, is, like all other habits, most easily acquired in early life. If not formed then, it cannot be in after life, but by constant watchfulness and painful discipline; the process of self-culture, meanwhile, is at a stand, or but tardily progressive. Argue as we may concerning different systems of instruction, no system is of much value which does not aim at making education a self-discipline, at making every man, in truth, a self-taught man. The chief value of books is to assist, not to supersede, the process of self-culture. Great is the theory of self-taught men, and full of wisdom. Little are they indebted to Faust's wondrous art; they derive their knowledge from that universal revelation of knowledge in man and nature, of which books only copy and often misquote the language. And have they not been, in all ages, the mighty of the earth, the seers and prophets of mankind? "Not out of those, on whom systems of education have exhausted their culture, comes the helpful giant to destroy the old, or build the new; but out of unhandseled savage nature, out of terrible Druids and Berserkirs, come at last Alfred and Shakespeare."

The child, the infant, is constantly making observations; the whole of his studious play is a process of induction. Instead of fostering this habit, do not the practiced systems of education tend directly to prevent its formation, to crush the awakening energies of the intellect, to connect learning with the most disagreeable and painful associations? . . . Give the child a set of pothooks and the range of the kitchen at home, and in most cases he will work out for himself more elements of knowledge in a day, than he can, with grief and indignation, compass in half the term of his scholastic inflictions. . . .

Why do we not here, as elsewhere, found our systems upon induction? Why, instead of counteracting, do we not follow and assist the instinctive developments of the young mind? That is ever active, ever seeking knowledge by observation. From the moment the child begins to crawl, he lays hold of everything, feels, tastes everything, and from everything gets knowledge, is teaching himself, learning the nature and properties of substance, acquiring ideas of extension, solidity, and the other mysteries of matter. . . . Books are now his delight, because they present to him several new problems in mechanics and natural philosophy, and also enable him to demonstrate his own force in pulling them to pieces. It may be announced as a general, if not a universal, proposition, that he learns more from books at this time, than in any subsequent equal period of his life. He masters their material riches. Is it not an evil, more or less, that any untoward associations should ever make them aught to him but large depositories of intellectual treasures? . . . The flower he plucks, and as we name it, *idly* throws away, is a textbook, from which he learns lessons, that "the whining schoolboy, creeping like a snail unwillingly to school," will probably forget, but will not be likely to learn. He studies the first written book, of which all printed books are only translations, more or less tolerably, some execrably done, but none conveying the full spirit, truth, and beauty of the original.

Let him stay in this school yet a little longer. Follow, assist the direction of nature, but do not thwart her. Give him a teacher, if you will, to help him to observe, and aid him in his interpreting. Indeed some such interpreter, or seeing teacher, not a pedagogue, would seem to be necessary. But do not quench his spirit in its springtime by immuring him between walls (of brick or wood and mortar), and compel him to turn from the living, God-written page, to the dark, dead, perplexing hieroglyphics, (nay, double hieroglyphics; for are not most words, to the child as to many men, as much hieroglyphic mysteries, as the literal symbols which compose them?) from which as yet he can only and reluctantly draw small rills of nourishment for his infinite curiosity. Let him acquire many of the first truths of nature, the elements of which books are made; let him have some conception of the proper use of letters and words, of the functions of books, and a strong yearning to enter the wide domains of thought of which books are the portals; in short let him learn to be an authentic and judging reader, before he learns to read; lest he bow his mind to authority, and fail to be a man,—"man thinking." Said he not truth, who wrote, "I had better never read a book, than to be warped by its instruction clean out of my own orbit, and made a satellite instead of a system?"

The only use of letters being to make us acquainted with books, in pursuance of the spirit of the first step, the substance of education is laid in books, so far as education is a system. If the first steps do not create an unconquerable distaste or disgust, the child learns to consider books as almost the only sources of knowledge. Hence a reverence is acquired for books, merely as books, paralyzing to the energies of the intellect, and not to be removed in after life, but with serious, painful, and long-continued discipline. Hence the whole process of education is mere instruction, authoritative teaching, dogmatical. It does not draw out the powers of one's own mind; the true purpose of education, as its etymology indicates. The memory is almost the only mental faculty called into active exercise, while the higher powers of induction, comparison, reasoning, abstraction are almost inert, or but partially developed, never attaining their full maturity, except in rarely fortunate circumstances, or in minds of superior native energy. "The intelligent soul is not roused to free and vigorous activity." Hence there is so little of self-reliance, so much of servile dependence on the thoughts of others, the reverence for the past, the slow and contentious progress of improvement, the acquiescence in authority, the seeing and hearing with the organs of others, the using of other men's heads instead of our own.

This dogmatical character pervades the whole course of instruction. The child believes what is told him on the authority of the teacher, the master, or the book, without being taught to inquire into the validity of the authority; whether the professed revelation made to him is authentic, a fact or a fable. The mind is nearly passive during the process. If the teacher or the book be authentic, it is better so to learn, than to be ignorant. But he is not able to judge whether they be or not. A true book, true teaching, as I have said, are but transcripts of the facts of nature, more or less legibly written, according to the clearness of the vision of the seer. Of the greater part of those facts every person may acquire a competent knowledge, by the proper use of those instruments, which are furnished to all; namely his five or six physical senses, and his intuitions. Books and teachers do not originate, create, but only declare; and nothing which is not, for the most part, accessible without their aid. For were not all the things contained in books known, or to be known, before they were recorded in books? Were they not in the universe, not hidden but only invisible, until the eye of some seer was opened upon them? Every eye, that chooses, may be a seer. To make all eyes such is the mission of education. . . .

Education should be practical, it is said; its proper function is to train up youth into practical men; and practical men are the only useful men in society. In one sense, unquestionably true; in another sense, unquestionably false. All scripture is given by inspiration. All knowledge is essentially practical, calculated to enable man to accomplish the purpose of man's being; and all knowledge is worthless, which is not made to polarize around the central law of his being. In this sense the proposition is un-impeachable, that education should be practical. But what is meant by *practicalness;* who is the practical man? Is it he who judges of what may be done, from what has been done, and deems every theory a chimera, every project impossible, for which he does not remember a precedent; who refers everything to the maxims and usages of the past? . . .

On the contrary, can any system of education be truly practi-cal, which has not reference to man in his whole capacity, obliga-tions, and destiny, as something more than a money-getting ani-mal; which does not aim to draw out into free activity the whole faculties of his mind? And is not he the only practical man, who has formed himself under such a system of culture; who has taken in the widest range of investigation and discovered most of the laws of nature and of the human mind; who has attained the clearest insight into the relations of things, and established his principles of judgment and conduct, upon the widest observa-tion of facts, material and spiritual? He has no dread of innova-tion, reform, whether in the applications of labor, or the institu-tions of society; because he has seen and knows that progress, improvement, is the constant obligation of man's being, individ-ually and socially. He is not satisfied with the present, of his own mind, or of social institutions; but looks forward, striving with patient hope, to a gleaming future, when "that which is perfect shall come, and that which is in part shall be done away." He is conscious that he knows but the minutest portion of the universe and its laws, and is not rash to pronounce anything impossible, however incredible it may appear, and contrary to all former experience. . . .

Be education practical; and the more practical any system is, the more perfect it is. This it can never be, unless it has reference to man in his whole nature and destiny; unless it aims at something higher than to fit men for the routine of petty occupations, for the handicrafts and mechanical business of society; unless it contemplates for man a nobler destiny than that so strikingly depicted by a living American writer. "Man thus metamorphosed, is a thing, many things. The planter is a man sent into the fields to gather food, and is seldom cheered with the idea of the true dignity of his mission. He sees his bushel and his cart, and sinks into a farmer, instead of *man on a farm*. The tradesman scarce gives an ideal value to his work, but is ridden by the routine of his craft, and his soul is subject to dollars. The priest becomes a form; the attorney a statute book; the mechanic a machine; the sailor a rope of a ship.". . .

But man was not made to be a machine, a fraction; to lose his separate existence, and be incorporated in a mass; nor to suffer his free volitions to be overwhelmed by his social sympathies. It is the mission of education to rescue him from this individual annihilation; to develop the great central law and attribute of his being; that man, each man by himself, in reference to all other men, is essentially and inalienably free, and the brother and equal of every man. This great first truth must be roused from its almost dead sleep in constitutions and popular declamation, and brought out again, with new annunciations, into the highways and byeways of society; into the humble roadside schoolhouse, and into the halls where high science has her throne. Instead of being a parchment formula, let it be made a living, all-pervading energy; presiding in the assemblies of legislation; and giving an irresistible but tranquil and legitimate power to public opinion. . . . I can form no conception of a freedom in society, of which the freedom of individual man is not the primary element; of man as man, with rights not derived from society, prior to society, beyond the control of all other men, beyond the reach of government, laws, or public opinion. It is no impeachment of the validity of these rights, that the individual may and does abuse them. The power to abuse them is a necessary element of liberty. "God leaves man in his freedom, and does not control it, though man, in abusing it, brings damnation to his soul." The legitimate exercise of freedom can never work harm to others, or to society. There can be no collision between the clear rights of one individual, and those of another, any more than in the use of the all-pervading elements; for the rights are identical and universal. "So long as one does not trespass upon the rights of others, nor place obstacles in the way of their full and free exercise, society has no authority to interfere with his course."

These principles are in the highest degree practical; for in man's freedom lies his power of full and perfect development. They should be made the starting-point, and fixed as landmarks along the whole course of practical education. They should cheer the schoolboy's wearisome discipline with hope and confidence. To man they should be a universal presence, filling him with the fullness of strength, courage, and indomitable energy for all the "sublime possibilities" of his being.

THE SCHOLAR'S MISSION
[1843]

[*Brownson's income as an editor never sufficed to support his large family. Like so many others in this period of the lyceum movement, he lectured widely to augment his income, and gained something of a reputation as an orator. He was an imposing figure, well over six feet tall, of vigorous physique, and his voice was powerful and resonant. Though he admired especially the oratorical style of Webster, his own style was far less dramatic than Webster's. Brownson relied more on the logical development of his thought than on emotional appeal or on brilliance of rhetoric.*

The following oration was delivered before the Gamma Sigma Society of Dartmouth College during commencement exercises on July 26, 1843. For the full text, see Works, XIX, *65–87. Both Webster and Rufus Choate spoke on the same occasion, and according to Henry F. Brownson, in congratulating Brownson they "assured him that his was unquestionably the oration of the day."* (Brownson's Early Life, *p. 380.) The doctrine here developed of the scholar as lay prophet bears many correspondences with that of Emerson in "The American Scholar." Brownson's style now seems somewhat archaic and orotund, and certainly lacks the crispness, the metaphorical vividness of Emerson's great address, yet the oration has an unmistakable vigor. The conception of providential men which Brownson develops in other essays during this period is here brought into relation with the scholar's function.*]

THOUGH but ill-qualified by my own scholastic attainments to do the subject justice, I have yet thought that I could not better comply with your wishes, and answer the request which brings me here, than by selecting for the theme of our reflections, THE SCHOLAR'S MISSION. This is a subject which must be fresh in your minds; which must have often occupied your thoughts, and given rise to both painful anxieties and joyful anticipations; and to which the attention of us all is naturally drawn, by the day, the place, the occasion, and their respective associations.

In treating this subject, I shall first consider the scholar's mission in general; and secondly, as modified by the peculiar tendencies of our own age and country.

I use this word scholar in no low or contracted sense. I mean by it, indeed, a *learner*, for truth is infinite, and we are finite; but on this occasion I mean by it the MASTER rather than the pupil; and not merely the one who has mastered some of the technicalities of a few of the more familiar sciences, but the one who has, as far as possible, mastered all the subjects of human thought and interest, and planted himself on the beach at the farthest distance as yet moistened by the ever advancing wave of science. I understand by the scholar no mere pedant, dilettante, literary epicure or dandy; but a serious, hearty, robust, full-grown man; who feels that life is a serious affair, and that he has a serious part to act in its eventful drama; and must therefore do his best to act well his part, so as to leave behind him, in the good he has done, a grateful remembrance of his having been. He may be a theologian, a politician, a naturalist, a poet, a moralist, or a metaphysician; but whichever or whatever he is, he is it with all his heart and soul, with high, noble,—in one word, *religious* aims and aspirations.

With this view of the scholar, though I would not be thought deficient in my respect for classical literature, I cannot call one a scholar, merely because he is familiar with Homer and the Greek tragedians, and can make a felicitous quotation from Horace or Juvenal. The scholarship is not in this familiarity, nor in this ability, though neither is to be despised; but in so having studied the classics as to have made them the means of throwing new

and needed light on some dark passage in human history or in
the human heart. We study the classics as scholars only when we
study them as the exponents of Greek and Roman life, of the
humanity that then and there was, lived and toiled, joyed and
sorrowed, came and went; and from deep sympathy with that
humanity acquire a deeper sympathy with the humanity that
now is, and strengthen our hearts and our hands for the necessary work of attaining to a nobler humanity hereafter. . . .

We talk much in these days and in this country, about equality, and some of us go so far as to contend that every man is fitted
by nature to succeed equally in everything. We lose individual
inequalities in the dead level of the mass, and believe that we
shall be able more effectually to carry the race forward by means
of this dead level, than by suffering individuals to stand out
from and above the multitude, the prophets of a more advanced
stage, and the ministers of God to help us to reach it. But this
theory of equality, popular as it may have become, will not abide
the wear and tear of active life; it is a mere dream, a silly dream,
unsustained by a single fact tangible to waking sense. All men
are equal only in this, that all are equally men, equally accountable to God, and no one is bound to obey any merely *human*
authority. The authority, to have the right to command, must
be more than human. For each man may say, "I also am a man.
Who as a simple human being is more? No one? Then has no
one, as a simple human being, the right to call himself my
master." In this sense, and in this only, is it true, "that all men
are created equal."

The universe is made up of infinite diversity. No two objects
can be found in nature which are absolutely indistinguishable, or
which perform one and the same office. In our own race the same
diversity obtains. One man does not merely repeat another. All
individual men participate of humanity, of human nature, and
are men only by virtue of such participation; but humanity, all

and entire, enters into no one man. No one man can say, I am all of humanity; for if it were so, you might kill off all save that one man, and humanity would suffer no loss. . . .

This being the constitution of humanity and of human society, it follows that in the order of divine Providence, each man must needs have his special mission, and that a mission which no one else has, or can be fitted to perform. Each is to labor for the advancement of all, not by attempting to do the work of all indiscriminately; but by confining himself to his own specially allotted work. To some is assigned one work, to others another. Some are called to be artists, some to be cultivators of science, others to be industrials. All cannot be prophets and priests; all cannot be kings and rulers, all cannot be poets and philosophers; and all, I dare add, cannot be *scholars,* in all or in any of the special departments of scholarship. The doctrine of St. Paul is as applicable in its principle here to society at large, as to the church. "Now there are diversities of gifts, but the same Spirit. For to one is given by the Spirit the word of wisdom; to another, the word of knowledge; to another, faith; to another, the gifts of healing; to another, the working of miracles; to another, prophecy; to another, discerning of spirits; to another, divers kinds of tongues; to another, the interpretation of tongues; but all these worketh that one and the self-same Spirit, *dividing to every man severally as he will.*". . .

Without this diversity, and the inequality necessarily growing out of it, it were idle to talk of the progress of humanity. The mass are not carried forward without individuals, who rise above the general average. Where would have been the race now, had it not been for such men as Pythagoras, Socrates, and Plato, Abélard and St. Thomas, Bacon and Descartes, Locke and Leibnitz; Alexander and Caesar, Alfred and Charlemagne, Napoleon and Washington; Homer, Aeschylus, Sophocles, and Pindar, Virgil and Homer, Dante, Shakespeare, and Milton, Goethe

and Schiller; not to speak of the immeasurably higher order of
providential men, whom we bring not into the category of these,
—inspired prophets and messengers, specially called, and illuminated in their several degrees, by the Holy Ghost,—such as
Noah and Abraham, Moses and David, Paul and John, Augustine and Bernard, George Fox, and others. It is only by the life,
love, labors, and sacrifices of these, and such as these, that the
race is quickened, instructed, inspired, and enabled to make its
way through the ages to the accomplishment of its destiny. . . .

But when I speak of the mass, of the many, I pray you not to
misinterpret me. They whom I include in the term *many*, or on
whom my mind specially rests in speaking of the many, are not
exclusively those whom the world calls the poor and illiterate.
Never measure a man's capacity, attainments, or virtues, by his
apparent rank, wealth, or education. I am no great believer in
the superior capacities or virtues, of what are called the upper
classes. Nine-tenths of the graduates of our colleges, are as innocent as the child unborn of any, the least, the faintest conception
of the real problems of metaphysical science; and it were as easy
to make him who is stone deaf, relish the performance of one of
Beethoven's symphonies, as to make them even conceive of these
problems, to say nothing of their solving them. Only a few pe-
culiarly constituted minds, coming at rare intervals of time and
space, can seek successfully their solution; and these perhaps
come oftenest, when and whence they are least expected. To
these, come when or whence they may, belongs the solution of
the problems of which I speak; the results or benefit of the solution belong to the many. So say we of theology, ethics, and politics. The *science* is for the few, the *results* for all men. The
science is to be sought by the few alone, but solely and expressly
for the many, who will not, and cannot, successfully seek it for
themselves. To the few then the honor and glory of the labor;

to the many the right to enter into the labors of the few, and enjoy the fruit. . . .

The scholar's mission is to instruct and inspire the race in reference to the general end,—progress,—for which God has made and placed us here. This is the fact that too many of those who pass for scholars, overlook: and hence the prejudice we find in our own day and country against them. This prejudice does not grow out of any dislike to the general law of Providence, that the race is to be carried forward by individuals, who stand out from and above the mass. Every republican glories in the name of Washington; every democrat delights to honor Jefferson. No man is really offended, that there is inequality in men's capacities, attainments, and virtues. But the prejudice grows out of the fact that our educated men are exceedingly prone to forget, that their superior capacities and attainments are to be held by them, not for their own private benefit, but as sacred trusts, to be used for the moral, religious, social, and intellectual advancement of mankind. They for the most part look upon their superior capacities and scholastic attainments, as special marks of divine favor upon themselves personally, conferred for their own special good, because God perchance loves them better than he does others. This is a grievous error. God is no repecter of persons; and if he gives this man one capacity, and that man another, it is not because he loves one man more or less than he does another; for it is always while the children are yet unborn, before they have done either good or evil, that it is written, "the elder shall serve the younger." But it is because he has so ordered it, that his purposes in regard to humanity are to be carried on only by a division of labor, by establishing among men a diversity of gifts and callings, by assigning to one man one work, and to another man another work. The mortal sin of every aristocracy, whether literary, scientific, military, or political, is by no means in the inequality it implies, produces, or perpetuates; but in the fact, that it regards itself as a *privileged* order, specially endowed for its own special benefit. Hence, every aristocracy seeks always to consolidate itself, and to secure to itself all the advantages of the state, or of society. It seeks to make itself a caste, and to rule, not as the servant of others, but as their master. . . .

The scholarship that rests with the scholar, that seeks only the scholar's own ease, pleasure, convenience, or renown, is worthy only of the unmitigated contempt of all men. Of all men, the scholar is he who needs most thoroughly to understand and practice the abnegation of self; who more than any other is to be laborious and self-sacrificing, feeling himself charged to work out a higher good for his brethren; and that wherever he is, or whatever he does, the infinite Eye rests upon him, and his honor as a man, as well as a scholar, is staked on the wisdom and fidelity, with which he labors to execute his mission.

Thus far I have considered the mission of the scholar only in its general character, as we find it at all times, and in all places; but it is time that we proceed now to consider it as modified by the peculiar tendencies of our own age and country. The scholar, let him do his best, will be more or less affected by the peculiar tendencies of the age in which he lives, and the country in which he was brought up, and must act; and in these peculiar tendencies he finds, and must find, his special mission, the special work to which God in his providence calls him. His general mission, we have said, is to instruct and inspire his race. To ascertain his special mission, he must ask, In relation to what does my age or my country most need to be instructed and inspired? . . .

It never is, it never can be, the mission of the scholar to do over again for the progress of his race, what has already been done; but that which has not as yet been done, and which must be done, before another step forward can be taken. What is the

special work for me to do *here* and *now?* This is *here* and *now*
my work as a scholar.

The scholar, I repeat, is one who stands out from and above
the mass, as it were, a prophet and a priest to instruct and inspire
them. He is not, then, and cannot be, one who joins in with the
multitude, and suffers himself to be borne blindly and passively
along by their pressure. Do not mistake me. The scholar is not
one who stands above the people, and looks down on the people
with contempt. He has no contempt for the people; but a deep
and an all-enduring love for them, which commands him to live
and labor, and, if need be, suffer and die, for their redemption;
but he never forgets that he is their instructor, their guide, their
chief, not their echo, their slave, their tool. He believes, and proceeds on the belief, that there is a standard of truth and justice,
of wisdom and virtue, above popular convictions, aye, or popular
instincts; and that to this standard both he and the people are
bound to conform. To this standard he aims to bring his own
convictions, and by it to rectify his own judgments; and, having
so done, instead of going with the multitude when they depart
from it, swimming with the popular current when it sets in
against it, he throws himself before the multitude, and with a
bold face and a firm voice commands them to pause, for their
onward course is their death. He resists the popular current, he
braves the popular opinion, wherever he believes it wrong or
mischievous, be the consequences to himself what they may. This
he must do, for Providence, in giving him the capacity and
means to be a scholar, that is, a leader, and chief of his race, has
made him responsible, to the full measure of his ability, for the
wisdom and virtue of the multitude.

Here is the law that must govern the scholar. He must labor
to lead public opinion where right, and correct it where wrong.
Keeping this in view, he can without difficulty comprehend what,

in these days and in this country, is the special work for the
scholar. The tendency of our age and country is a *leveling* tendency. This is seen everywhere and in every thing; in literature,
religion, morals, and philosophy,—in church and in state. There
is no mistaking this fact. In *literature* the tendency is to bring
all down to the level of the *common* intelligence, to adapt all to
the lowest round of intellect. What is profound we eschew;
what requires time and patient thought to comprehend, we
forego. . . .

In religion and the church, we find the same tendency to level
all distinctions. The minister of God, who was clothed with authority to teach, has become the minister of the *congregation,*
and responsible to those, whose sins he is to rebuke, for the doctrines he holds, and the reproofs he administers; and instead of
being at liberty to consult only the glory of his Master in the
salvation of sinners, he must study to render himself popular, so
as to please men as well as God. In the sanctuary, as well as on
the hustings, we hear, *vox populi est vox Dei.* The pulpit is thus
forced, instead of proclaiming, with an authoritative voice, the
word of God, our supreme law, to echo popular convictions and
prejudices, popular passions and errors, and to vary its tone with
the varying moods of the congregation. . . .

The religious *press* feels the same influence; echoes the popular sentiment; and is as superficial as the popular mind. Scarcely
a question is solidly and learnedly discussed; very few of our
theologians are up with the literature of their profession; fewer
still are able to make any contributions to theological science.
We every day value less and less sound theological knowledge.
Our congregations cry out against *doctrinal* sermons; religious
readers will hear nothing of controversial theology; and the conviction has become quite general, that it matters much less what
one thinks, than what one feels; what are one's doctrines, than
what are one's emotions. . . .

The conviction, or feeling seems to have become quite general, that a public man should have no mind of his own, no will, no conscience, but that of his party. To disregard the wishes of one's party, when that party is assumed to be in the majority, though in obedience to the constitution, to one's oath of office, and conscientious convictions of duty, is proclaimed to be base, unpardonable treachery. . . . In a word, it has come to this, our study is to *follow*, to *echo* the public opinion, not to *form* it.

Now, I do not say, that this tendency is accompanied by no good, nor that it has originated in a source wholly evil. So far as it has been effectual in elevating the great mass of the people, in actually ameliorating, in any degree, their moral, intellectual, or social condition, I certainly am not the man to declaim against it, but to thank my God for it. Whatever tends, directly or indirectly, to benefit the masses, so long neglected and downtrodden, however hard it may bear on individuals, I am prepared in both religion and morals to defend. But I deny, that this tendency has resulted in any general elevation of the poorer and more numerous classes, of those who hitherto in the world's history, have been "the hewers of wood and drawers of water" to the few. On the contrary, I contend that it has been for the most part exceedingly hostile to them, and tended to put far off the day of their complete emancipation. It is in their name, and in their interests, and not in the name or the interests of the aristocracy, with whom I have no sympathy, that I condemn it. I accept, with all my heart, democracy; but democracy, as I understand and accept it, requires me to sacrifice myself *for* the masses, not *to* them. Who knows not, that if you would save the people, you must often oppose them? No advance has ever yet been made, but it has been opposed by them, especially by those they follow as their trusted leaders. Every true prophet and priest, is at first martyred by them. They were the people, who condemned Socrates to drink hemlock; they were the people, who cried out against one infinitely greater than Socrates, "Crucify, crucify him." The real benefactor of his race, is always calumniated as a public enemy. Nor does it help the matter by saying, this is not the fault of the people themselves, but of those who have their confidence; for if the people were themselves as discerning, and as virtuous, as is contended, how should they come to confide in leaders, who would induce them to crucify their redeemers? The future is elaborated in the present; but its elaborators must work in dark laboratories, in silent retreats, wander the earth in sheepskins, . . . and dwell in the mountains, or in the caves, of whom the world is not worthy. It cannot be otherwise. They are of the future, and must look to the future for their reward. Their views, hopes, wishes, are dark mysteries to their contemporaries, and how can they be the favorites of their age, the men one meets at the head of processions, or in the chief seats in the synagogues? They are the prophets of a better age, of which they must be the builders, as well as the heralds.

You see then, my young friends, if ye will be scholars, and acquit you like men, what here and now, is your mission. You are *to withstand this leveling tendency,* so far, but only so far, as it is a tendency to level downwards, and not upwards. Do not, however, mistake, on this point, the real purport of your mission. Withstand no tendency to sweep away barbarous castes and factitious distinctions, which divide and make enemies of those, who else were friends and brothers; advocate no artificial inequality; contend for no privileged orders; but do all in your power to enable all men to stand up, side by side, with their feet on the same level. Consent never that a man, short by nature, shall plant his feet on your, or another man's, shoulders, draw himself up, and with great self-complacency, look round on the multitude, and exclaim, "See, how tall I am!" But, if when all men thus stand up, acknowledged to be men, with their feet on the same broad level of humanity, some are taller than you by the head and shoulders, envy them not; but thank God that your race is blessed with men taller than you. . . .

But the tendency I ask you to withstand, is not merely a tendency to sweep away privileged orders, to bring down all who are elevated only for their *private* advantage, and to place all men with their feet on the same level; but it is a tendency to level from the other extremity, to obtain equality by lopping off all heads, that rise above the general average, and to resist the elevation of any to a sufficient height, to enable them to labor with advantage for the elevation of others. It is this leveling tendency, I ask you to withstand. But this tendency is so strong and decided, that you will find it no easy matter, no child's play, to withstand it. The public mind is unsound, the public conscience is perverted, and in order to set either right, you must appeal from the dominant sentiment of your age and country, to that higher tribunal, to which you and the public are both alike accountable. . . .

Bind on, if need be, your tunic of coarse serge, and feed on water in which pulse has been boiled, as did Saint Bernard de Clairvaux, or sew you up a suit, "one perennial suit," of leather, as did the sturdy old George Fox, and putting your trust in God, thus defy the world, trample Satan and his temptations under your feet, and maintain, in all their plenitude, the freedom and dignity of scholarship. Ask not what your age wants, but what it needs; not what it will reward, but what, without which, it cannot be saved; and that go and do; do it well; do it thoroughly; and find your reward in the consciousness of having done your duty, and above all in the reflection, that you have been accounted worthy to suffer somewhat for mankind. . . .

PUBLIC AND PAROCHIAL
SCHOOLS
[1859]

[*In the opening paragraphs of the following essay, which appeared in* Brownson's Quarterly Review *for July, 1859* (Works,
XII, 200–216), *Brownson calls attention to the "very energetic
and decided language on the subject of public schools" employed
by Archbishop J. B. Purcell of Cincinnati in his* Pastoral Letter
on the Decrees of the Second Provincial Council of Cincinnati,
Cincinnati, *1859. He also remarks on the fact that his own recent
essays on the school question had brought on him the charge that
he was taking "a non-Catholic ground," and that his was no
longer "a Catholic Review." The tone of the essay is typical of
most of Brownson's writings during the period from 1855 to
1864. His 1856 essay on "The Mission of America" had dis-
pleased his bishop, Archbishop Hughes, and the Bishop objected
equally to the following essay. Since Archbishop Hughes had
for long endeavored to obtain support for parochial schools from
public funds, Brownson's reservations about the merits of the
parochial schools as they then existed, and his defense of the
public-school system, were interpreted by some as an attack on
the whole parochial-school movement. One of Brownson's most
frequently reiterated charges was that the defense of Catholic
education was often linked with the attempt to perpetuate,
among American Catholics, European traditions erroneously associated with the Catholic Faith. For a full discussion of Brownson's attitude, see Edward J. Power's University of Notre Dame
doctoral study,* The Educational Views and Attitudes of Orestes
A. Brownson, *first published in* The Records of the American
Catholic Historical Society of Philadelphia, LXII (*1951*) and
LXIII (*1952*), and later reprinted in a single volume.*]

WE RECOGNIZE in the church all the authority over the subject of education she claims, that is, plenary authority in respect to all that pertains to the moral and religious training of the young. Faith and morals saved, I have the right, in purely secular education, to educate my children as I judge best; but I am not free, even in secular education, to send my children to schools which she interdicts, or to which the Prelates the Holy Ghost has placed over me declare I cannot send them without gravely imperiling their faith or morals. On this point we see not how there can be any question among Catholics. The church has the full and supreme control of the moral instruction and religious education of the young, as included in her divine mission, and she has full and supreme authority to say what secular schools are or are not imminently dangerous to faith and morals, and to those she declares to be thus dangerous no Catholic parent can lawfully send his child. Now, how stands the case with the public schools, or, as we usually say, the district schools? Have our prelates interdicted them? If so, we are ignorant of the fact. The pastoral before us does not go that length, and it goes as far as any thing we have seen. . . .

We know our pastors are not satisfied with the district schools as they are, and we know that many of them are doing all they can to establish separate Catholic schools for our Catholic children. Have we ever taken ground against them, pretended the district schools as they are satisfy even ourselves? Or have we in any way whatever opposed their movement to establish separate Catholic schools? We assuredly have done no such thing. We have never felt that we were free to oppose, and, moreover, have never wished to oppose or take ground against them. Whence, then, the tremendous outcry against us? Whence comes it that we are charged with taking a non-Catholic ground, and that our *Review* is referred to as being no longer a Catholic periodical, in consequence of its views on the subject of the dis-

trict schools? It comes not from any opposition we have offered
to our prelates, to Catholic education, or to Catholic schools; but
it comes, if the truth must be told, from the source whence has
come the greater part of the opposition to us for the last five
years,—that is, from our steady and determined opposition to
any and every movement the direct tendency of which is to de-
nationalize the American Catholic, and to keep Catholics a foreign colony in the United States, or Catholicity here in this New
World linked with that old effete Europeanism which has always, wherever it has existed, been a drag on it, and which all
that is true, good, generous, and noble in our American political
and social order repudiates. . . .

Rightly or wrongly, we believe that the best safeguard, aside
from purely Catholic instruction and the sacraments, of the faith
and morals of our children, is not in building up a wall of separation, not required by Catholic doctrine, between them and the
non-Catholic community, but in training them to feel, from the
earliest possible moment, that the American nationality is their
nationality, that Catholics are really and truly an integral portion of the great American people, and that we can be, whatever
the Know-Nothings may say to the contrary, without the slightest difficulty, at once good Catholics and loyal Americans, and
the enlightened and earnest defenders of political, civil, and religious liberty.

We are, and always have been, decidedly in favor of really
Catholic schools, that is, schools in which our children are sure
to be taught, and well taught, their religion, and we cannot understand how any Catholic at all worthy of the name can be
otherwise than earnestly in favor of such schools; but we have
not favored, and, till further advised, we cannot favor, under
pretext of providing for Catholic education, a system of schools
which will train up our children to be foreigners in the land of
their birth, for such schools cannot fail, in the long run, to do

more injury than good to the interests of religion. We quarrel
with no man for being a foreigner, but we recognize the moral
right in no class of American citizens to train up their children
to be foreigners, and then to claim for them all the rights, franchises, and immunities of American citizens. . . .

Although we do not pretend, and never have pretended, that
the district schools are all that Catholics need for their children,
we yet cannot approve the wholesale condemnation of them in
which some of our friends indulge. Much of that condemnation
is, we think, dictated by European notions and habits, and proceeds from not considering that many things which in the Old
World have a good and desirable tendency would have a contrary tendency here, and that many things which could not there
be tolerated for a moment without the gravest consequences re-
sulting, are wholly innocuous here, because in harmony with the
general spirit and constitution of our society. Immorality and irreligion are, no doubt, on the increase in the Union, but it is
wrong to attribute the fact to the influence of our common school
system. These schools do not, indeed, wholly prevent it; but we
think there would be much more immorality and irreligion
among us if we were without these schools. Even Catholic
schools have not always proved effectual in preventing immorality and irreligion in Catholic states. Education is not omnipotent,
and can never be a substitute for the sacraments. No system of
schools ever devised, or that ever will be devised, can be completely successful in making or keeping a people moral and religious. Experience has disappointed the too sanguine expecta-
tions of the philanthropists. Too much is, perhaps, still expected
from education. Our friends, also, make too much of individual
cases of immorality in our public schools, and which are only
rare exceptions to the general rule. We ourselves were educated
in a district school, and as teacher or as committeeman, we have
since been connected with the common schools in New York,

Michigan, Vermont, New Hampshire, and Massachusetts for over twenty years of our life; we have had eight children partly educated in them, and we claim to have some personal knowledge of them, and although we do not consider them by any means faultless, we are very far from recognizing as just the description of them which we usually meet in our Catholic journals. No schools, not even our Catholic schools, are perfect. . . .

In what we have written on the public schools we have had no intention of opposing the hierarchy, or of discouraging or interfering with their efforts to provide for Catholic education, which seems to us to have been greatly and even culpably neglected. We have written with a far different purpose. The district school system is an American pet; it is the pride of the American people, their boast, and really their glory. It is dear to their hearts, and we cannot strike them in a tenderer point than in striking this system, or do anything more effectual in stirring up their wrath against us, or in confirming their prejudices against our religion,—a system devised and adopted for themselves without any view favorable or unfavorable to Catholics, for it was devised and adopted when there were scarcely any Catholics in the country. Common prudence, if nothing else, should prevent us from exaggerating its defects, and shutting our eyes to its good points. We do not pretend, we never have pretended, that the public schools can satisfy all our wants as Catholics, and we have never pretended that we could use them, save where we have not and are not able to have good schools of our own, in which the positive doctrines of our religion can be taught. But we have believed that some of our Catholic friends have assailed them unjustly, with a zeal, a vehemence, and a bitterness alike impolitic and unwarranted, and we have wished to say something to neutralize their undue severity, and by frankly acknowledging the merits of the system to allay the wrath unnecessarily excited against us and our church. We have also felt on this subject as an American as well as a Catholic, and have wished to vindicate the honor of our country against the unjust aspersions cast on it by men who are indebted to her free institutions and the protection of her just laws for the very liberty they use in insulting and abusing her. In order to do this we have felt it necessary to bring up the side usually overlooked by our journalists, and to remind our Catholic friends that something may be said for as well as against our countrymen in relation to the public schools. . . .

We cannot hope what we have said will be acceptable to those of our friends who judge that the true policy for Catholics here is to make war on everything highly esteemed by non-Catholic Americans, or to those who would abolish the American system of public schools, and leave the whole matter of education to parents and the religious bodies to which the parents belong. We favor in principle a system of public schools, and are not prepared to maintain that the state should withdraw entirely from the whole matter of schools and education. We assert its right and its duty to see, as far as in its power, that all its children receive at least a good common-school education, though we deny most energetically its right to interfere with the conscience of any class of its citizens, and we maintain with equal energy the plenary authority of the church in all that pertains to the moral and religious instruction and education of the children of Catholic parents.

We cannot hope any more to satisfy those who look upon intelligence and independence as guilty tendencies, and make war, in religion, in morals, in science, in philosophy, in politics, on the whole natural order, and think we can be good Catholics only by denouncing all the works of unbelievers as sins. We are not among those who fancy that Catholicity can flourish here only by rooting out everything American, and completely revolutionizing American society and institutions. We believe American society, as natural society, is better organized, and organized more in accordance with the needs of Catholic society, than is any other society on the face of the globe, and we are anxious to preserve and perfect it according to its original type. We are disposed, also, to remember that the people who, under the providence of God, organized American society, in which Catholics enjoy a freedom they have nowhere else in the world, were themselves almost to a man non-Catholics, and at the time they organized it, there was probably no Catholic nation is existence that could have sent out a colony capable of organizing a society so much in accordance with the natural rights of man and the freedom and independence of religion. Certainly no Catholic colonies did do it, or by the mother country were permitted to do it. It does not become Catholics, who have subsequently, by virtue of its own free constitution, been received into this society on a footing of perfect equality, to forget this fact, or to show themselves ungrateful to the memory of its founders by constantly holding them up to ridicule, and seeking to undo their work, as the so-called Catholic press frequently does our Puritan ancestors. The late Know-Nothing movement, unjustifiable as we regard it, should be turned to profit, and instead of exciting our hostility to Americans and everything American, and making us sigh for a *régime* like that introduced into France by the Nephew of his Uncle, should induce us to re-examine our conduct, and inquire if we have not been pursuing a line of policy admirably fitted to provoke such a movement. It would do us no harm to inquire if there have not been faults on our side, and if there have been, to seek to avoid them in the future.

CATHOLIC SCHOOLS AND
EDUCATION
[1862]

[*The following essay, the full text of which is in* Works, *XII,
496–514, is one of the most challenging Brownson wrote on education. It suggests a standard at which Catholic higher education should aim, and levels the most severe criticisms at the
American Catholic colleges of the period. Most of these, it must
be emphasized, had only been established in the previous two
decades, and had as yet neither the material resources nor the
faculty personnel they would need if they were to develop into
strong institutions. How just was Brownson's criticism of the
actual practices of the colleges is largely an historical question.
There is a striking similarity, however, between Newman's and
Brownson's understanding of the purposes of Catholic higher
education. Just as Newman, having affirmed in the opening discourses of the* Idea of a University, *the central place of theology,
goes on in the remaining discourses to insist on "intellectual en-
largement" and the development of "the philosophical habit of
mind" as the aim of university education, so Brownson empha-
sizes the need for living men, thinking men who are competent
to contribute to the civilization of their own age. Like Newman,
Brownson saw the great need for liberally educated Catholics
with philosophical, scientific, and literary understanding, men
worthy of being recognized as intellectually equal to or superior
to those educated in secular universities.*

*Brownson never gave to his educational theory the consum-
mate expression Newman achieved in his* Idea of a University,
*yet his occasional essays are often imbued with Newman's spirit,
and he looked to Newman as the foremost expositor in his time
of the aims of Catholic education.*]

THE IMPORTANCE of education in general needs in no sense to be dwelt on in our country, for no people are or can be more alive to its utility and even necessity than are the American people, especially in the non-slaveholding states; and no people have, upon the whole, made more liberal provisions for its general diffusion. There would seem to be just as little need of dwelling on the importance and necessity of Catholic schools and Catholic education for our Catholic population. All Catholics feel, or should feel, that education, either under the point of view of religion or of civilization, is useful and desirable no further than it is Catholic. Catholic truth is universal truth, is all truth, and no education not in accordance with it is or can be a true or a useful education, for error is never useful, but always more or less hurtful. Every Catholic, then, indeed every man who loves truth and wishes to conform to it, must be in favor of Catholic schools and Catholic education, if they are Catholic in reality as well as in name.

So believing, our bishops and clergy, supported by various religious communities, have lost no time in making the imposing effort to provide under their own direction schools, academies, colleges, and universities for all our Catholic children and youth. They have felt the necessity of giving our children a Catholic education, as the best and surest way of securing their temporal and spiritual welfare, of promoting Catholic interests, and of converting this whole country to the Catholic faith. Yet, strangely enough, they are very far from receiving the hearty and undivided support of our whole Catholic community. Great dissatisfaction has been expressed, and in quarters entitled to respect, with our colleges and female academies, and not a few whose love of Catholicity and devotion to the church cannot be questioned, refuse to join in the movements for parochial schools, or the establishment of separate schools for our children under the care of our clergy. Whence comes this division of sentiment? Whence comes it that our colleges and conventual schools do not meet the unanimous approbation of Catholic parents and guardians? Whence comes it that so many amongst us prefer the public schools of the country to schools conducted by Catholics? What is the explanation of these facts? How are they to be accounted for? If these schools, whether for the higher or the lower branches of education, are really Catholic, and educate throughout in accordance with Catholic truth, how should it be possible that honest and intelligent Catholics should differ among themselves as to the policy of establishing them, or that any should hesitate to give them their cordial support? These are questions which need and must receive an answer.

There are a great many people, honest people, but not over and above stocked with practical wisdom, who imagine that whatever is done or approved by Catholics in any age or country, in any particular time or locality, must needs be Catholic, and that opposition to it is necessarily opposition to Catholicity itself. These people never doubt that schools and colleges, under the patronage and direction of the bishops, religious orders and congregations, and the regular and secular clergy, must necessarily be truly Catholic in character and tendency, and hence they conclude that dissatisfaction with them or opposition to them must indicate a heterodox tendency, or the absence of a thoroughly Catholic disposition. They transfer to the bishops and clergy as individuals the veneration and respect due only to the priesthood and the prelacy, and to the individual members of the church the infallibility that can be predicated only of the church as the living body of Christ. But we are permitted neither by Catholic faith nor by Catholic duty to make this transfer, and all experience proves that there is neither wisdom nor justice in making it. It does not necessarily follow that schools and colleges are Catholic because founded and directed by religious orders and congregations approved by the church, or by bishops and parish priests; and therefore it does not follow that dissatisfaction with the schools and colleges, or even opposition to them, is any indication of a heterodox tendency, or of any want of true Catholic faith and devotion. Such schools may themselves fail to educate in a truly Catholic spirit, or to give a truly Catholic character to their pupils, and thus leave it possible that the dissatisfaction or the opposition should arise not from the fact that they are Catholic, but from the fact that they are not Catholic, or that, in spite of their name and profession, they are really sectarian and heterodox. The dissatisfaction, in such case, instead of being a reproach to those who feel and express it, would be no mean proof of their Catholic discernment, their strong desire for really Catholic education, and earnest devotion to Catholic interests.

There need be no question as to the purity of motive and honesty of intention on the part of those who are engaged in founding or supporting schools and colleges for imparting a Catholic education, or even of those who tolerate the expression of no opinion adverse to the system of schools adopted, or to the quality of the education imparted. . . . Any hostile criticism which should in any sense impeach their motives or intentions would be manifestly unjust, and should not be tolerated. But the subject of Catholic education itself cannot be prudently withdrawn from discussion, either private or public; nor can its discussion be confined to the prelates and clergy alone. The laity have, to say the least, as deep an interest in it as have ecclesiastics or the religious, and they have in regard to it the common right of all men to judge for themselves. Parents have certain duties growing out of their relation as parents which they cannot throw upon others, and they must themselves discharge them according to the best of their ability. They are bound by the law of God to give their children, as far as in their power, a truly Catholic education, and they are free to criticize and to refuse to support

schools, though professing to be Catholic, in which such education is not and cannot be expected to be given. They are not
obliged to patronize schools, because founded or directed by
Catholics, any more than they are to support a tailoring or a
hatting establishment, because owned by a Catholic who employs
Catholic workmen, or because recommended by bishops and parish priests. We protest against the assumption that so-called
Catholic schools, collegiate or conventual, parochial or private,
because under the control of Catholics, participate in the immunities of the church, of the priesthood, or of the prelacy, and
are sacred from public investigation and public criticism; or that
we are necessarily bound by our Catholic faith and Catholic piety
to patronize or defend them any further than we find them
Catholic institutions in fact as well as in name.

The first question, then, for us Catholics to settle relates to
the catholicity of the education imparted in our so-called Catholic schools. Catholicity, as we have elsewhere shown, is the idea
in its plenitude, and therefore the catechism tells us that the
church is catholic, because "she subsists in all ages, teaches all
nations, and maintains all truth." She, then, is catholic (potentially) in space and time, and (actually) in idea—as she must be,
since her life is the life of the Word made flesh, of him who was
at once "perfect God and perfect man"—and therefore the
whole truth living and individuated in both the divine and human orders in their dialectic union. It is for this reason that the
catechism says she "maintains all truth"; and it is because she
maintains all truth, and all truth in its unity and integrity, that
she is called the *Catholic* Church; and it is because she is catholic
in idea, that is, embracing in her ideal all truth, human and divine, that she is actually or potentially catholic in space and time.

Catholic would say *universal*, and when predicated of truth
means universal truth, all truth, and all truth in and for all ages
and nations. They whose views are not universally true, are not

applicable to all times and places, and to all subjects, may have truth under some of its aspects, but they are not Catholics. They are heterodox, sectarian, or national. Men cease to be Catholics, in the full sense of the term, by denying the universality of the idea or life the church is living, the principle she is evolving and actualizing in the life of humanity, and alike whether they deny this universality in relation to space or in relation to time, in relation to the natural, or in relation to the supernatural. . . . The rule of St. Vincent of Lérins says *quod* SEMPER, as well as *quod* UBIQUE. Catholic truth is simply truth, all truth in the intelligible order and in the super-intelligible, in religion and civilization, in time and eternity, in God and in his creative act.

Catholic education must recognize the catholicity of truth under all its aspects, and tend to actualize it in all the relations of life, in religion and civilization. Its tendency is to aid the church in the fulfillment of her mission, which is the continuous evolution and actualization of the idea, or the life of the Word made flesh, in the life of humanity, or completion in mankind of the incarnation completed in the individual man assumed by the Word. . . . All education, to be Catholic, must tend to this end, the union, without absorption of either, or intermixture or confusion of the two natures, of the human and the divine, and therefore of civilization and religion. It must be dialectic, and tend to harmonize all opposites, the creature with the creator, the natural with the supernatural, the individual with the race, social duties with religious duties, order with liberty, authority with freedom, the immutability of the dogma, that is, of the mysteries, with the progress of intelligence, conservatism with reform; for such is the aim of the church herself, and such the mission given her by the Word made flesh, whose spouse she is. Fully and completely up to this idea we expect not education in any age or in any nation to come, but this is the type it should aim to realize, and be constantly and, as far as human frailty admits, actually realizing. Such is the character and tendency of what we term Catholic education.

It is with this ideal standard of Catholic education that we have the right to compare our Catholic schools, and we must judge them as they, by the instruction they give, and the influence they exert, tend or do not tend to its realization. We hazard little in saying that our so-called Catholic schools, in their actual effect, tend rather to depart from this standard than to approach it. They practically fail to recognize human progress, and thus fail to recognize the continuous and successive evolution of the idea in the life of humanity. They practically question the universality of the idea by failing to recognize as Catholic the great principles or ideas natural society is evolving and actualizing in its career through the ages. They do not educate their pupils to be at home and at their ease in their own age and country, to train them to be living, thinking, and energetic men, prepared for the work which actually awaits them in either church or state. As far as we are able to trace the effect of the most approved Catholic education of our days, whether at home or abroad, it tends to repress rather than to quicken the life of the pupil, to unfit rather than to prepare him for the active and zealous discharge either of his religious or his social duties. They who are educated in our schools seem misplaced and mistimed in the world, as if born and educated for a world that has ceased to exist. . . . Do we find them up to the level of contemporary civilization, and foremost in all those movements fitted to advance intelligence, morality, and the general well-being of society? Do we find them showing by their superior intelligence, their superior morals, and their loftier aspirations the superiority of their religion and the salutary influence it is fitted to exert on civilization? With very few exceptions, we fear we must answer: This is not the case. Comparatively few of them take their stand as scholars or as men on a level with the graduates of non-

Catholic colleges, and those who do take that stand, in most cases, do it by throwing aside nearly all they learned from their alma mater, and adopting the ideas and principles, the modes of thought and action they find in the general civilization of the country in which they live.

Whence comes it that such, in general terms, has been thus far in our country the effect of what we proudly call Catholic education? We cannot ascribe it to any innate incompatibility between Catholic truth and the civilization of the country, for that would be to deny the catholicity of the idea; nor to any repugnance between it and modern society, because that would be to deny its catholicity in time. The cause cannot be in Catholicity itself, nor can it be in our American order of civilization, for Catholicity, if catholic, is adapted to all times and to all nations, —as the catechism tells us, when it says, she "subsists in all ages, and teaches all nations." If we educated in conformity with Catholic truth, those we educate would be fitted for their precise duties in their own time and country, and they would be the active, the living, and the foremost men among their contemporaries and fellow citizens. When such is not the case, we may be sure that our education fails, in some respects, to be Catholic, and is directed to the restoration of a past severed from the present, and therefore an education that breaks the continuity of life either of the church or of humanity; and therefore is essentially a schismatic and heterodox education. . . . The cause of the failure of what we term Catholic education is, in our judgment, in the fact that we educate not for the present or the future, but for a past which can never be restored, and therefore in our education are guilty of a gross anachronism.

The fault we find with modern Catholic education is not that it does not faithfully preserve the symbol, that it does not retain all the dogmas or mysteries, so far as sound words go, but that it treats them as isolated or dead facts, not as living principles, and overlooks the fact that the life of the church consists in their continuous evolution and progressive development and actualization in the life of society and of individuals. They themselves, since they are principles and pertain to the ideal the church is evolving and actualizing, must be immutable, and the same for all times, places, and men. They are the principles of progress, but not themselves progressive, for the truth was completely expressed and individuated in the Incarnation. The progress is not in them, but in their explication and actualization in the life of humanity. The truth contained in them is always the same, can neither be enlarged nor diminished; but our understanding of them may be more or less adequate, and their explication and application to our own life and to the life of society may be more or less complete. Their evolution is successive, progressive, and continuous. This fact, which lies at the bottom of Dr. Newman's theory of development, though not always presented by him in an orthodox sense, is what our Catholic education seems to us to overlook, and practically to deny. It seems to us to proceed as if the work of evolution were finished, and there remained nothing for the Christian to do, but to repeat the past. It aims not at the continuous evolution and realization of the Catholic ideal; but to restore a past age, an order of things which the world has left behind, and which it is neither possible nor desirable to restore, for it could be restored, if at all, only as a second childhood. It is now "behind the times," and unfits rather than prepares the student for taking an active part in the work of his own day and generation. It either gives its subjects no work to do, or a work in which humanity takes no interest and will not work with them,—a work which all the living and onward tendencies of the age obstinately resist, and which, if there is any truth in what we have said, is adverse alike to the present interests of both religion and civilization. . . .

These remarks apply to Catholic education not in our own

country only, but throughout no small part of Christendom. In scarcely any part of the Christian world can we find Catholics, —we mean men who are earnest Catholics, firm in their faith, and unfaltering in their devotion to the church,—among the active and influential men of the age. In all, or nearly all countries the Catholic population is the weaker, and the less efficient portion of the population in all that relates to the war of ideas, and the struggle of opinions. Those Catholics who see this and have the courage to place themselves in harmony with the times, are looked upon as, at least, of doubtful orthodoxy, and not unfrequently are held up to clerical denunciation. Even when they are not cried down as heterodox, they are pushed aside as imprudent or unsafe men. It is very widely and, we fear, very generally believed, that true Catholic duty requires us to take our stand for a past civilization, a past order of ideas, and to resist with all our might the undeniable tendencies and instincts of the human race in our day. . . .

But the objection we urge has a peculiar force and application to Catholic education in our country. Our Catholic population, to a great extent, is practically a foreign body and brings with it a civilization foreign from the American, and in some respects inferior to it. The great majority of our congregations are of foreign birth, or the children of foreign-born parents, and the greater part of our bishops and clergy, and of our professors and teachers, have been born, or at least educated, abroad, and they all naturally seek to perpetuate the civilization in which they have been brought up. Those even of our clergy and of our professors and teachers who have been born and educated in the country, have been educated in schools founded on a foreign model, and conducted by foreigners, and are, in regard to civilization, more foreign than native. . . . Catholics from the Old World necessarily bring with them their own civilization, which, whether we speak of France or Italy, Ireland or Germany, is, to say the least, different from ours, and, in some respects, even hostile to it.

But this is not all. The civilization they actually bring with them, and which without intending it they seek to continue, is, we being judges, of a lower order than ours. It may be our national prejudice and our ignorance of other nations, but it is nevertheless our firm conviction, from which we cannot easily be driven, that, regarded in relation to its type, the American civilization is the most advanced civilization the world has yet seen, and comes nearer to the realization of the Catholic ideal than any which has been heretofore developed and actualized. We speak not of civilization in the sense of simple *civility*, polish of manners, and personal accomplishments, in which we may not compare always favorably with the upper classes of other nations; but of the type or idea we are realizing, our social and political constitution, our arrangements to secure freedom and scope for the development and progress of true manhood. In these respects American civilization is, we say not the term of human progress, but, in our judgment, the furthest point in advance as yet reached by any age or nation. Those who come here from abroad necessarily bring with them, therefore, a civilization . . . of the past. If they educate, then, according to their own civilization, as they must do, they necessarily educate for a civilization behind the times and below that of the country. . . .

That we are to have schools and colleges of our own, under the control of Catholics, we take it is a "fixed fact." Whether the movement for them is premature or not, it is idle, if nothing worse, to war against it. Let us say, then, to those who regard the education actually given by Catholics as we do, and who have not seen their way clear to the support of primary schools under the control of Catholics as a substitute, in the case of Catholic children, for the common schools of the country, that we regard it as our duty now to accept the movement, and labor not to arrest it, or to embarrass it, but to reform and render truly Catholic the whole system of Catholic education, from the highest grade to the lowest. . . .

The reform in our schools and in education will go on just in proportion as it goes on in our Catholic community itself, and perhaps even much faster. The dissatisfaction we hear expressed with our collegiate education for boys, and with that of our conventual schools for girls, is an encouraging symptom; it proves that there is, after all, a growing americanization of our Catholic population, and that the need of an education less European and more truly American is daily becoming more widely and more deeply felt. It will be more widely and more deeply felt still as time goes on, and as Catholics become more generally naturalized in habit, feeling, and association, as well as in law. It indicates also the revival of Catholic life in our population, that Catholics are becoming more earnest and living men, and unwilling that their orthodoxy should be wrapped up in a clean napkin and buried in the earth. In proportion as their Catholic life revives and grows more active, they will demand an education more in accordance with Catholic truth in all its branches, than is that now given. The demand will create a supply. . . . Then our schools will send out living men, alive with the love of God and of man,—men of large minds, of liberal studies, and generous aims,—men inspired by faith and genius, who will take the command of their age, breathe their whole souls into it, inform it with their own love of truth, and raise it to the level of their own high and noble aspirations. Let us console ourselves for what Catholic education now is with what it may become, and with what we may by well-directed effort aid it in becoming. This is the conclusion to which we ourselves have come, and if we are not satisfied with Catholic schools and education as they are, we are satisfied with their capabilities, and shall henceforth content ourselves with doing what in us lies to bring them under the great law of progress, which we have insisted on, and which is the law of all life, even of the divine life,—as is proved in the eternal generation of the Word, and the procession of the Holy Ghost, or in the assertion of theologians that "God is most pure act," *actus purissimus*.

Literature and Literary Men

LITERATURE AND
LITERARY MEN

EDITOR'S PREFACE

WHEN Brownson established his *Boston Quarterly* in 1838, he announced that it would be concerned with Religion, Philosophy, Politics, and General Literature. The announcement indicates the subordinate place literature occupied among Brownson's interests. His quarterlies were always general reviews rather than literary reviews, and consistently devoted more attention to religious, philosophical, social, and political problems than to literature. Yet Brownson wrote many literary essays during his journalistic career, and most of them are marked by vigor of style and independence of judgment, though rarely by imaginative sensitivity. His essays on American literature, his evaluations of the work of such figures as Emerson, Carlyle, and Wordsworth, and his later effort as a Catholic journalist to bring religious and ethical principles to bear upon the criticism of fiction constitute his most significant contribution to literary studies.

Keenly aware of the part literature could play in the emergence of an indigenous American culture, he presents a view of American literature in his early writings that parallels his social criticism of the period. It is a proletarian and sociological approach which differs sharply in many ways from Emerson's. Emerson's "American Scholar" has long been recognized as the classic statement of the conditions under which a great American literature might emerge. Yet in 1839 Brownson considered Emerson's view to be too individualistic, and held that a great literature would come inevitably when social, political, or religious crises agitated the nation and when writers identified themselves with, rather than isolating themselves from, the hopes and aspirations of the people.

As editor of *The Boston Quarterly,* Brownson was instrumental in spreading the doctrines of Transcendentalism. The emphasis, however, was always unmistakably his own. Emerson, Alcott, and English writers like Carlyle and Wordsworth were given generous space in review articles on their work. But in treating these writers, Brownson was always primarily interested in their ideas. His early criticism of Wordsworth, for example, centers not on the poetry but on the reactionary social philosophy Brownson holds to be implicit in Wordsworth's poetry even when "he sings wagoners, pedlers, and beggars."

After 1844, as editor of a Catholic quarterly, Brownson focused his attention on the popular fiction of the time and especially on the so-called Catholic novel. What he frequently looked for in the latter was an integrally Catholic vision of experience. What he nearly always found was sentimentality combined with a "dose of theology." Brownson attempted in his later work, often crudely it must be admitted, to do what T. S. Eliot holds, in "Religion and Literature," the Christian reader must do. "What I believe to be incumbent upon all Christians," writes Eliot, "is the duty of maintaining consciously certain standards and criteria of criticism over and above those applied by the rest of the world; and that by these criteria and standards everything that we read must be tested." (*Essays Ancient and Modern*, New York, 1932, p. 112.) Brownson tried to establish such criteria, but though he says in one passage that the novel "should conform to the essential laws of poetry," all too frequently he forgets the work under discussion and launches into a moralizing discourse or a tedious jeremiad against the romantic attitude toward love. He tends to separate "form" and "content" too mechanically, and to concern himself only with the latter. While his judgments of the importance of the novel as an art form vary widely, his underlying assumption seems to be that the novel is not, in itself, worthy of prolonged and serious attention.

Nearly all of Brownson's literary criticism is to be found in Volume XIX of his *Works*. Virgil Michel's *The Critical Principles of Orestes A. Brownson* (Washington, D.C., 1918) is valuable as an attempt to analyze the fundamental principles of all of Brownson's literary criticism. More recently, in "The Literary Criticism of Orestes A. Brownson," *Review of Politics*, XV (1954), pp. 334-51, Chester A. Soleta, C.S.C., has made a judicious evaluation of Brownson's merits and limitations as a critic.

CARLYLE'S FRENCH
REVOLUTION
[1838]

[*Brownson, in his early years, shared with many others of the New England school a vital interest in the works of Thomas Carlyle. The fact that* Sartor Resartus *first appeared in book form not in England, but in America, in 1836, with a preface by Emerson, is indicative of the role of the Transcendentalists in establishing Carlyle's reputation in this country. It was Carlyle's social criticism that gained an immediate response from Brownson. His essay on "The Laboring Classes" began as a review of Carlyle's "Chartism" (1839); and he also wrote a review article on* Past and Present (*1843*).

The following essay first appeared in the Boston Quarterly Review *for October, 1838. It is included in* Works, XIX, *40–47. Some doubt has been raised as to Brownson's authorship of the essay because of Theodore Parker's marginal note in his own copy of the* Review, *indicating W. H. Channing as the author.* (*See C. L. F. Gohdes,* Periodicals of American Transcendentalism [*1931*], *p. 49.*) *But presumably Henry F. Brownson had evidence in his father's papers of its authorship.*

Brownson's later estimates of Carlyle are much less favorable than the one he makes here. His rejection of Transcendentalism involved the rejection of much that was fundamental to Carlyle's thought, and he came to regard Carlyle's "natural supernaturalism" as a typical expression of the religious confusion of the period. He was also severe in his judgment of Carlyle's later political thought, declaring in 1871 that "he has deified force, and consecrated the worship of might in the place of right." (See Works, III, *328–9.*)]

W HAT INDUCED Thomas Carlyle to select such a subject as
the French Revolution?" we have heard asked by those
who, having read only the *Sartor Resartus,* think him a poeti-
cal mystic. "Did he write it for bread, or from sympathy with
that social movement?" To those who know him it is plain
enough that our good friend, however pinched by want, could
not let out his mind to do job-work. His Pegasus would break
down at the plow. Carlyle's heart is always, must always be, in
what he does. . . .

Carlyle, we feel sure, has dropped all conventional spectacles,
and opened his eyes to the true characteristics of our times,—
which is, that the "better sort" are being elbowed more and more
for room by the "poorer sort," as they step forward to gather a
share of the manna on life's wilderness. Perhaps he thinks it high
time that they who are clad in decencies and good manners
should busy themselves in teaching their brother "sans-culottes"
to wear suitable garments. We believe, then, that our author was
led to a study and history of the French revolution, because he
saw it illustrating in such characters of fire the irrepressible instinct of all men to assert and exercise their natural rights;—and
the absolute necessity which there is, therefore, that man's essential equality with man should be recognized.

Mr. Carlyle has evidently done his work like a man. He appears to have read most voraciously, and sifted most scrupu-
lously. And when one thinks of the multifarious mass which he
must have digested in the process of composition, we cannot but
equally admire his sagacity, and respect his faithfulness. Add the
consideration, that the first volume, when fully prepared, was by
an unfortunate accident destroyed; and that the author, without
copy or plan, was thus forced to tread over when jaded the path
he had climbed in the first flush of untried adventure; and that
yet with this additional labor he has only been occupied some

two years and more upon the book, and our estimate of his ability, his genius, his energy, cannot but be great.

And now what has he produced? A history? Thiers, Mignet, Guizot forbid! We ourselves call this French Revolution an epic poem; or, rather say the root, trunk, and branches of such a poem, not yet fully clothed with rhythm and melody indeed, but still hanging out its tassels and budding on the sprays. . . .

And once more, let us say in our attempt to describe this unique production, it is *a seer's second sight of the past*. We speak of prophetic vision. This is a *historic vision*, where events rise not as thin abstractions, but as visible embodiments; and the ghosts of a buried generation pass before us, summoned to react in silent pantomime their noisy life.

The point of view, from which Carlyle has written his history, is one which few men strive to gain, and which fewer still are competent to reach. He has looked upon the French Revolution, not as a man of one nation surveys the public deeds of another; nor as a man of one age reviews the vicissitudes of a time gone by. Still less has he viewed it as a religionist, from the cold heights, where he awaits his hour of translation, throws pitying regards on the bustling vanities of earth; or as a philanthropist, from his inflated theory of life, spies out, while he soars, the battle of ideas. And it is not either in the passionless and pure and patient watching, with which a spirit, whose faith has passed into knowledge, awaits the harmonious unfolding of heaven's purposes, that he has sent his gaze upon that social movement. But it is as a *human spirit*, that Carlyle has endeavored to enter into the conscious purpose, the unconscious strivings of *human spirits;* with wonder and awe at the mighty forces which work so peacefully, yet burst out so madly in one and all at times. He has set him down before this terrible display of human energy, as at a mighty chasm which revealed the inner deeps of man, where gigantic passions heave and stir under mountains of custom;

while free-will, attracted to move around the center of holiness, binds their elements of discord into a habitable world. As a *man* Carlyle would study *man*. It is as if he were ever murmuring to himself: "Sons of Adam, daughters of Eve, what are ye? Angels ye plainly are not. Demons truth cannot call you. Strange angelic-demoniac beings, on! on! Never fear! Something will come of you." Carlyle does not pretend to fathom man. His plummet sinks below soundings. We do not know a writer, who so unaffectedly expresses his wonder at the mystery of man. Now this appears to us a peculiar and a novel point of view, and a far higher one than that of the "progress of the human race." Not that he does not admit progress. The poor quibbles of those, who see in one age only the transmigration of the past, do not bewilder him. But he feels how little we can know, and do know, of this marvelous human race,—in their springs, and tendencies, and issues. This awe of man blends beautifully with reverence for Providence. There is no unconscious law of fate, no wild chance to him, but ever brightening "aurora splendors" of divine love. Enough, however, of this point of view. We will but add that its effect is to give the most conscientious desire of seeing things exactly as they are, and describing them with scrupulous truth. Hence we suppose his intense effort to transfuse his soul, and animate the very eyes and ears of the men who lived in that stormy time, and mingle up his whole being with theirs. Hence, too, the pictorial statement of what he gathers by that experience; and hence, in fine, a mode of historical composition, wholly original, which must revolutionize the old modes of historicizing, so "stale, flat, and unprofitable" do theories and affected clearness appear, after we have once seen this flash of truth's sunlight into the dark cave of the buried years.

Of the *spirit* in which this book is written, we would say that it breathes throughout the truest, deepest sympathy with man. Wholly free from the cant, which would whine, and slap its breast, and wring its hands, saint-like, over the weaknesses, which the canter is full of,—it yet is strict in its code of right. Most *strict* indeed, though somewhat peculiar. It is not the proper or decorous, which he prizes, but it is the true. And of all writers he is the most unflinching in his castigations of pretence. He never flatters, he never minces; but yet he speaks his hard truth lovingly, and with an eye of hope. He does not spare men, because he sees more life in them than they wot of. While he says to the moral paralytic, "sin no more, lest a worse thing befall thee," he adds, "rise, take up thy bed, and walk." He is kind, and pitiful, and tolerant of weakness, if it only does not affect to seem what it is not, and paint the livid cheek with mock hues of health. This leads us to say a word of his irony and humor, and he is full of both, though chiefly of the latter. No man has a keener eye for incongruities. It is not the feebleness of men, or the smallness of their achievements, which excites his mirth;— for where there is humbleness in the aspiration, he is of all most ready to see the Psyche in the crawling worm. But what appears to him so droll is the complacence and boastfulness, with which crowds build their Babel to climb to heaven, and the shouts of "glory" with which they put on the cap-stone, when their tower is after all so very far beneath the clouds. He loves so truly what is good in man, that he can afford to laugh at his meannesses. His respect for the essential and genuine grows with his success in exposing the artificial. Under the quaint puffings and paddings of "vanity fair," he does really see living men. He joins in the carnival. He looks upon it as a masquerade, and it is with real frolic that he snatches off the false nose or the reverend beard, and shows the real features of the dolt who would pass for a Solomon. He evidently does enjoy a practical joke on primness. But if he would, like the doctor in the tale, make his gouty patient hop on the heated floor, it is only for his *cure*. Carlyle seems to us full of true benevolence. He loves every thing but insincerity. This he cannot abide. It is the very devil, and he has but one word, *Apage, Satana*. He stands among the Pharisees with the indignant words bursting from his heart, "Ye Hypocrites." In this relation it is too true that our friend is nowise angelic, but only too much a man. His contempt is too bitter. We do not readily tolerate in a frail mortal the scornful mirth with which Carlyle sometimes shows us the cloven hoof under the surplice. Not that the indignation is not merited. But is a man ever pure enough from all taint of falsehood himself, thus to wield the spear of Michael against the dragon? Yet honor to this brave and true man. It is because he has struggled so hard, and withal so well, to disentangle himself from the last thread of cant, that he has so little patience with the poor flies yet buzzing in the web. This loathing of the formal, which a vigorous nature and a bold effort have freed him from, is, we take it, the true and very simple explanation of that occasional rudeness, and even levity, with which, it must be confessed, he speaks of so-called worshipers and worship.

And this introduces us to a consideration of his religious spirit. Some perhaps would say, have said, that Carlyle's writings are not baptized into that "spirit of adoption which cries Abba, Father." But to us no writings are more truly reverential. It surely is from no want of faith in the fullness of divine love, from no insensibility as to the nearness of almighty aid, from no doubt as to the destiny of the soul, and its responsibilities and perils, that he uses so little of the technical and prescribed language of piety. Oh, how far, far from it! But he will not name the Unnamable. He will not express more than he feels, or desecrate by familiarity what he does feel, yet knows not how adequately to utter. His sense is so abiding of our present imperfect development, his hope is so vast in that good which Providence has in store in its slow but harmonious processes, that he will not "enter the kingdom of God by violence. . . ."

AMERICAN LITERATURE
[1839]

[*The following pages represent the final third of an essay in the* Boston Quarterly Review *for January, 1839, reviewing Emerson's "Literary Ethics; An Oration delivered before the Literary Societies of Dartmouth College, July 24, 1838." The complete text is in* Works, XIX, *1–21. Brownson questions the soundness of Emerson's doctrine that the creation of a national literature is dependent on individuals, and develops his own sociological theory of literature as the organic expression of the national life. The theory here developed can profitably be compared with Brownson's remarks four years later, in "The Scholar's Mission," on the leveling tendency in a democracy.*]

FEW THINGS are less dependent on mere will or arbitrariness than literature. It is the expression and embodiment of the national life. Its character is not determined by this man or that, but by the national spirit. The time and manner of its creation are determined by as necessary and invariable laws, as the motions of the sun, the revolutions of the earth, the growth of a tree, or the blowing of a flower. It is not by accident that this man sings and that one philosophizes; that this song is sung, and this system of philosophy is brought out now and in this country; and that another song is sung and another system of philosophy is broached, at another time and in another country. The thing is predetermined by the spirit of the age and nation. It depended not on Homer alone to sing. He sang because his song was in him and would be uttered. The god moved, and he must needs give forth his oracle. The choice of his subject, and the manner of treating it, depended not alone on his individual will. It was given him by the belief in which he had been brought up, the education which he had received, the spirit, habits, beliefs, prejudices, tastes, cravings of the age and country in which he lived, or for which he sang. Had he been born at the court of Augustus, or of Louis XIV, he had not sung the wrath of Achilles and prowess of Hector; or if he had, it would have been to listless ears. His song would have taken no hold on the affections, and would have died without an echo. He might even not have been a poet at all.

This notion, which some entertain, that a national literature is the creation of a few great men, is altogether fallacious. Chaucer, Shakespeare, and Milton, Spenser, Pope, and Johnson are not the creators of English literature; but they are themselves the creatures of the spirit of the English nation, and of their times. Bacon, Hobbes, and Locke are not the authors of English philosophy, they are but its interpreters. Great men do not make their age; they are its effect. They doubtless react on their age, and modify its character; but they owe their greatness not to their individuality, but to their harmony with their age, and to their power of embodying the spirit, the reigning views of their age and country. Know the great men of a country, and you know the country; not because the great men make it, but because they embody and interpret it. A great man is merely the glass which concentrates the rays of greatness scattered through the minds and hearts of the people; not the central sun from which they radiate. To obtain an elevated national literature, it is not necessary then to look to great men, or to call for distinguished scholars; but to appeal to the mass, wake up just sentiments, quicken elevated thoughts in them, and direct their attention to great and noble deeds; the literature will follow as a necessary consequence. When a national literature has been

quickened in the national mind and heart, the great man is sure
to appear as its organ, to give it utterance, form, embodiment.
Before then his appearance is impossible.

We find also some difficulty in admitting the notion that the
scholar must be a solitary soul, living apart and in himself alone;
that he must shun the multitude and mingle never in the crowd,
or if he mingle, never as one of the crowd; that to him the
thronged mart and the peopled city must be a solitude; that he
must commune only with his own thoughts, and study only the
mysteries of his own being. We have no faith in this ascetic
discipline. Its tendency is to concentrate the scholar entirely
within himself, to make him a mere individual, without con-
nexions or sympathies with his race; and to make him utter his
own individual life, not the life of the nation, much less the universal life of humanity. He who retires into the solitude of his
own being, in order to learn to speak, shall never find a companion to whom he can say, "How charming is this solitude!"
He who disdains the people shall find the people scorning to be
his audience. He who will not sympathize with the people in
their sentiments and passions, their joys and sorrows, their hopes
and fears, their truths and prejudices, their good and bad, their
weal and woe, shall gain no power over the mind or heart of his
nation. He may prophesy, but it shall be in an unknown tongue;
he may sing, but he shall catch no echo to his song; he may reason, but he shall find his arguments producing no conviction.
This is the inflexible decree of God. We can make the people
listen to us only so far as we are one of them. When God sent us
a Redeemer, he did not make him of the seed of angels, but of
the seed of Abraham. He gave him a human nature, made him
a partaker of flesh and blood, in like manner as those he was to
redeem were partakers of flesh and blood, so that he might be
touched with a sense of human infirmities, sympathize with our
weakness, and through sympathy redeem us. So he who would

move the people, influence them for good or for evil, must have like passions with them; feel as they feel; crave what they crave; and resolve what they resolve. He must be their representative, their impersonation.

He who has no sympathies with the people, and who finds himself without popular influence, may console himself, doubtless, with the reflection that he is wiser than the people; that he is above and in advance of his age; that a few choice minds understand and appreciate him; and that a succeeding generation shall disentomb him,—posterity do him justice and dedicate a temple to his memory. Far be it from us to deprive any man of such consolation as this; but for ourselves, if we cannot succeed in commanding to some extent the attention of our own age, we have no hope of succeeding better with a future and more advanced age. He who is neglected by his own age, is more likely to be below his age than above it. We recollect not an instance or record of remarkable posthumous literary fame, in opposition to the decision of the people during the man's lifetime. Posterity often reverses the judgments our own age renders in our favor; rarely, if ever, the judgments rendered against us. We speak not here of the judgments rendered by professional judges, but by the real, living, beating heart of the people. We therefore, notwithstanding we have experienced our full share of neglect, derive very little consolation from the hope that a coming age will do us better justice. Alas, it is that "better justice" we most dread. If we have failed to interest our own age, how can we hope to interest the age to come? Is it not as likely to be our fault as that of the age, that we do not reach its heart? We always distrust the extraordinary merits of those, who attribute their failures not to their defects, but to their excellences, to the fact that they are above the vulgar herd, and too profound to be comprehended, till the age has advanced and called into exercise greater and more varied intellectual powers. We are disposed to believe that of our scholars the greater part may attribute their failures to the fact, that they have drawn their inspirations from books, from the past, from a clique or coterie, and not from the present, not from the really living, moving, toiling and sweating, joying and sorrowing people around them. Did they disdain the people less, did they enter more into the feelings of the people, and regard themselves strictly as of the people, and as setting up for no superiority over them, they would find their success altogether more commensurate with their desires, their productions altogether more creditable to themselves, and deserving of immortality.

Moreover, we doubt whether we show our wisdom in making direct and conscious efforts to create an American literature. Literature cannot come before its time. We cannot obtain the oracle before the pythoness feels the god. Men must see and feel the truth before they can utter it. There must be a necessity upon them, before they will speak or write, at least before they will speak or write anything worth remembering. Literature is never to be sought as an end. We cannot conceive anything more ridiculous than for the leading minds of a nation to set out consciously, gravely, deliberately, to produce a national literature. A real national literature is always the spontaneous expression of the national life. As is the nation so will be its literature. Men, indeed, create it; not as an end, but as a means. It is never the direct object of their exertions, but a mere incident. Before they create it, they must feel a craving to do something to the accomplishment of which speaking and writing, poetry and eloquence, logic and philosophy are necessary as means. Their souls must be swelling with great thoughts—struggling for utterance; haunted by visions of beauty they are burning to realize; their hearts must be wedded to a great and noble cause they are ambitious to make prevail, a far-reaching truth they would set forth, a new moral, religious, or social principle they

would bring out and make the basis of actual life, and to the success of which speech, the essay, the treatise, the song are in-
dispensably necessary, before they can create a national literature.

We feel a deep and absorbing interest in this matter of American literature; we would see American scholars in the highest
and best sense of the term; and we shall see them, for it is in the
destiny of this country to produce them; but they will come not
because we seek them, and they will be produced not in consequence of any specific discipline we may prescribe. They will
come when there is a work for them to do, and in consequence of
the fact that the people are everywhere struggling to perform
that work. How eloquently that man speaks! His words are fitly
chosen; his periods are well balanced; his metaphors are appropriate and striking; his tones are sweet and kindling; for he is
speaking on a subject in which his soul is absorbed; he has a
cause he pleads, an idea he would communicate, a truth he
would make men feel, an end he would carry. He is speaking out
for truth, for justice, for liberty, for country, for God, for
eternity; and humanity opens wide her ears, and her mighty
heart listens. So must it be with all men who aspire to contribute
to a national literature.

The scholar must have an end to which his scholarship serves
as a means. Mr. Emerson and his friends seem to us to forget
this. Forgetfulness of this is the reigning vice of Goethe and
Carlyle. They bid the scholar make all things subsidiary to himself. He must be an artist, his sole end is to produce a work of
art. He must scorn to create for a purpose, to compel his genius
to serve, to work for an end beyond the work itself. All this
which is designed to dignify art is false, and tends to render art
impossible. Did Phidias create but for the purpose of creating a
statue? Was he not haunted by a vision of beauty which his soul
burned to realize? Had the old Italian masters no end apart

from and above that of making pictures? Did Homer sing merely that he might hear the sound of his own voice? Did Herodotus and Thucydides write but for the sake of writing, and Demosthenes and Cicero speak but for the purpose of producing inimitable specimens of art? Never yet has there appeared a noble work of art which came not from the artist's attempt to gain an end separate from that of producing a work of art. Always does the artist seek to affect the minds or the hearts of his like, to move, persuade, convince, please, instruct, or ennoble. To this end he chants a poem, composes a melody, laughs in a comedy, weeps in a tragedy, gives us an oration, a treatise, a picture, a statue, a temple. In all the masterpieces of ancient and modern literature, we see the artist has been in earnest, a real man, filled with an idea, wedded to some great cause, ambitious to gain some end. Always has he found his inspiration in his cause, and his success may always be measured by the magnitude of that cause, and the ardor of his attachment to it.

American scholars we shall have; but only in proportion as the scholar weds himself to American principles, and becomes the interpreter of American life. A national literature, we have said, is the expression of the national life. It is the attempt to embody the great idea, or ideas, on which the nation is founded; and it proceeds from the vigorous and continued efforts of scholars to realize that idea, or those ideas, in practical life. The idea of this nation is that of democratic freedom, the equal rights of all men. No man, however learned he may be, however great in all the senses of greatness, viewed simply as an individual, who does not entertain this great idea, who does not love it, and struggle to realize it in all our social institutions, in our whole practical life, can be a contributor to American literature. We care not how much he may write; how rapid and extensive a sale his works may find; how beautifully in point of style they may be written; how much they may be praised in reviews, or admired in saloons; they shall not live and be placed among the national classics. They have no vitality for the nation, for they meet no great national want, satisfy no national craving.

In order to rear up American scholars, and produce a truly American literature, we would not do as the author of the oration before us, declaim against American literature as it is, against the servility, and want of originality and independence of the American mind; nor would we impose a specific discipline on the aspirants to scholarship. We would talk little about the want of freedom; we would not trouble ourselves at all about literature, as such. We would engage heart and soul in the great American work. We would make all the young men around us see and feel that there is here a great work, a glorious work, to be done. We would show them a work *they* can do, and fire them with the zeal and energy to do it. We would present them a great and kindling cause to espouse; wake up in them a love for their like, make them see a divine worth in every brother man, long to raise up every man to the true position of a man, to secure the complete triumph of the democracy, and to enable every man to comprehend and respect himself, and be a man. If we can succeed in doing this, we can make them true scholars, and scholars who shall do honor to their country, and add glory to humanity. When our educated men acquire faith in democratic institutions, and a love for the Christian doctrine of the brotherhood of the human race, we shall have scholars enough, and a literature which will disclose to the whole world the superiority of freedom over slavery.

Let Mr. Emerson, let all who have the honor of their country or of their race at heart, turn their whole attention to the work of convincing the educated and the fashionable, that democracy is worthy of their sincerest homage, and of making them feel the longing to labor in its ennobling cause; and then he and they may cease to be anxious as to the literary results. It will be because a man has felt with the American people, espoused their cause, bound himself to it for life or for death, time or eternity, that he becomes able to adorn American literature; not because he has lived apart, refused "to serve society," held lone reveries, and looked on sunsets, and sunrise. If he speak a word, "posterity shall not willingly let die," it will not be because he has prepared himself to speak, by a scholastic asceticism, but by loving his countrymen and sympathizing with them.

CATHOLIC SECULAR
LITERATURE
[1849]

[*After his conversion Brownson, as editor of a Catholic quarterly, turns his attention to what he calls "the schism between the spiritual order and the secular which characterizes all modern society," and which he finds especially in contemporary literature. Immediately after his conversion, he is almost Jansenistic in his treatment of nature and grace, and in his characterization of Protestant literature as "essentially heathen—a reproduction, under varied forms, of the literature of pagan antiquity." (Works, XIX, 101.)*

By 1849, the date of the following essay, Brownson's tone begins to be more moderate, and in "Catholicity and Literature" (1856) he writes that "the office of popular literature is not precisely to spiritualize, but to civilize a people." (Works, XIX, 454.) "Grace supposes nature, and consequently leaves a large margin to natural sentiments and affections. . . . The highest rank is to be assigned to those literary works which have, so to speak, the infused habit of grace, and stand on the elevated plane of the Christian virtues, which proceed from nature elevated by grace, not from nature alone; but we are not at liberty to deny a certain degree of merit to works of a less elevated character; or to condemn, as sinful, any works which, though they proceed from nature alone, do not oppose grace or the supernatural." (Works, XIX, 449–50.)

Such essays as the following, while they reveal serious limitations in Brownson as a literary critic, also show his awareness of basic critical questions usually ignored in his own time. If these questions are treated by Catholic critics with more precision and

sensitivity in our own time than Brownson brought to them, it is
partly because of that very renewal of intellectual life which
Brownson did so much to encourage.]

A SLIGHT GLANCE at our Catholic literature—we mean that which is accessible to the mere English student—is sufficient to satisfy us that we have very little literature adapted to seculars, to the great body of the laity living in the world and taking part in its affairs. The religious are amply provided for. Our ascetic literature is rich, varied, and extensive. We have admirable manuals of devotion for all ages and classes, and suitable to all stages and modes of the spiritual life; we have, too, an abundance of theological works, speculative and practical, dogmatical and polemical; but we have no secular literature in English. The monastery is richly endowed; our secular life has nothing but the crumbs that fall from its table, or the soup dealt out at its gate. Secular literature, whether its authors are Catholics or Protestants, breathes, for the most part, an unchristian spirit, and is dangerous to Christian truth and Christian piety. Here is the literary defect we have wished on various occasions to point out, and which we wish our authors to undertake to remedy.

The novels we censured were intended to remedy this defect, —to supply seculars with amusing, interesting, and instructive reading, which should keep their minds free from error, their hearts protected from impure influences, and both in a healthy state, alike compatible with religious duties and worldy avocations. So far as the intention of their authors was concerned, they were admirable; but in execution they were failures, because they were marked by the schism between the spiritual order and the secular, which characterizes all modern society. On their religious side they smelt of the schools or the convent; on their secular side, of unregenerate human nature; and could as well have been written by pagans, Protestants, or unbelievers, as by

Catholics. They lacked unity, failed to temper the two orders together, to blend them in one, or, in other words, to baptize the secular, to infuse into it the Catholic spirit, and yet suffer it to remain secular. . . .

The secular order, in its subordinate and subservient sphere, exists by divine right; and within that sphere we have no more right to labor to destroy it, than we have to labor to destroy the spiritual order itself. We have, on the other hand, no right to assert its independence and supremacy. It has the right to exist as a servant, no right to exist as a master. Here are the two truths which it is always necessary to keep in view. The recognition of the spiritual alone leads, in effect, to the same result as the recognition of the secular alone; for the secular will always, in spite of us, remain and assert itself; and when not subject to law, it will assert itself without law, or, if need be, against law. The only way to escape infidelity or licentiousness is, not to demand exclusive spirituality of the mass of mankind, but to accept within it sphere the secular, and, by christianizing, render it not only innocuous, but even serviceable to religion. . . .

One of the most powerful instruments of bringing about the unity we contend for is literature, and in this we agree perfectly with the authors of the Catholic novels we have censured. We censured them because they did not furnish the kind of literature we needed. On one side they give us religion, but religion that excludes the secular order; on the other side, they give us the secular order independent of religion. Their religion is for religious, their secularity for the infidel and licentious; and instead of tempering the two orders together by infusing the spiritual into the secular, they only alternately sacrifice one order to the other, now the secular to the spiritual, and now the spiritual to the secular. Here is their defect, a defect which proceeds, not from the intention of their authors, but from the duality which introduces antagonism into their own life,—from the schism which, unsuspected by them, runs through their own interior moral and intellectual world, sundering the two orders, and maintaining them in perpetual hostility one to the other. What we want is a literature which is the exponent of the harmony in the mind and heart of the two orders, which is adapted to the secular in its subordinate and subservient sphere, and which, without any formal dogmatizing or express ascetic dissertations, exhortations, or admonitions, shall excite the secular only under the authority of religion, and move it only in directions that religion approves, or at least does not disapprove.

We are far from pretending that works pertaining to a literature of this sort should supersede dogmatical, controversial, or ascetic works,—that they are works of the highest order, or even works that are always and everywhere needed. We hold, of course, that the religious state is higher than the secular, and that general literature is a temporary and accidental want. But here and now, taking into consideration the age and country, such works are much needed and would be of very high utility. They would amuse, interest, instruct, cultivate in accordance with truth the mind and the affections, elevate the tone of the community, and, when they did not directly promote virtue, they would still be powerful to preserve and defend innocence,—often a primary duty. They would weed out from the modern world what it still retains of medieval barbarism, advance true civilization, open to thousands a source of rational enjoyment, and preserve a healthy and vigorous state of the public mind and heart. In a word, they would contribute to what we need, a Christian *secular* culture, perhaps the greatest want of our times, and that which would more than any one thing else—the grace of God supposed—aid, not only in preserving the faith in those who have it, but in winning to it those who now have it not. Purely spiritual culture is amply provided for; but owing to the barbarism of past ages, and the incredulity and license of the last century and the present, secular culture in unison with the Christian spirit is, and ever has been, only partially provided for, and but imperfectly attained. It seems to us that the best way for our Catholic writers —not theologians by profession, and whose works come and must come under the head of general literature—to serve the cause of truth and virtue is to devote themselves, not to controversial or ascetic works, of which we have enough, but to the *Christian secular culture* of the age, or, in a word, to the advancement of Christian civilization. They need not aspire to teach Catholic theology; let it satisfy them to breathe into literature the true Catholic spirit, and, as far as possible, inform the secular world itself with the genuine Christian life. . . .

The aim of the literature we demand is not positive or strictly scientific instruction in religion and morals. The purpose is to cultivate the secular element of individual and social life,—to press that element into the service of religion and morality, on the principle that the church makes use of poetry and music in celebrating her divine offices, or art in the construction and decoration of her altars and temples. The great artist, if he is to aid religion, if he is to subserve her influence by removing the obstacles which the flesh interposes, subduing the passions, and setting the affections to the keynote of devotion, must, it is true, understand his religion well, and in some sense be himself eminently religious; he must also, if he would be great even as an artist, whatever the sphere or tendency of his art, be a man of genuine science; for art is the expression of the true under the form of the beautiful, and it is obvious that a man cannot express, under the form of the beautiful, or any other form, what he does not apprehend. . . .

Instructive [literature] should be, by all means; but as Beethoven's Symphonies, Haydn's Masses, or Mozart's Requiem are instructive,—instructive by the moral power they excite, the lofty thoughts they suggest, the tone and direction they impart to the whole interior man.

Or, if more direct instruction is aimed at, it should be of that general kind, and in those general departments of knowledge, which are open to men who may be widely apart as to their special views. The Catholic cultivator of secular literature should, of course, be always governed, influenced, by his religion, and should always take care not to utter a single sentiment not in perfect harmony with his Catholic faith and morals; but his aim should not be the direct exposition or propagation of his faith, any more than it is when he is cultivating his field, attending to his merchandise, or taking part in the political affairs of his country. He must not affect to be the theological doctor, the missionary, or the spiritual director. He must remember that he is a layman, or at least is to act here as a layman, not as a professional man. He may instruct, but it is with regard to those matters which are properly within the province of laymen. He may even be controversial; but let the controversy be on matters where he may carry with him the suffrages of all men who recognize the law of nature or the authority of natural reason,—where he may have intelligent and well-disposed men, who are not of his communion, for readers and for friends. There is a vast field in which we can labor, a field which is our own, but in which we may have for fellow laborers many who, in the immediate province of religion, would be against us. Not that we are to make any concession to them, or to go out of our way to please them,—far from it; but it is lawful and profitable to bring out the truth which they and we hold or may hold in common. We must follow out our own principles, and should never court or seek to gain them; but if, in following out our own principles on literary, moral, historical, or political subjects, we gain them thus far, it is an advantage for us, if not for them, that we are under no obligation to forego. Thus Lingard, in writing the History of England, did well to keep to his character as an historian, and to waive in that work his character as a Catholic doctor. His business in his work was to write true history, not theology. If the truth of history redounded to the credit of his church, all well and good; so far the defense of his church was legitimate; but beyond that he had nothing to say on the subject. We wish he had been always mindful of this, and had suffered the theologian to appear less often; for then he would have avoided certain judgments not called for by the purposes of his history, not essential to the full and impartial statement of historic truth, and which, however pleasant they may be to Protestants, are not a little painful to Catholics. . . .

It is time that the friends of truth try to prove themselves men, and to take the lead in affairs; and we are sure that Catholic secular writers in our day can render no better service even to religion than to possess themselves of the secular literature of the age, and to make it speak the language of truth, of wisdom, of moral majesty,—not in faint, timid tones, or feeble, apologetic whispers, that will be lost in the infidel, socialistic, and revolutionary din of the times, but in free, bold, manly tones, that will ring through all men's hearts, and recall them to their senses, to think and to act. Resist the devil and he will flee from you; show yourself afraid of him, cower and crouch before him, and you are gone. Pray, trust in God, by all means; but be also active, strong, energetic men, quick to perceive and fearless to perform what duty commands. . . .

EMERSON'S PROSE WORKS
[1870]

[*No American writer engaged Brownson's interest so deeply or so continuously as did Emerson. Brownson's criticisms of Emerson's work extend in time from 1838, when he reviewed the "Divinity School Address," to 1870, when the following essay was published in* The Catholic World. (Works, *III, 424–38.) The seventy-odd pages of the* Boston Quarterly Review *devoted to Emerson's early work, most of which were by Brownson, have been called by C. L. F. Gohdes "perhaps the most convincing criticism of Emerson brought out during the period."* (The Periodicals of American Transcendentalism [*1931*], *p. 81*.)

Profound philosophical and religious disagreement, increasing as Brownson moved toward the Catholic Church, combined with a love and respect for the man and recognition of his genius—this, in brief, sums up Brownson's attitude toward Emerson. There is a deeply personal quality in all that Brownson writes of Emerson. He seems, as in the following essay, always to be trying to reach the man, to persuade him that the Christianity he abandoned was not the fullness of the Christian faith, and that the eclecticism he embraced could never satisfy his spiritual needs. In a word, Brownson never ceased trying to convert Emerson.

The most illuminating essay on the religious and philosophical issues underlying Brownson's criticism of Emerson is A. Robert Caponigri's "Brownson and Emerson: Nature and History," New England Quarterly, *XVIII (1945), pp. 368–90.*]

M R. EMERSON's literary reputation is established, and placed beyond the reach of criticism. No living writer surpasses him in his mastery of pure and classic English, or equals him in the exquisite delicacy and finish of his chiseled sentences, or the metallic ring of his style. It is only as a thinker and teacher that we can venture any inquiry into his merits; and as such we cannot suffer ourselves to be imposed upon by his oracular manner, nor by the apparent originality either of his views or his expressions.

Mr. Emerson has had a swarm both of admirers and of detractors. With many he is a philosopher and sage, almost a god; while with others he is regarded as an unintelligible mystic, babbling nonsense just fitted to captivate beardless young men and silly maidens with pretty curls, who constituted years ago the great body of his hearers and worshipers. We rank ourselves in neither class, though we regard him as no ordinary man, and as one of the deepest thinkers, as well as one of the first poets, of our country. We know him as a polished gentleman, a genial companion, and a warm-hearted friend, whose kindness does not pass over individuals and waste itself in a vague philanthropy. So much, at least, we can say of the man, and from former personal acquaintance as well as from the study of his writings.

Mr. Emerson is no theorist, and is rather of a practical than of a speculative turn of mind. What he has sought all his life, and perhaps is still seeking, is the real, the universal, and the permanent in the events of life and the objects of experience. The son of a Protestant minister, brought up in a Protestant community, and himself for some years a Protestant minister, he early learned that the real, the universal, and permanent are not to be found in Protestantism; and assuming that Protestantism, in some or all its forms, is the truest exponent of the Christian religion, he very naturally came to the conclusion that they are not to be found in Christianity. . . . He passed then naturally to the conclusion that all pretensions to a supernaturally revealed religion are founded only in ignorance or craft, and rejected all of all religions, except what may be found in them that accords with the soul or the natural reason of all men. . . .

He agrees with Plato that the real thing is in the methexis, not in the mimesis; that is, in the idea, not in the individual and the sensible, the variable and the perishable. He wants unity and catholicity, and the science that does not attain to them is no real science at all. But as the mimesis, in his language the hieroglyphic, copies or imitates the methexic, we can, by studying it, arrive at the methexic, the reality copied or imitated. . . .

Mr. Emerson, indeed, uses neither of these Platonic terms, though if he had, he would, with his knowledge of the Christian doctrine of creation, have detected the error of Plato, and most likely have escaped his own. The term *methexis*—participation— excludes the old error that God generates the universe, which is rather favored by the terms genera and species. We use the term *mimesis* because it serves to us to express the fact that the lower copies or imitates the higher, and therefore the doctrine of St. Thomas, that *Deus est similitudo rerum omnium*, or that God is himself the type or model after which the universe is created, and which each and every existence in its own order and degree strives to copy or represent. The error of Plato is, that he makes the methexis an emanation rather than a creature, and the plastic power that produces the mimesis; the error of Mr. Emerson, as we view the matter, is, that he makes the mimetic purely phenomenal, therefore unreal, sinks it in the methexic, and the methexis itself in God, as the one only being or substance, the *natura naturans* of Spinoza. . . .

It were an easy task to show that whatever errors there may be, or may be supposed to be, in Mr. Emerson's works grow out of the two fundamental errors we have indicated—the identification of soul, freed from its personal limitations, as in Adam,

John, and Richard, with God, or the real being, substance, force, or activity, and the assumption that whatever is distinguishable from God is purely phenomenal, an apparition, a sense-show, a mere bubble on the surface of the ocean of being, as we pointed out in our comments on the proceedings of the Free Religionists, to which we beg leave to refer our readers.

Yet, though we have known Mr. Emerson personally ever since 1836, have held more than one conversation with him, listened to several courses of lectures from him, and read and even studied the greater part, if not all of his works, as they issued from the press, we must confess that, in reperusing them preparatory to writing this brief notice, we have been struck, as we never were before, with the depth and breadth of his thought, as well as with the singular force and beauty of his expression. We appreciate him much higher both as a thinker and as an observer, and we give him credit for a depth of feeling, an honesty of purpose, an earnest seeking after truth, we had not previously awarded him in so great a degree, either publicly or privately. We are also struck with his near approach to the truth as we are taught it. He seems to us to come as near to the truth as one can who is so unhappy as to miss it.

We consider it as Mr. Emerson's great misfortune, that his early Protestant training led him to regard the Catholic question as *res adjugicata*, and to take Protestantism, in some one or all of its forms, as the truest and best exponent of Christianity. Protestantism is narrow, superficial, unintellectual, vague, indefinite, sectarian, and it was easy for a mind like his to pierce through its hollow pretensions, to discover its unspiritual character, its want of life, its formality, and its emptiness. It was not difficult to comprehend that it was only a dead corse, and a mutilated corse at that. The Christian mysteries it professed to retain, as it held them, were lifeless dogmas, with no practical bearing on life, and no reason in the world for believing them. Such a system, having no relation with the living and moving world, and no reason in the nature or constitution of things, could not satisfy a living and thinking man, in downright earnest for a truth at least as broad and as living as his own soul. It was too little, too insignificant, too *mesquine*, too much of a dead and putrefying body to satisfy either his intellect or his heart. If that is the true exponent of Christianity, and the most enlightened portion of mankind say it is, why shall he belie his own under-standing, his own better nature, by professing to believe and reverence it? No; let him be a man, be true to himself, to his own reason and instincts, not a miserable time-server or a con-temptible hypocrite.

If Mr. Emerson had not been led to regard the Catholic ques-tion as closed, except to the dwellers among tombs, and to the ignorant and superstitious, and had studied the church with half the diligence he has Plato, Mohammed, or Swedenborg, it is pos-sible that he would have found in Christianity the life and truth, the reality, unity, and catholicity he has so long and so earnestly sought elsewhere and found not. Certain it is, that whatever af-firmative truth he holds is held and taught by the church in its proper place, its real relations, and in its integrity. The church does not live in the past nor dwell only among tombs; she is an ever-present and ever-living church, and presents to us not a dead historical Christ, but the ever-living and ever-present Christ, as really and truly present to us as he was to the disciples and apostles with whom he conversed when he went about in Judea doing good, without having where to lay his head, and not more veiled from our sight now than he was then from theirs. Does she not hold the sublime mystery of the Real Pres-ence, which, if an individual fact, is also a universal princi-ple? . . .

In the Catholic church we have found the real presence, and unity, and catholicity which we sought long and earnestly, and could find nowhere else, and which Mr. Emerson, after a still longer and equally earnest search, has not found at all. He looks not beyond nature, and nature is not catholic, universal, or the whole. It is not one, but manifold and variable. It cannot tell its origin, medium, or end. With all the light Mr. Emerson has derived from nature, or from nature and soul united, there is infinite darkness behind, infinite darkness before, and infinite darkness all around him. He says, "Every man's condition is a solution in hieroglyphic of those inquiries he would put." Suppose it is so, what avail is that to him who has lost or never had the key to the hieroglyph? Knows he to interpret the hieroglyph in which the solution is concealed? Can he read the riddle of the sphinx? He has tried his hand at it in his poem of the Sphinx, and has only been able to answer that

Each answer is a lie.

It avails us little to be told where the solution is, if we are not told what it is, or if only told that every solution is false as soon as told. Hear him; to man he says,

Thou art the unanswered question; couldst see thy proper eye,
  Alway it asketh, asketh; and each answer is a lie:
So take thy quest through nature, it through a thousand natures ply;
  Ask on, thou clothed eternity; time is the false reply.

The answer, if it means anything, means that man is "a clothed eternity," whatever that may mean, eternally seeking an answer to the mystery of his own being, and each answer he can obtain is a lie; for only eternity can comprehend eternity and tell what it is. Whence has he learned that man, the man-child, is "a clothed eternity," and therefore God, who only is eternal?

Now, eternity is above time, and above the world of time, consequently above nature. Catholicity, by the very force of the term, must include all truth, and therefore the truth of the supernatural as well as of the natural. But Mr. Emerson denies the supernatural, and does not, of course, even profess to have any knowledge that transcends nature. How, then, can he pretend to have attained to catholic truth? He himself restricts nature to the external universe, which is phenomenal, and to soul, by which he means himself. But are there no phenomena without being or substance which appears or which shows itself in them? Is this being or substance the soul, or, in the barbarism he adopts, the ME? If so, the NOT-ME is only the phenomena of the ME, and of course identical with himself, as he implies in what he says of the "one man." Then in himself, and emanating from himself, are all men, and the whole of nature. How does he know this? Does he learn it from nature?

Of course, Mr. Emerson means not this, even if his various utterances imply it. He uses the word *creation,* and we suppose he intends, notwithstanding his systematic views, if such he has, contradict it, to use it in its proper sense. Then he must hold the universe, including, according to his division, nature and soul, has been created, and if created, it has a creator. The creator must be superior, above nature and soul, and therefore in the strictest sense of the word supernatural; and as reason is the highest faculty of the soul, the supernatural must also be supra-rational.

Does the creator create for a purpose, for an end? and if so, what is that end or purpose, and the medium or means of fulfilling it, whether on his part or on the part of the creature? Here, then, we have the assertion of a whole order of truth, very real and very important to be known, which transcends the truth Mr. Emerson professes to have, and which is not included in it. We say again, then, that he has not attained to catholicity, and we also say that, by the only method he admits, he cannot attain to it. How can he pretend to have attained to catholicity, and that he has already a truth more universal than Christianity reveals, when he must confess that without the knowledge of a super-natural and supra-rational truth he cannot explain his origin or end, or know the conditions of his existence, or the means of gaining his end?

Mr. Emerson says, as we have quoted him,

Undoubtedly we have no questions to ask which are unanswerable. We must trust the perfection of the creation so far as to believe that whatever curiosity the order of things has awakened in our minds, the order of things can satisfy.

Alway it asketh, asketh; and each answer is a lie.

There is here a grand mistake. If he had said the Creator instead of creation, there would have been truth and great propriety in the author's assertion. Nature—and we mean by nature the whole created order—excites us to ask many very troublesome questions, which nature is quite incompetent to answer. The fact that nature is created, proves that she is, both as a whole and in all her parts, dependent, not independent, and therefore does not and cannot suffice for herself. Unable to suffice for herself, she cannot suffice for the science of herself; for science must be of that which is, not of that which is not.

Mr. Emerson, we presume, struck with the narrowness and inconsistencies of all the religions he had studied, and finding that they are all variable and transitory in their forms, yet thought that he also discovered something in them, or underlying them all, which is universal, invariable, and permanent, and which they are all honest efforts of the great soul to realize. He therefore came to the conclusion that the sage can accept none of these narrow, variable, and transitory forms, and yet can reject none of them as to the great, invariable, and underlying principles, which in fact is all they have that is real or profitable. To distinguish between the transient and permanent in religion was the common aim of the Boston movement from 1830 to

1841, when we ourselves began to turn our own mind, though very timidly and at a great distance, toward the church. Mr. Emerson, Miss Margaret Fuller, A. Bronson Alcott, and Mr. Theodore Parker regarded the permanent elements of all religions as the natural patrimony or products of human nature. We differed from them, by ascribing their origin to supernatural revelation made to our first parents in the garden, universally diffused by the dispersion of the race, and transmitted to us by the traditions of all nations. Following out this view, the grace of God moving and assisting, we found our way to the Catholic church, in which the form and the invariable and permanent principle, or rather, the form growing out of the principle, are inseparable, and are fitted by the divine hand to each other.

The others, falling back on a sort of transcendental illuminism, sank into pure naturalism, where such of them as are still living, and a whole brood of young disciples who have sprung up since, remain, and, like the old Gnostics, suppose themselves spiritual men and women in possession of the secret of the universe. There was much life, mental activity, and honest purpose in the movement; but those who had the most influence in directing its course could not believe that anything good could come out of Nazareth, and so turned their backs on the church. They thought they could find something deeper, broader, and more living than Christianity, and have lost not only the transient, but even the permanent in religion.

Philosophy

PHILOSOPHY

EDITOR'S PREFACE

IN BROWNSON's philosophical writings there is to be noted a development similar in many ways to the development of his political and religious thought.

The first important phase of his philosophical studies began with his residence in Canton. Having studied Constant, he went on to examine the work of Victor Cousin (1792–1867), and became one of the chief advocates and expositors of Cousin's eclecticism in America. Like many of the Transcendentalists, he thought he found in Cousin a philosophical foundation for that confidence in intuition as a means of arriving at objective truth which characterized the whole movement. Moreover, Cousin's eclecticism seemed to furnish a method adapted to such religious theories as Brownson elaborated in his *New Views of Christianity* (1836). Brownson's writings on Cousin attracted wide attention, and Cousin himself was so pleased with the work of his American expositor that he suggested in 1838 to Charles Sumner that Brownson should be recommended for the chair of philosophy at Harvard College.

That Brownson was a more rigorous philosophical thinker than almost any of the Transcendentalist group is indicated by the criticism to which he soon subjected not only Cousin but also Kant, Hegel, Fichte, and Schelling. On the problem of epistemology he centered much of his attention prior to his conversion. How the mind knows, and the relation between the objective order of things and our mental conceptions of them, seemed to him a fundamental problem not satisfactorily answered by the philosophies he had been following. Without some assurance of the objectivity of knowledge there could properly be no philosophy. "Is there really any cause," he asks in "The Eclectic Philosophy" (1839), "to respond to our notion of cause? Is the infinite a reality? This is the ontological question." (*Works*, II, 551.) The establishment of the mind's relation to the object became almost his sole preoccupation from 1842 to 1844. In Pierre Leroux he thought he discovered the foundation of true realism in opposition to Cousin's and to Kant's subjective idealism.

Brownson finally came to an analysis of subject, object, and their relation which solved for him the problems left unanswered from the time of Descartes. Although he was not aware at this time of the scholastic distinction between the existential modalities of objects in the universe of things and in the mind, he glimpsed the truth that the escape from radical idealism could come only through a theory of knowledge that affirmed the intentional existence of the object in the mind. He did not, however, abandon his reliance on intuition. Rather, he tried to combine his intuitionism with realism, and it is generally agreed that at least during the period from 1842 to 1844, when he held that we have immediate intuition of God, he was an ontologist in the sense improbated by the Catholic Church in 1861. Yet Brownson affirms in *The Convert* (*Works*, V, 172) that his philosophical studies during this period were a preamble to faith. "As I gained a real philosophy, a philosophy which takes its principles from the order of being, from life, from things as they exist, instead of the abstractions of the schools, faith flowed in, and I seized with joy and gladness the Christian Church and her dogmas."

The question of whether Brownson was an ontologist after his conversion has largely tended to thrust into the background any other considerations of his philosophical thought. He studied scholastic philosophy after his conversion, and for a time tried to employ only scholastic terminology in his philosophical writings. How thoroughly he knew St. Thomas's original texts and how much he relied on contemporary manuals of scholasticism is not clear. Scholastic philosophy was then at a low ebb. Newman writes from Rome in 1847 that even there philosophy was being studied in "bits," as he put it, and some of Brownson's dissatisfaction undoubtedly came from his sense of the routine nature of current scholastic thought. He tried, at any rate, around 1850 to take up again some of the problems he thought were being ignored, and began to use his own terminology. This brought upon him charges of ontologism, which he continued to disavow in essay after essay until his death. Even today, however, opinion is sharply divided. Sidney A. Raemers, for example, in *America's Foremost Philosopher* (Washington, D.C., 1931) makes out an elaborate case to prove that Brownson as a Catholic was not an ontologist, and insists on the validity of his epistemological approach. In a more recent study, however, *Orestes Brownson's Approach to the Problem of God* (Washington, D.C., 1950), Reverend Bertin Farrell, C.P., compares Brownson's epistemology with that of St. Thomas, and concludes that Brownson was an ontologist.

Further study of Brownson's philosophical writings in the context of nineteenth-century thought is needed before such questions as that of his alleged ontologism can finally be settled. It may be that his most important contribution is in his analysis of the idealistic tendencies of modern philosophy since Descartes. Even if his search for a moderate realism was not entirely successful, his criticisms of such philosophers as Descartes, Locke, Kant, Hegel, and Cousin, may still prove to be of great cogency today.

THE PHILOSOPHY OF
HISTORY
[1843]

[*Such essays as the following, in which Brownson attempts a comparison of various philosophies of history, may best be read in the whole context of his criticism of Transcendentalism. This essay, in fact, represents a significant step in his movement toward the historical Church. He develops here the providential conception of history which he had already touched upon in "Leroux on Humanity" (1842) and "The Mediatorial Life of Jesus" (1842). Before doing so, however, Brownson analyzes those current theories of history which he considers most influential, referring to them as the war theory of Michelet, the humanitarian theory of Jouffroy, and the rationalist theory of Cousin. In one sense, the essay is part of Brownson's entire criticism of the Transcendentalist approach to religion, inasmuch as it repudiates the characteristically ahistorical search for spiritual principles in "nature," and affirms the continuous operation of God's Providence in human history. His "theory of the supernatural defines the basis upon which he is prepared to accept and finally does accept the historical claims of Catholicism: that there is a providential and supernatural intervention and agency in human history, directed to some extraordinary and crucial historical end." (A. R. Caponigri, "Brownson and Emerson: Nature and History,"* New England Quarterly, *XVIII [1945], p. 388.) The full text of the essay, which appeared in two parts in the* Democratic Review *for May and June, 1843, is in* Works, *IV, 361–423.*]

THE CONCEPTION of a Universal History of humanity belongs almost to our own times, and is said to be due to the Cartesian school of philosophy; although that school, by taking its point of departure in the pure reason as manifested in the individual consciousness, was and needs must be altogether unhistorical in both its principle and tendency. . . .

By the Universal History of humanity, we do not understand so much a complete narration of all the facts or events of the life of humanity in time and space, as their scientific explication. In constructing it, we assume the facts to be known, spread out as it were before us, and we merely ask, as we contemplate them, what mean these facts? What is their principle? What is their law? Do they develop, or realize a plan? Can they be reduced under a general law, and referred to a common origin? If so, what is this origin, this law, or, in one word, this plan? By Universal History, then, we understand not what commonly passes for history, but the *Philosophy* of History.

Universal history, in the sense here taken, is possible only on condition that the various facts and events of the life of mankind, originate in some permanent principle, according to some universal law, in subordination to a general plan or design; and on condition that the plan, the law, and the principle are ascertainable. . . .

What is this plan? What purpose was the life of humanity intended to serve? What grand scheme does it realize or develop? . . .

The answer to the question here raised, is virtually the answer to the question, what is the final cause of man and of men? . . . Here is the question of questions. . . . Many answers have been suggested, many an Oedipus has guessed at the riddle of the Sphinx, but she sits as ever at the wayside proposing it anew. The mystery of the Man-child remains, for all that philosophy has done or can do, yet unexplained. . . .

We have no intention of answering this question, which, if we were able to do, we could not do without leaving the field of philosophy, and trenching too far on the field of theology, for our present purpose, and also for the general design of the Journal in which we are writing. . . . This much let it suffice us to say, that we believe life taken in its largest sense, as the life both of the individual and of the race, has a plan, a wise and good plan, worthy of the infinite Wisdom and Love in which it originated. So far as our present purpose is concerned, it is enough to say that man was made for progress, for growth. . . .

We must determine in some degree the end for which man was made, before ever we can determine what is or is not progress. But through the Lion of the tribe of Judah, through the Gospel, that end, for Christendom at least, is determined, and the solution of the problem is at the bottom of every *Christian* conscience. . . .

THE PROVIDENTIAL THEORY

The providential theory, which probably in some form is recognized or intended to be recognized by all philosophers, may be contemplated under two different points of view: 1. The pantheistic view. 2. The religious view. In what we have to offer on each, we shall make Cousin our representative of the first, and Bossuet of the second.

1. Cousin is a professed eclectic, and it is the boast of his system of history, that it excludes no element from its appropriate share. Under a certain point of view, he assuredly does admit all the elements that can be conceived of as at work in human affairs. But granting that he admits all the elements, does he in his account of them, recognize and describe them all in their true character? In order to answer this question, we must return upon his system for a few moments, and contemplate it under a different point of view from that under which we have already

contemplated it. He recognizes five elements in human history, five original ideas, whence have proceeded, and to which may be referred as their source, all the facts of the life of humanity considered collectively or individually. 1. The idea of the useful; 2. The idea of the just; 3. The idea of the beautiful; 4. The idea of the holy; 5. The idea of the true.

The first creates industry, and the mathematical and physical sciences; the second, the state, government, jurisprudence; the third, the fine arts; the fourth, religion (*cultus*); the fifth, philosophy, which clears up, accounts for, and verifies the other four. That these five elements exhaust human nature, there can be no doubt. . . . But in the creation of industry, politics, art, religion, philosophy, does humanity work alone and on her own funds; or does Providence come to her assistance? If Providence intervenes, is it in the form of a fixed, permanent, and necessary law of humanity; or in the form of a free, sovereign power, distinct from humanity, graciously supplying her from time to time with new strength and materials to work with? Here lies the whole question between Providence in the pantheistic sense, and Providence in the religious sense.

Under the point of view we are now considering the subject, Cousin is to no small extent a disciple of John Baptist Vico, born at Naples, 1668, educated in the study of the ancient languages, the scholastic philosophy, theology, and jurisprudence, known as the author of the *Scienza Nuova*, or New Science, a work of vast compass, of immense power, and a mine of rich and profound thought, too little prized and studied by even our best scholars. Vico, though recognizing religion, and the action of Providence, yet starts from the principle that humanity is, so to speak, her own work. God acts upon the race, but only by it, in its instinctive operations. He explains nearly all the facts of human history from the political point of view; but he traces the various laws of nations, the manners and customs, and all the materials which enter into the history of humanity, to the "common sense of nations." Humanity is divine, but there is no divine man. The great men of ancient history, poets, prophets, sages, legislators, are not to be taken as individuals. They are mythical personages, creations of the national thought of their respective nations and epochs, formed by the slow accretions of centuries. . . .

It is a capital objection to this theory of Providence, that, while it is brought forward to show, among other things a safe and solid ground in the very wants of the human soul, and instinctive indications of the race, for religion, it is, when once admitted, fatal to all religious exercises. . . . If God intervenes in human affairs only through the transcendental side, only in the inherent and necessary laws of human nature itself; if he be only the fixed, and permanent, the necessary in human action, where is the room for prayer, praise, sacrifice, or devotion? . . .

We see here the fundamental vice of modern philosophy itself, and in its later as well as in its earlier developments. Its grand error is found in the point of departure of Cartesianism. Descartes assumes the sufficiency of reason, as manifested in the individual consciousness, to account for all that can appear in the life of humanity. Obviously, then, nothing can be admitted as an integral, an essential, or as a permanent and necessary part of human life, that does not come in through humanity as the operating cause. The old French philosophers, a much wiser and worthier set of men than we commonly allow—plain, straightforward, outspoken, and the sworn enemies of all cant and humbug,—saw very clearly, that *on this principle,* religion, since its very essence is in the recognition and worship of a supernatural and superhuman Providence, could not subsist a moment after men had once come to see whence had originated their religious institutions, faith, and disciplines; and, therefore, they said all plainly that religion originates in human weakness and ignorance. They considered religion, therefore, a reproach and a shame, and as such condemned it, and labored to teach men philosophy; so that they should be able to cast it off, and live without it. The Germans saw this, but shrank from the conclusion. Warm, and somewhat devout of heart, they would retain religion; subtle of brain, and speculatively inclined by temper and education, they would retain philosophy; so they set themselves with downright German earnestness at work to reconcile the two. They sought the source of religion, as a fact of human history, in human nature itself, and found man endowed by nature with a religious sense or faculty, which some of them called *religiosity*. Now, said they, the controversy must end. Here is religion a very element of man's nature; it grows out of a fundamental want of his being, and therefore religion he has, and must, and will have, as long as he continues to be human. This philosophy was imported into France by Madame de Staël and Benjamin Constant, and in a modified form was accepted by Cousin and Jouffroy. But, after all, this was merely a new version of the very doctrine of the old *philosophes*. At first, it seemed to be something else, and many an inquirer thought he had found what he was looking after. But, alas! the discovery of the origin of religion *in human nature* destroyed the possibility of *religiousness*. The *religiosity* was struck from the list of human faculties the moment it was discovered to be a faculty; because then it lost all its character of sacredness and authority, and men who understood the secret, could regard only as a mere sham or pretense all religious exercises. Religion was no longer a law imposed on man by a lawgiver, but something growing out of his nature, standing on a level with industry, politics, art, and the like. Here was no God to worship, but an instinct to follow; no extra-mundane sovereign to obey, but an internal law to develop. . . .

But, as we have already shown, though from another point of view, this theory of the non-intervention of Providence, save through the fixed and permanent laws of human nature, will not suffice to explain and account for the facts of human history. By it we may explain and account for what is fixed, permanent, uniform in history; but how explain by its light, or account for what is exceptional, variable, individual, diverse? Vico, by his "common sense of nations," can only explain what is common to all nations; not by any means what each nation has in its life that is peculiar to itself. We have seen that we cannot do it merely by the aid of climate and geography. The difference of races may do somewhat; but if we assume, or even if we do not assume, that all the varieties of the human race have sprung from the same family, this difference will be insufficient to account for all the diversities which we find in the lives of different nations and individuals. On this ground, we ask again, what shall we do with *providential men,* who come at long intervals of time and space, and by their superhuman virtue, intelligence, wisdom, love, and power of sacrifice, found systems and eras, redeem and advance their race? History presents us, at least *tradition* presents us, these men standing by the cradles of all nations, as the founders of their respective civilizations. These men cannot come as the ordinary developments of humanity, for humanity cannot of itself surpass its uniform type. What shall we say of them? Shall we boldly deny their existence as individuals, and with Vico declare them vast collective beings; understanding by Homer, not "the blind old bard of Scio's rocky isle," but a long series of bards and rhapsodists, the Homerides; nay, not the Homerides merely, but the whole Greek people embodying itself and history, through the whole epoch of its earlier and heroic life, in a sublime Iliad, and a didactic Odyssey? Shall we say that there was no Moses, but the Jewish people, emancipating themselves from servitude, who obtain after various trials and vicissitudes a country, and establish a fixed code of laws, political, civil, and religious? . . . As well strike the Divinity from heaven as dispeople the earth of its heroes. No; these providential men, these angels of God, these messengers of truth and love, were not mere fictions, the mere impersonations of the thoughts, feelings, and deeds of the masses in their respective nations; but they were great and glorious *realities*, almost the only realities on which the eye can seize and repose, through all the long vista of the past. No; critics and philosophers, having spoiled us of our God, do in common charity spare us the glorious army of saints and martyrs, heroes, prophets, apostles, and sages, by whom our race has been redeemed and blessed. To spare us these is not to rob the masses of their glory, for their glory is that they love, and reverence, and cherish the memory of these, and profit by their diviner lives. . . .

The error of the advocates of this theory, arises from their assuming that all in the life of humanity must be a development of humanity itself. But humanity does not suffice for itself. The Creator has not merely created man, placed him here, and left him to the natural workings of the original principles of his being, as the Epicureans teach, but he remains ever near him, watching over him with a tender love; and intervenes to aid his growth, and the accomplishment of his destiny. This brings us to

2. The religious view of Providence. We have objected to Cousin's doctrine that it gave no place to human freedom; we object to it now, that it gives no place to divine freedom. Unquestionably, Cousin asserts that the human *me*, as Leibnitz contends, is a force, a cause, and really is no further than it is free; but in tracing virtually, if not expressly, all the facts of history to the impersonal reason, and assigning to the reflective reason, in which alone the *me* intervenes, only a retrospective agency, he renders this liberty of the *me* altogether unproductive, and therefore as good as no *me* at all. Unquestionably also, he asserts, and it is a capital point in his philosophy, that

God is cause, and substance, or being, only in that he is cause; therefore necessarily asserting his freedom, for a cause not free is no cause—the cause being not in *it*, but in that which binds or necessitates it. But in his account of the divine intervention, he recognizes that intervention only in creation. It is, as we have seen, solely an ontological intervention, coming through the side of our permanent nature, affecting us in the fixed and unalterable laws of our being, and not through our life, our actions, and reaching our substantive existence through our phenomenal existence. Therefore, whatever freedom there was in creating us, there can be none in governing or controlling us. The divine action is limited, restrained by the laws or nature of the creature. God can act only in these laws; nay, these laws are *his* action. There is and can be no divine influx but these laws themselves. Consequently, God is not and cannot be free to correct their action, or to give them a new direction, or an *additional* force, as may be required for the greatest good of the race, unless we lose them entirely, and fall into absolute pantheism. From the first point of view, we lose man, from the last, we lose God. . . .

We have made Bossuet, a celebrated Catholic bishop, author of the *Discours sur l'Histoire Universelle,* the representative of this religious view of Providence, because it is from it, as his point of sight, that his history is conceived and written; also because he is among the earliest of those who have attempted a universal history. This work has had a great reputation, and it must be owned that it is written with great eloquence and power, with the force and dignity becoming an eminent prelate of the church; yet regarded as a history, it is unquestionably very defective—defective considering the state of historical knowledge at the time it was written, and much more so now. Its merit is that it is written from the point of view of Providence, and designed to show the active intervention of Providence in the affairs of this world to reward and to punish, to solace and to succor, and especially its intervention in the rise, progress, and decline of states and empires. But the prelate sees seldom the *people,*—seldom condescends to bestow a thought on the domestic and everyday life of the masses; he dwells in the Temple, or follows the Court and the Camp.

The French claim for Bossuet the high honor of having been the first to conceive the plan of a universal history, written in a philosophic spirit, from a given point of view; but possibly without sufficient foundation. Bossuet's originality is more in the execution than in the conception of his work, the plan of which was given him by the church herself, was indicated in Genesis, and had been rough-sketched, at least, by St. Augustine in his *De Civitate Dei.* Moreover, the *History of the World,* by Sir Walter Raleigh, which preceded the *Discours sur l'Histoire Universelle* by more than half a century, is conceived in the same spirit, written from the same point of view, and with virtually the same thought. Sir Walter finished only a third part of his work as originally designed; but he has, in the masterly preface to the part completed, sketched the plan of the whole. As a mere history, though by no means without its merit, it unquestionably falls far below the work of the Catholic prelate; but the preface and introductory chapters, philosophical and theological, are written with great vigor and majesty of thought, with a pathos, a richness, and a magnificence of style and language, hardly surpassed, if equaled, by anything of the kind we are acquainted with, and show, among other things, how little philosophy has really advanced since the pretended reforms introduced by Bacon and Descartes. . . .

St. Augustine had conceived, and to some extent sketched, the history of the rise and progress of TWO CITIES, one of which he called the "City of this world," whose end is destruction, the other of which he called the "City of God," whose end is to remain forever the empire of the saints, and the habitation of the just. Here is unquestionably the germ of the *Discours sur l'Histoire Universelle*. But St. Augustine wrote not as the historian, but as the polemic and the dogmatist; while Bossuet writes almost always as the simple historian, only as the historian of principles rather than of mere facts and details. He is writing for the instruction of the Dauphin, and his design is indeed to prepare his royal pupil, should Providence call him to the throne, for the proper discharge of his duties as sovereign of France. He writes, therefore, from the point of view of religion and politics, with the evident design of showing from the history of God's providence, and that of renowned states and empires, that no policy of a prince, however wise to mere human apprehension, can ever be successful, if it in any respect runs counter to the laws of God, as displayed in his providential dealings with mankind. He sought to inculcate the wholesome lesson, always inculcated by the Catholic church, and always needing to be inculcated, whether the political sovereignty be vested in the one, the few, or the many, that there is a King of kings, a Power above the state, who is the true Sovereign, and whose laws can never be transgressed with impunity. Nor this only; he everywhere sought to show, by implication, however, rather than by express assertion, what the English Solomon, James the First, in his *Remonstrance for the Divine Right of Kings, in reply to an Oration of the Cardinal du Perron,* undertakes to controvert, namely, that this true Sovereign, this King of kings, Law of laws, to which the civil magistrate owes allegiance, has on earth even, a visible embodiment, and a representative, other than that which may be conceived of as existing in the state itself. He therefore contends for two empires—1. The empire of the people of God, the religious. 2. The empire of men, the political.

In his view, these two empires are not co-ordinate, though co-existing; nor does he make the first subordinate to the second, raising the civil power over the ecclesiastical—the human over the divine—as do the Anglicans in their theory of the reformation; and as does James, especially in his *Remonstrance,* or defense of kings; but he makes the religious empire, which derives its authority immediately from God himself, supreme, and proclaims it from his episcopal chair as the law of the political power;—a doctrine humbling to the pride of kings, and which, through the long period from the establishment of the barbarians on the ruins of the Roman empire down to the reformation in the sixteenth century, had caused an almost unbroken war between the civil government and the ecclesiastical. . . .

From this point of view, Bossuet proceeds to sketch the two empires, but more especially the religious empire, and to trace the uninterrupted succession of the people of God, the depositaries of the supreme Law. In the history of this empire he finds the history of God's providential intervention in human affairs. The design of this providential intervention is to raise up, educate, and conduct to truth, and justice, and love, an elect people, eminently and strictly the *People of God.* Bossuet traces the history of this people from the Creation, down through Seth, Noah, the patriarchs, Moses, the Jewish nation, to the coming of Christ, and then no longer in a single nation, but in the apostles and the church, gathering and forming into one compact body the people of God from *all* nations; for in the seed of Abraham, which is Christ, all the families, kindreds, and nations of earth were to be blessed.

It will be seen from this statement that the Catholic bishop writes his history solely from the point of view of the Christian church. His point of departure is in Genesis, and his point of arrival is the consummation of the people of God in Jesus Christ, through the Gospel. We, of course, have no fault to find with this point of view. It is the only point of view from which the history of humanity can be written, or should be written. But, then, we must understand it well, and be careful that we overlook nothing which it permits us to see. Undoubtedly, Providence intervenes through the medium of an elect people; undoubtedly, too, the Jewish people prior to the coming of Christ, and the Christian church, are to be regarded as standing at the head of this people; but it would be unjust to leave all the rest of mankind to the mere law of nature, and untrue, to say that no rays of divine light had penetrated to them but through the inherent and necessary laws of nature and humanity. The false religions of antiquity were not altogether the creations of the devil, but corruptions, or imperfect, incomplete embodiments of the true religion. . . .

Now, assume a providential man, that is, a man qualified by the special interposition of his Maker, to exhibit to the world a higher order of spiritual and moral life than the world had hitherto known or been capable of. They who should come into personal communion with him, would live by him, and their life would partake of his fullness. He would be the object—not the *end* in reference to which—but the object *in conjunction* with which, they would live; consequently his higher and diviner character would be communicated to their acts, so that in acting they would act him as well as themselves, would literally live his life. Here is the secret of the well-known influence of example. The *fact* of this influence has always been known and insisted on; the *law* or *philosophy* of this fact has not, till quite recently, been discovered. "Evil communications corrupt good manners." Wherefore? Because our life is composed of two elements, one the subject, which is ourselves, the other the object we are in relation with, which is not ourselves; and as the life partakes of the character of both the subject and the object, it follows necessarily that, if the object be corrupt, that part of our act depending on it will also be corrupt. So good communications have the opposite effect, and purify our manners, and for the same reason. The object in relation with which we live being better than we are, more elevated and holy, evidently, as our acts must derive somewhat from it, our life will be purified and elevated. The fact here stated everybody knows; the *reason* of the fact is all that is novel in the statement. Who of us has ever conversed for one half-hour with a really great and good man, but has felt that a virtue has come out of him to us, and that we ourselves are lifted up, and are no longer, and never can be again, what we were before? This law, which we call the spiritual communicability of life, creates what we denominate, from a French legal term, the mutual *solidarity* of the life of the human race. By this all are not only ontologically, that is, in the common principles of their nature, members of one race; but all are members of one and the same community, and members one of another, living, in their various degrees, one and the same *life*.

Now, admitting the providential intervention to be in the form and manner asserted by Bossuet, that is, through a peculiar, an elect people of God, it does not follow that it was necessarily confined to that people. . . . While, then, we accept the prelate's general point of view, and readily admit that Providence is specially manifested in the religious empire, represented by the Jewish people prior to the coming of Christ, and by the Christian church since, yet we are not willing to regard the effects of this providential interference as shut up within the limits of this empire, or as confined exclusively to the peculiar people of God. The patriarchs, the Jews, and the church were made the depositaries, so to speak, of Providence, not for themselves as ends, but as the instruments and ministers of God in accomplishing his purposes, which concern the entire human race. . . .

The historian, who wishes to give really a universal history of mankind, must unquestionably treat that history under the five-fold division of Industry, Politics, Art, Religion, and Philosophy, as contended by Cousin, for these are all indestructible elements of the *life* of humanity; but in considering these in relation to their origin, their cause, their progress, it will not be enough to consider them as originating in certain permanent and indestructible wants of human nature. In other words, nature given as their theater, and man also given with his inherent and permanent wants, still all the facts of the life of mankind would not be given; we should yet have no industry, no politics, no art, no religion, no philosophy. It is here we separate from Cousin. If we understand him, since Providence intervenes only in nature and in the permanent laws of humanity, nature and humanity given, all the facts of human history are given. This we deny. Human history is explained only by the recognition of three elements as at work in its production. 1. Nature; 2. Humanity; 3. Providence.

Jouffroy excludes nature and Providence; for he finds the principle of change in human things only in the human intelligence; Cousin, by tracing all to the impersonal reason, and recognizing the divine action only in the fixed, the permanent, and the necessary, virtually, while contending for them, excludes both humanity and Providence; Bossuet takes no note of nature, and makes quite little of humanity, and therefore gives us an exaggerated view of Providence. But neither can be excluded without vitiating our philosophy of history.

1. Nature is not the mere passive theater on which man is placed to display his activity, but is herself an active force, and progressive even. . . . All substance, in the last analysis, will be found to be immaterial, possessing inherent activity, capable of making an effort (*conatus*) from its own center.

Nature is not only active, but progressive. This is demonstrable from the very conception which we have, and cannot but have, of God, if we conceive of him at all. Our only conception of God is of him as cause, creator, but as an infinitely powerful, wise, and good cause. He is essentially cause, and not merely a potential cause, but actually, eternally, and universally a cause.

In causing or creating, he is realizing his own infinite ideal in space and time. But space and time are limited, and can contain only the finite. Creation, therefore, or the universe, viewed either as a whole or in detail, must be incomplete—can be only a finite realization of the infinite; consequently, only an *imperfect* realization of the divine ideal. . . .

2. While we reject the notion that all in the life of humanity is developed from itself, and is nothing but its own creation in answer to its own inherent wants, we must still recognize humanity in every fact of human history, and there too as a free, active, productive cause, though a limited cause, working in conjunction with other causes, never alone. To a great extent, human history depends on human volition. If Miltiades had not defeated the Persians at Marathon, or if Themistocles had not destroyed the Persian fleet at Salamis, the whole course of ancient history would have run differently; and yet this depended, to no inconsiderable extent, on the skill and bravery of a few Greek leaders and a mere handful of followers. . . . These Greeks might have proved cowards and traitors, been false to themselves and to humanity; and had they been so, we should all have fared the worse. If Alexander had not invaded Asia and Africa, and by so doing founded the Egypto-Grecian and the Syro-Grecian empires, who will say that the course of human history would have flowed on all the same? . . .

3. Providence undoubtedly intervenes so as to secure in the details of history, the execution of the divine purposes; but it does not follow from this that nothing is to be found in human history not there by the express will and appointment of God. For were it so there would be small space left for human agency, and there would and could be no *crimes*. Human action on the large scale on which history contemplates it, as well as on the narrow scale on which it is contemplated by practical ethics, is alike the action of individuals. Humanity, though itself

transcending all individuals, yet lives and actualizes itself only in individuals. . . .

In recognizing the intervention of Providence, then, we must not so recognize it, as to imply that all goes on in obedience to the laws of God, as if man and men were at every moment doing what God wills or commands them to do. The purpose of God, it is admitted, is not frustrated; but this purpose is to leave man free within given limits, and to reward him if he exercise his freedom properly, and to chastise him if he abuse it. Providence is unquestionably to be found in all the facts of human history, but not there to contravene human freedom, and by a sovereign agency to compel men to do this or to do that. He is there to make the very wrath of man to praise him, and to restrain indeed the effects of that wrath so far as it cannot be made subservient to the divine economy for the government of humanity. The general course of humanity is onward, towards the realization in individual and social life of the perfect law of liberty. When the Jews refuse to perform a certain work in this progress, God rejects them and calls the gentiles. He has given us Americans a certain work for humanity; he is with us ready to grant us all the assistance we need in executing it; but if we refuse to do it, he will cast us off, and raise up another people to inherit the glory that might have been ours. Whether we execute this work or not, will depend on ourselves, on our own intelligence and virtue. . . .

If we find in human history three agencies at work, namely, nature, humanity, Providence, we must bear in mind that these all three intervene and work after one and the same original law, type or model, eternal and *essential* in the infinite mind or Logos. . . . Could we but hear the voice of the veriest grain of sand, we should hear the same Word that in the beginning said, "Let there be light and there was light," or that, clothed with flesh, over the wild tempestuous sea of Galilee, said to the winds and waves, "Peace, be still," or at the grave of Lazarus to the sleeping dead, "Come forth.". . .

In conclusion, if we have made intelligible the thought with which we have written, we may say that the course of human history depends in no slight degree on the voluntary activity of individuals. Nature and Providence are in it, but men may by their wickedness pervert its course, though not with impunity; and by their wisdom, and virtue, and energy, they may aid it onward in obedience to the will of God, and the good of their race. Here we find, what theorists have denied us, the room, the motive, and the sanction needed for human virtue. The *room* is, in the space we allow in history to human freedom; the *motive* is obedience to God, and the welfare of humanity, which last must always receive damage from individual ignorance, vice or crime; and the *sanction* is in the ever-present Providence to aid and reward us in well-doing, and to chastise us, or to cut us off, as a people, or as individuals, in evil-doing. Here we are free to counsel, to warn, to rebuke. Humanity lives only in the life of individuals. Then let statesmen, kings, emperors, priests, philosophers, and scholars, nay, all individuals, whatever their degree, position, or ability, lose no time in making all possible efforts to enable and to induce all men, in public or in private, to live in strict obedience to the perfect law of liberty; and in making these efforts, let them know that God and nature work with them, and they may do all things. And let them know also that if they will not make them, not only shall all humanity fare the worse, but the Judge of all the earth will do right, and will one day demand of them wherefore they have been unprofitable servants.

KANT'S CRITIQUE OF PURE REASON
[1844]

[*Just as his essay on "The Philosophy of History" gives evidence of Brownson's attempt, prior to his conversion, to confront the problem of history, so his essays on Kant represent his attempt to confront the problem of knowledge. During 1844, the year of his conversion, Brownson published in his newly established* Brownson's Quarterly Review *three closely reasoned articles on Kant's* Critique of Pure Reason. *The first article sketched out the history of philosophy from Descartes to Kant. The following selection is abridged from the second article. The full text of all three is in* Works, I, 130–213.

This study of Kant was in many ways a philosophical milestone for Brownson, and measures his departure from eclecticism and subjectivism. "Nearly all through the year 1844," writes his son, "the great subject of talk in the dinng-room was Kant." (Early Life, p. 413.) René Wellek remarks that "Brownson had a stronger philosophical bent than his friends and associates, and a genuine gift for speculation, as well as an altogether unusual grasp, in his time and place, of philosophical technicalities. He alone of all the Transcendentalists seems to have been seriously disturbed by the problem of knowledge and truth, and he alone made a close examination of Kant's actual text." ("The Minor Transcendentalists and German Philosophy," New England Quarterly, XV [1942], pp. 652–80.)]

WE HAVE CLASSED the several modern doctrines of Science, sketched their history from Descartes down to Kant, and determined Kant's position and problem. His problem is, as we have seen, the purely scientific problem; that is, Is science possible? Yet it is not precisely in this form that he himself proposes it. To even a tolerably attentive reader of the *Critic of Pure Reason*, the real problem will appear to concern the conditions, extent, and bounds of human science, rather than the possibility of human science itself.

By a rigid analysis of the intellectual phenomenon, Kant discovers that every fact of knowledge involves a synthetic judgment, and hence he proceeds to inquire, How are synthetic judgments formed? What is their reach? What their validity? In asking and answering these questions, he disguises, both from himself and his readers, the real problem with which he is concerned. The science, that is, the *knowing*, properly so called, is all and entirely in this very synthetic judgment. If this judgment be impossible, if it be invalid, then is science impossible, and human knowledge a mere delusion. So, after all, Kant is inquiring into the possibility, as well as into the conditions, validity, extent, and bounds of science.

Assuming this, we may say, in the outset, that the whole inquiry into which Kant enters is founded in a capital blunder, and can end in no solid or useful result. To ask if the human mind be capable of science is absurd; for we have only the human mind with which to answer the question. And it needs science to answer this question, as much as it does to answer any other question. Suppose we should undertake to answer this question, and should demonstrate by an invincible logic, as Kant himself professes to have done, that science is impossible, our demonstration would be a complete demonstration of its own unsoundness; for the demonstration must itself be scientific, or be no demonstration at all. If the demonstration be scientific, it establishes the fact of science in demonstrating to the contrary; if it be not scientific, then it is of no value, and decides nothing, as to our scientific capacity, one way or the other.

Kant professes to start at a point equally distant from both dogmatism and skepticism. He neither affirms nor denies; he merely criticizes, that is, investigates. But is the critic blind? To criticize, to investigate,—what is this but to discriminate, to distinguish, to judge? Can there be an act of discrimination, of judgment, without science? If you assume, then, your capacity to enter into a critical investigation of the power of the human mind to know, you necessarily begin by assuming the possibility of science, and therefore by what logicians term a *petitio principii*. Kant attempts the investigation, and in so doing assumes his capacity to make it; and, therefore, contrary to his profession, begins in pure dogmatism. He begins by assuming the possibility of science, as the condition of demonstrating its impossibility,—for the impossibility of science is what he professes to have demonstrated, as the result of all his labors.

We might hesitate a moment before bringing this charge of absurdity against a man of Kant's unquestionable superiority, did we not seem to ourselves not only to perceive the absurdity, but also its cause. Kant's fundamental error, and the source of all his other errors, is in attempting, like most psychologists, to distinguish between the subject and its own inneity, and to find the object in the subject,—and *not-me* in the *me*. We believe his much-wronged and misapprehended disciple, Fichte, was the first to detect and expose this error. If Kant had comprehended, in the outset, the simple fact subsequently stated by Fichte in the postulate, the *me* is *me*, he never would, he never could, have written the *Critic of Pure Reason;* for he would have seen that if the *me* is *me*, the *not-me* is not *me*, and therefore that the object, or whatever is objective, since distinguished from the subject, is not and cannot be *me*, nor the inneity of the *me*. This simple truism, which is nothing but saying, what is, is, completely refutes the whole Critical Philosophy. We would therefore commend to the admirers of the *Critik der reinen Vernunft* of the master, the careful study of the *Wissenschaftslehre* of the disciple.

Kant's great and leading doctrine is, that, in the fact of knowledge, the form, under which the object is cognized, is determined not by what it is in itself, but by the laws of the subject cognizing. He complains that hitherto metaphysicians have supposed, that the form of the cognition depended on the object, and that our cognitions must conform to the intrinsic character of the objects cognized. . . . The external world, for instance, is not necessarily in itself what it appears to us, but it appears to us as it does because our inneity, or intuitive power, compels it so to appear. . . . Change our inneity, and you change all objects of knowledge. This is the great, the leading Kantian doctrine; and the reason why metaphysical science has made no more advance is, because metaphysicians have overlooked this doctrine, and obstinately persisted in believing that there is really some difference between fish and flesh, wine and water, besides what is inherent in the taste of the eater or drinker!

But if the form of the object is determined by the forms of the subject, then, instead of going into an investigation of the innumerable and diversified objects of knowledge, in order to determine the foundations and conditions of science, we should go into an investigation of the subject itself, of this very inneity which the subject imposes upon all its cognitions. The grounds, conditions, and laws of science, are then to be obtained from the study of the subject instead of the object. We must know ourselves, as the condition of knowing all else. The object of the *Critic* is, therefore, to investigate the subject, and determine its part in the fact of experience. . . .

All actual knowledge begins with experience, and prior to experience there is no actual knowledge; but every actual cognition, or fact of experience, if we understand Kant, is composed of two parts, one *empirical*, obtained from the sensible impression, the other *a priori*, furnished by the understanding itself from its own resources. The marks or criteria of the cognition *a priori* are universality and necessity. Whatever is conceived of as absolutely universal and necessary is *a priori*. . . . This means, if we comprehend it, all simply, that we never do, and never can, conceive of the particular and contingent, save through conception of the universal and the necessary. This fact we are not disposed to question; but the further statement which Kant makes is not quite so evident, namely, that the conceptions of the universal and necessary are underivable from experience, and must, therefore, be cognitions *a priori*. . . .

Kant holds, 1. That we are in possession of cognitions *a priori;* 2. That these cognitions are the indispensable ground and conditions of all actual cognition; 3. That they stretch away beyond the field of even possible experience; 4. That among these which extend beyond even possible experience are those cognitions which lie at the foundation of our loftiest faith and sublimest hopes concerning God, Freedom, and Immortality; 5. That it is precisely of these that philosophy needs a science which shall determine their possibility, principles, and extent; and 6. Till we have such a science, we have no solid foundation for any religious or ethical faith, indeed for any branch of knowledge whatever.

The inquiry into which Kant enters concerns precisely these cognitions *a priori*, and his aim is to construct the science of their possibility, principles, and extent. His aim is high, and his inquiry one of no mean importance,—if the case stands as he assumes. Are these cognitions *a priori*, which extend beyond all actual, beyond all possible experience, able to sustain our religious, ethical, and scientific superstructures? Here is the question Kant raises, and which he says should have been raised, and answered, long ago, but which, unhappily, has remained hitherto neglected, and consequently hitherto *no progress* has been made in metaphysical science.

The assumption of Kant, that thus far no progress has been made in metaphysical science, is in the outset a strong presumptive proof that he himself is in the wrong. A man who comes forward with a pretended discovery in any branch of human science, requiring him to consider all who have hitherto cultivated that branch to have been wholly in the wrong, proves by that fact alone that his discovery is to be looked upon with no little doubt and distrust. It is reserved for no man, in our day and generation, to take the initiative in any branch of human thought; and he who can discover no merit in his predecessors gives very good evidence that he has no merit of his own. Kant's unqualified condemnation of all the metaphysical labors of humanity, prior to himself, is, for us, a sufficient proof that his own system has no solid foundation, and that his labors have no permanent value.

But we must examine these cognitions *a priori* a little closer. What are they? They are a constituent part of every actual cognition, and, in addition, its ground and condition. *It is only by virtue of these that experience is possible.* We pray our readers to remember this. Deny these, you deny the possibility of experience; deny, then, the validity of these, and you deny the validity of experience. And yet, these cognitions are supplied by the subject, and have no objective validity! The cognition (*Erkenntniss*), which stretches beyond even possible experience, has, according to Kant, no objective validity, that is to say, has no value in relation to any reality exterior to the subject. The moment we venture forth with Plato, on the wings of Ideas, beyond the world of the senses, we are in the empty space of the pure reason, and as unable to succeed as would be the light dove, which cleaves the air, to fly in mere airless space. A cognition, extending beyond the sensible world, is a pure conception, and a pure conception is an *empty* conception, a conception in which nothing is conceived. Of this class are all our judgments *a priori*, which are again the ground of all our judgments *a posteriori!*

Our cognitions *a priori* are of two kinds, analytic and synthetic. The analytic judgments do not extend our knowledge; they only clear up and place distinctly before the mind what was previously conceived, though confusedly; only the synthetic judgments add to the sum of our knowledge. In these there is, at least, a *seeming* extension of knowledge. Take the proposition, All that which happens has a cause. Now the conception of cause is different from the conception of something happening. In this proposition, then, I add the conception of cause to the conception, Something happens. Now, how am I able to do this? And what is the real value of this synthesis, or addition? I cannot obtain this synthesis from experience, for experience can give me only the conception, Something happens; never, the conception, All that which happens *has a cause*. This last conception, namely, of causality, without which there would, and could, be no extension of knowledge, must be supplied, Kant tells us, by the understanding itself, in which it lies *a priori*, ready to be applied to experience of an actual case of causation. Then what is its value? It is—and this is the great doctrine of the *Critik der reinen Vernunft—it is a mere conception, an empty conception in which nothing is conceived.* Here, then, we are. The whole fabric of human science rests on cognitions *a priori*, and these cognitions are but mere empty conceptions. Here, then, we are, following this great modern philosopher, *in dem leeren Raum des reinen Verstandes.* If there be meaning in language, this is nothing but the Hindoo doctrine of Maya, namely, that all science is mere illusion. It is hardly worth one's while to master the crabbed style and barbarous terminology of Kant, to be taught this, which after all, like all other teaching, must needs be a delusion.

The full discussion of the facts which Kant has had in view, when asserting cognitions *a priori*, we reserve, till in a subsequent article, we come to consider the categories of the pure understanding. Here we can only remark, that, while we admit what Kant calls cognition *a priori,* we deny it to be a cognition *a priori.* We deny both the reality and the possibility of cognitions *a priori.* Cognition *a priori* is a contradiction in terms. Cognition is the act of cognizing. If nothing be cognized, it is not cognition. Conception in which nothing is conceived is an impossibility: Can there be *seeing* where there is not somewhat that is *seen?* If the cognition be cognition, it must be *a posteriori;* for it must needs be preceded both by that which cognizes and by that which is cognized. . . .

Now, the question we raise concerning the cognition *a priori,* that is, the *pure* cognition, and the transcendental cognition, is, whether they are really intelligible objects, νοήματα, or whether they are not. Kant decides, at once, that they are not; for, if they were, they would not be *a priori.* What, then, are they? Remember, they precede all actual cognition, and are the grounds and conditions of the possibility of actual cognition. They are not on the side of the object, are not derived from the object, but exist prior to the apprehension of the object, in the understanding, from which they are supplied. What are they, or what can they be, but the power of the subject to cognize?

We must bear in mind that our inquiry lies wholly within the region of the subjective faculty of intelligence. It does not concern the *knowing,* but the *power* or ability to know; not experience, but the possibility and conditions of experience. This possibility and these conditions are not the object, nor derivable from the object, but, according to Kant, lie already *a priori* in the understanding; that is to say, they lie already in the understanding, prior to any actual fact of experience. These pure and transcendental cognitions are not, then, if we understand Kant, produced by the understanding, nor are they the understanding in operation, that is to say, operating on occasion of a fact of experience; they are not the actual thinking of non-empirical elements, on occasion of the empirical fact; but they are the *power* or *ability* of the subject, in a fact of experience, to think and apply to that fact what is not contained in it, nor derived or derivable from it, and yet without thinking which, the fact of experience itself could not have occurred. They are not the *thinking* of that which transcends experience, but the *ability* to think it. This, in simple terms, is all that we can understand by the pure and transcendental cognitions. If we are right in this, and we are confident we are, then these cognitions are nothing more or less than the constituent elements of the cognitive faculty, of the understanding, without which it would not be the power to understand. They are, then, the understanding itself; that is, the power of the subject to understand; that is, again, all simply, as we say, the inneity of the subject.

Kant calls his work a *critic*, and of course designedly; he calls it a critic of the *pure* reason; that is, of reason, when abstraction is made of all experience, of all exercise of reason, and of all that results from its exercise. In other words, pure reason is the faculty itself, as we may say, *"in potentia, non in actu"*; that is, reason as the *vis cognitrix*, the force that knows, taken entirely independent of the *act* of knowing, or cognition. Now, it is reason in this sense, reason as the power of reason, that Kant undertakes to criticize. He assumes in this, that the pure reason may be subjected to analysis. He then assumes the pure reason itself, that is, the subjective faculty of reason, of intelligence, to be complex, and therefore susceptible of decomposition. The decomposition of this faculty gives, as its original, fundamental elements, the cognitions in question; which shows us that these cognitions, in Kant's view, are not products of reason, nor reason operating, but its constituent elements, therefore it itself.

This last conclusion, however, is ours, not Kant's. Kant's labor is that of analysis; his aim is, to decompose the power of thought. He is not, with Condillac and others, decomposing thought as a fact, but the power, of the exercise of which, thought is the product. He is decomposing, not the act, but the principle of the act; not the thinking, but, properly speaking, the force that thinks. But here is the precise point where his error commences. The understanding, taken substantively, is the cognitive force; but Kant does, and does not, so take it. He fancies a distinction between the force cognizing and that by virtue of which it is able to cognize. Reason, therefore, is reason by virtue of a somewhat that is distinguishable from it as intelligent force. In other words, the power to know is the power to know, by virtue of containing in itself elements which we may distinguish from itself. Hence, while he would make the pure and transcendental cognitions constituent elements, so to speak, of the cognitive power, he would still make them rather the instruments it uses, than it itself. In his view, they are a somewhat medial between the cognitive force as substance, and cognition, or the knowing, taken phenomenally. They are neither the *vis* nor the *actus*, but the endowments, attributes, or properties of the force cognizing. This is Kant's actual doctrine as exactly seized and stated as it is possible for us to seize and state it.

But here is a grand error, the very error we have so frequently pointed out as the source of all the errors of our modern psychologists, the assumption of a distinction between the subject and the inneity of the subject. Kant, through his whole *Critic*, assumes that the faculty is distinguishable, though not separable, from the subject. But there is no ground for this assumption. The distinction of faculties in man, as of properties in animals and inanimate beings, we of course admit; but this distinction of faculties, or of properties, is a distinction *in* not *from* the subject. This is the great and essential fact, which Kant either overlooks or denies. Thus, he defines the conception of substance to be the conception of the *substratum* that underlies and upholds the properties or faculties. Thus, we may abstract from an object, corporeal or incorporeal, all the qualities revealed to us by experience, and still the conception of substance will remain, and the object still be considered as existing. Now, this we deny *in toto*. Abstract from a given object, corporeal or incorporeal, or, to make the statement as strong as possible in Kant's favor, abstract from your conception of object in general all conception of qualities and properties, and there will remain the conception of—NOTHING. Substance defined, as Kant defines it, to be a mere substratum, is nothing but the veriest logical abstraction. Even the definition in the schools, of substance (*substans*, standing under), as that which supports accidents, is inadmissible, unless we are careful to distinguish between essential properties, qualities, or faculties, and *accidents*. The property, or quality, is not an accident, and therefore distinguishable from the substance in which it inheres, or upon which it may be supposed to be superinduced. The quality, or property, is not distinguishable *from* the substance. We may conceive of substance in which we may distinguish qualities, or properties, different from those we distinguish in other substances; but we cannot conceive of one and the same substance with different properties, much less, a substance with no properties. . . .

The actual cognition, we have seen, consists of two parts, the cognition *a priori*, and the cognition *a posteriori*,—the portion derived from experience, and the portion supplied by the subject experiencing. The empirical portion is merely the sensation, consequently, the actual cognition is sensation *plus* the subject,— the old doctrine attributed to Aristotle, with the famous reserve suggested by Leibnitz: *Nihil est in intellectu, quod prius non fuerit in sensu,*—NISI IPSE INTELLECTUS: Nothing can be in the mind but what is first in the senses,—except the mind itself. Here is the germ of the *Critik der reinen Vernunft*, and all that Kant has done has been to develop and systematize the doctrine contained in this celebrated maxim.

We commend this fact to those zealous Kantians among us who are loud in condemning Locke for his alleged sensism. The charge of sensism against Locke comes with an ill grace from a follower of Kant; for, so far as it concerns the *objects* of knowledge, the Englishman is much less liable to it than the German. Locke, indeed, recognized only sensation as a source of primary ideas, yet he held that logic, or what he calls Reflection, is capable of extending our knowledge, and of attaining, by way of deduction, of inference, from sensible *data*, to realities transcending the limits of sensation itself,—which Kant denies, and labors at length to refute, in his "Transcendental Dialectics."

The great and important fact, which Kant seems to us to have recognized, is that contained in the reserve of Leibnitz already quoted,—*nisi ipse intellectus;*—namely, that, in every fact of experience, the subject enters for a part, and must count for something; and that, prior to experience, the understanding is not, as Locke alleged, a mere blank sheet void of all characters and of all ideas. It is the assertion of this fact that has deceived so many in regard to the true character and worth of the Critical Philosophy, and made them look upon the *Critik der reinen Vernunft* as a successful refutation of the *Essay on the Human Understanding*. Yet even here the difference between the two is more apparent than real, and, so far as real at all, is to the advantage of Locke. . . .

The simple truth is, that, touching objective knowledge, the only matter which Locke termed knowledge, Kant has made no advance on Locke, but virtually adopts Locke's general doctrine. He leaves, in the beginning, Locke where he is, and attempts to get behind experience, and make a critic of the experience-power; not the cognition, but the cognitive power (*Erkenntnis-vermögen*); that is to say, to determine whether the sensation and reflection of Locke, or the knowledge, so called, obtained by them, or rather through them, could claim any validity, or be worthy of any reliance. At best, he would only have left us the power of communicating with what lies outside of us, which Locke asserted; but, in reality, he has not left us even so much. For he has attempted to show that no experience is or can be valid without both synthetic judgments and synthetic conceptions, *a priori*, and that these judgments and conceptions are of no value, being nothing but pure, that is, empty conceptions. So that, with him we are worse off than we were with Locke; for if Locke was defective in not recognizing the subject in its completeness, Kant is still more defective, in that he, with Hume, recognizes in man no power of intelligence at all. Kant himself believed, many have since believed, that his *Critic* is a refutation of Hume; *we* regard it as the most masterly defense of Hume that man may be expected to produce. If Kant is right, man is incapable of demonstrating the reality of any existence outside of the subject, and the subject, for the want of a resisting medium, finally loses all apperception of itself, for Kant contends that the *me* can have intuition of itself only in the intuition of the diverse, that is, of the *not me;* and so all science vanishes, all certainty disappears, the sun goes out, the bright stars are extinguished, and we are afloat in the darkness, on the wild and tempest-roused ocean of universal Doubt and Nescience. Alas! we do not misrepresent the philosopher of Königsberg, for he himself, in the preface to his second edition, tells us that the result of his whole investigation is, to rebuke dogmatism, "to demolish science to make way for faith."

The *Critic of Pure Reason,* we all know, is confessedly atheistic; it leaves no space for faith in God, and Kant was obliged to write his *Critic of the Practical Reason* in order to restore the faith it had overthrown.

TRANSCENDENTALISM
[1845]

[*The selection that follows is an abridgment of the first of a series of three articles on Transcendentalism which appeared in* Brownson's Quarterly *in 1845 and 1846 as a review of Theodore Parker's* A Discourse of Matters pertaining to Religion (*Boston, 1842*). *Parker (1810–1860) was, after Emerson, one of the leaders of the Transcendentalist movement. He had been a contributor to the* Boston Quarterly *and a personal friend of Brownson. Brownson had already devoted the entire final number of the* Boston Quarterly Review *to a review of Parker's book, and a comparison of Brownson's criticisms in 1842 and in 1845–1846 indicates the development of his whole critique of Transcendentalism in these years. As early as 1840 Brownson had written: "So far as Transcendentalism is understood to be the recognition in man of the capacity of knowing truth intuitively, or of attaining to a scientific knowledge of an order of existence transcending the reach of the senses, and of which we can have no sensible experience, we are Transcendentalists. But when it is understood to mean, that feeling is to be placed above reason, dreaming above reflection, and instinctive intimation above scientific exposition; in a word, when it means the substitution of a lawless fancy for an enlightened understanding . . . we must disown it, and deny that we are Transcendentalists."* (Boston Quarterly Review, *III, pp. 322–3.*) *That Parker's book played a decisive part in Brownson's complete break with the movement is clear from his discussion of it in* The Convert (*1857*). *There Brownson says that, listening in the autumn of 1841 to the lectures which Parker later published as the first part of his book, he realized they "contained nothing but a learned and eloquent statement" of the very doctrine which he*

*had defended for many years, and which he had called "the
religion of humanity." "But," Brownson adds, "strange as it may
seem, the moment I heard that doctrine from his lips, I felt
an invincible repugnance to it, and saw, at a glance, that it was
unphilosophical and anti-religious." (Works, V, 151.)]*

W E ARE NOT a little perplexed, the moment we undertake
to analyze Mr. Parker's book, and reduce it to fundamental propositions which may be clearly apprehended and distinctly stated. It is a book of many pieces. Its author abounds
in contradictions no less than in loose and intangible statements,
and sometimes brings together in the same sentence not less than
two or three mutually contradictory systems. Nevertheless,
after much toil and pains, aided by our own familiar acquaintance with the general subject, we believe we may compress what
is systematic in the book, what the author most values, what
constitute the bases of the transcendental doctrines generally,
within the three following propositions; namely:

I. Man is the measure of truth and goodness.

II. Religion is a fact or principle of human nature.

III. All religious institutions, which have been or are, have
their principle and cause in human nature.

A single glance at these propositions reveals the character of
the system. It is sheer naturalism, and Mr. Parker himself calls
it "the natural-religious view." Its advocates, however, profess
to be religious, to be the especial friends of religion, and to have
put a final conclusion to the controversy between believers and
infidels, by having discovered a solid and imperishable foundation for religion in the permanent and essential nature of man.
Man is religious because he is man, and must be religious or
cease to be man. According to them, religion has its foundation,
not in supernatural revelation, but in human nature, and rests
for its authority, therefore, not on the veracity of God, but on

the veracity of man; and as man can neither deceive nor be deceived, it of course must be eternally and immutably true! They also affect to discover truth in all religions, and to accept it. But this does not take their system out of the category of naturalism, because, 1, they recognize no religion as having been supernaturally given; and, 2, because they acknowledge in religious institutions, which have been or are, nothing to be truth, which transcends the natural order, or which the natural faculties of man are not adequate to discover, and of whose *intrinsic* truth they are not competent to judge. All the rest they hold to be misapprehension or exaggeration of natural phenomena, or a mere symbolic way of expressing simple truths lying within the reach of natural reason. . . .

Whatever, then, the merits of the system under examination, it is naturalism,—nothing more, nothing less. The question, then, between us and transcendentalism is the old question between naturalism and supernaturalism. Is man's natural relation the only relation he sustains to his Creator? Have there been supernatural revelations, or are the so-called supernatural revelations explicable on natural principles? Do man's natural forces—that is, what he is and receives by virtue of his natural relation to God—suffice for the fulfilment of his destiny; or needs he the gracious, that is, supernatural, interposition and assistance of his Maker? These are the real questions at issue; and these questions Mr. Parker and the transcendentalists answer in favor of nature against grace, of man against God. The validity and value of their answer is, then, what we propose to examine.

With these remarks, we proceed to take up, *seriatim*, the propositions themselves. We begin with the first.

1. *Man is the Measure of Truth and Goodness.*

We do not understand the transcendentalists to assert by this proposition, that man actually knows all truth and goodness, though from many things they say we might infer this; but that man is the measure, the standard, the criterion of all truth and goodness,—the touchstone on which we are to try whatever is alleged to be true and good, and to determine whether it be true and good, or false and evil. Nor do we mean to assert that they are prepared to maintain even this in general thesis; but that they do assert it, that they everywhere imply it, and that without assuming it their whole system would be a baseless fabric, and their doctrines and speculations the sheerest absurdities. . . .

We are not ignorant that the *humanitarian* division of the transcendentalists exhort us to sink the individual and to fall back on our common humanity, and seem to teach that this common humanity is not merely that which each individual man realizes, but that it is, as it were, a mighty entity, a vast reservoir of wisdom, virtue, and strength, which individuals do not and cannot exhaust. We ourselves, especially during the interval between our rejection of eclecticism and our conversion to Christianity, following Plato, the Neo-Platonists, Leroux, and the Saint-Simonians, and some half glimpses of the teachings of the old realists, whose doctrines we did not understand, fell into this absurdity, and sought to make it appear that humanity, not as the collective mass of individuals, but as genus, as out of all individuals, has a real, an entitative existence, and can operate as subject; and that in this sense humanity is not what is common to all individuals, but a somewhat that transcends all individuals, and *makes* all individuals, manifesting itself in various degrees,—in one individual under one aspect, in another under another, and so on. An individual we regarded as a particular manifestation of a particular aspect or phase of humanity, as a particular act of an individual manifests some particular aspect or phase of the individual; and the mission of the individual we declared to be, through his whole life, the realization of his own thoughts, words, and deeds of that particular phase or aspect of humanity he represents. It was in this way we solved the old question of individuation, and found, as we supposed, a basis for the state, and *legitimated*, so to speak, individual liberty. Taking this view, we necessarily held humanity to be greater than the individual, nay, greater than all individuals together. Substantially, all transcendentalists, so far as they admit a human existence at all, do the same. They all say man is greater than men.

The common source of all our errors on this point is easily discovered;—it is in the well-known doctrine of the transcendentalists, that the possible exists, not merely as possible, but in point of fact as real, and that what is possible is altogether more perfect than the actual. What you conceive is possible; then it *is* —possible. Then you affirm that it exists, though not yet realized, —is real *in potentia*, and what is real *in potentia* is superior to what is *in actu*. Therefore, regard not the actual, but fall back on the possible. To conceal the absurdity, we gave to the possible the name of the ideal, and then said, live not in and for the actual, but in and for the ideal. All very fine, no doubt, and admirably calculated to make old men see visions, and young men and maidens dream dreams, and, what is worse, tell their dreams.

But what is *in potentia* is no more *in re* than *in actu*, for it is a contradiction in terms to call the *potential* real. Moreover, the ideal, the possible, is always below the real, the actual, because it has never in itself the force to realize or actualize itself. The power to act is below act, because it must receive what it has not, before it becomes act, or is reduced to act. Here is the fundamental error, in denying this, and assuming *potentia* to stand above *actus*,—which is the terminus or last complement of *potentia*. Now, humanity *in abstracto* is at best only man *in potentia*. To assume, then, its superiority over individuals, who are its terminus, or last complement, or that, in sinking individualized humanity and falling back on humanity as abstracted from all individuals, or rather as emancipated from all individuality, we fall back on something higher, broader, and richer, is precisely the error of placing *potentia* above *actus*, the possible above the actual. *Potentia* is void; *actus* is full. Void is therefore superior to full, emptiness to fullness! . . .

We think it not difficult now to comprehend the essential character of transcendentalism. It exhorts us to sink our personality, and abandon ourselves to the impersonal soul, the unconscious energy that underlies it. The essential characteristic of personality is reason, and therefore to sink personality is, as we have seen, practically to sink reason itself. If we discard reason, we must also discard will, for will is not simply acting from one's self as subject, nor from one's self as subject *to* an end; but from one's self as subject *propter finem*, to an end and on account of it, which is not possible without reason. Eliminate from man, that is, from what comes properly within the definition of man, reason and will, and nothing remains of man but passion, or, if you will, passion and phantasy, or imagination. At most, then, we have for the impersonal nature, on which to fall back, only passion and imagination; for passion and imagination, together with reason and will, are the whole man, all that can be covered, in any sense, by the word *man*, or by the term *human nature*. But, in order to be as liberal as possible, we will gratuitously suppose, after reason is discarded, will remains; it can remain only as a simple executive force, for that is all it is at any time. Reason discarded, it can remain only as the executor of the suggestions of passion and imagination. The plain, simple transcendental doctrine, then, is, *passion and imagination are superior to reason*. Give loose reins to passion and imagination, and your head will be filled with wilder dreams and stranger fancies than if you subject them to the surveillance and restraints of reason; and these dreams and fancies are to be regarded as superior to the dictates of reason, because these are spontaneous and the dictates of reason are personal!

Passion and imagination, or what remains of man, after the elimination of reason,—are precisely what the schoolmen call the inferior soul, and hold to be the seat of concupiscence. What Christian theology calls the superior soul is the rational nature as distinguished from the sensitive soul, or, as termed by some modern psychologists, internal sensibility, or principle of the sentiments or feelings as distinguished from sensations, or perceptions of sense. It has three faculties,—will, understanding, and memory. To make passion and imagination the superior is simply asserting the superiority of the sensitive nature over the rational. The subject now begins to open, and we approach a territory very well known. The distinction contended for is now quite intelligible, and though not properly a distinction between the personal and impersonal, yet a very real distinction, and one not now noted for the first time. It is the distinction which renders possible and intelligible that spiritual conflict which has been noted in all ages, and which every man experiences who undertakes to live a Christian life. The impersonal soul of the transcendentalists is the "carnal mind" of the Sacred Scriptures, the inferior nature, which, according to Christian faith, has been disordered by the fall, and become prone to evil and that continually,—that "old man of sin," the seat of all inordinate desires and affections,—"the flesh," which our religion commands us to "put off," to "mortify with its deeds," and to bring into subjection to the law of Jesus Christ after the inner man. This is what it is, and all that it is, and under these names it is no new acquaintance.

Now, the peculiarity, we cannot say the *originality*, of transcendentalism consists precisely in declaring the flesh superior to the spirit; this *inferior* soul, or what Christianity pronounces the inferior soul, superior to the rational soul, or what Christianity declares to be the *superior* soul; in giving as its higher nature . . . to which we are to abandon ourselves, and which we are to take. as the infallible revelation of the will of our Maker, and the measure of truth and goodness, this very carnal mind . . . against which the saint wars, which he mortifies, and through his whole life labors incessantly to subdue, to subject to reason and will. . . . It makes this struggle not only unnecessary, but wrong; and requires us, as the rule of life, to give up reason, and abandon ourselves to the solicitations of the flesh!

The mist now vanishes; and this transcendentalism, which has puzzled so many simple-minded people, becomes as plain and as unmistakable as the nose on a man's face. It has revealed no mystery, has detected no new facts or elements in human nature, but has simply called *higher* what the Gospel calls *lower*, that true and good which the Gospel calls false and evil, and *vice versa*. It would simply liberate us from the restraints of reason, and deliver us to the license of passion and imagination, free us from the struggle, and permit us to follow nature instead of commanding us to crucify it. It merely gives the lie to our blessed Saviour; and where he says, "Deny thyself," it says, "Obey thyself." It ridicules the notion that a holy life must be a life of incessant warfare against one's self, and teaches that we are to gain heaven by swimming with the current, not against it; a pleasant doctrine, and, if universally adopted and acted on, would, no doubt, produce some effects.

People who do not believe much in the modern doctrine of progress, and who are not aware that we live in the age of light, may be strongly inclined to believe that we misrepresent the transcendentalists; but they should bear in mind that it was fore-told thousands of years ago that there would come a race of men who would call the churl liberal, evil good, and bitter sweet. The doctrine we charge upon the transcendentalists is but a necessary logical inference from the principles they lay down in the passages we have quoted from their writings. Absolute religion and morality are, we presume, the highest expression of truth and goodness; and absolute religion and morality, Mr. Parker tells us, are "religion as it exists in the facts of man's nature," "what answers exactly to the religious sentiment." By sentiment, we presume also, he means sentiment, for he so calls it, defines it to be a want, and distinguishes it from cognition, discursive reason, and volition; if a sentiment, then a fact of the sensitive or inferior soul, which is the seat or principle of all the sentiments, whether good or bad. If absolute religion and morality answer exactly to the religious sentiment, or if that which answers exactly to the religious sentiment is absolute religion and morality, then the sensitive soul is their measure, and then the measure of truth and goodness.

The transcendentalists, moreover, claim to be *spiritualists*, and they call their doctrine *spiritualism*. Their impersonal soul, it is well known, they term spirit, and distinguish, on the one hand, from reason, and on the other from external sense. They pretend to have detected here an element in man, or a faculty of man's soul, which is overlooked by the rationalists and the materialists, as also by the supernaturalists, whom Mr. Parker classes with the materialists. This element or faculty is the principle of their doctrine, and that which characterizes their school. In their view it *transcends* reason and external sense, and hence their name of *transcendentalists*. They are *pneumatici*, differing from those of the old Gnostic stamp only in claiming for all men what the old Gnostics claimed for merely a select few.

Now strike out reason and external sense, and you have nothing left of man but this very sensitive soul to which you can possibly apply the term spirit; for these and it are the whole man. Therefore the transcendentalists must mean this, if they mean anything, by the spirit; for there is nothing else in man they can mean. . . .

Mr. Emerson, the real chief, or sovereign pontiff, of transcendentalism, denies in plain terms the struggle.

People, [says he] represent virtue as a struggle, and take to themselves great airs on their attainments, and the question is everywhere vexed, when a noble nature is commended, Whether the man is not better who strives with temptation? But there is no merit in the matter. Either God is there, or he is not there. We love characters in proportion as they are *impulsive* and *spontaneous*. . . . When we see a soul whose acts are all regal, graceful and pleasant as roses, we must thank God that such things can be and are, and not turn sourly on the angel, and say, "Crump is a better man with his resistance to all his native devils."—*Essays*, p. 109.

This is conclusive. Now, since the transcendentalists avowedly contemn personality, whose basis is reason, and do not condemn in any respect the sensitive soul, and since they call upon us to obey the soul, and since the sensitive soul, after personality is discarded, is all the soul there is left for us to obey, it follows necessarily that they do, intentionally or unintentionally, raise the sensitive soul over the rational, as we have alleged.

1. It may be objected to this, that the transcendentalists also call their impersonal soul *reason*, and therefore do not intend to distinguish it from the rational nature. They distinguish between reason and understanding. Understanding is the intellectual principle of sensation; reason, of spiritual cognition, and is above understanding. Reason, as understanding, they discard; reason, as the principle of spiritual cognition, of intuition, they do not discard, because it is precisely what they mean by *spirit*. We deny the validity of this distinction, which is supported by no facts alleged, or which can be alleged. Reason is the principle of understanding, and without reason man would cease not only to be rational, but to be intelligent,—for intelligence in man is not the intelligence of animals *plus* reason, but reason itself, as

is affirmed when man is affirmed to be of a rational nature. There is not in man an intelligent nature *and* a rational nature; but the intelligent nature in man is essentially and integrally rational nature. The intelligent principle is, then, one and the same, whatever the conditions of its operation, or the sphere or degree of knowledge.

2. But we may be told, again, that the transcendentalists contend that man's *whole* nature should be retained and exercised, and that his supreme good consists in the harmonious development and action of all his faculties; therefore they cannot assert the superiority of the sensitive soul alleged. We deny the conclusion; for they contend, that, though man's whole nature is to be retained and exercised,—which, by the way, is hardly consistent with what else they say,—yet all is to be retained and exercised *in subordination to the instinctive nature*, which we have identified with the sensitive soul. "We love characters," says Mr. Emerson, "in proportion as they are impulsive and spontaneous." "Absolute religion," says Mr. Parker, "is that which answers exactly to the religious *sentiment*." Instinctive, sensitive nature is evidently, then, placed above personal nature, which is identical, as we have seen, with rational nature,—and this is all our argument asserts. . . .

Mr. Parker seeks to sustain his theory of natural inspiration by alleging that God is immanent in his works, the *causa immanens* of nature, not merely the *causa transiens;* and being immanent in all, and therefore in man, is necessarily present in man to supply all man's deficiencies. But we must distinguish. If immanent as creator and sustainer of man and all beings, each in the distinctive nature he gives them, we concede his immanence; if immanent in each being as subject, we deny it. To assume that God is immanent in his creatures as the subject which acts in them and produces what are called their acts is Spinozism, a doctrine which admits no existence but God and his modes,—

and which, though unquestionably implied by transcendentalism generally, we understand Mr. Parker expressly to disavow. Moreover, it is a doctrine neither he nor the other transcendentalists can admit, without falling into gross contradictions, and refuting themselves; for they find little in the actual world they do not condemn; and yet, if they admit this doctrine, they cannot condemn anything without condemning God. If they admit God can do wrong, then they gain nothing in favor of the impersonal soul as the measure of truth and goodness by identifying it with God.

If they concede that God is not immanent in his creatures as subject, but simply as cause, creator, and sustainer, then his immanence merely creates and sustains them in their several natures,—that is, each order of being, and each individual being, in its being and distinct nature. In this case, his immanence is no pledge of the natural influx of divinity assumed. For then nothing could be received naturally of God but the nature itself. Whatever more may be received must be supernaturally received, through faith or elevation of nature, which the transcendentalists cannot admit.

Mr. Parker's doctrine on this point seems to be that man's faculties open on God, and in proportion as he opens them God flows in, and man may thus be strong with the strength of omnipotence, wise with the wisdom of omniscience, and good with the goodness of infinite goodness, and all this as naturally as the lungs inhale the atmosphere, or the stomach secretes the gastric juice. But this is absurd; for it implies that the finite subject may appropriate infinite attributes, the infinite God himself, and live and act with infinite power, wisdom, and goodness. It would imply that the infinite is communicable, and communicable to the finite, without absorbing the finite, leaving it finite still, and a finite personality! The immanence of God in his works is a pledge that they will be upheld, and is a ground of hope, since it implies that he is ever present to afford us the supernatural aid we need, and in a supernatural manner, if we seek this aid in the way and through the channels he has appointed; but this is all, and it is nothing to the purpose of the transcendentalists. . . .

We know now the transcendental rule of faith and practice. We have ascertained its *method;* and knowledge of this rule, of this method, throws no little light over the whole subject of transcendentalism. The more difficult part of our labor is accomplished; we shall be able to dispose of the two remaining propositions with comparative ease. But we must reserve the consideration of these to a future occasion. . . .

DIGNITY OF HUMAN
REASON
[1857]

[*The essays of Brownson which have been cited as evidence of his ontologism are too numerous to be represented adequately here. Nor is it any easier to represent Brownson's many answers to the charge of ontologism. The following essay develops Brownson's intuitive method, and indicates his defense of the method against contemporary criticism. It is the first of two articles reviewing H. L. C. Maret's* Philosophie et religion, *Paris, 1856. The complete text of the review articles is in* Works, *I, 438–89. A fuller development of Brownson's philosophical thought will be found in such essays as "The Existence of God" (1852), "Schools of Philosophy" (1854), and "The Problem of Causality" (1855) in* Works, Volume I, *and in "Ontologism and Psychologism" (1874) in Volume II.*

Briefly, ontologism teaches that the human mind has by its very nature a direct and immediate intuition of God's existence, whereas according to the philosophy of Aristotle and St. Thomas the mind knows God by natural reason mediately and analogically. The studies by Raemers and Farrell cited in the preface to this section treat in detail Brownson's relation to ontologism.]

MANY WORTHY PERSONS, we are aware, hesitate to adopt the intuitive method, because they fear that it would require them to maintain that we can have the intuitive vision of God enjoyed by the Saints in Heaven by our simple natural light, which all our theologians teach is possible only by the light of glory or *ens supernaturale*. We respect their hesitation, but their fear is unfounded. No man in his senses maintains that the intuitive vision of God enjoyed by the Blest is possible by the simple light of natural reason, or even by natural reason illumined by the supernatural light of faith. We assert by the natural intuition of God nothing of the sort. That vision is intrinsic, the view of God as he is in himself, his own interior life and essence; but our natural intuition of God is extrinsic, apprehensive, not comprehensive, and is a view of God as he is in relation to our intellect, as the principle and immediate object of our intelligence, not as he is in himself, or in his essence. We see him only as the Idea, the Intelligible, the type and cause of creatures, and therefore as the principle and necessary element of our intelligence. This element to which is reducible what philosophers call necessary ideas, necessary truths, first truths, eternal truths, &c., is intuitively presented, for without it there is and can be no intellectual operation, and in point of fact no human intellect itself; and hence it is that we are never able to stop with the finite and the contingent, but are obliged, as the inductive philosophers allege, to assert at every moment the infinite and the necessary, not as an abstraction, a mental conception, but as an objective reality. All the reasonings ever adopted or that ever can be adopted to prove the existence of God demand, as their principle, the conception of the infinite and the necessary, and this conception, if formed by the mind from the generalization of the finite and the contingent, without intuition of real and necessary being, is an abstraction, and, like all abstractions, objectively null.

The failure to recognize this intuition is what ruined the dialectic philosophy of the seventeenth century, which Père Gratry is laboring so enthusiastically to revive, and the logical consequences of which are to be seen in the Sensism and Atheism which followed, and from which we are even now only slowly recovering. That philosophy overlooks intuition and founds all on conceptions defined to be modes or affections of the subject.

Hence the God it asserts is simply a mental conception, an abstraction, and no real, living God at all. Descartes no doubt labored hard to prove that the idea in the mind of the infinite and the necessary, is not a purely mental conception, but his success did not respond to his industry or his good intention. Conceptions can give only conceptions,—$o \times o = o$. As a man, as a Christian, Descartes believed, no doubt, in a living God; but as a philosopher he asserted only an abstract God.

Others, again, hesitate to adopt the intuitive method, because they fail to observe that nobody pretends that we can know without reflection, study, or instruction, that the Idea, the Intelligible, the necessary entity, or real and necessary being, affirmed to us in intuition, is God, or that it can be proved to be God without reasoning, both inductive and deductive, that is, without dialectics and the syllogism. No one thinks of superseding the necessity of reasoning on the subject, and we certainly do not dispute, in its place and with its proper conditions, the validity of the reasoning of St. Anselm, St. Thomas, or even the Bridgewater Treatises in proof of the existence of God. We only say that to the validity of that reasoning a prior fact, tacitly assumed by it, but of which it takes no account, must be recognized, namely, the intuition of the Intelligible, the infinite, the necessary, the perfect, that is, real and necessary being, the intelligible element of all thought and the principle of all reasoning. That must be intuitively presented, but we do not say that we do or that we must know intuitively that it is God. St. Anselm concludes the existence of God from the idea of the most perfect being, than which nothing greater can be conceived. If he stops there, he concludes only an abstract God, and offers no refutation of Atheism. St. Thomas sees this, and hence refutes and rejects St. Anselm's argument, as he understands it. The conclusion is valid only on the condition that the idea is taken to be the intuition of most perfect or real and necessary being. Taking the idea as an intuition, the argument is conclusive; taking it as a mental conception, or as a conception formed from the intuition of the finite, the imperfect, or the contingent alone, it is not so much as an ingenious sophism. St. Anselm, Descartes, and all Père Gratry's dialectic philosophers, fail to recognize distinctly the fact that conceptions or ideas without intuitions are null, are abstractions, and affirm no reality beyond the human mind itself. This point Kant has forever settled, and it is really one of the most important steps made by modern philosophy.

Aristotle, and St. Thomas after him, concludes the existence of God from the necessity of a prime mover or of the actual to reduce the potential to act. We accept the argument, providing you concede us intuition of the principle on which it rests, namely, the *necessity* alleged. This necessity is, in the argument, the universal, and must itself be intuitive, or nothing can be concluded from it. But this necessity itself, what is it? Does it exist only in the mind, or does it exist out of it? If only in the mind, it is subjective, and your conclusion contains no objective reality. If out of the mind, it must be being, real and necessary being, and intuition of it is intuition of that which is God, therefore, in reality, of God himself. Either then we have intuition of real and necessary being, which is God, or his existence cannot be proved by natural reason, since every conceivable argument for his existence demands that intuition as its principle. No doubt, the judgment, real and necessary being is, and the judgment, God is, or real and necessary being is God, are formally or subjectively distinguishable; and it is precisely on this fact that the conceptualists found their objections to the intuitionists. The judgment, real and necessary being is, is an intuitive judgment; the judgment, real and necessary being is God, or God is, is not an intuitive, but a reflective judgment. Hence as this formal judgment is obtained only by reflection, by reasoning, by argument, the conceptualists assert truly, from the psychological point of view, that the existence of God is not intuitively given. Not intuitively given as a conception, conceded, for no conception is intuitive; but not really given, or given intuitively as an objective reality we deny; for objectively, in the real order, the judgment, real and necessary being is, and the judgment God is, are one and the same, since all theologians agree that God is real and necessary being—*ens necessarium et reale*, or *ens simpliciter*, as distinguished from *ens secundum quid*,—creature, or created existence; and this is all that the intuitionist ever dreams of asserting, when he asserts that God affirms himself to us in direct and immediate intuition. We never pretend that he affirms himself, conceptually as God, but really, as real and necessary being, as the Idea, or the Intelligible. The difficulty of the conceptualists or psychologists arises from the fact that they confound intuition with conception, and will not allow that anything is given in the intuition, which is not formally embraced in the conception. In other words, they confound the intuitive order with the reflective, and the ontological with the psychological.

The conceptualists would be relieved of this and many other difficulties, if they could for once place themselves at the point of view of the intuitionists or ontologists, or if they would take the pains to understand before attempting to refute them. Ontologists profess to speak according to the order of things, not according to the order of conceptions. When Gioberti speaks of the ideal formula, defines it to be *ens creat existentias*, and calls it the *primum philosophicum*, he speaks of the real, intuitive formula, not of the conceptual. He presents this formula as the *primum* both of things and of science. It should be noted that the formula in question is asserted as the ideal or real formula, and the real not the conceptional principle, the non-empirical not the empirical element of all human thought. The formula is what Kant would call a synthetic judgment *a priori*, not an empirical judgment, but a judgment which precedes all experience, and is the necessary condition of all experience, or that which renders experience possible. It enters into all experience as its ideal principle and basis. It is at once the *primum* of things and the *primum* of science, the *primum ontologicum* and the *primum psychologicum*,—ontological in that it is real and necessary being affirming itself, and psychological in that it is real and necessary being affirming itself to our intellect, which it in affirming itself creates and constitutes. It is the permanent ideal element of all our knowledge, but not therefore does it follow that every conception, every fact of experience, takes the form, Being creates existence, or existences. Perhaps the majority of men never in their whole lives conceive it distinctly, or distinguish it from the facts of experience.

The ideal formula is intended, by those who defend it, to express the intuitive principle of all our judgments, the Divine judgment which all our judgments copy or imitate. As the ideal, the intelligible, it is the basis of all our knowledge, and enters into all our judgments; but not therefore is it the empirical form of all our judgments, nor are all our judgments intuitive. It is not *our* judgment at all, but is precisely that in our judgment which is not ours. Our judgments demand it, presuppose it, but in so far as ours they are formed by reflection, by contemplation, by experience.

The conceptualists find it difficult to understand the intuitive method because they do not regard ideas as objective, or if they do, they fail to perceive their identity with the Divine Intelligence, and therefore with God himself. They regard them as affections or products of our intellect, or, it may be, as something distinct from God which he implants in our minds, and therefore termed innate. They think that they sufficiently explain the matter by saying that they are furnished by the *in-*

tellectus agens, or active intellect, asserted by the Peripatetics. But what is this *intellectus agens* itself? Is it our intellect, the noetic faculty of the human soul? Then the ideas, the intelligibles, the necessary truths it furnishes, are products of the subject, the mind's own products or affections, not objects apprehended by it, and therefore introduce us to no objective reality at all. Is the *intellectus agens* the Divine Intellect, presenting us the necessary ideas in presenting itself? Then you must accept the intuitive method, and the very ideal formula you seek to cover with ridicule. You assert the very doctrine you labor to refute. Is it neither one nor the other,—the *ens in genere* of Rosmini, the impersonal reason of Cousin, which is Divine and yet not God? But what is neither God nor creature is not at all. Between God and creature there is and can be no middle existence, and no middle term but the creative act of God. What is not God is creature, and what is not creature is God. There is no *mundus logicus* between them. The possible world exists only in God, and what exists in God is God himself. The world of abstractions which is sometimes talked about as if it were neither God nor creature, but something independent of both, and even governing both, is, in so far as neither one nor the other, nothing. There are no abstractions in nature, and abstractions are simply the conceptions of our own minds operating on intuition. The scholastics, though not careful always to note this fact, do not maintain anything to the contrary, and usually take it for granted. St. Thomas, if we understand him, does not regard the *intellectus agens* as a created intellect, but as our participation of the Divine, uncreated Intellect, that is to say, God himself in his relation to our intellect, or as we say, God as the Intelligible. It is not every man who calls himself a Thomist that understands St. Thomas.

But our psychologists proceed on the supposition that in the facts of knowledge, man, supposing him to be sustained in existence, suffices for himself, and they never understand that the Divine concurrence as the Intelligible is as necessary in order to enable him to know, as is the Divine concurrence as Being in order to enable him to exist. As profoundly as many of them have investigated the conditions of knowledge on the side of the subject, they have forgotten generally to investigate them on the side of the object. They make all facts of knowledge purely human, and leave God out of the account, and they, furthermore, make them all purely psychological, and recognize no activity in their production, but the activity of the soul itself. Here is their capital mistake,—a mistake as capital as would be that of regarding the soul as an independent existence. There can no more be a fact of knowledge without an objective activity, than there can be without a subjective activity. This is recognized by Cousin, and has been proved, although abused, by Pierre Leroux, and in proving it, he has made a contribution to modern philosophy that his wildness and extravagance in regard to other matters have prevented from being generally appreciated according to its merits. In consequence of overlooking the activity of the Intelligible in the fact of intuition, and placing all the activity on the side of the subject in intuition as well as in conception, the psychologists have failed to recognize the objectivity of ideas, which Plato had long ago clearly established, and which Aristotle really accepts, though he rejects the term *idea*, and substitutes that of *principle*.

We are not writing for tyros in philosophy, and therefore do not deem it necessary to enumerate the ideas and principles which compose the ideal or intelligible world. Everybody likely to read our philosophical articles knows that there is in some form and in some manner present to our minds a non-sensible world, a world of necessary ideas, or eternal truths, which enters into all our intellectual operations, and is the principle and basis of all our sciences, physical, metaphysical, and ethical. We can-

not speak of an effect without thinking cause, of a particular cause
without thinking a universal cause; of the contingent without
thinking the necessary; of the finite without thinking the infinite; of beautiful things without thinking beauty, that by which
all beautiful things are beautiful—the beautiful in itself; of good
actions without thinking goodness, that by which all good actions are good, the good in itself, and so in many other instances,
which will readily occur to the reader. The question to be settled
is, what are these absolute, these necessary ideas? Are they
objects of the human mind, realities existing independent of it?
Or, are they the necessary forms or conceptions of our understanding? The psychologists or conceptualists hold the latter,
and this we regard as their fundamental error, an error held by
Abélard, and opposed by Guillaume de Champeaux and the old
Realists. Plato held them to be objects of the noetic faculty of
the soul, really existing independently of the human mind. This
was the doctrine of St. Augustine, of St. Anselm, and in reality
of St. Thomas, although St. Thomas seems at times to regard
them as representatives of the objective realities rather than as
those realities themselves. Balmes regards them generally as
representatives of the object, seldom as the object itself. He appears to have been led to take this view by the old Peripatetic
doctrine, that the soul knows only in itself, and therefore never
sees immediately things themselves, and sees them at all only
through their representatives, their *species* or *phantasms*. This
Peripatetic doctrine seems to have originated in the truth, not
well comprehended by Aristotle and his followers, that created
or contingent things are not intelligible in or of themselves, and
hence cannot be apprehended by the mind without an intelligible medium. This we hold to be true, but not precisely in the
Aristotelian sense. Reid dispelled, forever, the Peripatetic
phantasms, and proved that in sensibles we perceive the things
themselves, not their images, phantasms, or immaterial repre-

sentatives. Malebranche, after Plato and St. Augustine and others, had previously done the same thing in regard to the non-sensible world. The things supposed to be represented by the intelligible species, or by ideas, are themselves intelligibles, and therefore cognizable or evident *per se*. They are all resolvable, as far as we are now considering them, into real and necessary being, and real and necessary being is intelligible by its own light, and all that is intelligible by its own light. It needs only to be presented to the mind to be beheld. There is no need and no room between it and our mind for representative ideas. The being itself is as intelligible as can be its idea or representation. Nothing can make it plainer, more intelligible, or bring it into closer contact with the mind. In a word the realities, if realities, represented by the ideas we speak of, are themselves as near and as open to the mind as the ideas or representatives. The *intellectus agens*, supposed to furnish the representative ideas, if not the human intellect, as St. Thomas certainly did not hold it to be, is itself the idea, and the idea is not the representative of the intelligible reality, but that reality itself. The ideas are in that intellect, and it presents them in presenting itself intuitively to our intellect, and hence the *intellectus agens* of Aristotle and the schoolmen is identically the Intelligible, or God affirming himself intuitively as the Intelligible, as maintained by Gioberti, and virtually by Cousin, who represents these ideas to be constitutive of the impersonal or objective reason, which he calls Divine. The only error of Cousin on this point is, first, in not sufficiently distinguishing the objective from the subjective reason, and second, in hesitating to assert the identity of the objective reason with the Divine Intelligence, and therefore with God himself. What is necessary to place philosophy on a solid basis is to explode entirely the representative theory, invented by Aristotle to reconcile his maxim, *nihil est in intellectu, quod prius non fuerit in sensu,* with the undeniable truth in the

Platonic theory, and retained by St. Thomas, in his unsuccessful attempt to harmonize Aristotle and St. Augustine. . . .

The intuitive faculty is the faculty of intelligence itself, and conception, reflection, reasoning, judging, comparing, abstracting, &c., are only the different modes in which we apply this faculty; but intuition itself is a fact, not a faculty, and it is not, like conception, primarily a psychological fact. It is not by our faculty taking the initiative that the object is beheld. The immediate intuitive object is always and everywhere the Intelligible, and the intuition is the Intelligible affirming itself to us, not we affirming immediately the Intelligible. In intuition it is not the human mind that by its own inherent power immediately seizes hold of the Intelligible, but the Intelligible immediately affirming itself and thereby constituting our intelligence. Hence the intuition is primarily an ontological fact, though affirming simultaneously the ontological and the psychological. M. Maret does not seem to us to place this ontological character of the fact of intuition in so clear and so strong a light as is desirable, and we seem after all to detect in his expression, if not in his thought, a reminiscence of that psychologism against which he so justly protests. The fact is, the Intelligible is God creating, and in the fact of intuition he creates our intellect, or makes it an actually existing intellect, capable of acting, of apprehending. Our intellect is created, constituted in the fact of intuition, and cannot be conceived as acting or even as existing prior to it. In like manner as we depend on God, as being, for our existence, do we depend on him, as the intelligible, for our intelligence, and he is as immanent and must be as immanent in us under the one relation as the other. This is what is implied in the scholastic doctrine of the *intellectus agens*, what Balmes himself really teaches, and what all the philosophers and theologians mean when they speak of reason as a participation in the Divine Reason. . . .

SCIENCE AND THE
SCIENCES
[1863]

[*Aside from his essay on the "Pretensions of Phrenology,"
which appeared in the* Boston Quarterly Review *in 1839, and
in which he charged the phrenologists with confusing physiology
and philosophy, Brownson devoted little attention to the new
scientific works until relatively late in his career. It was only
after the appearance of Darwin's* Origin of Species (1859),
*when the Victorian debate over "science and religion" entered
its acute phase, that Brownson felt called upon to speak. Beginning with the essay printed here, he went on in succeeding years
to review numerous scientific essays, among them works by Darwin, Huxley, Spencer, Lubbock, and Draper.*

*Brownson was no obscurantist. His profound respect for logic
and for true scientific method led him to receive many of the
new discoveries in geology and biology with enthusiasm. Moreover, he saw that they could not be reconciled with many received opinions as to Biblical chronology, and he was as much
concerned to distinguish between the authoritative teachings of
the Catholic Church and the opinions of certain theologians, as
to distinguish between genuine science and the opinions of scien-
tists. Brownson saw clearly the philosophical assumptions concealed in the work of Huxley and Spencer, for example, even
when they professed to speak as biologists. He endeavored to
distinguish between the data and method of theology, philosophy, and the special sciences, and to make clear the legitimate
domain of each. It was, Brownson emphasized, the function
of the special sciences to treat second causes, not first causes,
which were in the domain of philosophy. Thus he wrote in "Faith
and the Sciences" (1867): "We do not deduce our physics from*

*our metaphysics; but our metaphysics or philosophy gives the
law to the inductive or empirical sciences, and prescribes the
bounds beyond which they cannot pass without ceasing to be
sciences.*" (Works, *IX*, 270.)

The full text of the essay that follows, which appeared in
Brownson's Quarterly Review *for July, 1863, is in* Works, *IX,
254–268. It need hardly be remarked that the title might also
have been given as "Philosophy and the Special Sciences." Mari-
tain's chapter so entitled, in his* Introduction to Philosophy
(*London, Sheed & Ward, 1930*), *can profitably be read in connection with Brownson's essay.*]

THERE ARE MANY CATHOLICS, and very good Catholics too,
we learn from the *New York Tablet*, who care very little
for the objections to our faith drawn from the discoveries, or alleged discoveries, and inductions of modern science, especially
the science of geology, and regard it as a waste of time even to
listen to them. There can be, they say, no conflict, if both are
true, between faith and science. We know our faith is from God,
and that it is true, and therefore that whatever science conflicts
with it is false science, and should be dismissed without cere-
mony, as an impudent pretender. There is, no doubt, truth in
this argument, and we might justly content ourselves with it if
we had to deal only with sciolists and cavilers, or if all Catholics
were good and staunch Catholics like those described by the
Tablet; if there were no weak Catholics; if there were no non-
Catholics; if Catholics had no interest in science and owed no
duties to civilization; if only the whole needed a physician; or
if charity were a vice or weakness, and not a Christian virtue.
The argument is conclusive for all those who care nothing for
science or civilization, for human intelligence and social well-
being, and whose faith having been entertained without reason,
no reason can disturb; but these Catholics, however numerous
and respectable they may be, are not all the world, nor all who

are Catholics, and their wants are not the only wants to be consulted. . . .

The argument is, also, one that can be retorted, and used with as much practical effect against faith as against science. There can, if both are true, be no conflict between science and faith. We know our science is true, and therefore that your faith, so far as it conflicts with it, is a false faith, an impudent pretender. It will be difficult to persuade the man of science that the argument is not as valid for him as it is for you, or even to satisfy all who are inside of the church that it is not a fair retort. Few Catholics, we apprehend, can see their faith clearly contradicted by the alleged discoveries and inductions of science without being more or less disturbed; and many, we know, have been led to abandon their faith by objections drawn from the sciences, which they had no scientific means of refuting. . . . Science, or what passes for science, is, and for a long time has been, *extra ecclesiasm*, and in its spirit and tendency *contra ecclesiam*. The public opinion of the scientific world is against us, and carries away not a few of our own children, and prevents those not in the church from ever listening to our argument in her favor.

It is certainly true that science does not and never can conflict with the revelation of God, and whenever an apparent conflict arises we must always conclude that either what is alleged as science is not science, but the opinion and conjectures of scientific men; or that what passes for faith is, after all, only the opinion or conjectures of theologians. . . . Yet it is well to bear in mind that the certainty of faith neither objectively nor subjectively surpasses the certainty of science. Men have been able to deny the true faith, which they have once believed; no man ever denies or abandons what he sees and knows to be scientifically true. The believer who finds his science contradicting his faith, yields his faith rather than his science; for, in such a case, to continue to believe would be to cease to reason, would be to deny the very intellect, without which not even faith would be possible.

Then, again, we must bear in mind that, though faith and science can never be in contradiction, yet much that passes for faith may be in contradiction with science, and much that passes for science may be in contradiction with faith. This contradiction, indeed, affects neither what is really faith nor what is really science, but in minds not sufficiently instructed to draw sharply, on the one hand, the line between what is faith and what is only theological opinion, and, on the other, between what is science and what is only the opinion or conjecture of scientific men, it has the inevitable effect of creating, on the one side, a prejudice against science and, on the other, a prejudice against faith. Hence the *good* Catholics, of whom the *Tablet* speaks, are really opposed to all scientific investigations, to all exercise of reason, and seek their only natural support for faith in ignorance and pious affection. It is therefore the church comes to be looked upon as the enemy of intelligence, as in some sense an institution for the perpetuation of ignorance and diffusion of general stupidity. She thus loses her hold on the intelligence of the age, on a large portion of the free, independent, ingenuous, and cultivated young men, even in her own communion, and fails almost entirely to command the respect or the attention of a similar class brought up in heterodoxy or unbelief. Therefore it is that the modern world has lapsed into unbelief, and remains outside of the church and bitterly prejudiced against her.

We owe it to the generous and noble youth growing up in the church, and who, as things go, are sure one of these days of being found among her enemies, to these immortal souls whom our Lord hath redeemed with his precious blood, to show them what we are constantly telling them is true, namely, that science never is and never can be in conflict with faith; that there really is no conflict between what we are required by our church to receive as the word of God, or hold as divine faith, and real science, whether physical or metaphysical, whether ethical or historical. . . . We must make ourselves masters of science, not simply as it was before the flood, or as it was in the ages of barbarism, but as it is now, as held by the recognized masters of today, and thus gain the ability to meet the scientific on their own ground. We must not, in order to save their faith, discourage our youth from cultivating either science or the sciences, or content ourselves with merely declaiming against modern science as anti-Catholic, as infidel, and with refuting it with a condemnation pronounced by authority against it, or declaring it *contra fidem*. We must go further, and meet it scientifically, with superior science, and refute it, where it errs, on scientific principles, by scientific reasons.

It is not enough to show that what passes for science is in contradiction with systems constructed by eminent theologians, which have widely obtained in the church, and which are still held by multitudes in her communion without censure or reproof; for theologians, even the most eminent, are men and fallible as all men are, and it is well known that there are opinions in the church which are not the opinions of the church, —*sententiae in ecclesia,* not *sententiae ecclesiae.* We must either show theologically that what is contradicted is not of faith, and has never been taught as of faith by the church in her official teaching, or scientifically that what contradicts is not science, or no just induction from the real facts in the case. . . .

There can be no question that Catholics have lost the vantageground they once held, and lost it through their own fault. To a fearful extent, they have failed to comprehend their mission, and proved unfaithful to their trust. They have incurred the reproach of our Lord, that of failing to "discern the signs of the times." They have in their practice too often confounded the human with the divine, and done evil by endeavoring to give to political institutions and scientific theories and opinions of an ignorant and semi-barbarous age the stability and immutability which belong only to the church of God, or to Catholic faith. Faith is stable, invariable, permanent; opinion is fickle, variable, transitory. But we have held on to opinions in the church and associated with faith, though confessedly human, and staked as far as possible, the Catholic cause on their maintenance. When advancing science assails them we cry out infidelity, and instead of calmly re-examining them, and modifying them as demanded by the new light thrown on them by the investigations and discoveries of the scientific, we declaim against the arrogant pretensions of the cultivators of science, and get off any number of wise saws against the uncertainty of science, the weakness of human reason, and the folly and sin of setting up its conclusions above the word of God, forgetting that what we are defending is itself only human opinion in the church, not the divine faith the church teaches. Hence is created a public opinion hostile to the church, and which, as against her, is unjust, and wholly unwarranted. This hostile public opinion, a mere prejudice as against the church, and yet not wholly unfounded as against Catholics, tends to keep the heterodox and unbelieving out of the way of salvation, and to deprive them of the divine light of the gospel. . . .

We owe this, finally, to science itself. We must not suppose because we have the revelation of the eternal things of God, are Catholic believers, and seeking eternal rest in heaven, that we are withdrawn from the affairs of this world, and that we have no concern with society and its interests, or with science and civilization. God has not made it necessary that the great majority of mankind should be heretics or infidels in order to take care of the earth, and leave us believers free to devote ourselves solely to ascetic exercises and the salvation of our souls. This world has its place in the Christian economy, and is God's world, not Satan's. The earth, according to the Copernican system, is one of the celestial bodies. Natural society is not our end, but it is as necessary to it as the cosmos is to palingenesia. Civilization is initial religion. Science is an essential element of civilization, which is the supremacy of faith and knowledge, of intelligence and love, over ignorance, rudeness, barbarism, and superstition. If we as Catholics have no duties to civilization, pray, tell us who have? If we are not bound to labor for its progress, who is? If we neglect modern civilization, what right have we to stand and declaim against it as heretical or infidel? If we denounce science, or refuse to cultivate it, what right have we to complain that it becomes our enemy instead of our friend and ally? . . .

Nevertheless, though we urge upon Catholics the duty of laboring for the continuous progress of civilization, and of making themselves able to meet and master the scientific on their own special ground, yet we are far from accepting as science all that passes for science, or from conceding that there has been in our times anything like that wonderful progress in science or the sciences, which is very generally asserted. Modern cultivators of science have pushed their investigations far into the material order, and amassed a considerable body of tolerably well-ascertained facts in the history of the globe and its inhabitants, but these facts, though of great value to science, indispensable to it, if you will, are not themselves science. Science does not consist in the simple observation of facts and inductions therefrom; but in their explanation and co-ordination under the dialectic law of the universe, which has not been done, and cannot be done on the so-called Baconian method, the method modern science boasts of adopting and rigidly following. . . .

The error of our men of science is not in adopting the Baconian method, but in adopting it as an exclusive method, and in attempting by it alone to attain to science. That method begins by the study of phenomena, and gives us at best only an arbitrary classification of appearances. But the simple study and classification of phenomena is not science, for the excellent reason that nothing exists as pure phenomenon or appearance. Appearance without something that appears is nothing, a sheer nullity. There is no phenomenon without its noumenon, no appearance without that which appears, no particular without the universal, no mimesis without methexis, no individual without the genus or species, no universe without God; and Kant, after Leibnitz, the greatest of German philosophers, has proved once for all that the second series of terms can never, either by way of deduction or of induction, be rationally concluded from the first; that neither by way of deduction nor of induction is God obtainable from the universe, the methexic from the mimetic, the universal from the particular, the noumenon from the phenomenon. This is the real significance of that little understood and much misunderstood work, the *Critik der reinen Vernunft*. . . .

The fault of modern science is in separating,—not simply distinguishing, but separating,—in its method the contingent from the necessary, the empirical from the ideal, or the mimetic from the methexic, and hence its inductions and generalizations are nothing but unscientific and arbitrary classifications of phenomena or particulars. Our complaint of the modern cultivators of science, whether in or out of the church, is that they have no philosophy, as our pretended philosophers have no theology. It is our complaint of the modern world itself. Our age has no philosophy, and having no philosophy it has no genuine science. We have separated the sciences from philosophy, that is, from science, and philosophy from theology, reason from revelation, and have therefore been compelled to attempt the construction of science and the sciences empirically, by the study and classification of particulars. We have thus eliminated from the science we study every ideal or non-contingent element, and attempted to explain the universe with the contingent alone, without God or his creative act, as may be seen in the *Cosmos* of Alexander von Humboldt, and in the positivism of Auguste Comte.

All truth is in relation. All things exist in the real synthesis instituted by the creative act of God, and nothing can be truly seen, observed, and known except in the real relations, or the relations in which it actually exists. Even what we call facts, cannot be understood, or represented, cannot be seen, as they are, detached from these relations, taken in detail, and studied in their isolation, because as isolated, detached, they are no facts at all. Hence the science of geology, zoology, physiology, philology, ethnology, ethics, or history can never be completed and mastered as a separate and detached science. Each of these sciences, to be successfully studied, must be studied in its real relations, and not one of them can deserve the name of science, if constructed by the effort to rise from the particular to the universal. . . .

What we insist upon is that the human mind never has its normal action when compelled by false or exclusive theories to operate with only a small portion of the light furnished it. We found not science on revelation, but we maintain that it is impossible to attain to the true system of the universe without the light of revelation. We demand the free normal action of reason, but reason never does and never can have its free normal action, when left to itself alone, with no aid from the revealed word of God. In all that is contingent, reason has need of experience, observation, experiment, investigation; but with these alone, we can never rise above the empirical, or attain to scientific results. . . . Ideal science—philosophy,—and revelation are both necessary to the successful cultivation of the sciences; and the reason why the sciences make so little real progress, why they are so uncertain, and why they are received with so much distrust by metaphysicians and theologians, is that the men who cultivate them insist on cultivating them as separate and independent sciences, and will accept no aid from philosophy or from faith. Descartes ruined philosophy when he separated it from theology, and made it a creation of reason isolated from faith; Bacon ruined the sciences as sciences, when he separated them from philosophy or ideal science and made them purely empirical. Facts or one side of facts may have been examined, and the scientific men of today have no doubt, in their possession a larger mass of materials for the construction of the sciences, than had their predecessors, but they have less science than had the great medieval doctors and professors. St. Thomas had more science than Sir Charles Lyell, or Professor Owen. The recent work of Sir Charles on the *Antiquity of Man,* as well as that of Darwin on the *Origin of Species,* shows not the progress, but the deterioration of science. The same thing is shown by Agassiz in his elaborate essay on *Classification,* and by the trouble naturalists have to settle the proper classification of man. The naturalists are unwearied in their investigations, and shrink from no sacrifice to advance their respective sciences, but we meet not one of their works that does not prove that they have lost the true key to the scientific sense of the universe. They are men whose ability, whose patience, whose labors we respect; they do all that men can do with their method; they do much for which we are grateful to them, and we are by no means among those who detract from their merits, or denounce them as the enemies of religion; but we must tell them that they will never, in the way they proceed, attain'to the science to which their lives are so generously devoted. . . .

Yet we are not asserting revelation as a foreign authority, or insisting that the naturalists, or physicists, are in their own departments to bow to the *dicta* of the metaphysicians. We would impose no fetters on reason, no trammels on science; for the assertion of revelation as a trammel on reason, or philosophy as a restraint on science, would be to assert that very separation we complain of, that very divorce of religion and civilization which Bacon and Descartes so successfully inaugurated, and from which all modern society now suffers. What we assert is the synthesis of religion and civilization, of revelation and science, of faith and reason. The human mind operates in all, and operates freely, according to its own intrinsic laws. Faith does not restrain reason in matters of science; does not say to it, Thus far, but no further; but bids it use all the light it has, and aids it to go further than by its own light it could go. We are not contending that reason should cease to be reason, or that reason should close her eyes, fold her hands, and fetter her feet, but that she keep both of her eyes open, and use both of her hands, and both of her feet. We do not wish her to extinguish her own light and envelop herself in darkness, in order to see by the light of revelation. If to attain to true science reason needs immediate intuition of principles and the supernatural revelation of the superintelligible, it is reason that receives and uses them. In the field of science as distinguished from that of faith, revelation is adjutative rather than imperative. Its light and that of reason coalesce and shine as one light. The naturalist studies man, for instance, as an animal, and can give no scientific account of him, and is at a loss how or where to class him, whether in a distinct order of animals by himself, or in the family of baboons. This must be so, because man is not a pure animal, and cannot be classed as such. We know from revelation that he is composed of body and soul, or body and spirit, and that the animal in him is the animal transformed. The animal when separated from the soul or spirit is not a living, but a dead animal. Take this fact from revelation, not as a dogma, unless you please, but as a theorem, and you will find all the facts you can observe in the case harmonize with it, and tend to confirm it. So universally,

in every department of science. The key to the scientific classification and explanation of the phenomena of nature is in the
superintelligible, and is furnished only by supernatural revelation.

It is because revelation places the mind in the true position,
or gives it the true point of departure, for the study of nature,
and enables the naturalists or physicists to pursue their investigations scientifically, according to a rule, not at random, that we
so strenuously urge upon Catholics the duty of taking the sciences into their own hands. They and they only can cultivate
them scientifically, for they and they only have the revelation
of God in its unity and integrity, and occupy a position from
which the universe can be seen as it is. . . . What we must do
is to combine our faith and science, unite, without confounding
them in our method, the light of revelation and the light of
reason. Were we to do this as did the great Greek and Latin
fathers, and as did the more eminent medieval doctors and professors, we could soon, with the vast body of facts or materials
accumulated by modern students and at our disposal, heal the
deplorable schism between faith and reason, revelation and science; reunite what should never have been separated, and render civilization really Catholic. We could place the public opinion of the civilized world once more on the side of the church,
and our youth would grow up believers, and demand reasons
for *not* believing instead as now of demanding reasons *for* believing. This is an end worthy of the noblest and most earnest
efforts of Catholics. Let them not, we pray them, lose sight of it.

Religion

RELIGION

A BRIEF SKETCH of the steps in Brownson's conversion to the Catholic Church is to be found in the general introduction, where I have emphasized the unique part that his social, political, and philosophical speculations played in his approach to the Church. Some of the essays on these themes are included in other sections of this volume. Among these, the essay on "Transcendentalism," though written after his conversion, and "New Views" are of first importance. In the following section, "The Mediatorial Life of Jesus" represents a significant stage in his religious thought prior to conversion, though numerous other essays, like "Leroux on Humanity" (1842), "No Church, No Reform" (1844), and "The Church Question" (1844), might be included.

Because his conversion so nearly coincided with Newman's, close comparisons of the first years of both in the Church and the methods by which they studied and defended Catholicity could be of immense value, but no such studies have yet been made. Brownson's criticism of Newman's *Development of Christian Doctrine,* for example, is illuminated by a study of how Brownson abandoned his own approaches to the Church, and turned immediately to the study of scholastic philosophy. The complete break with his own past modes of thought irked him, as he makes clear in *The Convert* and elsewhere, and something of his resentment may have found its way into his insistence that Newman follow the same course.

The question of originality, in the ordinary sense, does not, of course, enter into a judgment of Brownson's religious thought after his conversion. What he attempted was a work of recovery and assimilation, in a period when the Catholic theological and liturgical revival was still far in the future. That he should be called upon to write on the most difficult theological problems as a recent convert and a layman makes his contribution in many ways a remarkable one. His work as a Catholic journalist is marked by an unflagging effort to understand the traditional teaching of the Church, and to interpret the significance of this teaching for the individual and society. He was willing—some would say imprudently willing—to confront the most difficult problems in his reviews of contemporary theological works. Moreover, his practice of reviewing not only Catholic but also Protestant theological works, evaluating both by norms which he was himself in the process of making intellectually his own, showed his desire to answer, not only the traditional objections to the Church, but those he found currently being urged.

He reviewed dozens of volumes of theology and was keen to detect the theological assumptions in philosophical and scientific works. In review after review he criticized naturalism and rationalism in their various forms, attempting to make clear that however valid the claim that supernatural religion did violence to nature and to reason might be against Jansenism or Calvinism, it was not valid against orthodox Catholic doctrine. *Gratia supponit naturam,* grace presupposes nature, became central to much of his theological writing, and his discussion of the revealed law and the natural law in "Nature and Grace" (1868) suggests that he had meditated long on such works as St. Thomas Aquinas' *Treatise on Law.* Many of these later essays, especially those treating "Faith and Reason," give evidence of what Newman would call "real assent" as opposed to "notional assent," partly because Brownson had held to and had himself taught many of the views he now analyzed and refuted. Yet as late as 1873 he could confess that the real relation of reason and faith "is one of the mysteries of life that we do not find ourselves able to explain." (*Works*, III, 543.)

THE MEDIATORIAL LIFE
OF JESUS

[*The following letter, addressed to William Ellery Channing only a short time before Channing's death, was published as a pamphlet on June 1, 1842. It is included in* Works, *IV, 140–72. It is an eloquent testimony of Brownson's debt to Channing, and gives evidence of how Brownson, in his own words, "disputed the ground inch by inch" as he moved from Unitarianism to Transcendentalism and then toward the Catholic Church. In retrospect, Brownson believed that the central idea of his letter, the doctrine of life by communion, while it did not bring him into the Church, did remove all of his a priori objections, and brought him to the recognition of the Church as authoritative.* (The Convert, Works, *V, 163.) For Channing's friendly letter of acknowledgment, see H. F. Brownson,* Early Life, *pp. 443–4.*

The elder Channing (1780–1842) was minister of the Federal Street Society of Boston from 1803 until 1842, and a leading figure in New England Unitarianism. In the words of Perry Miller, "The Transcendental generation grew up in adoration of him, improved his every hint to an imperative, and continued to worship him even after he shuddered at their excesses." (The Transcendentalists, *Harvard University Press, 1950, p. 22.) Miller calls Channing's sermon on* Likeness to God, *to which Brownson refers in his letter, the epitome of Channing's message, and includes a portion of it in his anthology. In 1880, in* Historic Notes of Life and Letters in New England, *Emerson said of Channing: "We could not then spare a single word he uttered in public, not so much as the reading a lesson in Scripture, or a hymn, and it is curious that his printed writings are almost a history of the times. . . ." But of Brownson's letter to Channing, Emerson wrote to Elizabeth Peabody: "With such questions I find myself unrelated. They are for those whom they concern. It is all positive, local and idolatrous.*" (Letters, *III, 63–4.*) *Quoting this passage, Maynard adds that Emerson "could not but recognize that 'The Mediatorial Life of Jesus' was Brownson's repudiation of Transcendentalism.*" (Orestes Brownson, *p. 127.*)]

A *Letter to* Rev. WILLIAM ELLERY CHANNING, D.D., *June,* 1842

Reverend and Dear Sir:—My apology, if an apology be needed, for addressing you on the Mediatorial Life of Jesus, is in the position which you occupy among the friends of liberal inquiry, the influence your writings have had in forming my own religious opinions and character, and the generous friendship which you have long shown me personally, in good report and in evil.

You, sir, have been my spiritual father. Your writings were the first to suggest to me those trains of thought, which have finally ended in raising me from the darkness of doubt to the warm sunlight of a living faith in God, in the Bible as God's Word, and in Jesus Christ as the mediator between God and men, and as the real Saviour of the world through his life, death, and resurrection. I can never cease to be grateful for the important services you have rendered me, nor can I forget the respect and indulgence you have shown me notwithstanding all my shortcomings, and the steadiness with which you have cheered and sustained me, when the world grew dark around me, and hope was dying out of my soul.

You know, sir, somewhat of the long and painful struggles I have had in working my way up from unbelief to the high tableland of the Christian's faith and hopes; you have borne with me in my weakness, and have not been disposed to condemn me because I was not able, with a single bound, to place myself on that elevation. You have not been one to despise my

lispings and stammerings; but while others have treated me
rudely, denying me all love of truth, and all sense of goodness,
you have continued to believe me at bottom honest and sincere.
From my heart, sir, I thank you. I feel that you have been a
true friend, and that I may open my mind and heart to you
without reserve. You will receive with respect whatever comes
forth from an ingenuous heart, whether it find a response in
your own severer judgment or not.

You know that many years ago I was a confirmed unbeliever.
I had lost, not my unbelief, but my hostility to religion, and
had even to a certain extent recovered my early religious feelings, when a friend, now no more, read me one day your sermon on *Likeness to God*, preached at the ordination of Fred-
eric A. Farley, Providence, R.I., 1828. My friend was an excellent reader, and he entered fully into the spirit of the sermon.
I listened as one enchanted. A thrill of indescribable delight ran
through my whole soul. I could have leaped for joy. I seemed
suddenly to have found a Father. To me this was much. I had
never known an earthly father, and often had I wept when I
had heard, in my boyhood, my playmates, one after another, say
"my father." But now, lone and deserted as I had felt myself, I
too had become a son, and could look up and say, "my father"—
around and say, "my brothers."

The train of thought then suggested, pursued with fidelity,
led me to believe myself a Christian, and to resume my profession as a Christian preacher. But when I first came into this
community as a preacher, my Christianity was pretty much all
comprised in two articles, the divinity of humanity, and the
brotherhood of the race—which I had learned from your sermon. . . . So far as sincerity of purpose and honesty of conviction were concerned, I knew myself a believer, and thought
I had a right to be treated as a believer. You were one of the few
to acknowledge that right.

In looking back, sir, on the ten years which have passed, or nearly passed away, since I had the honor and the pleasure of first meeting you personally, I am now satisfied that I came among my Unitarian brethren with a faith quite too contracted for the wants of a real Christian, and with my bosom torn by two contrary tendencies. I had a strong tendency to religion, and to religious faith; but at the same time, unconsciously, another tendency, of quite an opposite character. This last tendency, really the weaker of the two, was almost the only one noted by the public, and hence, the almost universal accusation of infidelity of which I became the subject. This last tendency has shown itself in my efforts to find the grounds of religion in human nature, to discover in the pure reason the evidences of religious faith, and to resolve the providences of God, as manifested in extraordinary men, prophets, and messiahs, into the ordinary operations of nature. But, in my preaching and writings, I have given altogether more prominence to this tendency than it really had in my own mind, in the persuasion that by so doing, I could recommend the Gospel to unbelievers. I am now satisfied that in this I not only exposed myself to undeserved reproach, but committed a great mistake as a matter of mere policy. The best way to convert unbelievers to the Gospel is to preach the Gospel, the whole Gospel, and nothing but the Gospel. . . .

The truth is, sir, that I have come but slowly and perhaps reluctantly into the Christian faith. I embraced at once the two articles I have named, but I have been slow to go far beyond. I have disputed the ground inch by inch, and have yielded only when I had no longer any ground on which to stand. The debate in my mind has been going on for the last ten years, which have been to me, taken as a whole, years of much severer internal conflict than they have been of external conflict, severe as this last, as you well know, has actually been. . . .

I have, sir, finally attained to a view of the plan of a world's salvation through a Mediator, which I think reconciles all conflicting theories, discloses new wisdom in that plan, and enables us to take, in its most obvious and literal sense, without any subtlety or refinement, what the scriptures say of Jesus, and of salvation through his life. The Gospel becomes to me now a reality, and the teachings of the New Testament throughout realities, having their corresponding facts in the positive world. The views to which I have attained appear to me to be new, grand, and of the greatest importance. If I am not deceived they enable us to demonstrate with as much certainty as we have for our own existence several great and leading doctrines of the church universal, which have heretofore been asserted as great and holy mysteries, but unproved and unexplained. I think I can show that no small portion of the Bible, which is generally taken figuratively, is susceptible of literal interpretation, and that certain views of the Mediator, and his Life, from which our Unitarian friends have shrunk, are nevertheless true, and susceptible of a philosophical demonstration. I think, sir, I am able to show that the doctrine that human nature became depraved through the sin of Adam, and that it is redeemed only through the obedience of Christ; that the doctrine which teaches us that the Mediator is truly and indissolubly God-man, and saves the world by giving literally his life to the world, are the great "central truths" of Christianty, and philosophically demonstrable. . . .

What I have to offer on the main subject of this Letter, I shall take the liberty to arrange under three general heads.

First.—Whence comes the Mediator? *Second.*—What is his work? *Third.*—What is the method by which he performs it?

These three inquiries will cover the whole ground that I wish at present to occupy, or that is necessary to enable me to bring out all the peculiar views I am anxious to set forth concerning Jesus as the Mediator and Saviour of the world.

First.—Whence comes the Mediator? I should not detain you a moment with this inquiry, were it not that there is a tendency in some minds among us, to rank Jesus in the category of ordinary men. I do not say that any among us question his vast superiority over all other men of whom history retains any record, but in this superiority they see nothing supernatural, no special interposition of Providence. Jesus was a man of greater natural endowments, and of more devout piety, truer and deeper philanthropy than other men. He has exerted a great and beneficial influence on the world, will perhaps continue to exert a beneficial influence for some time to come; but he is divine, it is said, in no sense in which all men are not divine, in no sense in which nature is not divine. He had a larger nature, and was truer to it, than other men, and this is all wherein he was distinguished from other men, or had any special divinity. . . .

It seems to me, sir, that this tendency, which neither you nor I have wholly escaped, is a tendency to resolve God into the laws of nature,—the laws of the moral world, and those of the natural world. Now what is this but a tendency to sink God in nature, to lose him entirely, that is, to become atheists? I do not mean to say that you or I have been affected by this tendency to any very great extent, but you know that it has manifested itself in our midst. We have found it in our friends; we have met with it in our parochial visits; we have seen it in the doctrines put forth by men who profess to have outgrown the past; and indeed it has been the decided tendency of the literature and science of Christendom for the last century and a half. Men have deified nature, boasted the perfection and harmony of her laws, forgetful that there are such things as volcanoes, earthquakes, noxious damps and poisonous effluvia, blight and mildew. They shrink from admitting the doctrine of Providence. In reading ancient history they seek to resolve all that is marvelous or prodigious into natural laws, and some entire religious sects are so afraid of the interposition of God, that they say men are rewarded and punished according to the "natural laws." They see no longer the hand of God, but great Nature.

But I need hardly say to you that this whole tendency is antireligious, and productive, in every heart that indulges it, of decided irreligion. The Scriptures everywhere represent the agents and ministries of our instruction and improvement as sent by a heavenly Father. Noah, Abraham, Moses, David, Isaiah, Peter, James, John, and Paul, are always called of God, and sent. They come to us not of their own accord; they speak to us not in their own name, but as ambassadors for God. God gives to each a special mission, and sends him on an errand of love and mercy to his tribe, nation, or race. This is the only view compatible with religion.

When we resolve God into the laws of nature, whether as called the laws of the moral world or of the natural world, we have nothing remaining but nature. Nature, when there is no God seen behind it, to control it, to do with it as he will, in fact, that wills to overrule its seeming evil for real good, is a mere fate, an inexorable destiny, a dark, inscrutable, resistless necessity. It has no freedom, no justice. . . .

In fact, sir, not a few among us, though they admit, in words, that there is a God, do virtually deny his existence, by failing to believe in his freedom. You have contended for human freedom, and declared that man is annihilated just in proportion as his freedom is abridged. You may say as much of God. Freedom and sovereignty are one and the same. It has been felt that God has hedged himself in by natural laws, laws of his own establishing, so that he is no longer free to hear and answer prayer, or to comfort and forgive the penitent. God acts undoubtedly in accordance with invariable and eternal laws, but these laws are not the *natural* laws, not laws which he has enacted, but the laws of his own being; that is to say, he acts ever in conformity with himself, according to his own immutable will. The laws which he is not free to violate are not laws out of himself, but which he himself is. That is to say again, God is not free to be other than himself, and in this fact he is proved to be absolutely free. . . .

According to this view, we must regard Jesus, not as *coming*, but as *sent*, not as raising himself up to be the Mediator, but as having been raised up by the Father in heaven. He is from God, who commends his love to us by him. It is God's grace, not human effort or human genius, that provides the Mediator. It is impossible then to press Jesus into the category of ordinary men. He stands out alone, distinct, peculiar. This much, I must be permitted to assume in regard to Jesus, if I am to concern myself with Christianity at all. In answer then to the question, Whence comes the Mediator? I reply, from God, "who so loved the world that he gave his only begotten Son to die, that whosoever should believe on him might not perish, but have everlasting life."

Second.—But, assuming that God sent the Mediator, what did he send him to do? What was the work to be done for human redemption and sanctification? In other words, what is the condition in which the Gospel assumes the human race to be *without Christ,* and from which God, through the mediation of Christ, is represented as saving it? A great question this, and one on which I feel that I cannot so fully sympathize with your views as I once did. You say, in the sermon to which I have already alluded, that "In ourselves are the elements of the Divinity. God, then, does not sustain a figurative resemblance to man. It is the resemblance of a parent to a child, the likeness of a kindred nature." I am not sure that I catch your precise meaning in these sentences, but from these and from your writings generally, I infer that you hold man to be created with a *nature* akin to that of the Divinity. . . .

I certainly shall not deny that there is something divine in man; but I do deny that what is divine in man is original in his nature, save as all nature is divine, inasmuch as it is the work of God, and made at bottom,—if one may so speak, and mean anything,—out of divine substance. But neither you nor I have ever intended to favor pantheism. We do not therefore confound nature with God, any more than we do God with nature. I see not, then, how it is possible for man in any intelligible or legitimate sense of the word, to be *naturally* divine. The two terms seem to me to involve a direct contradiction. There is something divine in the life of man, I am willing to own; but this divinity which you find there, I think has been communicated to man, superinduced upon his nature, if I may so speak, by the grace of God through our Lord Jesus Christ. . . .

Allow me to say, that I think it is an error to assume that Christianity takes the divinity of humanity as its point of departure. Christianity seems to me to assume throughout as its point of departure, man's sinfulness, depravity, alienation from God and heaven. . . .

I am now prepared to answer the question, what is the work to be done? It is to redeem human nature from its inherent depravity, communicate to it a new and divine life, through which individuals may be saved from actual transgression, and raised to fellowship with the Father, by which they shall become really sons of God, and joint-heirs of a heavenly inheritance.

Third.—Having now determined the work there was for a Mediator to perform, I pass in the third and last place to consider the method by which he performs it; and I think I shall succeed in demonstrating the truth of the four following positions which are held by the church generally.

1. Man naturally does not and cannot commune directly with God, and therefore can come into fellowship with him only through a Mediator.

2. This Mediator must be at once and indissolubly, in the plain literal sense of the terms, very God of very God, and very man of very man; and so being very God of very God, and very man of very man, he can literally and truly mediate between God and men.

3. Jesus saves man, redeems him from sin, and enables him to have fellowship, as John says, with the Father, by giving his life literally not only for him but to him.

4. Men have eternal life, that is, live a true normal life, only so far forth as they live the identical life of Jesus. "He that hath the Son hath life"; "he that hath not the Son hath not life"; "except ye eat the flesh and drink the blood of the Son of Man ye have no life in you.". . .

Jesus says, in answer to a question put to him by Thomas, "I am the way, the truth, and the life." These words have a profound significance, and a literal truth, which I confess I for one have been but slow to comprehend. I confess, sir, that I have honestly believed that we might have a very sufficient Christianity without including the historical person we call Jesus; not indeed that I have ever failed, in my own view of Christianity, to include him. But I have taught from the pulpit, and from the press, that Christianity did not necessarily and could not be made to stand or fall with the fact whether there ever was or was not such a person as Jesus. This I now see was a grave error. Christ, the literal person we call Christ, *is* Christianity. All begins and ends with him. To reject him historically is to reject Christianity. This is the truth which they have had who have accused some of us of advocating the "latest form of infidelity," though under other aspects we who have been so accused, have been much further from infidelity than our accusers. . . .

In my *New Views*, Jesus has for me a high *representative* value. But having once attained to the principle represented, to the everlasting truth signified, I felt that the representative became as unnecessary as the scaffolding after the temple is erected.

On the other hand were our Unitarian friends of what has been called the old school. These with great truth hung on to the person and life of Jesus, and accused us who sought to resolve Jesus into an abstract law of the moral world, of rejecting Christianity altogether. But they did not help our difficulties. True they retained a personal Jesus, but they did not seem to us to retain any great matter for him to do; and when they talked of the importance of his life they failed to show us that importance. With the best intentions in the world, we could not see how, except in words, they made out that Jesus was anything more than a very exemplary sort of a man, a very zealous and able reformer, whom we should do well to respect and to remember along with Plato, Alfred, Luther, and Swedenborg. We felt that there must be a deeper, a more permanent Christ than this, and we sought him, as I have intimated, in abstract philosophy. . . .

I begin by assuming that the finite cannot commune directly with the infinite. Like does not and cannot commune with unlike. Moreover, the finite when regarded as depraved, all will agree, cannot commune, hold fellowship with infinite holiness. Man then could not commune directly with God; both because finite and because sinful. Then he must remain ever alienated from God, or a medium of communion, that is, a Mediator, must be provided. And this Mediator must of course be provided by the infinite and not by the finite. It would be absurd to say that man, unable to commune with God, can nevertheless provide a medium of communion with him. God must provide it. That is, he must condescend, come down to the finite, down to man, and by so doing, take man up to himself. . . .

Now Jesus being at once God and man in his life, answers precisely the condition of a Mediator between God and men. God and man are nothing to us save so far as they are living. They exist for us only so far forth as they live. Jesus is all to us in his life. The Jesus men saw and communed with was the life of Jesus, the living Jesus, that is to say, the Christ. Being human he was within the reach of human beings, and being at the same time indissolubly God, by communing with him they necessarily communed with God. Whoso touched him, laid his hand on God. "Have I been so long with thee, and yet hast thou not known me, Philip? He that hath seen me, hath seen the Father." . . .

The coming of Jesus has communicated a new life to the race, which by means of *communion* of man with man shall extend to all individuals. . . . Human nature in some sense then, I own, possesses today the divine worth you claim for it; not by virtue of its own inherent right, but by virtue of its union through the law of life to Christ, who is our head, and who is one with God. This union, virtually complete, is actually incomplete. To complete it, and therefore to make all men one in Christ, and through him one with the Father, thus fulfilling his prayer, as recorded in the seventeenth chapter of John's Gospel, is the work to be done, toward which Christian civilization is tending, and to which all true Christians direct all their efforts, individual and social. . . .

I have now, I feel, a doctrine to preach. I can preach now, not merely make discursions on ethics and metaphysics. The Gospel contains now to me not a cold abstract system of doctrine, a collection of moral apothegms, and striking examples of piety and virtue. It points me to Life itself. Metaphysical studies have indeed brought me, through the blessing of God, to the understanding of the doctrine, but having come to it, it suffices for itself. I now need to know nothing but Jesus and him crucified. . . .

I feel, too, that I can now go and utter the very word this age demands. That word is COMMUNION. The age is waiting for it. It is sick of divisions, sick of mere forms, wearied and disgusted with mere cant; no better pleased with mere metaphysical speculations; impatient of dry disquisitions, and of cold, naked abstractions. It demands Life and Reality. . . . The great doctrine of Life may now be preached, and whoso preaches that will bring the world to the Life, and through the Life save it from death and raise it to God. . . .

More I would say, but enough. I have addressed you with freedom, but I trust not with disrespect. I have spoken freely of myself, for I have wished to make certain explanations to the public concerning my faith. I have spoken earnestly, for the view which I have presented of the Mediatorial Life of Jesus has deeply affected me. I have been verging toward it for years; some of my friends tell me they have obtained it some time ago from my public communications; but I myself have not seen it clearly until within a few weeks. Had I seen it earlier, the obscurities and seeming inconsistencies with which I have been charged, I think would never have occurred. I have found it a view which clears up for me my own past, and enables me to preserve the continuity between the past of humanity, its present, and its future. . . . My early profession I therefore resume, with a love for it I never felt before. I resume it because my heart is full, and would burst could it not overflow. I must preach the Gospel. Necessity is laid upon me, and woe is me if I do not.

Forgive the liberty I have taken, and believe me, as ever,

Yours, with sincere respect,

O. A. Brownson

NEWMAN'S DEVELOPMENT
OF CHRISTIAN DOCTRINE
[1846]

[*Brownson was received into the Catholic Church on October 20, 1844. During 1845 Newman, in retirement at Littlemore, worked unceasingly at his* Essay on the Development of Christian Doctrine. *When he entered the Church on October 9, 1845, the manuscript lay unfinished on his desk. Adding merely a final paragraph to the book and submitting it, in a postscript to the preface, to the judgment of the Church, he published it immediately.*

Brownson's essay in the July, 1846, number of his Review, *attacking the theory in vehement tones, started a controversy which continued for the next two years. See* Works, *XIV, 1–141, for the full text of this essay and for Brownson's later essays on Newman's theory. In 1864 Brownson was to admit, with generosity and humility, that he had misunderstood Newman, saying, "We have long suspected that we did him an injustice. . . . The fact is, his book was profounder than we supposed, and was designed to solve theological difficulties which we had not then encountered in our own intellectual life and experience."* (Works, *XX, 372.*) *It is interesting to compare Brownson's criticisms with the misinterpretations of Newman's theory by which such modernists as Tyrrell and Loisy attempted to justify their doctrines. And it is at least possible that Newman's careful revisions of his book in the definitive 1878 text were partly prompted by Brownson's comments. See Edmond D. Benard's* A Preface to Newman's Theology *(1945), especially pp. 97–105, for a discussion of Brownson's criticism, and Theodore Maynard's* Orestes Brownson, *pp. 198–205.*]

OUR READERS do not need to be informed that the distinguished author of this work on the development of Christian doctrine has, within the last year, been admitted to the communion of the holy Catholic Church; for who has not heard of the event, and what Catholic heart has it not filled with devout joy and gratitude? Mr. Newman has stood for several years before the public as a man of rare gifts and acquirements; he was at the head of a very influential party in the Anglican communion, and appears to have enjoyed a personal esteem, and exerted a personal influence, which seldom fall to the lot of any but the master minds of their age or country. We may well, then, look upon his conversion with more than ordinary gratitude to the great Head of the church, and as an event of more than ordinary significance. . . .

It is but simple justice to Mr. Newman to say that it is not for his sake that we are about to point out some objections to his theory of developments. The circumstances under which he wrote, his acknowledged learning and ability, the presumption that he had thoroughly surveyed his ground, and the *apparent* favor with which his essay has been received by the Catholic press in England, are not unlikely to convey to Protestant, and perhaps to some partially instructed and speculative Catholic minds, the impression, that, if the theory set forth is not exactly Catholic, it at least contains nothing which a Catholic may not accept. The fact that the author—whether legitimately or not —comes to Catholic conclusions, that he ends by entering the Catholic communion, that he puts forth his theory expressly for the purpose of removing the obstacles which others may find in following his example, and with this view publishes it to the world even after his conversion, can hardly fail to produce in many minds the conviction that the theory and conclusions are necessarily or at least legitimately connected. And several Protestant reviewers seem actually to entertain this conviction;

and they, therefore, hold the theory up to condemnation as the
"Romanist" theory; or, as they express themselves, "as the
ground on which modern Rome seeks to defend her manifest
corruptions of Christian doctrine." It is therefore due both to the
church and to Protestants to say, expressly,—and we do so with
the highest respect for Mr. Newman, and with warm admiration
for the truth, beauty, and force of many of the details of his
work,—that his peculiar theory is essentially anticatholic and
Protestant. It not only is not necessary to the defense of the
church, but is utterly repugnant to her claims to be the authoritative and infallible church of God. A brief examination of some
of the principal features of the theory will justify this strong and
apparently severe assertion. . . .

Mr. Newman proceeds on the assumption, that the revelation
committed to the charge of the church was not a distinct, formal
revelation, but a vague, loose, obscure revelation, which she at
first only imperfectly apprehended. This is evident from the
extracts we have made, and also from what he says when pointing out an error in a passage which he quotes from one of his
previous publications. "The writer considers the growth of the
doctrine [of Purgatory] an instance of the action of private
judgment; whereas I should now call it an instance of *the mind
of the church working out dogmatic truth from implicit feelings*,
under secret supernatural guidance." This is a pregnant passage,
and may be regarded as a key to Mr. Newman's doctrine of development, and also to his view of the teaching authority of the
church. The development, as is evident from the context, is
not the formal definition of the faith against a novel error, but
is a slow, painful, and laborious working out, by the church herself, of dogmatic truth from implicit feelings,—though what
kind of feeling an *implicit* feeling is, we are unable to say.
"Thus St. Justin or St. Irenaeus might be without any digested
idea of Purgatory, or Original Sin, yet have an *intense feeling*,

which they had not defined or located, both of the fault of our first nature and of the liabilities of our nature regenerate." It is obvious from the whole course of Mr. Newman's reasoning, that he would predicate of the church, in their time, what he here predicates of St. Justin and St. Irenaeus. The church had a vague yet intense feeling of the truth, but had not digested it into formal propositions or definite articles. She had a blind instinct, which, under secret supernatural guidance, enabled her to avoid error and to pursue the regular course of development. She had a secret feeling of the truth, as one may say, a natural taste for it, and a distaste for error; yet not that clear and distinct understanding which would have enabled her at any moment, on any given point, to define her faith. She only knew enough of truth to preserve the original idea, and to elaborate from her intense feelings, slowly and painfully as time went on, now one dogma and now another. What in one age is feeling in a succeeding age becomes opinion, and an article of faith in a still later age. This new article gives rise to a new intense feeling, which, in its turn, in a subsequent age becomes opinion, to be finally, in a later age yet, imposed as dogmatic truth. This is, so far as we can understand it, Mr. Newman's doctrine of development, and what he means by "working out dogmatic truth from implicit feelings." . . .

Mr. Newman evidently proceeds on the assumption, that Christianity can be abstracted from the church, and considered apart from the institution which concretes it, as if the church were accidental and not essential in our holy religion. "Christianity," he says, "though spoken of in prophecy as a kingdom, came into the world as an *idea* rather than an institution, and has had to wrap itself in clothing, and fit itself with armor of its own providing, and form the instruments and methods of its own prosperity and warfare." If he does not so consider it, all he says on the development of ideas in general has and can have no relation to his subject. "The more claim," he says, "an idea has to be considered living, the more various will be its aspects; and the more social and political is its nature, the more complicated and subtile will be its developments, and the larger and the more eventful will be its course. *Such is Christianity;* and whatever has been said about the development of ideas generally becomes, of course, an antecedent argument for its progressive development." Its divine Author then sent Christianity into the world a naked and unarmed idea. By its action on us, and ours on it, it gradually develops itself into an institution, which, feeble at first, as time and events roll on, strengthens and fortifies itself, now on this side, and now on that, pushes deep its roots into the heart of humanity, sends out its branches, now in one direction and now in another, till at length it grows up and expands into that all-embracing authority, those profound and comprehensive dogmas, those pure and sublime precepts, and that rich and touching ritual, which together make up what we today call the Roman Catholic and Apostolic Church. Hence the significance of what the author told us in his introduction: "Christianity has, from the first, . . . thrown itself upon the great concourse of men. Its home is in the world; and to know what it is we must seek it in the world, and hear the world's witness of it."

We meet here an old, familiar acquaintance,—a doctrine which we embraced for years before we became a Catholic, and which for years kept us out of the Catholic Church, as it now keeps out the greater part of our former friends and associates. Assuming that Christianity came into the world originally as an idea, and not as an institution, that it was thrown upon the great concourse of men, to be developed and embodied by the action of their minds, stimulated and directed by it, we held that, by seizing it anew, abstracting it from the institutions with which it has thus far clothed itself, and proclaiming it as eighteen hundred years of intense moral and intellectual activity have developed it, we might organize through it a new institution, a new church, in advance of the old by all the developments which these eighteen hundred years have effected; and we see not, even now, wherein we were wrong, if it be assumed that Christianity was originally given us as a naked and unarmed idea.

This doctrine rests on the assumption, that ideas, in themselves considered, are active and potent, and that they may, as our old friend, the author of *Orphic Sayings*, would express himself, "take unto themselves hands, build the temple, erect the altar, and instaurate the worship of God." This is not only bad theology, but false philosophy, as we attempted to show in an article entitled "No Church, No Reform," published in April, 1844. Ideas, not concreted, not instituted, are not potencies, are not active, but are really to us as if they were not. The ideal must become actual, before it can be operative. If Christianity had come into the world as an idea, it would have left the world as it found it. Moreover, if you assume it to have come as an idea, and to have been developed only by the action of the human mind on it, the institutions with which it is subsequently clothed, the authorities established in its name, the dogmas imposed, the precepts enjoined, and the rites prescribed are all really the products of the human mind; and instead of governing the mind, may be governed, modified, enlarged, or contracted by it at its pleasure. The church would be divine only in the sense philosophy or civil government is divine. If Mr. Newman had not been so preoccupied with the solution of the problem which his Anglicanism proposed, it seems to us he must have seen this, and shrunk from advancing his theory of developments. . . .

Our difficulties do not diminish when we take up Mr. Newman's definition of *idea*. An idea, according to him, is the habitual judgment which the mind forms of that which comes before it; and in this sense, he tells us, the term is used in his *Essay*. Christianity came into the world as an idea, therefore as an habitual judgment formed by the mind. This, if construed strictly, makes Christianity purely human; for, if it be an habitual judgment formed by the human mind, it has no existence out of the mind, and could have had none before being formed in it. This is a conclusion from which every believer must recoil with horror. . . .

Mr. Newman tells us again that ideas sometimes represent facts, and sometimes do not. Does Christianity represent a fact, or does it not? He doubtless intends to teach that it does. But what is the evidence? What is the criterion by which to distinguish an idea which represents a fact from one which does not? He answers:

When one and the same idea is held by persons who are independent of each other, and variously circumstanced, and have possessed themselves of it by different ways under very different aspects, without losing its substantial unity and its identity, and when it is thus variously presented, and yet recommended to persons similarly circumstanced; and when it is presented to persons variously circumstanced, under aspects discordant at first sight, but reconcilable after such explanations as their respective states of mind require; then it seems to have a claim to be considered the representative of objective truth.

This is pure *Lamennaisism* which makes the *consensus hominum* the criterion of truth. It would also authorize us to infer, that, if Christianity, as at its first promulgation, be embraced only by a few, and these mutually connected and similarly circumstanced, and if, at the same time, these all receive it by the same way and under the same aspect, or agree among themselves in their views of it, it would have no "claim to be considered the representative of objective truth." The faith of the Blessed Virgin, the twelve apostles, and the seventy disciples, must, then, have labored under very serious disadvantages. Moreover, if all the world should be converted, all gathered into the same communion, become of "one mind," as well as of "one heart," there would be room to question whether Christianity represents a fact or a no-fact. Is this Catholic teaching?

Nor are we better satisfied with what Mr. Newman says of the process of development. Christianity came into the world as an idea, an habitual judgment; and we may say of it in particular all he says of development in ideas in general. . . . It is plain . . . that Mr. Newman means to teach that the church, in order to attain to an adequate expression of the Christian idea or of Christian doctrine, must institute and carry on the precise process of development which he has predicated of ideas generally; for he contends, and he told us as much in the beginning, that she is forced to do so by the nature of the human mind itself. The revelation is not and cannot be taken in all at once. The church can neither learn nor teach it, except under particular aspects, none of which, he says, can go the depth of the idea,—that is, we presume, of the fact or no-fact which the idea represents; for it is hardly to be supposed that a judgment cannot go the depth of itself; and it is only by collecting and adjusting these particular aspects, that she can attain to an adequate expression of Christian doctrine. This is naked eclecticism, not in philosophy only, but even in faith.

But this development is effected only gradually, and "after a sufficient time." Some centuries elapse, and the doctrine of purgatory is "opened upon the apprehension of the church." She at first cannot take in all revealed truth. She has it all stowed away somewhere, but she only partially apprehends it. As time goes on, as individuals differently circumstanced view it under different particular aspects and from opposite poles, as new controversies arise, bold and obstinate heretics start up, some clamorous for one particular aspect, and some for another, she is able to enlarge her view, to augment the number of her dogmas, and tell us more truly what is the revelation she has received. And this we are to say of a church we are defending as authoritative and infallible, and which we hold has received the formal commission to teach all nations all things whatsoever our Lord commanded his apostles! In plain words, was the church able to teach truly and infallibly in the age of Saints Clement and Polycarp, or of Saints Justin and Irenaeus, the whole Catholic faith, and the precise Catholic faith, on any and every point which could be made,—or was she not? If she was, there can have been no development of doctrine; if she was not, she was not then competent to discharge the commission she received. Was what she then taught the faithful sufficient for salvation? Is not what was then sufficient all that is really necessary now? If so, and if she teaches doctrines now which she did not then, or insists on our believing now what she did not then, how will you exonerate her from the charge brought by Protestants, that she has added to the primitive faith, and teaches as of necessity to salvation what is not necessary, and therefore imposes a burden on men's shoulders they ought not to be required to bear? Moreover, where are these developments to stop? Have we reached the end? Has the church finally brought out the whole body of dogmatic truth, or are we, like the Puritan Robinson, "to look for new light" to break in upon her vision? Mr. Newman seems to think new developments are needed; for he mentions several fundamental matters, which he says he supposes "remain more or less undeveloped, or at least undefined, by the church."

Mr. Newman, after Leibnitz, represents heresy as consisting in taking and following out a partial view of Christian truth. Will he permit us to ask him to tell us how, at that period, when the church apprehended the truth only under particular aspects, heresy was distinguishable from orthodoxy? Moreover, if there ever was a time when the church did not teach the whole faith, how he can maintain her catholicity; since to her catholicity, as we learn from the catechism, it is not only essential that she subsist through all ages, and teach all nations, but that she teach all truth? . . .

After all, it is clear that Mr. Newman's πρῶτον ψεῦδος, his mother error, is in assuming that the Christian doctrine was given originally and exclusively through the medium of the written word. How far he assumes this absolutely for himself, or how far his assumption is intended to be a concession to his Anglican friends, it is impossible for us to say; and we confess that, on reading and rereading the book, we are at a loss to determine whether he is really putting forth a theory which he holds to be true, or only a theory which he thinks may remove, on Anglican premises, the difficulties which the Anglican finds in the way of Catholicity. But this much is certain,—his theory is framed on the supposition, that the revelation was first given in the written word exclusively, and that the church has herself had to learn it from written documents. Hence, as the doctrine in these is evidently not drawn out and stated in formal propositions or digested articles of faith, but is given only generally, vaguely, obscurely, in detached portions and loose hints, developments have been absolutely indispensable, and must have been foreseen and intended by the Author of our religion. This is what he labors to prove in the chapter entitled, *On the Development of Christian ideas antecedently considered.* But this is sheer Protestantism, not Catholicity, and is never to be assumed or conceded by a Catholic, in an argument for the church. Catholicity teaches that the whole revelation was made to the church, irrespective of written documents, and there never was a time when Christianity was confined to "the letter of documents and the reasonings of individual minds," as Mr. Newman presupposes. The depository of the revelation is not the Holy Scriptures, *plus* tradition. The divine traditions cover the *whole* revelation, and not merely that portion of it not found in the Holy Scriptures; and it is because the church has the whole faith in these divine traditions, which, by supernatural assistance, she faithfully keeps and transmits, and infallibly interprets, that she can establish the rule of Scriptural interpretation, and say what doctrines may and what may not be drawn from the written word. The greater part of her teachings are found in the Holy Scriptures, and she for the most part teaches through them, but was never under the necessity of learning her faith from them, as anyone might infer from the very face of the sacred books themselves, which were all addressed to *believers,* and therefore necessarily imply that the faith had been revealed, propounded, and embraced before they were written. The church must precede the Scriptures; for it is only on her authority that their inspiration can be affirmed. They are a part of her divine teaching, not the sources whence she learns what she is commanded to teach. If Mr. Newman had borne this in mind, he would hardly have insisted so strongly on his theory of developments, and would have spared himself the rather serious error of maintaining that the church appeals to the mystical sense of Scripture in *proof* of her doctrines. The source of heresy is not in the literal interpretation of Scripture, as he imagines, but in attempting to deduce the faith from Scripture by private judgment, independently of the church. The doctors of the church are accustomed to adduce the mystical sense of Scripture in *illustration* of Christian doctrine, but never in *proof,* except where the mystical sense is affirmed and defined by positive revelation.

We have been forcibly struck, in reading this essay, with the wisdom of the plan of instructing by the living teacher, which our Lord has adopted. If any man could have learned Catholicity from books or documentary teaching, we should have said that man was John Henry Newman. He had every qualification for the task which could be demanded,—genius, talent, learning, acuteness, patience of research, and all the books necessary at his hand; and yet, with the best intentions, in a work designed expressly to justify his change of religion to the world, and to open an easy passageway for others to follow him, he has mistaken Catholicity in its most essential points, and, in fact, written a book which will prove one of the hardest books *for him,* as a Catholic, to answer, he will be likely to find. If, instead of ransacking the libraries of all ages and nations, and amassing an erudition which he was not in the condition to digest, and for the interpretation of which he had no certain guide, he had gone to the first Catholic priest within his reach, and asked him to teach him the catechism, and to explain to him the creed of Pius IV, he would in one week have learned more of genuine Catholicity than he learned in the years he spent in the preparation of this work. No man should ever persuade himself that he knows anything really and truly of Catholicity, till he has listened patiently and reverently to the living teacher authorized by Almighty God to teach him. The faith is learned by *hearing* not by *reading.* . . .

It is plain to the Catholic reader, that Mr. Newman errs in consequence of his neglect to distinguish in his own mind,—or, if not in his own mind, in his book,—on the one hand, between Christian doctrine, that is, divine revelation, and Christian theology and discipline; and, on the other, between what the church teaches as of divine revelation, and the speculations of individual fathers and doctors. Take the whole history of the Christian world, so called, from the time of our blessed Lord down to the present moment, including the sects as well as the church, and considering all that has been going on with all who have borne the Christian name, and in every department of life, there is no doubt but such developments and processes as Mr. Newman describes have to some extent taken place. But he seems to have studied his theory chiefly in the history of the sects, where it is unquestionably applicable, and to have concluded that the church in its life in the world must be governed by a law analogous to the one by which they are governed, and that his theory may apply to her as well as to them. He forgets that she sprung into existence full grown, and armed at all points, as Minerva from the brain of Jupiter; and that she is withdrawn from the ordinary law of human systems and institutions by her supernatural origin, nature, character, and protection. If he had left out the church, and entitled his book, *An Essay on the Development of Christian Doctrine, when withdrawn from the Authority and Supervision of the Church*, he would have written, with slight modifications, a great and valuable book. It would then have been a sort of natural history of sectarism, and been substantially true. But applying his theory to the church, and thus subjecting her to the law which presides over all human systems and institutions, he has, unintentionally, struck at her divine and supernatural character. The church has no natural history, for she is not in the order of nature, but of grace. Or, if he had simply distinguished between Christian doctrine, in which there is no development, which is always and everywhere the same, and in which not the least shadow of a variation can be admitted, and confined his remarks to theology as a human science deduced from supernatural principles, to the variations of external discipline and worship, and to the greater or less predominance of this or that Christian principle in the practice of individual Christians in different ages of the church, much that he has said might be accepted, and no very grave error would be taught. . . .

THE CONVERT · Chapter XVIII
[1857]

[*Brownson published his autobiographical volume,* The Convert: or, Leaves from My Experience *in November, 1857. I have included here, from the twenty chapters that make up the book, one complete chapter, that recounting the story of his conversion. The full text of* The Convert *is in* Works, *V, 1–200.*

While Brownson was prompted to write The Convert *by no such dramatic occurrence as the attack by Kingsley that led Newman to write the* Apologia, *and while the book is not a vindication or defense in the sense that Newman's is, the fact that it was written in 1857 is not without significance. Brownson's decision in 1855 to leave Boston for New York, in search of more congenial surroundings; the different emphasis noticeable at this time in his essays; his review in 1855 of Isaac Hecker's "Questions of the Soul" in which Brownson favorably contrasts Hecker's sympathetic tone in addressing non-Catholics with his own polemical and logical method; and especially the letters between Brownson and Hecker during these years—all indicate that Brownson felt keenly at this time his failure, since his conversion, to gain from Protestants the hearing that he once hoped for. It was, in short, his desire to affirm the rational basis of his movement toward the Catholic Church, and to show the connecting link between his past and his present life that led him to write* The Convert. *Theodore Maynard's discussion of these points is particularly convincing.* (Orestes Brownson, *pp. 257–66.*)]

THE WORK of conversion is, of course, the work of grace, and without grace no man can come into the church any more than he can enter heaven. No merely human process does or can suffice for it, and I am far enough from pretending that I became a Catholic by my own unassisted efforts. Without the grace divinely bestowed, and bestowed without any merit of mine, all my labors would have been in vain. It was divine grace that conducted me, rolled back the darkness before me, and inclined my heart to believe. But grace does not exclude reason, or voluntary co-operation; and conversion itself, though a work of free grace, includes, inasmuch as it is the conversion of a rational subject, a rational process, though not always distinctly noted by the convert. All I am doing is to detail the rational process by which, not without, but with divine grace, I came into the church, and that not for those who are within, but for those who are without. Those who are within have no need in their own case of the process, for they have the life, and the life evidences itself, and they know in whom they believe, and are certain. But this sort of evidence they who are without have not, and we cannot allege it as evidence to them. They could take it only on our word, and they have no more reason to take our word than they have to take that of Evangelicals, who pretend to the same sort of evidence in their favor. It is necessary, therefore, to show them that there is a rational process included in the case, and to show them as clearly as may be what that process is.

The process I have detailed, or life by communion, did not, as I have said, bring me into the church, but, taken in connection with the admitted historical facts in the case, it did remove all my *a priori* objections, and bring me to the recognition of the church as authoritative, by virtue of the divine-human life it lived, for natural reason. This was not all that I needed, but it was much, and required me to go further and submit myself to her, and take her own explanation of herself and of her dogmas. I saw this clear enough, but my reluctance to become a Roman Catholic prevented me from doing so at once. Yet, even from the first, even from the moment I came to the recognition of the church as authoritative, I felt, though I refused personally to change my position, that I must take what had evidently been her positive teaching for my guide, and in no instance contradict it.

It was evident, without any special instruction, that the church, that the whole Christian world, proposed a very different end as the true end of life, from the one I had proposed to myself, and for which, during nearly twenty years, in my feeble way, I had been laboring. As a practical fact, the church, no doubt, really does aid the progress of society, and tend to give us a heaven even on earth, but this is not the end she proposes, or what she directly aims to effect. The end she proposes is not attainable in this world, and the heaven she points to is a reward to be received only after this life. There could be no doubt that she taught endless beatitude as the reward of the good, and endless misery as the punishment of the wicked. The good are they who in this world live the life of Christ, the wicked are they who live it not, and even refuse to live it. There needs no church or priest to tell me that I am not living that life, and that, if I die as I am, I shall assuredly go to hell. Now as I have no wish to go to hell, something must be done, and done without delay.

It is all very well, no doubt, to follow the example of the weeping Isis, and seek to gather up the fragments of the torn body of our Lord, and restore it to its unity and integrity; but what will it avail me if I remain severed from that body, and refuse to do what the church commands? How can I consistently ask the obedience of others while I refuse my own? Rewards and punishments are personal, and meted out to men as individuals, not as collective bodies. There is, then, but one rational course for me to take, that of going to the church, and begging her to take charge of me, and do with me what she judges proper. As the Roman Catholic Church is clearly the church of history, the only church that can have the slightest historical claim to be regarded as the body of Christ, it is to her I must go, and her teachings, as given through her pastors, that I must accept as authoritative for natural reason. It was, no doubt, unpleasant to take such a step, but to be eternally damned would, after all, be a great deal unpleasanter. Accordingly, with fear and trembling, and yet with firmness of purpose, in the last week of May, 1844, I sought an interview with the late Right Reverend Benedict Joseph Fenwick, the learned Bishop of Boston, and in the following week visited him again, avowed my wish to become a Catholic, and begged him to be so kind as to introduce me to someone who would take the trouble to instruct me, and prepare me for reception, if found worthy, into the communion of the church. He immediately introduced me to his coadjutor, who has succeeded him, the Right Reverend John Bernard Fitzpatrick. Of Bishop Fenwick, who died in the peace of the Lord, August 12, 1846, and who has left a memory precious to the American church, I have given, in my *Review* for the following October, a sketch to which I can add nothing, and from which I have nothing to abate. He was a native of Maryland, descended from an old Catholic family that came over with the first settlers of the colony, and to whom the American church is indebted for some of her brightest ornaments. He was a great and good man, a man of various and solid learning, a tender heart, unaffected piety, and untiring zeal in his ministry. Delicacy and his own retiring character prevent me from speaking of his successor, the present Bishop of Boston, in the terms which naturally present themselves. He was my instructor, my confessor, my spiritual director, and my personal friend, for eleven years; my intercourse with him was intimate, cordial, and affectionate, and I owe him more than it is possible for me to owe any other man. I have met men of more various erudition and higher scientific attainments; I have met men of bolder fancy and more creative imaginations; but I have never met a man of a clearer head, a firmer intellectual grasp, a sounder judgment, or a warmer heart. He taught me my catechism and my theology; and, though I have found men who made a far greater display of theological erudition, I have never met an abler or sounder theologian. However for a moment I may have been attracted by one or another theological school, I have invariably found myself obliged to come back at last to the views he taught me. If my *Review* has any theological merit, if it has earned any reputation as a stanch and uncompromising defender of the Catholic faith, that merit is principally due, under God, to him, to his instructions, to his advice, to his encouragement, and his uniform support. Its faults, its shortcomings, or its demerits, are my own. I know that, in saying this, I offend his modesty, his unaffected Christian humility; but less I could not say without violence to my own feelings, the deep reverence, the warm love, and profound gratitude with which I always recall, and trust I always shall recall his name and his services to me.

Bishop Fitzpatrick received me with civility, but with a certain degree of distrust. He had been a little prejudiced against me, and doubted the motives which led so proud and so conceited a man, as he regarded me, to seek admission into the communion of the church. It was two or three months before we could come to a mutual understanding. There was a difficulty in the way that I did not dare explain to him, and he instinctively detected in me a want of entire frankness and unreserve. I had been led to the church by application I had made of my doctrine of life by communion, and I will own that I thought that I found in it a method of leading others to the church which

Catholics had overlooked or neglected to use. I really thought that I had made some philosophical discoveries which would be of value even to Catholic theologians in convincing and converting unbelievers, and I dreaded to have them rejected by the Catholic Bishop. But I perceived almost instantly that he either was ignorant of my doctrine of life, or placed no confidence in it; and I felt that he was far more likely, bred as he had been in a different philosophical school from myself, to oppose than to accept it. I had indeed, however highly I esteemed the doctrine, no special attachment to it for its own sake, and could, so far as it was concerned, give it up at a word, without a single regret; but, if I rejected or waived it, what reason had I for regarding the church as authoritative for natural reason, or for recognizing any authority in the Bishop himself to teach me? Here was the difficulty.

This difficulty remained a good while. I dared not state it, lest the Catholic Bishop himself should deprive me of all reason for becoming a Catholic, and send me back into the world utterly naked and destitute. I had made up my mind that the church was my last plank of safety, that it was communion with the church or death. I must be a Catholic, and yet could not and would not be one blindly. I had gone it blind once, and had lost all, and would not do so again. My trouble was great, and the Bishop could not relieve me, for I dared not disclose to him its source. But Providence did not desert me; and I soon discovered that there was another method, by which, even waiving the one which I had thus far followed, I could arrive at the authority of the church, and prove, even in a clearer and more direct manner, her divine commission to teach all men and nations in all things pertaining to eternal salvation. This new process or method I found was as satisfactory to reason as my own. I adopted it, and henceforth used it as the rational basis of my argument for the church. So, in point of fact, I was not received into the church on the strength of the philosophical doctrine I had embraced, but on the strength of another, and, perhaps, a more convincing process.

It is not necessary to develop this new process here, for it is the ordinary process adopted by Catholic theologians, and may be found drawn out at length in almost every modern course of theology. It may, also, be found developed under some of its aspects in almost any article I have since written in my *Review*, but more especially in an article entitled "The Church against No-Church." I found it principally in Billuart's treatises *de Deo*, *de Fide*, *de Regulis Fidei*, and *de Ecclesia*; and an excellent summary and lucid statement of it, or what are usually called "motives of credibility," may be found in Pointer's *Evidences of Christianity*, and also in the *Evidences of Catholicity*, by Dr. Spalding, the present able and learned Bishop of Louisville. Though I accepted this method and was satisfied by it before I entered the church, yet it was not that by which I was brought from unbelief to the church; and it only served to justify and confirm by another process the convictions to which I had been brought by my application to history and the traditions of the race, of the doctrine of life obtained from the simple analysis of thought as a fact of consciousness. What would have been its practical effect on my mind, had I encountered it before I had in fact become a believer and in reality had no need of it for my personal conviction, I am unable to say, though I suspect it would never have brought me to the church,—not because it is not logical, not because it is not objectively complete and conclusive, but because I wanted the internal or subjective disposition to understand and receive it. It would not have found, if I may so say, the needed subjective response, and would have failed to remove to my understanding the *a priori* objections I entertained to a supernatural authoritative revelation itself. It would, I think, have struck me as crushing instead of enlightening, silencing instead of convincing, my reason. Certainly, I have never found the method effectual in the case of any non-Catholic not already disposed to become a Catholic, or actually, in his belief, on the way to the church.

The argument of our theologians is scholastic, severe, and conclusive for the pure intellect that is in the condition to listen to it; but it seems to me better adapted, practically, to confirm believers and guard them against the specious objections of their enemies, than to convince unbelievers. Man is not pure intellect; he is body as well as soul, and full of prejudices and passions. His subjective objections are more weighty than his objective objections, and the main difficulties of the unbeliever lie, in our times, further back than the ordinary motives of credibility reach. It strikes me that my method, though it can by no means supersede theirs, might be advantageously used as a preparation for theirs; not as an Evangelical Preparation, but as a preparation for the usual Evangelical Preparation presented by theologians, especially in this age when the objections are drawn from philosophy rather than from history, from feeling rather than from logic.

Having, however, found the other method of justifying my recognition of the church as authority for reason, I dropped for the time the doctrine of life, and soon came, without any discussion of its merits or demerits, to a good understanding with the Bishop, who, after a few weeks of further instruction, heard my confession, which included the whole period of my life from the time of my joining the Presbyterians, received my abjuration, administered to me conditional Baptism, and the sacrament of Confirmation, on Sunday, October 20, 1844, when I had just entered the forty-second year of my age, and just twenty-two years after I had joined the Presbyterians. The next morning at early Mass I received Holy Communion from the hands of Rev. Nicholas A. O'Brien, then Pastor of the Church in East

Boston. The great step had been taken, and I had entered upon a new life, subdued indeed, but full of a sweet and calm joy. No difficulties with regard to the particular doctrines of the church had at any time arisen, for, satisfied that Almighty God had commissioned the church to teach, and that the Holy Ghost was ever present by his supernatural aid to assist her to teach, I knew that she could never teach anything but truth. The fact that she taught a doctrine was a sufficient reason for accepting it, and I had only to be assured of her teaching it, in order to believe it.

As I did not make use in the last moment of my doctrine of communion, and as I had no occasion for it afterwards for my own mind, I made no further use of it; and when I addressed the public again, proceeded to defend my Catholic faith by the method ordinarily adopted by Catholic writers. I did this, because, seeing the Catholic Church and her dogmas to be infinitely more than that doctrine had enabled me to conceive, I attached for the moment no great importance to it. It certainly was not all I had supposed it, and it might prove to be nothing at all. It had served as a scaffolding, but now the temple was completed, it might serve only to obscure its beauty and fair proportions. At any rate, that and other philosophical theories which I had formed while yet unacquainted with the church, should be suffered to sleep, till I had time and opportunity to re-examine them in the light of Catholic faith and theology. It did not comport with the modesty and humility of a recent convert to be intruding theories of his own upon the Catholic public, or to insist on methods of defending Catholic doctrine, adopted while he was a non-Catholic, and not recognized by Catholic theologians. Was it likely I had discovered anything of value that had escaped the great theologians and doctors of the church?

But this suppression of my own philosophic theory, a suppres-

sion under every point of view commendable and even necessary
at the time, became the occasion of my being placed in a false
position toward my non-Catholic friends. Many had read me,
seen well enough whither I was tending, and were not surprised
to find me professing myself a Catholic. The doctrine I brought
out, and which they had followed, appeared to them, as it did
to me, to authorize me to do so, and perhaps not a few of them
were making up their minds to follow me; but they were
thrown all aback the first time they heard me speaking as a
Catholic, by finding me defending my conversion on grounds
of which I had given no public intimation, and which seemed to
them wholly unconnected with those I had published. Unable
to perceive any logical or intellectual connection between my
last utterances before entering the church and my first utterances
afterwards, they looked upon my conversion, after all, as a sudden caprice, or rash act taken from a momentary impulse or in
a fit of intellectual despair, for which I had in reality no good
reason to offer. So they turned away in disgust, and refused to
trouble themselves any longer with the reasonings of one on
whom so little reliance could be placed, and who could act without any rational motive for his action.

Evidently this was unpleasant, but I could not set the matter
right at the time, by showing that there really had been a continuity in my intellectual life, and that I had not broken with
my former self so abruptly or so completely as they supposed.
Till I had had time to review my past writings in the light of
my new faith, the matter was uncertain in my own mind, and it
was my duty, so far as the public was concerned, to let the doctrine sleep, and to write and publish nothing but what I had a
warrant for in the approved writers of the church. I acted
prudently, as it was proper I should act, and I should continue
to do so still, and not have written the present book and taken
up the connecting link, had not nearly thirteen years of Catholic

experience and study enabled me to perceive that the doctrine of life I asserted is in no way incompatible with any Catholic principle or doctrine I have become acquainted with, and that it did legitimately lead me to the Catholic Church. I do not mean that, as a doctrine of philosophy, it bridges over the gulf between the natural and supernatural, for that no philosophy can do, since philosophy is only the expression of natural reason; but I honestly believe, as I believed in 1844, that it does, better than any other philosophical doctrine, show the harmony between the natural and the supernatural, and remove those obstacles to the reception of the church, and her doctrines on her authority, which all intelligent and thinking men brought up outside of the church in our day do really encounter. I believe I am not only clearing myself of an unfounded suspicion of having acted capriciously, from mental instability, or mental despair, in joining the church, which were a small affair, but also a real service to a large class of minds who still remember me, by recalling it and showing them that in substance I still hold and cherish it.

My Catholic friends cannot look upon my doing so, after years of probation, as indicative of any departure from the diffidence and humility which at first restrained me from putting it forth. The doctrine is new only in form, not in substance, and is only a development and application of principles which every Catholic theologian does and must hold. The fact that it was first developed and applied by one outside of the church, and served to bring him to the church, since it is not repugnant to any principle of Catholic faith or theology, is rather in its favor, for it creates a presumption that it really contains something fitted to reach a certain class of minds at least, and to remove the obstacles they experience in yielding assent to the claims of the church. Non-Catholics do not, indeed, know Catholicity as well as Catholics know it, but they know better their own objections to it, and what is necessary to remove them. If, in investigating questions before them, in attempting to establish a system of their own, with no thought of seeking either to believe Catholicity, or to find an answer to the objections they feel to the church, they find these objections suddenly answered, and themselves forced, by principles which they have adopted, to recognize the church as authority for reason, it is good evidence that these principles, and the methods of reasoning they authorize, are well adapted to the purpose of the defenders of the faith, and not unworthy of the attention of Catholic controversialists, when, as in my case, they neither supersede nor interfere with the ordinary methods of theologians.

Motives of credibility or methods of proof should be adapted to the peculiar character and wants of the age, or class of persons addressed. Philosophy could never have attained to Christian revelation, or the sacred mysteries of our holy religion; but now that the revelation is made, that the mysteries are revealed, we know that all sound philosophy does and must accord with them,—must, as far as it goes, prepare the mind to receive them; and taken in connection with the historical facts in the case, must demand them as its own complement. Now, if I am not mistaken, a philosophy of this sort has become indispensable. The age is skeptical, I grant, but its skepticism relates rather to the prevailing philosophy than to reason, of which that philosophy professes to be the exponent. It distrusts reasoning rather than reason. It has no confidence in the refinements and subtilties of schoolmen, and, though often sophistical, it is in constant dread of being cheated out of its wits by the sophistry of the practised logician. Conclusions in matters of religion, which are arrived at only by virtue of a long train of reasoning, even when it perceives no defects in the premises and no flaw in the reasoning, do not command its assent, for it fears there may still be something wrong either in the reasoning or the premises, which escapes its sagacity. The ordinary motives of credibility do not move non-Catholics to believe, because these motives start from principles which they do not accept, or accept with so much vagueness and uncertainty, that they do not serve to warrant assent even to strictly logical conclusions drawn from them. Moreover, they do not reach their peculiar difficulties, do not touch their real objections; and though they seem overwhelming to Catholics, they leave all their objections remaining in full force, and their inability to believe undiminished.

The reason is in the fact that the philosophy which prevails, and after which the modern mind is, in some sense, moulded, is opposed to Christian revelation, and does not recognize as fundamental the principles or premises which warrant the conclusions drawn in favor of Christianity. The prevalent philosophy with very nearly the whole scientific culture of the age, is not only unchristian, but antichristian, and, if accepted, renders the Christian faith an impossibility for a logical mind. There is always lurking in the mind a suspicion of the antecedent improbability of the whole Evangelical doctrine. Apologists may say, and say truly, that there is and can be no contradiction between philosophy and faith; but, unhappily, the philosophy between which and faith there is no contradiction, is not generally recognized. Between the official and prevalent philosophy of the day, between the principles which have passed from that philosophy into the general mind, and Catholic faith, there is a contradiction; and not a few Catholics even retain their faith only in spite of their philosophy. The remedy is in revising our philosophy, and in placing it in harmony with the great principles of Catholic faith. I will not say with Bonnetty that the method of the scholastics leads to rationalism and infidelity, for that is not true; but I will say that that method, as developed and applied in the modern world, especially the non-Catholic world, does not serve as a preamble to faith, and does place the mind of the unbeliever in a state unfitted to give to the ordinary motives of credibility their due weight, or any weight at all.

Modern philosophy is mainly a method, and develops a method of reasoning instead of presenting principles to intellectual contemplation. It takes up the question of method before that of principles, and seeks by the method to determine the principles, instead of leaving the principles to determine the method. Hence it becomes simply a doctrine of science, *Wissenschaftslehre*, a doctrine of abstractions, or pure mental conceptions, instead of being, as it should be, a doctrine of reality, of things divine and human. It is cold, lifeless, and offers only dead forms, which satisfy neither the intellect nor the heart. It does not, and cannot move the mind toward life and reality. It obscures first principles, and impairs the native force and truthfulness of the intellect. The evil can be remedied only by returning from this philosophy of abstractions,—from modern psychology, or subjectivism, to the philosophy of reality, the philosophy of life, which presents to the mind the first principles of life and of all knowledge as identical.

Herein is the value of the process by which I arrived at the church. I repeat, again and again, that philosophy did not conduct me into the church, but, just in proportion as I advanced toward a sound philosophy, I did advance toward the church. As I gained a real philosophy, a philosophy which takes its principles from the order of being, from life, from things as they are or exist, instead of the abstractions of the schools, faith flowed in, and I seized with joy and gladness the Christian Church and her dogmas. The non-Catholic world is far less in love with heresy or infidelity than is commonly supposed, and our arguments, clear and conclusive as they are to us, fail because they fail to meet their objections, and convince their reason. They are not addressed to reason as it is developed in them, and answer not their objections as they themselves apprehend them.

The non-Catholic world is not deficient in logical force or mental acuteness, but it expresses itself in broad generalizations, rather than in precise and exact statements. Its objections are inductions from particulars, vaguely apprehended and loosely expressed, are more subjective than objective, and rarely admit of a rigid scientific statement or definition. To define them after the manner of the schools, and to reduce them to a strictly logical formula, is, in most cases, to refute them; but the non-Catholic is not thus convinced that they are untenable, for he feels them still remaining in his mind. He attributes their apparent refutation to some logical sleight-of-hand, or dialectic jugglery, which escapes his detection. He remains unconvinced, because his objection has been met by a refutation which has given no new light to his understanding, nor made him see any higher or broader principles than he was before in possession of.

An external refutation of the unbeliever's objections effects nothing, because the real objection is internal, and the refutation leaves the internal as it was before. The secret of convincing is not to put error out of the mind, but truth into it. There is little use in arguing against the objections of non-Catholics, or in laboring directly for their refutation. We can effectually remove them only by correcting the premises from which the unbeliever reasons, and giving him first principles, which really enlighten his reason, and, as they become operative, expel his error by their own light and force. This can be done only by bringing the age back, or up to·a philosophy which conforms the order of knowledge to the order of being, the logical order to the order of reality, and gives the first principles of things as the first principles of science. If Catholicity be from God, it does and must conform to the first principles of things, to the order of reality, to the laws of life or intelligence; and hence, a philosophy which conforms to the same order will conform to Catholicity, and supply all the rational elements of Catholic theology. Such a philosophy is the desideratum of the age, and we must have it, not as a substitute for faith, but as its preamble, as its handmaid, or we cannot recall the non-believing world to the church of God; because it is only by such a philosophy that we can really enlighten the mind of the unbeliever, and really and effectually remove his objections, or show that it is in fact true that there is no contradiction between Catholicity and philosophy.

The greatest and most serious difficulty in the way of the unbeliever is his inability to reconcile faith and reason, that is, the divine plan in the order of grace with the divine plan evident in the order of nature. The Christian order appears to him as an after-thought, as an anomaly, if not a contradiction, to the general plan of divine providence, incompatible with the perfections of God, which we must admit, if we admit a God at all. It strikes him as unforeseen, and not contemplated by the divine mind in the original intention to create, and as brought in to remedy the defects of creation, or to make amends for an unexpected and deplorable failure. The two orders, again, seem to stand apart, and to imply a dualism, in fact, an antagonism, which it is impossible to reconcile with the unity and perfections of God. If God is infinite in all his attributes, in wisdom, power, and goodness, why did he not make nature perfect, or all he desired it, in the beginning, so as to have no need to interfere to repair, or to amend it, or to create a new order in its place, or even to preserve it, and avert its total ruin? It is of no use to decry such thoughts and questions as irreverent, as impious, as blasphemous; for they arise spontaneously in the unbelieving mind, and denunciation will not suppress them. It will serve no purpose to bring in here the ordinary motives of credibility, drawn from the wants of nature, the insufficiency of reason, prophecies, miracles, and historical monuments, for these only create new and equally grave difficulties. What is wanted is not argument, but instruction and explanation. It is necessary to show, not merely assert, that the two orders are not mutually antagonistic; that one and the same principle of life runs through them both; that they correspond one to the other, and really constitute but two parts of one comprehensive whole, and are equally embraced in the original plan and purpose of God in creating. God could have created man, had he chosen, in a state of pure nature; but in point of fact he did not, and nature has never for a single instant existed as pure nature. It has, from the first moment of its existence, been under a supernatural providence; and even if man had not sinned, there would still have been a sufficient reason for the Incarnation, to raise human nature to union with God, to make it the nature of God, and to enable us, through its elevation, to enjoy endless beatitude in heaven.

The doctrine that all dependent life is life by communion of the subject with the object, shows that this is possible, shows the common principle of the two orders, and thus prepares the mind to receive and yield to the arguments drawn from the wants of nature, the insufficiency of reason, prophecies, miracles, and historical monuments; for it shows these to be in accordance with the original intent of the Creator, and that these wants and this insufficiency are wants and insufficiency, not in relation to the purely natural order, but in relation to the supernatural. Natural reason is sufficient for natural reason, but it is not sufficient for man; for man was intended from the beginning to live simultaneously in two orders, the one natural and the other supernatural.

Taking into consideration the fact that the skepticism of our age lies further back than the ordinary motives of credibility extend, further back than did the skepticism our ancestors had to meet, and shows itself under a different form, I believe the process by which I was conducted toward the church is not only a legitimate process in itself, but one which, in these times, in abler hands than mine, may be adopted with no little advantage. The present non-Catholic mind has as much difficulty in admitting the motives of credibility, as usually urged, as it has in accepting Christianity without them. Prior to adducing them, we must, it seems to me, prepare the way for them, by rectifying our philosophy, and giving to our youth a philosophical doctrine which reproduces the order of things, of reality, of life; not merely an order of dead abstractions. Such a philosophy, I think, will be found in that which underlies the process I have detailed; and I hope it is no presumption or lack of modesty on my part, to recommend it to the attention of the schools, as well as to the consideration of all whose office or vocation it is to combat the unbelief of the age and country.

READING AND STUDY OF
THE SCRIPTURES
[1861]

[In the July, 1861, number of his Review, *writing on "Catholic
Polemics," Brownson had asked many difficult questions con-
cerning the interpretation of Scripture. And this at a time when
Biblical scholarship was being pursued by the rationalistic meth-
ods of the higher criticism, and before the revival of Catholic
Biblical scholarship had begun.*

The following essay appeared in the October, 1861, issue of the
Review *and is in Volume XX, 171–187, of Brownson's* Works.
*Henry F. Brownson writes that it "was most orthodox in all re-
spects, and just such as he might have written after reading Pope
Leo XIII's Encyclical on the same subject, but containing one
passage which the Archbishop (Hughes) disliked, and which set
him against the whole essay."* (Brownson's Latter Life, *p. 271.)
This was the passage on "the downward tendency" of theological
studies from the early fathers to the modern professors "who
content themselves with giving compendiums of the compendiums given by the theologians." The passage was, in the words
of Henry F. Brownson, "tortured into a belittling of the scholastics and modern theologians."]*

T HE DOCTRINE of the church with regard to the Holy Scriptures has been much misunderstood and grossly misrepresented. She has never objected to or discouraged the reading of
the Scriptures, nor has she ever regarded their reading as un-
desirable or unprofitable. She approves, and always has approved, the use of the Bible, and objects, and has objected, only

to its misuse. She holds it to be written by inspiration, and profitable to teach, to reprove, to correct, to instruct in righteousness,
to perfect the man of God, and prepare him for every good
work. But she does not recognize it as the original medium of
divine revelation, or as sufficient to teach the true faith to one
who has received no preliminary instruction and no prior notice
of that faith. To put it into the hands of one who through the
living teacher, or through traditional instruction had received
no preparation for reading and understanding it, would be as
absurd as to put into the hands of the student a book on algebra
before he had learned the first four operations of simple arith-
metic. The principle on which she proceeds is adopted and acted
on by the various Christian sects, as well as by her, and to as
great an extent, else why do they have their Sunday schools,
their catechisms, their commentaries, their theological semi-
naries, their professors of theology, their preachers and teachers? The Presbyterian reads the Bible in the light of Presbyterian tradition; the Anglican, in the light of Anglican tradition; the Unitarian, in the light of Unitarian tradition; the
Methodist, in the light of Methodist tradition; and hence we
find that the children of Presbyterians tend naturally to grow
up Presbyterians, of Methodists to grow up Methodists, of Anglicans to grow up Anglicans, of Unitarians to grow up Unitarians. The only difference there is between the church and the
sects on this point is, that their traditions, in so far as they are
peculiar, date back only to the time of the reformers, whereas
her tradition dates back from the time of the apostles, and is
apostolic and therefore authentic.

The Evangelical sects, even while asserting the sufficiency of
the Scriptures, do really recognize their insufficiency. They all
recognize the necessity of a guide and interpreter to the understanding of Scripture not to be found in the Scriptures themselves; for they maintain that they are sufficient only when in-

terpreted to the understanding of the reader by the interior il-
lumination of the Holy Ghost. No man goes further in asserting
the weakness of the human understanding, or its insufficiency by
its own light to understand the Holy Scriptures, and deduce
therefrom the true Christian faith, than your stern, rigid, arrogant, and inflexible Presbyterian minister. No man is further
than he from accepting the doctrine of private judgment as held
by Unitarians and rationalists, and as ordinarily combated by
our Catholic controversialists. No man feels more deeply, or
maintains more rigidly or explicitly, the necessity of an infallible
guide and interpreter for whoever would read the Scriptures
with understanding and profit. "Thinkest thou that thou under-
standest what thou readest?"—"How can I unless someone
show me?" These questions are as significant for him as they
are for a Catholic, and he concedes that he cannot understand
what he reads, unless someone shows him or unfolds to him the
interior sense, the real meaning of the words he reads. This
someone he holds is the Holy Ghost, the Spirit of Truth, who
inspired the Scriptures themselves. The only controversy there
can be between him and us, is on a question of fact, not a question of law or principle. No doubt, if, as he supposes, he has the
Holy Ghost for his illuminator and instructor in reading the
Scriptures, his understanding of them is correct and worthy of
all confidence. Let him prove the fact, and there is no longer
any dispute between us. But he must excuse us, if we refuse to
accept it as a fact on his bare word, especially since we find
others, as much entitled to credit as he is, who claim to be illuminated and taught by the Holy Ghost, and whose understanding of the Scriptures is almost the very contradictory of his.

The principle insisted on by the church is a very plain and a
very reasonable principle, one that accords with the historical
facts in the case. The original revelation, she says, was not made
to mankind by writing, or through the medium of a book. It

was made in the beginning immediately by God himself to certain chosen individuals, who communicated it to others. Mankind knew and believed the truth, knew and believed the one true religion, at least in its substance, long before any book was written, or letters had been invented. The primitive believers under the Christian dispensation were taught the faith orally by those who had been orally instructed by our Lord himself. The faith thus orally taught and transmitted by the apostles to their successors, becomes the internal light by which the language of Scripture is interpreted and understood. Something of this sort is obviously necessary in the case of all language, whether written or unwritten. Written language is unintelligible to those who are ignorant of the characters in which it is written, or who have not learned to read. It is equally unintelligible to those who, though they know the characters and are able to read, yet do not understand the meaning of the words written. All words, whether written or unwritten, are signs or symbols; but they are signs or symbols only to intelligence; they signify, they symbolize nothing to one absolutely void of understanding. The interpretation of the sign or symbol comes from within, not from without; and if the sense be not, in some respect, already in the intelligence, there is and can be no real or true interpretation of the sign or symbol. Why, then, find fault with the church for adopting a rule which is universal, and which must be followed, or no instruction can be given through the medium of language, either written or unwritten? She has received the sense of the Holy Scriptures from the Holy Ghost, and by putting the faithful in possession of this, as she does, by means of analogies borrowed from nature, and accessible to the reason common to all men, she supplies the light and guidance necessary to enable them to read the Holy Scriptures with profit, and without perverting or wresting them to their own destruction.

The church undoubtedly requires her children to read the Scriptures with a reverential spirit, since they contain the revealed word of God, and it is God himself that is speaking through them. She also requires them to read the Holy Scriptures under her guidance, her direction, and not to interpret them in opposition to her teaching; because, as her teaching is from the Holy Ghost, by his assistance, and under his protection, any interpretation of Scripture contradicting that teaching would necessarily be a false interpretation, since the Scriptures are also from the Holy Ghost. But this does not mean that no one can read the Scriptures unless a priest stands at his back with a ferula in his hand, or that we have not the free use of our own reason and understanding in reading them, and developing and applying their sense. It does not mean that the errors of transcribers and of translators may not be corrected, or that we may not use all the helps to be derived from history and criticism, from science or erudition in correcting them. It does not mean that we may not use profane science and literature, the researches of geographers, the facts brought to light by travelers and the students of natural history, in illustrating and settling the literal meaning of the sacred text. It does not mean, any more, that we must understand and apply every text or passage, word or phrase, in the precise sense in which we find it understood or applied by the fathers and doctors of the church, or even by popes and councils. It means simply that we are not at liberty so to interpret Scripture as to derive from it any other doctrine than that which the church teaches, or to deduce from it any sense incompatible with faith and morals as she defines them. It is so we understand the doctrine of the church on the subject, and, so understood, her doctrine by no means cramps the intelligence, or restricts in any narrow or unreasonable degree the free and full exercise of our highest and best reason in understanding and applying the sublime truths they contain.

The abuse of the Holy Scriptures by the sects, and their exaggerated notions about Bible-reading, have no doubt had an influence on many Catholics, and tended, by way of reaction, to prevent them from reading and studying them as much as they otherwise would. The exaggerations of error tend always to discredit truth. The fear of being Bible-readers in the Protestant sense has, not unlikely, kept many from being Bible-readers in the Catholic sense. The necessity of repelling and refuting the exaggerations of Protestants has, in many instances, prevented us from insisting with due emphasis on the great advantage to be derived by the faithful from the daily reading and study of the written word of God, and substituted for them a whole host of devotional and ascetic works, many of which are of doubtful merit and doubtful utility. If faith has not suffered, piety, at least, has suffered therefrom; and we attribute no little of the weak and watery character of modern piety to the comparative neglect of the study of the Scriptures, and to the multiplication of works of sentimental piety. The piety these works nourish is just fit to accompany the meticulous orthodoxy now in vogue, and is a natural growth of the nursing and safeguard system now so generally insisted on. Faith, in our days, is weak and sickly, and piety dissolves into a watery sentimentality, rarely able to rise above "novenas and processions" in honor of some saint. It has become a sensitive plant; it lacks robustness and vigor, and is unable to meet the rough and tumble of the world.

The fathers studied and expounded the Scriptures, and they were strong men, the great men, the heroes of their times; the great medieval doctors studied, systematized, and epitomized the fathers, and, though still great, fell below those who were formed by the study of the Scriptures themselves; the theologians followed, gave compendiums of the doctors, and fell still lower; modern professors content themselves with giving compendiums of the compendiums given by the theologians, and have fallen as low as possible without falling into nothing and disappearing in the inane. In devotional and ascetic literature there has been the same process, the same downward tendency.

The remedy for the evil, in our judgment, is in returning anew to the study of the Scriptures themselves, and in drawing new life and vigor from their inspired pages. The words of man, however true or however noble, can never be made to equal the words of God; and the words of Scripture diluted down through twenty generations of men, each leaving out something of their divine significance, and adding something of human pettiness and weakness, can never be so effective in quickening and strengthening as they are as given us originally in the Scriptures by God himself. Orsini's or Gentilucci's *Life of the Madonna* is, no doubt, very beautiful; but it falls infinitely below in moral grandeur, in its inspiring effect, the few simple words touching our Lady given in any one of the Gospels themselves. There is much that is beautiful in our *Loves* and *Months of Mary*, but far less than in the *Magnificat*, the *Canticles*, or the *Psalms*; and all that is in them that has the slightest value for the soul is borrowed, and, we may say, diluted from these sources. Let us, then, go back to the Scriptures, study them as did the fathers, at least as did the great medieval doctors. Let us take in the sublime instruction as it was dictated by the Holy Ghost, and in language more beautiful and more sublime than ever did, or ever could, originate with uninspired men. Our faith will profit by it; it will become broader, purer, sublimer, and more comprehensive; it will become stronger, more robust, more energetic, and more able to withstand the seductions of error, or the temptations of vice. Our devotion will become more ardent, more solid, more enduring, flowing from a fixed and unalterable principle or conviction, not from mere temporary feeling or animal excitement; and our morals will conform to a higher standard, and we become capable of greater sacrifices and more heroic deeds.

What we in the English-speaking world most want is a good, faithful, and elegant translation of the Scriptures. To no mere English reader will the latinized language of our Douay version ever be attractive, especially if he has been early accustomed to read the Scriptures in the version made by order of James I of England. Archbishop Kenrick has done much to correct and improve this version, but still it falls, even in his amended edition, far short of what an English translation of the Holy Scriptures should be. His critical and explanatory notes are of great value, of greater value than their brevity and modest character would lead the majority of readers to suspect. But his language is not free, pure, idiomatic English. He has adopted many felicitous renderings from the Protestant version; he has, in some instances, substituted English for Latin words, and has gone as far as his plan permitted, and, perhaps, as far as he could go without too rudely disturbing the associations of those readers who know the Scriptures only in our Douay version; but it is to be regretted that he adopted so narrow a plan, and did not allow himself greater liberties in the same direction. We have heard much talk of a new translation to be undertaken and completed under the direction of Dr. Newman; but, as far as we can learn, this new translation has not as yet been commenced. In fact, we do not believe that it is possible in the present state of our language to make a new and original translation, which would be acceptable to those familiar with the Scriptures in their original tongues, or even the Latin Vulgate.

We have heretofore expressed our opinion, that in any attempt at a re-translation of the Scriptures into English for Catholics, King James's version should be taken as the basis, correcting it according to the readings of the Vulgate, and avoiding its mistranslations and its few grammatical and literary errors. Never was our language in so good a state for the translation of the Scriptures, as it was at the time when that translation was made. It had then a majestic simplicity, a naturalness, an ease, grace, and vigor which it has been gradually losing since, and which, if not wholly lost, we owe to the influence of that translation together with the Book of Common Prayer.

No translation of the Scriptures into the English of our best writers at the present day, could be endured by any reader of taste and judgment. Every day does our language depart more and more from the grandeur, strength, and simplicity which marked it in the sixteenth century and the beginning of the seventeenth; and proves very clearly, that the reading of the Scriptures, at least in the English version, is growing less and less common, or that scholars who have never familiarized themselves with that version, and formed their taste by its study, have gained the mastery in our modern literary world. Say what we will, since the time of Burke, the Celtic genius, aided by French influence, has been triumphing over the old Anglo-Saxon; and pompousness of diction, and diffuseness of style, have taken the place of terseness and simplicity. These facts render it impracticable for even our best scholars to produce a new translation of the Scriptures that could ever equal, in its literary merit, the Protestant version.

It is true, the version called the "Douay Bible" was made and published before that of the translators designated by King James,—the New Testament, at Rheims, in 1582, and the Old Testament, at Douay, in 1609; but it was made under great disadvantages, by Englishmen exiled from their own country, living, and, in part, educated abroad, and habitually speaking a foreign language. They were learned men, but they had, to a great extent, lost the genius and idioms of their own language, and evidently were more familiar with Latin and French than with their mother tongue. We give all honor to their memory, and we laud from our hearts their earnest and well-meant efforts; but we are unwilling to accept their translation even as they left it, as that in which the English-speaking world should study the Scriptures, far less as remodeled and emasculated by the excellent but tasteless Bishop Challoner, in which English and American Catholics now generally study them. In literary merit it can in no respect compare with the Protestant version; compared with that, it is weak, tasteless, and inharmonious. We might prove this by illustrations taken anywhere; but take, as it first occurs to us, the first verse of the first Psalm. In the Douay version it reads: "Blessed is the man who hath not walked in the counsel of the ungodly, nor stood in the way of sinners, nor sat in the chair of pestilence." In the Protestant version it reads: "Blessed is the man that walketh not in the counsel of the ungodly, nor standeth in the way of sinners, nor sitteth in the seat of the scornful." In this last version the parallelism of the Hebrew is better preserved, and the moral idea is carried out without change or interruption. But, in the first, the moral continuity is broken, and there is a sudden transition from the moral to the physical order, by substituting "the chair of pestilence" for "the seat of the scornful," which is not only better English, but a more faithful rendering of the original. Take another illustration, from the prayer of Habakkuk. In the Douay version it reads: "O Lord, I have heard thy hearing, and was afraid. O Lord, thy work, in the midst of the years, bring it to life. In the midst of the years thou shalt make it known; when thou art angry, thou wilt remember mercy. God will come from the South, and the Holy One from mount Pharan. His glory covered the heavens, and the earth is full of his praise. His brightness shall be as the light: horns are in his hands. There is his strength hid: death shall go before his face. And the devil shall go forth before his feet." The Protestant translation reads: "O Lord, I have heard thy speech, and was afraid: O Lord, revive thy work in the midst of the years, in the midst of the years make it known: in wrath remember mercy. God came from Teman, and the Holy One from mount Paran. Selah. His glory covered the heavens, and the earth was full of his praise. And his brightness was as the light; he had horns coming out of his hand: and there was the hiding of his power. Before him went the pestilence, and burning coals went forth at his feet.". . .

We have no intention, in anything we have said, to derogate from the authority of the Latin Vulgate. That text, corrected or amended according to the most authentic copies, is authoritative for all Catholics, and is, according to the judgment of the most eminent critics, upon the whole, the nearest approach to the exact reading of the original Scriptures which is now possible. It is, and must be, for Catholics, authority in all doctrinal discussions. We have not been speaking of it, but of an English translation, which may be read by English readers with pleasure and profit; but not of a translation that is ever to supersede for the theologian the Vulgate, or to be clothed with authority in controversies. Our simple suggestion is, that such translation should be made on the basis of the Protestant version, but conforming to the readings of the Vulgate where they differ from those of the received Greek and Hebrew texts. Such a translation, we think, would gradually come into general use, and ultimately supplant, in the English-speaking world, the Protestant version now in use. It would quietly settle the dispute between Catholics and Protestants as to the use of the Scriptures in the public schools, remove a great objection which Catholics now have to those schools, and go far to relieve us from the necessity we are now under of establishing separate schools for ourselves. But, however, this may be, we cannot close these desultory remarks,

without urging upon all Catholics the most attentive and as-
siduous study of the Holy Scriptures, as the best means of enlightening and confirming their faith, of elevating their devotion, of purifying and strengthening their piety, and giving robustness and vigor to their religious life.

Christianity and Civilization

CHRISTIANITY AND CIVILIZATION

EDITOR'S PREFACE

BROWNSON's earliest exposition of the relation between Christianity and civilization is humanitarian, ahistorical, and eclectic. With little understanding either of the history of western civilization or of the Church, Brownson interprets Christianity almost solely as a gospel of social reform. "New Views of Christianity, Society, and the Church" (1836) and "The Laboring Classes" (1840) represent this early position. In neither is there a clear distinction between the temporal and the spiritual order. "Church" and "State" are virtually convertible terms. As Brownson himself reminds us in *The Convert*, he meant by the term "Church" in 1836 essentially what he meant in 1840 by the term "State"; both terms expressed his doctrine of the single organization of mankind, or the unity of Church and state. "At the time I held it," Brownson writes, "though I accepted all the Christian mysteries in a sense of my own, I had no conception of the supernatural order." (*Works*, V, 111.)

In the first few years after his conversion, Brownson not only distinguishes between Church and state as two societies, the one concerned with man's supernatural, the other with man's natural good, but tends to separate them. His repudiation of his earlier exclusive concern for social reform and for the temporal good becomes itself exclusive. Individual salvation is of the Catholic Church; her mission is to call sinners to repentance, to sanctify individuals, to teach true doctrine. Essays like "Social-ism and the Church" (1849) not only condemn socialism as placing man's good solely in the natural order, but come close to a doctrine of flight from nature and society. The "world" is evil; the Christian must through emulation of the saints acquire the heroic virtues which make poverty and hardship indifferent.

With such essays as the "Mission of America" (1856)— which I omit because of limitations of space, and because its es-sential argument is to be found at the close of *The American Republic*—a different emphasis is discernible. Brownson sees the temporal common good of man as directed toward his ultimate good. As in his earlier writings, he now recognizes a Christian mission on the level of civilization, but he no longer makes so-cial reform an ultimate end. Although he devotes several essays to the relation of the Church to civilization in the medieval period, he repudiates "medievalism" as a solution to the modern problem. The relation of the Church to society must be a new one. Because it is in America that Church and state come closest to what he conceives as their normal relation, he holds that in America lies the greatest hope of the achievement of a new and more Christian civilization.

Because limitations of space prohibit a full representation of Brownson's thought on the theme of Christianity and civiliza-tion, I have selected the following essays chiefly from his later works, with the thought that for his earlier views the reader may refer to such essays as "The Laboring Classes."

NEW VIEWS OF CHRISTI-
ANITY, SOCIETY, AND
THE CHURCH
[1836]

["*New Views*" *was published as a pamphlet in Boston in November, 1836, the year that saw the publication of Emerson's
"Nature" and Bronson Alcott's "Conversations." It was Brownson's philosophical justification of "The Society for Christian
Union and Progress" which he organized in the previous July,
and of which, as he tells us in* The Convert, *he was the minister
until the latter part of 1843, "when I began to suspect that man
is an indifferent church-builder, and that God himself had already founded a church for us, some centuries ago, quite adequate to our wants, and adapted to our nature and destiny."*
(Works, *V, 82.*)
    *The title may have been suggested by Robert Owen's "A New
View of Society," though according to Brownson he derived his
ideas chiefly from "Benjamin Constant, Victor Cousin, Heinrich
Heine, and the publications of the Saint-Simonians." (*Works,
*V, 83.) The degree to which this essay epitomizes early nine-
teenth-century thought is suggested by the following quotation
from Christopher Dawson's* Progress and Religion: "*In the first
half of the 19th century the Idea of Progress had attained its
full development. It dominated the three main currents of European thought, Rationalist Liberalism, Revolutionary Socialism,
and Transcendental Idealism. It evoked all the enthusiasm and
faith of a genuine religion. Indeed it seemed to many that the
dream of St. Simon was on the eve of its fulfilment, and that
'the New Christianity,' the Religion of Progress, was to restore
to Europe the spiritual unity which she had lost since the Middle
Ages." (New York, 1938, pp. 210–11.)*]

CHRISTIANITY, as it existed in the mind of Jesus, was the type of the most perfect religious institution to which the human race will, probably, ever attain. It was the point where the sentiment and the institution, the idea and the symbol, the conception and its realization appear to meet and become one. But the contemporaries of Jesus were not equal to this profound thought. They could not comprehend the God-Man, the deep meaning of his assertion, "I and my Father are one.". . .

If the age in which Jesus appeared could not comprehend him, it is obvious that it could not fully embody him in its institutions. It could embody no more of him than it could receive, and as it could receive only a part of him, we must admit that the church has never been more than partially Christian. Never has it been the real body of Christ. Never has it reflected the God-Man perfectly. . . .

To comprehend Jesus, to seize the holy as it was in him, and consequently the true idea of Christianity, we must, from the heights to which we have risen by aid of the church, look back and down upon the age in which he came, ascertain what was the work which there was for him to perform, and from that obtain a key to what he proposed to accomplish.

Two systems then disputed the empire of the world: spiritualism [1] represented by the Eastern world, the old world of Asia, and materialism represented by Greece and Rome. Spiritualism regards purity or holiness as predicable of spirit alone, and matter as essentially impure, possessing and capable of receiving nothing of the holy,—the prison house of the soul, its only hindrance to a union with God, or absorption into his essence, the cause of all uncleanliness, sin, and evil, consequently to be contemned, degraded, and as far as possible annihilated. Material-

[1] I use these terms, Spiritualism and Materialism, to designate two social, rather than two philosophical systems. They designate two orders, which, from time out of mind, have been called *spiritual* and *temporal* or *carnal*, *holy* and *profane*, *heavenly* and *worldly*, &c.

ism takes the other extreme, does not recognize the claims of spirit, disregards the soul, counts the body everything, earth all, heaven nothing, and condenses itself into the advice, "Eat, and drink, for tomorrow we die.". . .

This antithesis generates perpetual and universal war. It is necessary then to remove it and harmonize, or unite the two terms. Now, if we conceive Jesus as standing between spirit and matter, the representative of both—God-Man—the point where both meet and lose their antithesis, laying a hand on each and saying, "Be one, as I and my Father are one," thus sanctifying both and marrying them in a mystic and holy union, we shall have his secret thought and the true idea of Christianity. The Scriptures uniformly present Jesus to us as a mediator, the middle term between two extremes, and they call his work a mediation, a reconciliation—an atonement. The church has ever considered Jesus as making an atonement. . . .

The aim of the church was to embody the holy as it existed in the mind of Jesus, and had it succeeded, it would have realized the atonement; that is, the reconciliation of spirit and matter and all their products. But the time was not yet. . . . Instead of understanding Jesus to assert the holiness of both spirit and matter, it understood him to admit that matter was rightfully cursed, and to predicate holiness of spirit alone. . . .

Everything must have its time. The church abused, degraded, vilified matter, but could not annihilate it. It existed in spite of the church. It increased in power, and at length rose against spiritualism and demanded the restoration of its rights. This rebellion of materialism, of the material order against the spiritual, is Protestantism. . . .

In Protestantism, Greece and Rome revived and again carried their victorious arms into the East. The reformation connects us with classical antiquity, with the beautiful and graceful forms of Grecian art and literature, and with Roman eloquence and jurisprudence, as the church had connected us with Judea, Egypt, and India. . . .

With Protestants, religion has existed; but as a reminiscence, a tradition. . . . If the religion of the Protestant world is a reminiscence, it must be the religion of the church. It is, in fact, only Catholicism continued. The same principle lies at the bottom of all Protestant churches, in so far as they are churches, which was at the bottom of the church of the middle ages. But materialism modifies their rites and dogmas. In the practice of all, there is an effort to make them appear reasonable. Hence commentaries, expositions, and defenses without number. Even where the authority of reason is denied, there is an instinctive sense of its authority and a desire to enlist it. In mere forms, pomp and splendor have gradually disappeared, and dry utility and even baldness have been consulted. In doctrines, those which exalt man and give him some share in the work of salvation have gained in credit and influence. Pelagianism, under some thin disguises or undisguised, has become almost universal. The doctrine of man's inherent total depravity, in the few cases in which it is asserted, is asserted more as a matter of duty than of conviction. Nobody, who can help it, preaches the old-fashioned doctrine of God's sovereignty, expressed in the dogma of unconditional election and reprobation. The vicarious Atonement has hardly a friend left. The Deity of Jesus is questioned, his simple humanity is asserted and is gaining credence. Orthodox is a term which implies as much reproach as commendation; people are beginning to laugh at the claims of councils and synods, and to be quite merry at the idea of excommunication. . . .

The real character of Protestantism, the result to which it must come, wherever it can have its full development, may be best seen in France, at the close of the last century. The church was converted into the pantheon, and made a resting place for the bodies of the great and renowned of earth; God was converted into a symbol of the human reason, and man into the man-machine; spiritualism fell, and the revolution marked the complete triumph of materialism. . . .

The eighteenth century will be marked in the annals of the world for its strong faith in the material order. Meliorations on the broadest scale were contemplated and viewed as already realized. Our republic sprang into being, and the world leaped with joy that "a man child was born." Social progress and the perfection of governments became the religious creed of the day; the weal of man on earth, the spring and aim of all hopes and labors. A new paradise was imaged forth for man, inaccessible to the serpent, more delightful than that which Adam lost, and more attractive than that which the pious Christian hopes to gain. We of this generation can form only a faint conception of the strong faith our fathers had in the progress of society, the high hopes of human improvement they indulged, and the joy too big for utterance, with which they heard France in loud and kindling tones proclaim *Liberty* and *Equality*. France for a moment became the center of the world. All eyes were fixed on her movements. The pulse stood still when she and her enemies met, and loud cheers burst from the universal heart of humanity when her tri-colored flag was seen to wave in triumph over the battlefield. There was then no stray thought for God and eternity. Man and the world filled the soul. They were too big for it. But while the voice of hope was yet ringing, and *Te Deum* shaking the arches of the old cathedrals,—the convention, the reign of Terror, the exile of patriots, the massacre of the gifted, the beautiful, and the good, Napoleon and the military despotism came, and humanity uttered a piercing shriek, and fell prostrate on the grave of her hopes!

The reaction produced by the catastrophe of this memorable drama was tremendous. . . . Men never feel what they felt but once. The pang which darts through their souls changes them into stone. From that moment enthusiasm died, hope in social melioration ceased to be indulged, and those who had been the most sanguine in their anticipations, hung down their heads and said nothing; the warmest friends of humanity apologized for their dreams of liberty and equality; democracy became an accusation, and faith in the perfectibility of mankind a proof of disordered intellect.

In consequence of this reaction, men again despaired of the earth; and when they despair of the earth, they always take refuge in heaven; when man fails them, they always fly to God. They had trusted materialism too far—they would now not trust it at all. They had hoped too much—they would now hope nothing. The future, which had been to them so bright and promising, was now overspread with black clouds; the ocean on which they were anxious to embark was lashed into rage by the storm, and presented only images of dismasted or sinking ships and drowning crews. They turned back and sighed for the serene past, the quiet and order of old times, for the mystic land of India, where the soul may dissolve in ecstasy and dream of no change.

At the very moment when the sigh had just escaped, that mystic land reappeared. The English, through the East India Company, had brought to light its old literature and philosophy, so diverse from the literature and philosophy of modern Europe or of classical antiquity, and men were captivated by their novelty and bewildered by their strangeness. . . .

The influence of the old Braminical or spiritual world, thus dug up from the grave of centuries, may be traced in all our philosophy, art and literature. It is remarkable in our poets. It moulds the form in Byron, penetrates to the ground in Wordsworth, and entirely predominates in the Schlegels. It causes us to feel a new interest in those writers and those epochs which partake the most of spiritualism. Those old English writers who were somewhat inclined to mysticism are revived; Plato, who traveled in the East and brought back its lore which he modified by western genius and moulded into Grecian forms, is re-edited, commented on, translated, and raised to the highest rank among philosophers. The middle ages are re-examined and found to contain a treasure of romance, acuteness, depth, and wisdom, and are deemed by some to be "dark ages" only because we have not light enough to read them. . . .

Indeed everywhere is seen a decided tendency to spiritualism. The age has become weary of uncertainty. It sighs for repose. Controversy is nearly ended, and a sentiment is extensively prevailing, that it is a matter of very little consequence what a man believes, or what formulas of worship he adopts, if he only have a right spirit. Men, who a few years ago were staunch rationalists, now talk of Spiritual Communion; and many, who could with difficulty be made to admit the inspiration of the Bible, are now ready to admit the inspiration of the sacred books of all nations; and instead of stumbling at the idea of God's speaking to a few individuals, they see no reason why he should not speak to everybody. . . .

We of the present century must either dispense with all religious instructions, reproduce spiritualism or materialism, or we must build a new church, organize a new institution free from the imperfections of those which have been. . . .

We cannot then go back either to exclusive spiritualism, or to exclusive materialism. Both these systems have received so full a development, have acquired so much strength, that neither can be subdued. Both have their foundation in our nature, and both will exist and exert their influence. Shall they exist as antagonist principles? Shall the spirit forever lust against the flesh, and the flesh against the spirit? Is the bosom of humanity to be eternally torn by these two contending factions? No. It cannot be. The war must end. Peace must be made.

This discloses our Mission. We are to reconcile spirit and matter; that is, we must realize the atonement. Nothing else remains for us to do. Stand still we cannot. To go back is equally impossible. We must go forward, but we can take not a step forward, but on the condition of uniting these two hitherto hostile principles. Progress is our law and our first step is Union. . . .

But we can do this only by a general doctrine which enables us to recognize and accept all the elements of humanity. If we leave out any one element of our nature, we shall have antagonism. Our system will be incomplete and the element excluded will be forever rising up in rebellion against it and collecting forces to destroy its authority. . . .

Unitarianism belongs to the material order. It is the last word of Protestantism, before Protestantism breaks entirely with the past. It is the point toward which all Protestant sects converge in proportion as they gain upon their reminiscences. Every consistent Protestant Christian must be a Unitarian. Unitarianism elevates man; it preaches morality; it vindicates the rights of the mind, accepts and uses the reason, contends for civil freedom, and is social, charitable, and humane. It saves the Son of man, but sometimes loses the Son of God.

But it is from the Unitarians that must come out the doctrine of universal reconciliation; for they are the only denomination in Christendom that labors to rest religious faith on rational conviction; that seeks to substitute reason for authority, to harmonize religion and science, or that has the requisite union of piety and mental freedom, to elaborate the doctrine which is to realize the atonement. . . .

But Unitarians are every day breaking away more and more from tradition, and every day making new progress in the creation of a philosophy which explains humanity, determines its wants and the means of supplying them. Mind at this moment is extremely active among them, and as it can act freely it will most certainly elaborate the great doctrine required. They began in rationalism. Their earlier doctrines were dry and cold. And this was necessary. They were called at first to a work of destruction. They were under the necessity of clearing away the rubbish of the old church, before they could obtain a site whereon to erect the new one. The Unitarian preacher was under the necessity of raising a stern and commanding voice in the wilderness, "Prepare ye the way of the Lord, make his paths straight." He raised that voice, and the chief priests and Pharisees in modern Judea heard and trembled, and some have gone forth to be baptized. The Unitarian has baptized them with water unto repentance, but he has borne witness that a mightier than he shall come after him, who shall baptize them with the Holy Ghost and with fire. . . .

I do not misread the age. I have not looked upon the world only out from the window of my closet; I have mingled in its busy scenes; I have rejoiced and wept with it; I have hoped and feared, and believed and doubted with it, and I am but what it has made me. I cannot misread it. It craves union. The heart of man is crying out for the heart of man. One and the same spirit is abroad, uttering the same voice in all languages. From all parts of the world voice answers to voice, and man responds to man. There is a universal language already in use. Men are beginning to understand one another, and their mutual understanding will beget mutual sympathy, and mutual sympathy will bind them together and to God.

And for progress too the whole world is struggling. Old institutions are examined, old opinions criticized, even the old church is laid bare to its very foundations, and its holy vestments and sacred symbols are exposed to the gaze of the multitude;

new systems are proclaimed, new institutions elaborated, new ideas are sent abroad, new experiments are made, and the whole world seems intent on the means by which it may accomplish its destiny. The individual is struggling to become a greater and a better being. Everywhere there are men laboring to perfect governments and laws. The poor man is admitted to be human, and millions of voices are demanding that he be treated as a brother. All eyes and hearts are turned to education. The cultivation of the child's moral and spiritual nature becomes the worship of God. The priest rises to the educator, and the schoolroom is the temple in which he is to minister. There is progress; there will be progress. Humanity must go forward. Encouraging is the future. He who takes his position on the "high tableland" of humanity, and beholds with a prophet's gaze his brothers, so long separated, coming together, and arm in arm marching onward and upward toward the perfect, toward God may hear celestial voices chanting a sweeter strain than that which announced to Judea's shepherds the birth of the Redeemer, and his heart full and overflowing, he may exclaim with old Simeon, "Lord, now lettest thou thy servant depart in peace, for mine eyes have seen thy salvation."

CATHOLIC POLEMICS
[1861]

[*In numerous essays written after 1855, Brownson stresses the
need on the part of Catholics of a creative and positive approach
to the intellectual and social problems of the time. There is an
unmistakable change of emphasis in all of his work, and the
vehemence of some of his criticism of Catholic contemporaries
even led some of his opponents to predict that he would leave
the Church. His distinction in the following essay between Catholic tradition and the traditions of Catholics is characteristic of
this period. In the full text of the essay* (Works, XX, 107–30)
*Brownson asks questions about Catholic doctrine on the punish-
ment of the damned and on the interpretation of Holy Scripture
which brought sharp criticism both in personal letters to him and
in the Catholic press. To the charges that the implied answers
to his questions were doctrinally unsound, Brownson replied at
length in the following* (October, 1861) *issue of his* Quarterly
(Works, XX, 130–70).]

WE HAVE no disposition to apologize for unbelievers and
rejecters of the truth; yet, we confess, we cannot wholly
approve a widely prevailing notion, that all error presupposes
malice, and that all who remain outside of the church do so
through hatred of the truth and love of iniquity. Any man who
has once been a Protestant and subsequently reconciled to the
church, knows well that his greatest difficulty in the way of accepting Catholic truth was in understanding it. He will tell you,
and tell you truly, that in proportion as he ascertained the real
meaning of the church he was prepared to accept it, and that

he wanted no argument to prove it after he had clearly seen it. The church to be loved needs but to be seen as she is; the truth to be believed needs but to be presented to the mind as it is in its real relations. This follows from the common doctrine of the scholastics that the object of the will is GOOD, and that the object of the intellect is TRUTH; as also from the doctrine of St. Thomas that all sin originates in ignorance. To convert a man it is necessary to enlighten him, and all theologians teach us that the grace which converts illustrates the understanding at the same time that it assists the will. Men reject or refuse to believe our doctrines because they do not understand them, that is, do not understand them in their relations with their own institutions or rational convictions, which, it seems to them, they cannot give up without a total abandonment of reason common to all men. May not, then, our failure to convert them, be, in great part, owing to the fact that we fail so to present them, that is, fail to present them so that they appear to them consistent with the dictates of reason and common sense? Must there not, then, be fault on our side as well as on theirs?

But here is our difficulty. It seems to be very generally understood in the Catholic community here and elsewhere, that the Catholic controversialist must never concede that Catholics can possibly err in their apprehension of Catholic truth, or in their mode of presenting it; that every Catholic writer or publicist must always proceed on the assumption that, as between them and their opponents, all Catholics are infallible and impeccable, and as wise as serpents and as harmless as doves; that to vary a single word or form of expression adopted by scholastic theologians would be to betray the Catholic cause; and that every attempt to present Catholic truth in a manner to be apprehensible by our age, and to remove the objections to it in the minds of non-Catholics by exhibiting it in a new light, or under new forms, would indicate a restless, uneasy, discontented, and querulous spirit, if not absolute disloyalty to the spouse of Christ. We are told on every side by those who affect to give tone and direction to Catholic thought and, action, that it is our duty as Catholic publicists to defend things as we find them; to raise no question which may excite controversy among ourselves; to enter into no philosophical or theological discussions not acceptable to all Catholics, whether learned or unlearned; never to criticize the doings or the sayings of our predecessors among Catholic polemists; never to take any deeper, broader, or loftier views than are taken by the most ignorant or uncultivated of Catholic believers; never to strike out any new lines of argument or to shift the ground of controversy with our opponents. We are required to follow tradition, not only in what is of faith, but in what pertains to the theological expression of revealed truth, and to the mode or manner of defending it. If we would be accounted orthodox, or stand well with the pretended exponents of Catholic public opinion, we must explain the causes of the Protestant rebellion according to the traditions of Catholics, and never deviate from that tradition in our manner of explaining and refuting its errors. We must be content to repeat the arguments stereotyped for our use, although those arguments may rest on historical blunders, metaphysical errors, and misreading of the fathers, or a doubtful interpretation of the sacred text. We are permitted to make no account of the researches of the moderns in the physical sciences, in history, natural or civil, in literary criticism, or Biblical literature; to pay no attention to the present state of the controversy between Catholics and non-Catholics, to the new questions which have arisen, to the new ground that has been taken, or to the new modes of warfare adopted by the rejecters of Catholic truth. We are required to take it for granted that all our controversy must be with Lutherans, Calvinists, or Anglicans, on the ground, we suppose, that error is as invariable as truth. We do not, of course, mean to say that there is any Catholic, cleric or laic, who would expressly maintain this; but this much we do mean to say, that anyone who does not conform to the rule here laid down will find that he has severer controversies to maintain with his own brethren than with the avowed enemies of the church, and there are few men who can maintain their credit for orthodoxy when a considerable number of their own brethren, and especially those who give tone and direction to Catholic action, are opposed to them. No men are more readily distrusted, no men are looked upon with more horror by Catholics than they who become the occasion of domestic controversy. The rule adopted seems to be not that which was laid down by the apostle, "Follow after the things that *make* for peace," but follow after peace, or seek peace at any price. . . .

In our historical reading we have found no epoch in which the directors of the Catholic world seem to have had so great a dread of intellect as our own. There seems to be almost universally the conviction expressed by Rousseau that "the man who thinks is a depraved animal." There is a widespread fear that he who thinks will think heretically. The study, therefore, of our times is to keep men orthodox by cultivating their pious affections with as little exercise of intelligence as possible. There is no doubt that for the last hundred years the intelligence, at least what is regarded as the intelligence of the world, has been divorced from orthodoxy. During this period the most successful cultivators of science, of history, literature, and art, have not been Catholics, or, if nominally Catholics, with little understanding of the teaching, or devotion to the practice, of the church. The natural sciences, zoology, geology, chemistry, natural history, ethnography, metaphysics, and to some extent history itself, have been anti-Catholic, while the popular literature, that which takes hold of the heart and forms the taste, the mind, and the morals of a nation, has been decidedly hostile to the church. It is very likely this fact, that has created the aversion in Catholic minds to free and independent thought, and driven them into the extreme that we complain of. They see how un-Catholic is thought in its modern forms and developments; they see how rapidly and how rashly the world rushes into the most fatal errors; and therefore they fear to trust thought, and consequently seek to restrain it. This is their excuse. Yet it is no full justification. The true policy, in our judgment, would be not to yield up thought and intelligence to Satan, but to redouble our efforts to bring them back to the side of the church, so as to restore her to her rightful spiritual and intellectual supremacy. Instead of foregoing thought and intelligence, and contenting ourselves with pious affection which, when divorced from thought, becomes a mere weak and watery sentimentality, we should grapple with them, master the age precisely in that in which it regards itself as strongest, increase our efforts to enlighten the people, and gain for them the superiority not merely in faith and piety, but in secular knowledge and science. Intelligence can be mastered only by intelligence, thought can be overcome only by thought.

There has never been an epoch in the world's history when the policy now generally pursued could have been more unwise, or likly to be more fatal, than the present. Now less than ever can we keep people in the faith by mere ignorance and prejudice, or even by early association and affection. We cannot keep our people ignorant of error if we would, and do what we will we cannot prevent them from being more or less affected by the spirit of the age. In no country have we an orthodox Caesar to protect the flock with his armed legions, or to keep down error by civil pains and penalties, even were that desirable. The civil government nowhere protects the church, any further than it hopes to use her for its own purposes. There is no longer any reliance to be placed upon the civil power, however deeply some

may regret it. The church is obliged to fall back on her own resources as a spiritual kingdom, and the last vestige of the old
union of church and state, will ere long be everywhere effaced.
The most the church can hope from the state hereafter is to be
let alone, and it will be much if Catholics are allowed to be free
in the general freedom of the citizen. . . . The authority of the
church, the divine institution of the clergy, the truth of the
sacred mysteries of religion, nay, the very providence and even
existence of God, are brought into public discussion. Doubts on
all points are entertained and boldly uttered. Nothing is regarded as fixed and certain. Now this state of things must be
met, and met effectually. But how can we meet it, if thought is
discouraged, free discussion prohibited, and our people kept as
far as possible in ignorance of all not absolutely necessary to
salvation? . . .

The existing state of things is not met by a mere negative
policy, or by a so-called safeguard system. No amount of pious
training or pious culture will protect the faithful, or preserve
them from the contamination of the age, if they are left inferior
to non-Catholics in secular learning and intellectual development. The faithful must be guarded and protected by being
trained and disciplined to grapple with the errors and false systems of the age. They must be not only more religiously, but
also more intellectually educated. They must be better armed
than their opponents,—surpass them in the strength and vigor of
their minds, and in the extent and variety of their knowledge.
They must, on all occasions and against all adversaries, be ready
to give a reason for the hope that is in them. They must be better scholars, more learned men, profounder philosophers, better
versed in the sciences, more thorough masters of history, abler
and more attractive writers and orators, and prove themselves in
every respect the *élite* of the race. It is in vain in our times to attempt to preserve them in their loyalty to the church by the

force of simple external authority, or even by their reverence for the prelates whom the Holy Ghost has placed over them. Both for those within and for those without, authority must vindicate itself,—must show that it is not merely a positive and arbitrary authority, but that it is authority in the reason and nature of things, intrinsic as well as extrinsic. Minds in our day are to be governed by respecting their freedom, not by restraining it, and men in authority must be more ready to convince than to command. Blind obedience is out of the question; submission to *men* is contrary to the spirit of the age; and the prelate must, if he would be obeyed, show that obedience to him is real, not reputed, obedience to God. There must be no shams, there must be no make-believes, but there must be everywhere the REAL PRESENCE.

We say not that it is not to be deplored that such is the case. We write not to vindicate the age, but to present it as it is. We say not but it would be far better if there were everywhere to be met only simple, unquestioning obedience; we say not that there is not something of impiety even in this questioning spirit of our times, which demands a reason even for obeying God, still more for obeying his ministers; we express, as we feel, no sympathy with this spirit; but it is the spirit that now reigns in Catholic populations hardly less than in non-Catholic populations. . . . Our Lord reasoned with the Jews; the apostles reasoned with the people to whom they were sent; and the greatest popes and prelates of the church have shown themselves, at all times, more studious to convince the understanding than to overcome the will.

No doubt this policy which we recommend imposes far greater labor on the ministers of our holy religion than the one we oppose, and that it is a policy that will never be acceptable to any who are not willing to spend and be spent in the service of God. Men who love their ease, who think only of performing a certain round of prescribed duties with as little trouble to themselves as possible, and feel not deeply the worth of human souls, cannot be expected to approve it. It can be adopted only by men who are in earnest, who take life seriously, and count no labors, no sacrifices in the service of their Lord. It is not a policy for amateurs and dilettanti. It is a policy only for strong men; men with robust souls, intrepid hearts, and indomitable love; men who feel that religion embraces all truth, and is the condition of all good; men who are above the world, whose affections are placed on things eternal, and whose conversation is in heaven. It will not meet the approbation of men who recognize only the *opus operatum*, and forget that men may be instrumental in the salvation of their brethren. But for those who understand that God works through means and carries on his designs by human agencies, and that men are in some sense responsible one for another, it will be an acceptable policy. These will not shrink from, but will joy to meet and perform the labors it requires. They will enter with alacrity upon the work, engage in it with their whole souls, with all the energy and strength God gives them. Heroic souls shrink not from difficulties; their courage rises with the danger, and their strength grows with the magnitude of the work before them.

Now if we look at the work that is to be done in our day and generation, we ask, how is it possible to do it, if we are to be tied down to old forms and old methods; if we are to be deterred by fear of disturbing the equanimity or self-complacency of narrow-minded and uninstructed publicists who are not aware that there have been any changes in the world for the last four hundred years? How are we to do it, if we are to open no discussions, enter upon no line of argument, offer no explanations, attempt no solutions of difficulties which are not already familiar to the age? How are we to do it, if we are allowed to engage in no controversy, to correct no error, to disturb no prejudice, to stir no thought? How are we to do it, if all that is permitted us is to repeat what we may find set down in our older and superannuated polemical works? How are we to do it, if we are only to follow servilely those who wrote before they could have any knowledge of the peculiar errors and peculiar wants of our times? How are we to do it, if we are bound to take the public opinions of Catholics in this or that locality instead of Catholic truth itself for our guide?

We find no fault with the great men, the great controversialists of other times. They did their work, and they did it well; they vindicated nobly, heroically, and successfully, the truth for their age; answered conclusively the objections which they had to answer, and in the form and way most intelligible to those who urged them. It is no reproach to them to say that they have not fully answered objections which were not raised in their time. What we ask is, that Catholic controversialists be allowed to follow their example, and that we be as free to grapple with the errors and speculations of our age as they were to grapple with the errors and speculations of theirs. They were free to do their work; let us be free to do ours. He who knows the age knows that there are objections to the church which are peculiar to our times, and to which no formal answer was or could have been given by our predecessors. Neither St. Augustine nor St. Thomas, neither Bellarmine nor Bossuet, had to meet objections of precisely the same sort as those we have to meet. Many things could be taken by them for granted which we are obliged to prove. Many things are denied now that nobody then questioned. Though error, in substance, may always be the same, it is continually varying its forms, and it appears now under forms under which it never before appeared. Shall we be permitted to meet these new forms in the only way in which they can be ef-

fectually met, or shall we be told that we must let them alone,
say nothing about them, and take all possible precautions to prevent the faithful from knowing of their existence? . . .

The difficulty is not that Catholics do not know the positive
doctrines of their church, but that they are not fully instructed
in regard to the errors and speculations now dominant in the
non-Catholic world. Our Catholic community, taken at large,
not only do not understand them, but are not sufficiently instructed to understand their refutation when given. Publicists,
who are as innocent of any knowledge of them as the child unborn, clamor against him who really refutes them, get up an
excitement against him, and cause all the lovers of peace to look
upon him as a dangerous and pestilent fellow; for usually the
friends of peace blame the party in the right, rarely the party in
the wrong. He who departs from routine is set down at once as
guilty, and they who misunderstand, misrepresent, and denounce him, are regarded as praiseworthy. . . . Just now popular opinion among Catholics, as among non-Catholics, identifies
Catholicity and despotism, and the controversialist who seeks to
prove that the Catholic religion has no natural association with
despotism but is favorable to liberty and the inherent rights of
man, runs the risk of being denounced on all hands as a bad
Catholic. The really formidable war waged upon the church is
waged by the cultivators of science and the German rationalists.
Yet he who should endeavor by his explanations of Catholic
theology, though adhering firmly to the Catholic faith, to dis-
arm them of their hostility and to show the perfect harmony of
science and reason with Catholicity, would most likely be accused by his own brethren of the errors he labors to refute. . . .

LACORDAIRE AND
CATHOLIC PROGRESS
[1862]

[*In many ways the following essay furnishes a clue not only to Brownson's thought before his conversion on the relation between democracy and Christianity, but also to the shift in emphasis which is so apparent in his "liberal period" from the midfifties to 1864. In the first part of the essay, which I have not been able to include, Brownson tells how he had followed with the greatest interest the attempt by Lammenais to make the Catholic Church in France the champion of political liberty and to "Christianize democracy." With the fall of Lamennais in 1832 he concluded "that the old Church was dead," and wasted, as he put it, a dozen years "in the endeavor to lay the foundation of a new church." What he did not realize was that Lacordaire and Montalembert, both associated with Lamennais at the time, accepted the papal condemnation of the extreme views of Lamennais' newspaper L'Avenir, yet continued their effort to give a courageous Christian leadership to the aspirations for democracy and liberty, but without committing Lamennais' error of trying to tie the Church to a particular political system. Brownson's "discovery" of these two men in the 1850's is, I believe, one of the most significant elements in his own attempt to reassert, within a Catholic context, many of the views he had repudiated immediately after his conversion. It is difficult not to speculate on how different his tone might have been from 1844 to 1850 had he been familiar with their thought and their work in France at that time.*

The essay appeared in Brownson's Quarterly *for July, 1862, and is to be found in* Works, *XX, 249–78. Since Brownson is reviewing Montalembert's volume,* Le Père Lacordaire (*Paris,*

1862), it is worth remarking that Newman begins his important note on "Liberalism" in his Apologia (1864) by quoting from the volume, and goes on to say: "I do not believe that it is possible for me to differ in any important matter from two men whom I so highly admire. In their general line of thought and conduct I enthusiastically concur, and consider them to be before their age. And it would be strange indeed if I did not read with a special interest, in M. de Montalembert's beautiful volume, of the unselfish aims, the thwarted projects, the unrequited toils, the grand and tender resignation of Lacordaire." (Apologia Pro Vita Sua, New York, Longmans, Green, 1947, p. 259.)]

THE GREAT CHANGE we look for in the mutual relations of the church and society, demanded by the progress of events, is not to be expected in a day. The old mixed civil and ecclesiastical government of society is that under which most Catholics have been trained, that to which in old Catholic countries they are still habituated, and that which almost everywhere the regular official instruction they receive presents as the beau-ideal of Catholic organization. All see and know that that order has been violently shaken, that it has in many places been overthrown, and is menaced everywhere; but probably the majority regard this as a fact to be deplored, and still cherish the hope of one day restoring the relations which have been disturbed or broken. Many may suspect the change threatened cannot be successfully resisted, but, regarding it as an evil, think it their duty to resist it as long as they can,—to put off the evil day to the remotest future possible. They who think with us that the change is not only inevitable, but desirable, and that it will prove not only a change, but a progress, are only a minority, and those not at the head of ecclesiastical affairs. The laity are much better prepared for it, and much more favorable to it, than the clergy; but it is not fitting that the laity should array themselves against the clergy, and in matters of this sort there is little good that can be accomplished without the co-operation of the hierarchy. The great evil, and that which delays the change, is the attempts of the laity to accomplish it without this co-operation, and in spite of it. These attempts are impolitic, and even uncatholic. They are in their nature revolutionary, and therefore always to be deprecated. If the clergy are not the whole church, there is no church without them, any more than there are children without parents. Much of the backwardness, slowness, and hesitancy of the clergy grows out of the impatience of the people, their disorderly demands, their revolutionary tendencies, creating in their minds the suspicion that the moving cause in the people is doubt of religion, and unwillingness to submit to its restraints, and to practice its precepts. The complete separation of church and state, leaving the church to find protection for her liberty in the general liberty secured to the citizen, we hold to be the only practicable solution of the problems of our age with equal advantage to civil and religious society; we believe that this solution is the one to which the whole progress of the world is tending; but we are not ourselves prepared to adopt it against the church, or without the consent of the hierarchy.

What we claim for ourselves is the right to urge it, the right to discuss it, to show its utility, its desirableness, and its inevitableness; to convince if we can, even the hierarchy of its utility, and persuade them to consent to it. The right to do this much, we maintain, is the right of every Catholic, whether cleric or laic, simply holding himself bound in the sphere of action to obey the constituted authorities. I am bound to obey the pontificate, and to venerate the sacerdocy, both of which are from God, but I am not bound to take no thought for the interests of religion and society, or, in this country at least, to refrain from expressing my honest convictions, when they in no sense impugn Catholic dogma, or what is unchangeable in the constitution of the church. There is a mission of genius, of intelligence in the church, which is not necessarily restricted to the clergy, and may be committed to laymen, or to clergymen in a sense outside of their sacerdotal character, for the church has a right to the service of the genius, the intelligence, the learning, the good-will, and the zeal of all her members, of laymen as well as of clergymen. We see nothing uncatholic in this non-hierarchical mission, any more than there was under the Old Law in the mission of the prophets, which was distinct from that of the ordinary priesthood, and, as we may say, extra-hierarchical. Indeed, in asserting it, we assert only what always has been and always will be. We claim no more for the laity than they have always done, except we claim publicity for what they do, or that what they do they do openly, before the whole world, not simply by private communication, by secret diplomacy, and sometimes by private intrigue. In discussion the layman, under responsibility, we hold, may take the initiative, and not await it from authority. He may open such questions as he deems important, and the business of authority is not to close his mouth, but to set him right, when and where he goes wrong. This is no more than princes and nobles have always been allowed, or assumed unrebuked the right to do, and princes and nobles are only laymen. What a crowned or a titled layman may do, a free American citizen, though uncrowned and untitled, may also do. I have as much right to make my suggestions, and offer my advice to the bishops or to the supreme pontiff as had Charlemagne and St. Louis, or as has Louis Napoleon or Francis Joseph to offer theirs. Before the church, if not before the state, all laymen are equal.

But this, though undeniably true, is so far removed from past usage, that to any but an inborn republican, it seems almost false, almost satanic, and it will need to be iterated and reiterated from many mouths and for a long time, before it will be generally accepted and practically conformed to. The memory of old systems and of the old relations between the temporal

and the spiritual is too vivid for even Catholics who have not
imbibed republican sentiments, and, as to that matter for many
who have imbibed them, to see in the assertion that the people
in relation to the ecclesiastical society, stand on a footing of perfect equality with princes and nobles, kings and kaisers, nothing
uncatholic or disrespectful to the hierarchy. All the old relations of church and state presuppose the state to have for its basis
not right and equality, but inequality and privilege. The greater
part of our ascetic literature or works designed especially for
spiritual instruction and edification, presuppose monarchy tempered or not tempered with aristocracy, as the constitution of
society, and are filled with allusions, illustrations and comparisons that are neither apt nor edifying to a republican mind. The
general tone of our theological literature, whether scholastic or
popular, speculative or polemical, produces an impression on the
reader that the church is confined to the government, and really
consists only of the clergy, hierarchically organized under their
chief, the supreme pontiff. The people seem to count for nothing
in the church, as formerly they counted for nothing in the state.
He who ventures to assert that the clergy are only functionaries
in the church and for the church, that the laity are an integral
part of the church, and not mere "hewers of wood and drawers
of water" to the hierarchy, with neither voice nor souls of their
own, is at once suspected of wishing to democratize the church, of
having Congregational predilections or reminiscences, if not of
being animated by an unavowed hostility to the hierarchical constitution of the church herself. It is hard to protest against an extreme in one direction, without being suspected of wishing to run
to an extreme in another. Hence it is that they who propose
changes or ask for changes demanded by the progress or changes
in civilization, are sure to be misunderstood, misrepresented, and
suspected of disloyalty to Catholicity.

No man ever lived who could more effectually bear witness

to the truth of what is here asserted than Père Lacordaire. He was sincere, earnest, and firm in his faith, simple and docile as a child, clear, distinct, and reverential in his expression, unbounded in his charity, full of tenderness of heart, gentle in his manners, eminent for his prudence, his sobriety, and for his earnestness, his singleness of purpose, and his disinterestedness, and yet he had his enemies, enemies who persevered in being his enemies during his life, who misunderstood him, misrepresented him, distrusted him as a Catholic, and did all in their power to lessen his influence, and defeat his purposes. How often have we heard him traduced, denounced as a radical, a Jacobin, a socialist, concealing the *bonnet rouge,* under the friar's hood. Yet he persevered, held fast to his integrity, held fast to his convictions, and continued on in the line of duty marked out for him, unshaken and unruffled, calm and serene, till he laid him down gently, and slept his sleep of sweet peace in the Lord who so tenderly loved him, and whom he so tenderly loved and has so heroically served. His example is full of inspiration and consolation, and proves that God is as near us today as of old, and has not abandoned our age. Great souls may be borne now as well as aforetime, and great and heroic deeds remain for the Christian today, not inferior to the greatest and most glorious performed by our fathers. Not in vain did Père Lacordaire live, toil, suffer, and die, and nothing better proves it than the touching words in the Albigensian *patois* uttered by a poor woman in the immense multitude that flocked to his obsequies at Sorèze. *Abion un rey, l'aben perdut,* "We had a king, we have lost him." No, my good woman, we have not lost him. He lives in the world; he lives in that free, manly spirit he quickened in the Catholic youth of France, in the souls he formed to take up his work, and carry it on to the glory of God, the honor of Jesus Christ, God made man, the redemption of souls and the revival of Catholic society.

We know the weakness and miseries of human nature; we know that principles, dogmas of faith are immutable; we know the government of the church is hierarchically constituted; and we recognize our duty to believe what God teaches us, and to obey those whom the Holy Ghost has commissioned to govern us; but we cannot persuade ourselves that he who for our sakes assumed our nature, made himself man that man might become God, requires us to suppress our nature, or that he ever intended to exclude from his religion all exercise of reason, all the living convictions of our own minds, all the warm affections and gushing tenderness of our own hearts. "Whom God has joined together let no man put asunder." In our Redeemer and Lord the divine nature and the human nature are joined together in one person forever, to be separated nevermore; and he who would separate them, that is, dissolve Christ, is not of God, but is antichrist. In the Incarnation, human nature, that nature which is equally the nature of all men, is elevated to be the nature of God, is, in the language of Pope St. Leo, "deified" actually and completely so in the Son of man, and potentially so in all men. How long shall we be in learning that this mystery of mysteries, in which the wisdom, the love, the mercy, and the creative power of God are, so to speak, exhausted, is not a mere isolated dogma, with no intimate relation to our practical and everyday life? In our religion there is the divine, but the divine with the human, and the human, but not the human without the divine; and we are as untrue to it when we take the divine without the human, as we are when we take the human without the divine. The religion that neglects civilization is in principle as uncatholic, as the civilization that neglects religion. He departs from the Gospel who asserts the divine authority to the exclusion of human freedom, as he who asserts human freedom to the exclusion of the authority of God. The Jesuits rendered the cause of orthodoxy a valuable service in their defense of nature and human liberty against the Jansenists. They might render it a still further service by reforming our ascetic literature, and placing modern spiritual direction in harmony with the principles they in their controversy with the Jansenists so vigorously, heroically, and successfully defended. . . .

CIVIL AND RELIGIOUS FREEDOM

[1864]

[*The following essay appeared in the July, 1864, number of* Brownson's Quarterly, *as a review of Montalembert's* L'Église libre dans l'État libre *(Paris, 1863). The full text is in* Works, *XX, 308–42. It is important as a forthright declaration by Brownson of his concurrence with Montalembert's position on an issue which was then the subject of the most acute controversy. Montalembert was a vigorous defender of civil and religious freedom throughout his life. He was a contributor from the time of his early youth to the review* Le Correspondant, *which had as its motto, "Civil and Religious Liberty for the whole world." He was a leader in the 1840's in the struggle for liberty of teaching and education. The volume which Brownson reviews is the text of discourses Montalembert delivered at the Congress of Belgian Catholics at Mechlin in August, 1863. These discourses raised a storm of controversy among Catholics, and cardinals and bishops, as well as clerical and lay journalists, opposed and defended Montalembert in a heated debate. The issues raised in this debate soon came to have a particular importance because of the publication in December, 1864, of the Encyclical* Quanta Cura *and the* Syllabus of Errors *against the errors of Liberalism.*

The July number of the Review *was the next to the last issue, until Brownson revived it in 1873. In the final issue for October, 1864, he wrote an essay called "Explanations to Catholics" (XX, 361–81) much of which is occupied with answering the objections made to the essay printed here.*]

HAT THE CHURCH has legislative authority, under the divine law, every Catholic maintains; but it is no part of Catholic faith that she is infallible in her legislation or in her disciplinary canons. Nothing forbids us to maintain, if such be our honest conviction, that any human law, borrowed from the Hebrew and Graeco-Roman civilizations, and incorporated into the discipline of the church, or at least for long ages approved by churchmen and acted on by civil government, is unnecessary, improper, or prejudicial to the best interests both of religion and of civilization. We find no trace of the doctrine on which the practice is founded among Christian writers, prior to the first Christian emperor. Many among the greatest doctors and fathers of the church have opposed it, and boldly asserted that the only lawful means of maintaining or re-establishing unity of faith are moral, spiritual weapons drawn from the armory of reason and revelation, and addressed to the understanding, the heart, and the conscience. So at one time, at least, held St. Augustine; so held the great St. Dominic, the reputed founder of the inquisition, who used all his influence to prevent the employment of force against the Albigenses, among whom he was sent to labor as a missionary; so held the illustrious St. Francis de Sales, who, if for a moment he called in the troops of the duke of Savoy to expel the Calvinistic ministers who gave him so much annoyance, instantly repented of his act, and gave himself no rest till the exiles were recalled and re-established in their homes; and so, it is well known, held the equally illustrious Fénelon, archbishop of Cambray, who would not undertake the mission for the conversion of the Huguenots, till Louis XIV consented to withdraw his dragoons. We feel, therefore, quite easy as to the past, and have no fear of compromising our orthodoxy by refusing to defend the doctrine, or by openly condemning it, as has been done by the late archbishop of Baltimore in his learned work on the *Primacy of the Apostolic See,* dedicated to the supreme pontiff himself.

That the doctrine we maintain, after M. de Montalembert, concedes the liberty of error, and places it and truth on the footing of equality before the civil authority, we grant, and we would have it so. We do not in this assert the indifference of truth and error, or that a man has the *moral* right to adhere to a false religion. Truth cannot tolerate even so much as the semblance of error, and in the theological order we are as intolerant as any Calvinist in the land, and hold firmly that out of the true church there is no salvation, any more than there is virtue without obedience to the moral law of God. Nor do we with Milton and Jefferson maintain that "error is harmless where truth is free to combat it." Error makes the circuit of the globe while Truth is pulling on her boots, and no error ever is or ever can be harmless. What we assert is, not what is called theological tolerance, but what is called civil tolerance. Error has no rights, but the man who errs has equal rights with him who errs not. The civil authority is incompetent to discriminate between truth and error, and the church is a spiritual kingdom without force, or the mission to employ it for the one or against the other. The weapons of her warfare are spiritual not carnal; consequently, before the secular or human authority, whether of churchmen or statesmen, truth and error must stand on the same footing and be equally protected in the equal rights of the citizen. All sects should be equal before the civil law, and each citizen protected in the right to choose and profess his own religion, which we call his conscience, as his natural right, so long as he respects the equal right of others. This is the American order, and we dare maintain that it is the Christian order; for when the disciples proposed to call down fire from heaven to consume the adversaries of our Lord, he rebuked them, and told them that they "knew not what manner of spirit they were of."

All the doctors of the church agree that faith is not to be forced, that it must be voluntarily accepted, and that no one can be compelled to receive baptism against his own free will. So much is certain; and hence Charlemagne, who placed before the conquered Saxons the alternative of baptism or perpetual slavery, is never regarded as having conducted himself as a good Christian or as a good Catholic. Yet it is not to be denied that theologians have argued, from the analogy of secular governments, that since by baptism the recipient is born again, and born a subject of Christ's kingdom, he may be compelled by force, when once baptized and become one of the faithful, to keep the unity of the faith, and submit to the authority of the church, as the natural-born subjects of a state may, if rebellious, be reduced to their civil allegiance by the strong hand of power, and, if need be, punished even with death for their treason. But have they not abused this analogy? "My kingdom," says our Lord, "is not of this world,"—is not a secular kingdom, for the government of men in their secular relations, but is a spiritual kingdom, founded to introduce and maintain in human affairs the spiritual or moral law of God. The church, which is clothed with the authority of this kingdom, or in a mystical sense, is it, has undoubtedly over her subjects the authority which secular governments have over theirs, only it is an authority of the same kind with her own nature and mission. Since her kingdom is moral and spiritual, she has and can have only moral or spiritual power. She can resort neither directly nor indirectly to physical force, for that would make her a secular kingdom,—a kingdom of this world,—and belie her own spiritual nature.

The mission of the state is one that can be executed by physical force, for its mission is restricted to external acts in the social order. The magistrate bears the sword against evildoers, and his mission is to watch over the safety of society, and to maintain justice between man and man, or to repress and redress external violence, either against individuals or against society itself. In this, physical force, when needed, may be employed, because there is a congruity between its employment and the end to be obtained. But it is not so with the church. Her mission being to introduce and maintain the law of God in the interior of man, she affects the exterior only through the interior, that is, the external act only through reason and conscience. This is wherefore she is called a spiritual, not a secular kingdom, or kingdom of this world. She teaches man the truth, tells him what he ought to believe, and what he must be and do in order to render himself acceptable to his Maker, his Redeemer, and his Saviour, or to gain the end for which he has been created. She administers to him the sacraments, through which he receives the new birth, is regenerated, restored, nourished, and strengthened in the life which ends in his supreme beatitude or supernatural union with God. But in all this she can address herself only to his moral or spiritual nature, to his reason or understanding, his free will, his heart, and his conscience. All physical force is here out of place, for physical force can affect only external acts, and all the acts she requires, to be of any value, must be internal, spring from the interior, from real conviction and love, and be the free, voluntary offering of the soul. Faith cannot be forced; she can by exterior force compel no one to receive the sacraments, for though they operate *ex opere operato*, they are inefficacious unless they are received with the proper interior dispositions. "My son, give me thy heart." Obedience in the moral or spiritual order cannot be forced, for it must be voluntary, from the heart; and a forced obedience, or an obedience that springs not from love, and is not yielded by free will, is simply, in her order, no obedience at all. In it the heart is not given. God demands a willing giver, is worshiped with the heart, in spirit and in truth, not with the lips only. External acts, genuflections, prostrations, singing of psalms and repetitions of the creed, the *Pater-noster*, and the *Ave-Maria*, are of no value if the heart be wanting, if love be absent, and there be not in them acts of free will,—all acts which by their own nature cannot be enforced, or produced by simple external authority or pressure. The church, then, cannot do her work, cannot produce faith or love, or maintain interior unity, by force, nor could she reduce by force her rebellious subjects to their allegiance and obedience if she would. The obedience must be voluntary, in the baptized no less than in the unbaptized.

The church precluded by her own spiritual nature and mission from the employment of force, and the state being incompetent in spirituals, no course is practicable, or even lawful, but that of placing before civil society, before external authority, truth and error on the same footing, and using for the promotion of the former and the correction of the latter moral power alone. Let the state leave the church free to wield her moral power according to her own divine nature against error, false doctrines, spiritual disobedience, or spiritual defection or rebellion, and it is all that in the divine economy is required or admissible. The state can demand only the faithful discharge of one's civil duties, and it can punish only civil offenses, and it has no right to make that a civil offense which is not so in its own nature. It has no right or competency to discriminate between the Catholic and the Calvinist, and, if each demeans himself as a good citizen, it is bound to maintain for each the same rights, and to place both in its own order, on the same footing. The responsibility of the religious error it must remit to the individual conscience, leaving each man to account, in the spiritual order, for himself to God, the only master of conscience. The spiritual offenses being in their very nature such as cannot be redressed by physical force, the church can use only moral power against them, that is, arguments addressed to reason and conscience. If these fail, she can do no more, and must, as the state, leave those whom she cannot convert to answer to God for themselves. She may, undoubtedly, use moral discipline to correct her delinquent subjects, or to advance them in virtue, and go even so far as to excommunicate those she judges incorrigible, that is, so far as to exclude them from her external communion. She may thus deprive them of many spiritual advantages; but she cannot exclude any from her internal communion unless they first exclude themselves, and she must raise the ban of excommunication from her external communion whenever the excommunicated demand it, and give satisfactory evidence of interior submission. Here her coercive power stops; and even so far her coercive power is moral not physical, and the moment it becomes physical, it is not in her mission. When the priest rides into a mob, and disperses it with the blows of his black-thorn stick or his horsewhip, he may do a very meritorious act, but he does it not in his priestly capacity, but as a peace officer, or as a chieftain of the clan.

The doctrine we contend for, and to which *La Civiltà Cattolica* objects, or which it permits to be held only as a concession or condescension of the church to the exceptional circumstances of particular localities, has its foundation in the very principle of the divine government itself. The spirit of Christ is the spirit of liberty. God governs the moral world by moral power, never by physical force. He made man free, endowed him with reason and free will, that he might have moral worth, be capable of virtue, and merit a reward; and he governs him according to the nature he has given him, as a free agent, and never forces his reason, or does violence to his free will. He governs him as a free man not as a slave, for he desires his love, and accepts from him only a rational, and voluntary service, *obsequium rationabile*, as says St. Paul. The church, whose mission it is to introduce and maintain the law of God in human affairs and the hearts of men, must imitate the divine government, and no more than God himself attempt to force reason, or by physical violence constrain free will. She is restricted by the very law of her existence to moral means, and can operate only through reason and conscience. God never suppresses error by the exertion of his omnipotence; he leaves the mind free, and corrects error only by the exhibition of his truth, and wins the heart by displaying his moral beauty. He lets the wheat and the tares grow in the same field; "maketh his sun to rise on the evil and on the good and sendeth his rain upon the just and the unjust." This is the law for the church, and she must bear with error and disobedience as God himself bears with them. . . .

CHURCH AND STATE
[1870]

[*From the moment when Christ, in answer to the question about the image of Caesar on the coin handed Him by the Pharisees, replied, "Render, therefore, to Caesar the things that are Caesar's, and to God the things that are God's," the relation of Church and state has been a classical problem of Christendom. To Newman, for example, it was certainly one of the crucial questions of the nineteenth century, and for Brownson no less so. Because it is a pervasive problem in all of his work, and one in which his position changes greatly, the following essay cannot be taken as typical of his thought even after his conversion. The essay* (Works, XIII, 263–84) *represents his thought on the subject in his last years, and the fact that it was published six years after the Encyclical* Quanta Cura *and the* Syllabus of Errors *suggests especially a comparison between his thought here and in the essay on "Civil and Religious Freedom" (1864). There, for example, he uses with approval the phrase "complete separation of church and state" (XX, 322) whereas the underlying idea of this essay is that in their normal relation they are distinct but not separate. Brownson's specific reference here to the* Syllabus of Errors, *one of numerous such references in his writings after 1864, raises the very important question of how he interpreted it. Briefly, his interpretation was similar to that of W. G. Ward of the* Dublin Review, *and those who came to be called "maximizers," and quite unlike that of Newman, Bishop Dupanloup, or Montalembert. For Newman's understanding of the* Syllabus, *his* Letter to the Duke of Norfolk (1875) *should be consulted. In "The Development of Newman's Political Thought,"* Review of Politics, VII (1945), *especially pp. 225–36, I have discussed an aspect of Newman's thought which may suggest significant comparisons with the essays by Brownson included in this section.*

"Orestes Brownson on Church and State," by Francis E. Mc-Mahon, Theological Studies, XV (1954), pp. 175–228, is a thorough and valuable recent study of Brownson's understanding of the problem throughout the entire body of his work.]

WE ASSUME in the outset that there really exist in human society two distinct orders, the spiritual and the temporal, each with its own distinctive functions, laws, and sphere of action. In Christian society, the representative of the spiritual order is the church, and the representative of the temporal is the state. In the rudest stages of society the elements of the two orders exist, but are not clearly apprehended as distinct orders, nor as having each its distinct and proper representative. It is only in Christian society, or society enlightened by the Gospel, that the two orders are duly distinguished, and each in its own representative is placed in its normal relation with the other.

The type, indeed the reason, of this distinction of two orders in society is in the double nature of man, or the fact that man exists only as soul and body, and needs to be cared for in each. The church, representing the spiritual, has charge of the souls of men, and looks after their minds, ideas, intelligence, motives, consciences, and consequently has the supervision of education, morals, literature, science, and art. The state, representing the temporal, has charge of men's bodies, and looks after the material wants and interests of individuals and society. We take this illustration from the fathers and medieval doctors. It is perfect. The analogy of church and state in the moral order, with the soul and body in the physical order, commends itself to the common sense of everyone, and carries in itself the evidence of its justness, especially when it is seen to correspond strictly in the moral order, to the distinction of soul and body in the physical order. We shall take, then, the relation of soul and body as the type throughout of the ideal relation of church and state.

Man lives not as body alone, nor as soul alone, but as the union of the two, in reciprocal commerce. Soul and body are distinct, but not separate. Each has its own distinctive properties and functions, and neither can replace the other; but their separation is death—the death of the body only, not of the soul indeed, for that is immortal. The body is material, and, separated from the soul, is dust and ashes, mere slime of the earth, from which it was formed. It is the same in the moral order with society, which is not state alone, nor church alone, but the union of the two in reciprocal commerce. The two are distinct, each has its distinctive nature, laws, and functions, and neither can perform the functions of the other, or take the other's place. But though distinct, they cannot in the normal state of society be separated. The separation of the state from the church is in the moral order what the separation of the body from the soul is in the physical order. It is death, the death of the state, not indeed of the church; for she, like the soul, nay, like God himself, is immortal. The separation of the state from the church destroys its moral life, and leaves society to become a mass of moral rottenness and corruption. Hence, the Holy Father includes the proposition to separate church and state, in his syllabus of condemned propositions.

The soul is defined by the church as the *forma corporis*, the informing or vital principle of the body. The church in the moral order is *forma civitatis*, the informing, the vital principle of the state or civil society, which has no moral life of its own, since all moral life, by its very term, proceeds from the spiritual order. There is in the physical order no existence, but from God through the medium of his creative act; so is there no moral life in society, but from the spiritual order which is founded by God as supreme lawgiver, and represented by the church, the guardian and judge alike of the natural law and the revealed law.

The soul is the nobler and superior part of man, and it belongs to it, not to make away with the body, or to assume its functions, but to exercise the *magisterium* over it, to direct and govern it according to the law of God; not to the body to assume the mastery over the soul, and to bring the law of the mind into captivity to the law in the members. So is the church, as representing the spiritual order, and charged with the care of souls, the nobler and superior part of society, and to her belongs the *magisterium* of entire human society; and it is for her in the moral order to direct and control civil society, by judicially declaring, and applying to its action, the law of God, of which she is, as we have just said, the guardian and judge, and to which it is bound by the supreme lawgiver to subordinate its entire official conduct.

We note here that this view condemns alike the absorption of the state in the church, and the absorption of the church in the state, and requires each to remain distinct from the other, each with its own organization, organs, faculties, and sphere of action. It favors, therefore, neither what is called theocracy, or *clerocracy* rather, to which Calvinistic Protestantism is strongly inclined, nor the supremacy of the state, to which the age tends, and which was assumed in all the states of gentile antiquity, whence came the persecution of Christians by the pagan emperors. We note further, that the church does not make the law; she only promulgates, declares, and applies it, and is herself as much bound by it as is the state itself. The law itself is prescribed for the government of all men and nations, by God himself as supreme lawgiver, or the end or final cause of creation, and binds equally states and individuals, churchmen and statesmen, sovereigns and subjects.

Such, as we have learned it, is the Catholic doctrine of the relation of church and state, and such is the relation that in the divine order really exists between the two orders, and which the church has always and everywhere labored with all her zeal and energy to introduce and maintain in society. It is her ideal of Catholic or truly Christian society, but which has never yet been perfectly realized, though an approach to its realization, the author thinks, was made under the Christian Roman emperors. The chronic condition of the two orders in society, instead of union and co-operation, or reciprocal commerce, has been that of mutual distrust or undisguised hostility. . . .

There is no opinion more firmly fixed in the minds of the people of today, at least according to the journals, than that the union of church and state is execrable and ought not to be suffered to exist. The words cannot be pronounced without sending a thrill of horror through society, and calling forth the most vigorous and indignant protest from every self-appointed defender of modern civilization, progress, liberty, equality, and fraternity. What is called the "liberal party," sometimes "the movement party," but what we call "the revolution," has everywhere for its *primum mobile,* its impulse and its motive, the dissolution of what remains of the union of church and state, the total separation of the state from the church and its assertion as the supreme and only legitimate authority in society, to which all orders and classes of men, and all matters, whether temporal or spiritual, must be subjected. The great words of the party, as pronounced by its apostles and chiefs, are "people-king," "people-priest," "people-God." There is no denying the fact. Science, or what passes for science, denies the double nature of man, the distinction between soul and body, and makes the soul the product of material organization, or a mere function of the body; and the more popular philosophy suppresses the spiritual order in society, and therefore rejects its pretended representative; and the progress of intelligence suppresses God, and leaves for society only political atheism pure and simple, as is evident from the savage war-whoop set up throughout the civilized world against the syllabus of condemned propositions published by our Holy Father, December, 1864. This syllabus touched the deep wound of modern society, probed it to the quick, and hence the writhings and contortions, the groans and screechings it occasioned. May God grant that it touched to heal, exposed the wound only to apply the remedy. . . .

For four hundred years, the church has sought to maintain peace and concord between herself and the state by concordats, as the wisest and best expedient she found practicable. But concordats, however useful or necessary, do not realize the ideal of Christian society. They do not effect the true union of church and state, and cannot be needed where that union exists. They imply not the union, but the separation of church and state, and are neither necessary nor admissible, except where the state claims to be separate from and independent of the church. They are a compromise in which the church concedes the exercise of certain rights to the state in consideration of its pledge to secure her in the free and peaceable exercise of the rest, and to render her the material force in the execution of her spiritual canons, which she may need but does not herself possess. They are defensible only as necessary expedients, to save the church and the state from falling into the relation of direct and open antagonism. . . .

For ourselves personally, we are partial to our own American system, which, unless we are blinded by our national prejudices, comes nearer to the realization of the true union as well as distinction of church and state than has heretofore or elsewhere been affected; and we own we should like to see it, if practicable there, introduced—by lawful means only—into the nations of Europe. The American system may not be practicable in Europe; but, if so, we think it would be an improvement. Foreigners do not generally, nor even do all Americans themselves, fully understand the relation of church and state, as it really subsists in the fundamental constitution of American society. Abroad and at home there is a strong disposition to interpret it by the theory of European liberalism, and both they who defend and they who oppose the union of church and state, regard it as based on their total separation. But the reverse of this, as we understand it, is the fact. American society is based on the principle of their union; and union, while it implies distinction, denies separation. Modern infidelity or secularism is, no doubt, at work here as elsewhere to effect their separation; but as yet the two orders are distinct, each with its distinct organization, sphere of action, representatives and functions, but not separate. Here the rights of neither are held to be grants from the other. The rights of the church are not franchises or concessions from the state, but are recognized by the state as held under a higher law than its own, and therefore rights prior to and above itself, which it is bound by the law constituting it to respect, obey, and, whenever necessary, to use its physical force to protect and vindicate.

The original settlers of the Anglo-American colonies were not infidels, but, for the most part, sincerely religious and Christian in their way, and in organizing society aimed not simply to escape the oppression of conscience, of which they had been the victims in the mother country, but to found a truly Christian commonwealth; and such commonwealth they actually founded, as perfect as was possible with their imperfect and often erroneous views of Christianity. The colonies of New England inclined, no doubt, to a theocracy, and tended to absorb the state in the church; in the southern colonies, the tendency was, as in England, to establish the supremacy of the civil order, and to make the church a function of the state. These two opposite tendencies meeting in the formation of American society, to a great extent, counterbalanced each other, and resulted in the assertion of the supremacy of the Christian idea, or the union and distinction under the law of God, of the two orders. In principle, at least, each order exists in American society in its normal relation to the other; and also in its integrity, with its own distinctive nature, laws, and functions, and therefore the temporal in its proper subordination to the spiritual.

This subordination is, indeed, not always observed in practice, nor always even theoretically admitted. Many Americans, at first thought, when it is broadly stated, will indignantly deny it. We shall find even Catholics who do not accept it, and gravely tell us that their religion has nothing to do with their politics; that is, their politics are independent of their religion; that is, again, politics are independent of God, and there is no God in the political order; as if a man could be an atheist in the state, and a devout Catholic in the church. But too many Catholics, at home and abroad, act as if this were indeed possible, and very reasonable, nay, their duty; and hence the political world is given over to the violence and corruption in which Satan finds a rich harvest. But let the state pass some act that openly and undisguisedly attacks the rights, the freedom, or independence of the church, in a practical way, it will be hard to find a single Catholic, in this country at least, who would not denounce it as an outrage on his conscience, which shows that the assertion of the separation of politics from religion so thoughtlessly made, really means only the distinction, not the separation of the two orders, or that politics are independent, so long as they do not run counter to the freedom and independence of religion, or fail to respect and protect the rights of the church. Inexactness of expression and bad logic do not necessarily indicate unsound faith.

Most non-Catholics will deny that the American state is founded on the recognition of the independence and superiority of the spiritual order, and therefore, of the church, and the confession of its own subordination to the spiritual, not only in the order of logic, as Cantù maintains, but also in the order of authority; yet a little reflection ought to satisfy everyone that such is the fact, and if it does not, it will be owing to a misconception of what is spiritual. The basis of the American state or constitution, the real unwritten, providential constitution, we mean, is what are called the natural and inalienable rights of man; and we know no American citizen who does not hold that these rights are prior to civil society, above it, and held independently of it; or that does not maintain that the great end for which civil society is instituted is to protect, defend, and vindicate, if need be, with its whole physical force, these sacred and inviolable rights for each and every citizen, however high, however low. This is our American boast, our American conception of political justice, glory. These rights, among which are life, liberty, and the pursuit of happiness, are the higher, the supreme law for civil society, which the state, however constituted, is bound to recognize and obey. They deny the absolutism of the state, define its sphere, restrict its power, and prescribe its duty.

But whence come these rights? and how can they bind the state, and prescribe its duty? We hold these rights by virtue of our manhood, it is said; they are inherent in it, and constitute it. But my rights bind you, and yours bind me, and yet you and I are equal; our manhoods are equal. How, then, can the manhood of either bind, or morally oblige the other? Of things equal one cannot be superior to another. They are in our nature as men, it is said again, or, simply, we hold them from nature. They are said to be natural rights and inalienable, and what is natural must be in or from nature. Nature is taken in two senses; as the physical order or the physical laws constitutive of the physical universe, and as the moral law under which all creatures endowed with reason and free-will are placed by the Creator, and which is cognizable by natural reason or the reason common to all men. In the first sense, these rights are not inherent in our nature as men, nor from nature, or in nature; for they are not physical. Physical rights are a contradiction in terms. They can be inherent in our nature only in the second sense, and in our moral nature only, and consequently are held under the law which founds and sustains moral nature, or the moral order as distinct from the physical order.

But the moral law, the so-called law of nature, *droit naturel*, which founds and sustains the moral order, the order of right, of justice, is not a law founded or prescribed by nature, but the law for the moral government of nature, under which all moral natures are placed by the Author of nature as supreme lawgiver. The law of nature is God's law; and whatever rights it founds or are held from it are his rights, and ours only because they are his. My rights, in relation to you, are your duties, what God prescribes as the law of your conduct to me; and your rights are, in relation to me, my duties to you, what God prescribes as the rule of my conduct to you. But what God prescribes he has the right to prescribe, and therefore can command me to respect no rights in you, and you to respect no rights in me, that are not his; and being his, civil society is bound by them, and cannot alienate them or deny them without violating his law, and robbing him of his rights. Hence, he who does an injury to another wrongs not him only, but wrongs his Maker, his Sovereign, and his Judge. . . .

If the rights of man are the rights of God in and over man as his creature, as they undeniably are, they lie in the spiritual order, are spiritual, not temporal. The American state, then, in recognizing the independence, superiority, and inviolability of the rights of man, does recognize, in principle, the independence, superiority, and inviolability of the spiritual order, and its own subordination to it, and obligation to consult it and conform to it. . . .

That the American state is true to the order it acknowledges, and never usurps any spiritual functions, we do not pretend. The American state copies in but too many instances the bad legislation of Europe. It from the outset showed the original vice of the American people, for while they very justly subjected the state to the law of God, they could subject it to that law only as they understood it, and their understanding of it was in many respects faulty, which was no wonder, since they had no infallible, no authoritative, in fact, no representative at all of the spiritual order, and knew the law of God only so far as taught it by natural reason, and spelt out by their imperfect light from an imperfect and mutilated text of the written word. They had a good major proposition, namely, the spiritual order duly represented is supreme, and should govern all men collectively and individually, as states and as citizens; but their minor was bad. But we with our reading of the Bible do duly represent that order. Therefore, &c. Now, we willingly admit that a people reverencing and reading the Bible as the word of God, will in most respects have a far truer and more adequate knowledge of the law of God than those who have neither church nor Bible, and only their reason and their mutilated, perverted, and even travestied traditions of the primitive revelation retained and transmitted by gentilism, and therefore that Protestantism as understood by the American colonists is much better for society than the liberalism asserted by the movement party either here or in Europe; but its knowledge will still be defective, and leave many painful gaps on many important points; and the state, having no better knowledge, will almost inevitably misconceive what on various matters the law of God actually prescribes or forbids. . . .

The state has no spiritual competency, and cannot decide either for itself or for its citizens which is or is not the church that authoritatively represents the spiritual order. The responsibility of that decision it does and must leave to its citizens, who must decide for themselves, and answer to God for the rectitude of their decision. Their decision is law for the state, and it must respect and obey it in the case alike of majorities and minorities; for it recognizes the equal rights of all its citizens, and cannot discriminate between them. The church that represents for the state the spiritual order is the church adopted by its citizens; and as they adopt different churches, it can recognize and enforce, through the civil courts, the canons and decrees of each only on its own members, and on them only so far as they do not infringe on the equal rights of the others. This is not all the state would do or ought to do in a perfect Christian society, but it is all that it can do where these different churches exist, and exist for it with equal rights. It can only recognize them, and protect and vindicate the rights of each only in relation to those citizens who acknowledge its authority. This recognizes and protects the Catholic Church in her entire freedom and independence and in teaching her faith, and in governing and disciplining Catholics according to her own canons and decrees, which, unless we are greatly misinformed, is more than the state does for her, in any old Catholic nation in the world. . . .

Undoubtedly, the liberals, or movement party, are, and have been, for nearly a century, struggling by all the means in their power, fair or foul, to overthrow European society, and reconstruct it after what they suppose to be the American model, but in reality on a basis, if possible, more pagan and less Christian than its present basis. They assert the absolute supremacy of the state in all things; only, instead of saying with Louis XIV, "*L'état, c'est moi,*" they say "*L'état, c'est le peuple,*" but they make the people, as the state, as absolute as any king or kaiser ever pretended to be.

The church would, in their reconstructed society, not have secured to her the rights that she holds under our system, by the fact that it is based on the equal and antecedent rights of all citizens, really the rights of God, which limit the power of the state, of the people in a democratic state, and prescribe both its province and its duty.

Even with us, the American system has its enemies, and perhaps only a minority of the people understand it as we do, and some of the courts are beginning to render decisions which, if in one part, they sustain it, in another part flatly contradict it. The supreme court of Ohio, in the recent case of the School Board of Cincinnati, has decided very properly that the board could not exclude religion; but, on the other hand, it maintains that a majority of the people in any locality may introduce what religion they please, and teach it to the children of the minority as well as to their own, which is manifestly wrong; for it gives the majority of the people the power to establish their own religion, and exclude that of the minority when, in matters of religion, that is, in matters of conscience, votes do not count. My conscience, though in a minority of one, is as sacred and inviolable as it would be if all the rest of the community were with me. As in the Polish diet, a single veto suffices to arrest the whole action of the state. The American democracy is not what it was in 1776. It was then Christian after a Protestant fashion; it is now infected with European liberalism, or popular absolutism; and if we had to introduce the American system now, we should not be able to do it.

There are serious difficulties on both sides. The church cannot confide in the revolution, and the governments cannot or will not protect her, save at the expense of her independence and freedom of action. They, if we must believe any thing the journals say, threaten her with their vengeance, if she dares to make and publish such or such a dogmatic decision, or to define on certain points which they think touch them, what her faith is and always has been. This is a manifest invasion of her right to teach the word of God in its integrity, and simply tells her with the sword suspended over her head, that she shall teach only what is agreeable to them, whether in God's word or not. This insolence, this arrogant assumption, applauded by the universal sectarian and secular press, if submitted to, would make the church the mere tool of the secular authority, and destroy all confidence in her teaching.

We know not how these difficulties on either side are to be overcome. The church cannot continue to be shorn of her freedom by the secular governments, and made to conform to their ambitious or timid politics, without losing more and more her hold on the European populations. Nor can she side with the revolution without perilling the interests of society from which her own cannot be separated. We see no way out of the dilemma but for her, trusting in the divine protection, to assert simply and energetically her independence of both parties alike, and confide in the faithful, as she did in the martyr ages, and as she does now in every heathen land. . . .

THE AMERICAN CATHOLIC TRADITION

An Arno Press Collection

Callahan, Nelson J., editor. **The Diary of Richard L. Burtsell, Priest of New York.** 1978

Curran, Robert Emmett. **Michael Augustine Corrigan and the Shaping of Conservative Catholicism in America, 1878-1902.** 1978

Ewens, Mary. **The Role of the Nun in Nineteenth-Century America** (Doctoral Thesis, The University of Minnesota, 1971). 1978

McNeal, Patricia F. **The American Catholic Peace Movement 1928-1972** (Doctoral Dissertation, Temple University, 1974). 1978

Meiring, Bernard Julius. **Educational Aspects of the Legislation of the Councils of Baltimore, 1829-1884** (Doctoral Dissertation, University of California, Berkeley, 1963). 1978

Murnion, Philip J., **The Catholic Priest and the Changing Structure of Pastoral Ministry, New York, 1920-1970** (Doctoral Dissertation, Columbia University, 1972). 1978

White, James A., **The Era of Good Intentions: A Survey of American Catholics' Writing Between the Years 1880-1915** (Doctoral Thesis, University of Notre Dame, 1957). 1978

Dyrud, Keith P., Michael Novak and Rudolph J. Vecoli, editors. **The Other Catholics.** 1978

Gleason, Philip, editor. **Documentary Reports on Early American Catholicism.** 1978

Bugg, Lelia Hardin, editor. **The People of Our Parish.** 1900

Cadden, John Paul. **The Historiography of the American Catholic Church: 1785-1943.** 1944

Caruso, Joseph. **The Priest.** 1956

Congress of Colored Catholics of the United States. **Three Catholic Afro-American Congresses.** [1893]

Day, Dorothy. **From Union Square to Rome.** 1940

Deshon, George. **Guide for Catholic Young Women.** 1897

Dorsey, Anna H[anson]. **The Flemmings.** [1869]

Egan, Maurice Francis. **The Disappearance of John Longworthy.** 1890

Ellard, Gerald. **Christian Life and Worship.** 1948

England, John. **The Works of the Right Rev. John England, First Bishop of Charleston.** 1849. 5 vols.

Fichter, Joseph H. **Dynamics of a City Church.** 1951

Furfey, Paul Hanly. **Fire on the Earth.** 1936

Garraghan, Gilbert J. **The Jesuits of the Middle United States.**
1938. 3 vols.

Gibbons, James. **The Faith of Our Fathers.** 1877

Hecker, I[saac] T[homas]. **Questions of the Soul.** 1855

Houtart, François. **Aspects Sociologiques Du Catholicisme Américain.**
1957

[Hughes, William H.] **Souvenir Volume. Three Great Events in the
History of the Catholic Church in the United States.** 1889

[Huntington, Jedediah Vincent]. **Alban: A Tale of the New World.** 1851

Kelley, Francis C., editor. **The First American Catholic Missionary
Congress.** 1909

Labbé, Dolores Egger. **Jim Crow Comes to Church.** 1971

LaFarge, John. **Interracial Justice.** 1937

Malone, Sylvester L. **Dr. Edward McGlynn.** 1918

The Mission-Book of the Congregation of the Most Holy Redeemer. 1862

O'Hara, Edwin V. **The Church and the Country Community.** 1927

Pise, Charles Constantine. **Father Rowland.** 1829

Ryan, Alvan S., editor. **The Brownson Reader.** 1955

Ryan, John A., **Distributive Justice.** 1916

Sadlier, [Mary Anne]. **Confessions of an Apostate.** 1903

**Sermons Preached at the Church of St. Paul the Apostle, New York,
During the Year 1863.** 1864

Shea, John Gilmary. **A History of the Catholic Church Within the
Limits of the United States.** 1886/1888/1890/1892. 4 Vols.

Shuster, George N. **The Catholic Spirit in America.** 1928

Spalding, J[ohn] L[ancaster]. **The Religious Mission of the Irish People
and Catholic Colonization.** 1880

Sullivan, Richard. **Summer After Summer.** 1942

[Sullivan, William L.] **The Priest.** 1911

Thorp, Willard. **Catholic Novelists in Defense of Their Faith, 1829-1865.**
1968

Tincker, Mary Agnes. **San Salvador.** 1892

Weninger, Franz Xaver. **Die Heilige Mission** and **Praktische Winke Für
Missionare.** 1885. 2 Vols. in 1

Wissel, Joseph. **The Redemptorist on the American Missions.**
1920. 3 Vols. in 2

The World's Columbian Catholic Congresses and Educational Exhibit.
1893

Zahm, J[ohn] A[ugustine]. **Evolution and Dogma.** 1896